Praise for J. Gregory Keyes's The Age of Unreason

Book One: *Newton's Cannon*

"The opening blast of his planned Age of Unreason [series] is powerful enough to make readers grab Book 2, *A Calculus of Angels*, when it arrives."

—*USA Today*

"A new myth-maker, a new star of the fantasy genre has arrived. Like Ursula K. Le Guin in the '60s, John Varley in the '70s, and Orson Scott Card in the '80s, author J. Gregory Keyes may well be the leading fantasy writer of the 1990s."

—*BookPage*

Book Two: *A Calculus of Angels*

"Masterful . . . A bravura performance . . . [An] ingenious mélange of Age of Unreason period details, stunning psychic and alchemical phenomena, [and] fetching poetic descriptions . . . Lavish and thoughtful."

—*Publishers Weekly* (starred review)

Book Three: *Empire of Unreason*

"Keyes's iconoclastic tale of science and sorcery leavened by a set of otherworldly villains offers deliciously skewed portraits of historical figures as well as a genuinely intriguing plot."

—*Library Journal*

"Keyes still is master of the details that make much of this universe believable, and the amount of action definitely makes the book exciting."

—*Booklist*

By J. Gregory Keyes
Published by The Ballantine Publishing Group:

The Chosen of the Changeling
THE WATERBORN
THE BLACKGOD

The Age of Unreason
NEWTON'S CANNON
A CALCULUS OF ANGELS
EMPIRE OF UNREASON
THE SHADOWS OF GOD*

BABYLON 5: DARK GENESIS
BABYLON 5: DEADLY RELATIONS
BABYLON 5: FINAL RECKONING

STAR WARS®: THE NEW JEDI ORDER:
EDGE OF VICTORY: CONQUEST
STAR WARS®: THE NEW JEDI ORDER:
EDGE OF VICTORY: REBIRTH*

**Forthcoming*

EMPIRE OF UNREASON

Book Three of
The Age of Unreason

J. Gregory Keyes

A Del Rey® Book
THE BALLANTINE PUBLISHING GROUP • NEW YORK

This book contains an excerpt from the forthcoming hardcover edition of *The Shadows of God* by J. Gregory Keyes. This excerpt has been specially set for this edition only and may not reflect the final content of the hardcover edition.

A Del Rey® Book
Published by The Ballantine Publishing Group

www.delreydigital.com

Library of Congress Catalog Card Number: 2001116711

ISBN 0-345-40610-9

Manufactured in the United States of America

First Hardcover Edition: May 2000
First Mass Market Edition: June 2001

10 9 8 7 6 5 4 3 2 1

For Veronica Chapman

Contents

Acknowledgments

Belated credits to Bob Kobres for his pointers on how to destroy London with an asteroid. Thanks to Steve Saffel, who had to jump on this boat in midstream, and in a pretty swift current. My appreciation to Kris Boldis, Ken Carleton, Professor Nell Keyes, and Nancy Landrum for reading. Thanks to Duane Wilkins of University Books in Seattle and Maryelizabeth Hart of Mysterious Galaxy in San Diego, not just for their dedication to science fiction and fantasy, but for their friendship. Finally, my thanks to Heather Ramsey, Tony Selto, Bill Nary, and everyone else at Salle Auriol Seattle for bruising my body but lightening my spirits.

Prologue

His body closed like a fist, each muscle trying to tear free of bone. He snarled through his teeth, watched the angel with slitted eyes.

"You can still change your mind," the angel said reasonably, "and obey me." It raised its feathery wings. Its face, as always, was a mask of light.

Peter tasted blood in his mouth, but he managed to get the words out as he wanted, clear and measured. "I am Peter Alexeyevich! I am the tsar of Russia. You cannot command me."

"I am an angel of God."

"You are not. You are a betrayer and a liar."

"I saved your life. I saved your empire. I helped you control your Old Believers. You were happy to tell *them* I was an angel."

Peter scooted against the cabin wall and dug his hands into the deep pockets of his coat. His face, which often slipped his control, spasmed terribly. "What do you want?" he demanded. "What do you devils really want?"

"Only the one thing I asked. Have I ever asked for anything else? Any reward for my services?"

"It isn't one thing. It's everything. I *know* you now."

"I doubt that. But, very well, if you insist on dying."

Peter pulled something from his pocket—a small cube with a circular depression in the top. It was humming, a single clear note.

The angel paused. "What is that?"

"Something a friend gave me. A wise friend, as it turns out." He placed a sphere the size of a musket ball in the depression, and a shriek cut through the fabric of the universe. Peter felt it in his bones. The angel felt it, too, and dripped fire into Peter's veins, even as a wind came that tore it apart, each feather dissolving into a line of smoke.

The death of the angel did not stop the pain. A wave of agony crested over Peter's head and dragged him under; and suddenly he had no weight at all, as if he were falling from a height with no end.

Red Shoes jerked awake to find himself already on his feet. He swayed there for a moment, trying to remember where he was, but the otherworld sight was still wrapped around him, making the trees, the earth he stood on, the stars themselves too strange to recognize.

He found his pipe and a pinch of Ancient Tobacco and lit it from an ember that had strayed from the remains of the fire. The warm, musky smoke strengthened the breath in him and curled from his nose. Gradually the world came clear.

He was Red Shoes, war prophet and miracle maker of the Choctaw people, and he stood on an earthen mound in the Natchez country, near the Great Water Road. The mound's top was as broad as a village, and around it lay swamp, the underworld kissing the earth from beneath.

A soft cough came behind him, and he turned to regard Skin Eater.

Skin Eater was a Natchez man, a descendant of the Sun, his dark skin mottled with even darker tattoos, blurred by the eighty winters of his life.

"I felt it," Skin Eater murmured. "Do you know what it was?"

"No," Red Shoes admitted. "Something important, something strong. My shadowchildren died bringing it to me."

"From the West."

"Yes. Since the strange news from the West began, I have sent my children out to watch. Now they have seen something."

"West is a big place," Skin Eater observed.

"I know. But my shadowchildren tell me no more than that. If only I knew *where* in the West . . ." Red Shoes trailed off, thinking.

Skin Eater reflected for a moment as he lit his own pipe. "You are more powerful than ever I was," he said, "perhaps the strongest there has ever been. But your people are younger than mine—there are things the Natchez remember that the Choctaw do not."

"I acknowledge that, great-uncle." It was a title of respect, only. He was not related to the old man.

Skin Eater swept his arms around. "This place is an image of the world—do you see? The deeps of the beginning times below and around us, the earth raised up with a face for each direction. The flat top here is the whole surface of the middle world. Like those paintings on paper the French use."

"You mean a map? But maps have things marked on them. Rivers, mountains, towns—"

"But if a town should move, will it move on a French map? Not unless they draw another map, yes? Here, however, you have only to know how to look. Here, the world can always be seen true."

Red Shoes frowned slightly as the implications of the old man's words sunk in. He took another puff of his pipe, and began chanting, walking in widening circles upon the top of the mound, giving smoke to the directions. His feet sank back into the world of spirit, of dream.

As he walked, the appearance of the mound changed. Below his feet, plains, mountains, and forests appeared and vanished, as if, indeed, he walked on an enormous and incredibly detailed map. Excited now, he strode west, looking for what he had seen. He crossed the Great Water Road, which the English called Mississippi. He towered above thinning trees, and then there were no trees at all, only grass. There, at last, he found an obscure place he could not see, a patch of nothing on the image of the world. This was the thing, the place where his shadowchildren had heard the scream, felt the strange power.

He made his way back, memorizing the directions as he went. The Natchez country was easy to find again, for it was in the middle of the mound; and for a moment he was dizzied, standing at the center of the center of the center. Then he shook himself alive again.

"Did you find it?" Skin Eater asked.

"What 'r' y' two talking about when a man is trying t' sleep?" A voice grumbled from nearby. Red Shoes turned to regard a big, broad-faced, knob-nosed Englishman, sitting up in his blankets.

"Good morning, Tug," Red Shoes said.

"Mornin'?" The Englishman glared around at the darkness. "Mornin' has *sunlight*, damn y'r In'yun soul." He looked around again, this time more worriedly. "What's got y' hup? Ghosts and ghoulies?"

"Something like that. How set were you on seeing New Paris?"

"W't y' mean? Han't we goin' to New Pa-ree?"

"Not anymore. I have to go someplace else."

"Oh, well, old Tug han't particular. Long's there's women an' rum."

"Well," Red Shoes began slowly, "now there is the problem. . . ."

Part One

MAGNETISMS

For it's well known that bodies act one upon another by the attractions of gravity, magnetism, and electricity; and these instances shew the tenor and course of Nature, and make it not improbable but that there may be more attractive forces than these.

—Sir Isaac Newton,
Optics 1717

Wherever law ends, tryanny begins . . .

—John Locke,
Second Treatise of Government 1689

1.

A Matter of Gravity

Benjamin Franklin felt awfully pleased with himself as he rose from the polished oak table to face his audience. The meeting room in the upper story of the Egyptian Coffeehouse was suffused with milky sunlight that poured through high, wide windows, blending with arabesques of pipe smoke and ephemeral vapors from a dozen bowls of coffee. He felt as if he were addressing a Dutch painting—one he himself had commissioned.

He paused at a small bench, and made as if to pluck at the cloth that covered the squarish object that lay upon it; but instead, repressing a devilish grin, he turned toward the assembly and cleared his throat. Coffee bowls clinked and settled as ten men and two women regarded him expectantly. He summoned up his best orator's voice.

"The opening questions of the Junto having been asked and answered, I now propose a modest demonstration. But first a query, my ladies and my gentlemen—and my otherwise—what is the most pressing problem of our day?"

"Get on with it, Mr. Franklin!" Shandy Tupman piped, in his reedy voice, shaking his fist in mock threat. "Han't no schoolroom, this!"

Franklin arched his brows. "And how would you know what the inside of a schoolhouse looked like, Mr. Tupman?"

That drew a few snickers.

"Only by rumor, sir," Shandy replied good-naturedly.

"Allow Mr. Franklin his glory, Mr. Tupman," a beetle-browed fellow named Dawkins said. "It's little enough of it he has, as it is."

A contagious chuckle passed around the room at that, and Franklin kept his smile small: he was not the least well-known man in the British Commonwealth of America.

"Very gracious," Franklin said. "And to my question?"

"Bed mites!" someone offered.

"Piss-thin beer!"

"Foolish, prattling, overblown husbands!" asserted a lightly built woman with sapphire eyes. Her exclamation was punctuated by assenting jeers.

"My dear," Franklin said, peering down his nose at her. "There's no cure for that sort of man but a sensible wife."

"Some cures take a lifetime to work, it seems," she said back sweetly, "especially when the patient is so deeply infected."

Franklin smiled. "Well, it may be. But one good husband is worth two good wives."

"And how do you reckon that, husband?" she said.

"Why, my dear Lenka, the scarcer something is, the greater its value."

He waited for the laughter to die, then put on a more somber face. "Now. In all seriousness."

"The malakim," August Stark said dourly. "That devilish brood and their warlock footmen are our greatest worry."

That chased all the good humor out of the room quickly enough.

"You're on the right track," Franklin agreed, "but I was thinking more specific."

Stark rubbed his hammer-heavy jaw. "Tsar Peter and his demon ships."

"There. Mr. Stark gets the prize."

"You have remedy for them?" Stark asked. "What have you to show us, Benjamin Franklin? Enough of this French wit. What have you invented?"

Franklin absorbed Stark's frank challenge with a modest

bow. He understood the man's attitude—Stark's father had died in Venice, fighting those demon ships. He was touchy on the subject, but a good man.

"No more delays," Franklin promised, "once I have two 'prentices to join me here."

"I'll sign no indenture papers with you, no more than I would sign for the devil," Stark said, "but if it'll get you on with it, I'll assist—"

"And me!" Tupman added.

The two men came up, as Franklin uncovered a simple wooden box, a yard long and half that wide and deep, with two handles.

"Take hold there, fellows," Franklin encouraged, "and try to lift her up."

They did. Tupman was a wiry little man, but Stark was a blacksmith with arms like the shanks of a plow horse. As much as they strained, neither could budge the box.

"Nailed down, ain't she," Shandy complained.

"Alley-oop," Franklin replied, and in a sudden motion, the box lifted from the bench, taking the two surprised men up with it. It rose without pause to the height of the ceiling—some fifteen feet—and stuck there, Stark and Tupman dangling from the handles, to the enthusiastic clapping and calling of the small crowd.

"And there you have it," Franklin said, bowing just a bit.

Roger Smalls raised his hands. "A flying box, very well. But there have been flying engines for nigh on ten years now."

"Ah, but not like this one," Franklin said. "Those globes on which the tsar hefts his ships are shells 'prisoning aethereal spirits—malakim. Every machine to this day which flies owes its motivation to those evil and untrustworthy creatures. We all know the malakim plot against us—I for one will not trust them to bear me up a mile above the Earth. This device owes them nothing. It repels directly against gravity."

"You solved the equation? You have the affinity of gravity?"

"Only last week."

"No wonder you've been all puffed up!" David Crowley said excitedly. "And well you deserve it! I admit to being impressed!"

"So must we all," Smalls vowed.

"I, for one," Stark called down from the ceiling, "would now like to see how well it reverses itself."

"At your command," Franklin said and, reaching into his pocket, pulled forth a small box and twisted a key set in it. The box floated back down, the two men with it.

"This is grand," Smalls went on. "Now the enemy loses his advantage, if the depneumifier y' spoke of last month works as well as this new flying engine. You can bring their ships crashing down as you float on up past 'em."

"The depneumifier needs testing," Franklin cautioned. "But, yes, we can at least build flying machines. I've got a good start on one, as a matter of fact."

"Will you publish it to us, Franklin? How it was done?"

"I would not have called you together otherwise. We members of the Junto do not hold back from one another, and I shan't hold this back. In fact, if you are all prepared, I shall—"

He was interrupted by the door suddenly banging open. In the doorway stood Robert Nairne in scarlet coat, Spanish rapier hanging rakishly at his side, a pistol in one hand.

"Pardon me," he said, a bit out of breath, "ladies and gentlemen of the Junto." He paused long enough to gaze around the room, to make certain that only members of that organization were present. "But a warlock walks among us."

Franklin's feeling of well-being vanished as the crowd broke into angry rattling. He held up his hands for quiet, and got enough to be heard. "Where?"

"He's in the Boar's Head, right down the street, plain as you please."

"You're certain?"

Robert pulled out a brass device that resembled a compass. "Look for yourselves."

Around the room, similar devices came from pockets and haversacks, and then a grim mutter of confirmation.

"Well," Franklin said coldly, "his bad luck, then. Robert, you and Shandy keep a watch on him. At nightfall we'll make our move." He glanced around. "We must delay discussions of matters scientific whilst we take up the *other* task of the Junto."

The bright copper sunset had tarnished to verdigris when Franklin pulled his greatcoat on and stepped into the streets of Charles Town. The day had been warm, but even here, in May, in the sunniest of colonies, evening brought chill. Boston, the town of his birth, languished beneath ice, as did New York and Philadelphia. The heart of America had been driven south by the cold years after the fall of the comet, and Benjamin Franklin had come south with it.

Lights were brightening in houses, and the streets were beginning to thicken with those seeking the joys and comforts of ale and wine, or the thousand darker sins it was said one could find in the city that had once been Blackbeard's capital. Young men in bright Venetian silks strolled arm in arm with their mistresses, damsels of every hue and nationality. Deerskin traders spit-washed their palms and faces, hoping some girl in a salon might be drunk enough to find them presentable. Sailors, adventurously seeking the taverns far from the docks, strutted unsteadily on legs not yet used to land—or perhaps already filled with waters stronger than the sea.

Franklin strode purposefully through the newly paved streets, comforted by the weight of the smallsword at his side, the arcane pistol in his belt, and the waistcoat aegis he wore beneath coat and greatcoat.

Outside of the Boar's Head, he met Robert.

"We've got him buttoned in," Robert told him, his mischievous green eyes more serious than usual. He tugged nervously at his long auburn braid, hung fashionably in front of his right shoulder. "I think he knows it but don't give no never mind."

"Interesting. They usually try to run when we discover them. They've learned to fear us, at least."

Robert shrugged. "Maybe this fellow is behind on his American news. What now?"

"I've a mind to say hello to this fellow."

"Did y' ever consider that's exactly what he might want? You within sword distance?"

"Well, then he shall get his wish."

"Are you a genie now, granting wishes?"

Franklin winked. "More a leprechaun, I hope." He turned and strode into the Boar's Head.

Six steps later, Robert was still with him.

"Alone," Franklin clarified.

Robert shook his head, a firm no. "I'll play Roger Pipe-smith with the ugliest girl in Charles Town before I let my best friend walk into a sea *that* deep over his head," Robert said. "I'll be quiet as a Quaker, but it's with you I'll be, no mistake. I'm a free man, last I heard from myself."

"I don't want him thinking me a coward," Franklin explained.

"You know what he is, and probably he knows you know what he is. The last warlock we met took seven bullets and a severe case of headlessness t' put down. He won't think either of us coward, goin' in only two t' one."

"You have a point there," Franklin admitted.

"Aye, an one here, too," Robert said, patting his sword.

"And here," Franklin finished, pointing to Robert's head. "Let's go, then."

The fellow wasn't hard to spot. The place had not begun to fill yet, and he sat all alone, lanthorn light glinting red in his eyes. For an instant Franklin was so filled with fury and loathing that he nearly pulled his pistol and murdered the thing on the spot. The first such creature like this he had met—a man-looking thing named Bracewell—had killed his brother, James, and done his level best to kill Franklin as well.

Even after more than a decade, he couldn't forget that weird look of surprise in James' dead eyes, or the red glow of Bracewell's familiars pursuing him through the night.

But he calmed himself, walked to the table, and sat down across from the creature.

The warlock looked up, his eyes now mild and normal. Blue. He had a high forehead and a slightly weak chin, and was young, surely no more than twenty.

"Benjamin Franklin, I think," the man said in a German-sounding accent.

"My father gave me that name, a good man, and I'd appreciate you keeping your tongue off it."

"What offense have I offered you, sir?"

"You know what you are. Your existence is an offense."

The fellow blinked. "One cannot help how one is born, sir, only what one does afterward."

"And what have you done?"

"I have come here to see you."

"Many of your kind have," Franklin said in a low voice, "and we have purged you. Go back to the Old World. Keep it. But America is not for you."

The man smiled. "Yes, you have the great ones talking out there in their palaces of night, Benjamin Franklin. You have them worried, I must say. In all of the lands in all the world, this is the corner they know the least about. And all due to you."

Franklin did not correct him. The Junto had members in every city of the Commonwealth, and other places besides, and their mission was the same—find and kill these agents of the malakim. He, Franklin, had begun it, but it was beyond him now. If he died this moment, the work would go on.

No use telling *it* that, however. " 'They' cannot see or know the world of matter without human—or animal—eyes and ears," Franklin said. "They cannot strike at what they cannot see."

"Oh, no. It is *difficult* to strike at what you cannot see, but it can surely be done. You have chafed them but not beaten them." He lifted his mug and took a long quaff of beer. "You have some method of detecting us, don't you?"

"Friend, you would be better off with your questions unanswered. We have been known to pack your kind back to whence you came alive. But, frankly, as much as I abhor killing, I'd as soon put you in the mouths of the worms, if you give me the least excuse. Now, you've been waiting for me here, it seems. What have you to say to me?"

"Just this. That things are not as simple as you might have them. Do you know what I really am?"

Franklin shrugged. "What word shall I use? 'Warlock' is popular, and 'sorcerer,' and 'demon.' From my reading, I suspect your kind have been faeries and goblins and all manner of things that slither in the night. What you are is a traitor to Man, and I care only to call you enemy."

The man sighed and took another drink of beer. He leaned forward on his elbows and stared intently into Franklin's eyes.

"They come to us when we are young, very young. I remember their voices from my mother's belly, I think. How is a child to know? How old was I before I knew that every boy did not have this voice in his head, this secret mother and friend? She taught me and made me what she could, my angel mother, and when I was old enough to travel and hold a sword, she sent me out into the wide, wide world to serve the secret emperor. And I was proud to do it." He leaned back. "Tell me, Franklin. You are not a poor man, as I hear it, nor an unimportant one. Why, then, do you dress in linsey-woolsey rather than silk and lace?"

"What divergence is this?"

"If you plan to kill me, you might at least answer that one question."

"Because I am Benjamin Franklin, the son of Josiah Franklin, a tallow chandler and a more honest man than any silk-gowned lord on Earth. Plain cloth is good enough for me. If I wore silk, I would still have all the same faults, with vanity added to them, and would have gained nothing but the respect of fools."

"A lovely sentiment, very Protestant. But once you wore fine, courtly garb, *ja?*"

"Once I was younger. Experience is an expensive school, but fools will learn in no other."

"So you thought yourself a fool for going 'gainst your father. He brought you up one way, and when you strayed from it, you eventually brought yourself to task, *ja?*"

"Will you compare my father to your damned familiar?" Franklin asked heatedly.

"Yes. How is a child to know? And once the child is man, how hard for him to doubt? You might leave your father behind, and stray from his ways under other influences, but me—"

"And yet I think you have come to convince me that you have, indeed, strayed? That you are no longer an enemy? Oh, this is sweet. How many years it has taken you to use honey instead of vinegar! What genius among your number came upon this stratagem? Your own 'mother'?"

"No. She is no more."

"You mean to say you dismissed her?"

"No. I mean to say she is dead."

"Dead?"

"Ha. And now I pique your interest, if I didn't already. Yes, they can die. They are strange, they are ancient, but not immortal. Wouldn't you like to know how to kill malakim?"

"I know how."

"Sir, with all respect, I do not think you do."

"I know how to kill *you*."

"I am *not* a malakim, nor ever was I. I am a man, or something they have made from a man. If you are confused in that, you are confused indeed."

"But—as I said—without *your* kind, there is little they can do."

"Not true. There are more sorts of malakim than you can

dream. Know you not of the cherubim who humbled mighty Gomorrah? Do you think you have met *them* in your travels? I assure you, you have not, or you would not walk on two legs. But you *will* meet them, sir—you will. Their way is being prepared."

"So you say. I have no proof of them."

"Ah, the scientific. If you have not seen it, 'tis not real."

"Why, yes. Why haven't I seen these death angels? If I am such a thorn in their sides, why do they continue to send such ineffectual assassins as yourself, when Michael himself might claim my soul?"

The man hesitated. "As you said, they normally have little influence in our world, the world of matter. But engines have been built—dark engines, which bring their hideous strength from the aether to atoms. A year ago, they had no such contrivances; a month from now—or two—they will. As well, their ancient law still restrains them, a law older than Adam. But that is changing, too, my friend."

"Call me 'friend' again, and I will have your heart."

The fellow blinked, and was suddenly a blur of motion, a long silver splinter in his hand. Robert moved quickly, too, but the difference was as a hummingbird to a starling.

Robert was not the hummingbird. He managed to slap away the blade darting for Franklin's throat, but the warlock's other hand snapped out faster than vision and cracked solid against Robert's jaw. Franklin had time to sprawl back and drag at his pistol, but had it only half from his belt before the warlock had bounded over the table like a cat and landed with the point of his smallsword pressing into the flesh that covered Franklin's heart. A small red stain began to spread on the white fabric. Franklin tried to look brave, waiting for the yard of steel to slide into his chest.

The warlock stepped back, saluted, and sheathed his blade. Franklin stared at him. About the same time, Robert wobbled up, *kraftpistole* drawn. Franklin held up his hand and signaled not to shoot; Robert understood, but kept the pointed tip of the weapon trained on the warlock.

The patrons and landlord of the Boar's Head were staring at the three of them, wide-eyed.

Frowning, Franklin took a step toward the man. "And now I am to trust you, I suppose?" he whispered. "Was that the outcome you hoped?"

The warlock unbuckled his sword belt and let it drop. He held up his hands. "No, I would not expect that," he replied. "But I place myself in your care."

Franklin nodded. "You will regret it, if I find this to be some sort of ruse, I promise you." He looked around at the crowd. "Thank you for your attention, ladies and gentlemen," he shouted. "My friend and I here had a wager to first blood. As you all will witness, I've a bet to pay. I'm sorry if we disturbed you."

Some nodded, and most looked dubious; but in Charles Town, one rarely asked questions about such things.

"Come along with me," Franklin commanded.

Once outside, Tupman and Stark joined them. "Is he for the ship or the dirt?" Stark growled, his intonation clearly indicating his preference.

"Neither, for the moment. He's for the jail we keep out on Nairne's plantation." He glanced meaningfully at their captive and rubbed the pricked spot on his breast. "For the moment," he repeated, with feeling.

The warlock turned back to him, and his eyes flashed feral red. "Don't keep me waiting too long, Mr. Franklin. Things are not as they were. My old masters are troubled and impatient. Their plan proceeds in a new direction as we speak. Their goal is in sight."

"What goal?"

"The eradication of that troublesome race of insect, Man."

2.

A Death

Adrienne rode a wheel of Ezekiel toward the top of the sky, angels burning beneath her feet. The midday sun brightened as they ascended, as the sky paradoxically darkened and the air grew chill. Below, the Earth showed her generous curve.

"Beautiful," Veronique de Crecy murmured from her armchair. Like Adrienne, she gazed thoughtfully out the thick windows of the carriage, her pale face tinted blue by the light thrown up from distant seas. "How much higher may we ascend?"

Adrienne glanced at the brass banks of dials thoughtfully. "Not much farther. We are near to six leagues above the Earth now. Outside of this carriage, we would die from lack of air. My djinni keep the atmosphere in the carriage thick, but must draw it from somewhere. If we advance much higher, they will have none to give us."

"A pity. I should like to walk upon the Moon and gaze earthward."

"One day." Adrienne shrugged.

"Before I am a hag, that I might seduce a moon man."

Adrienne was considering a remark at her friend's expense when the death appeared.

Adrienne could see more than most people. With better-than-mortal eyes she could gaze upon the intricate patterning of the aether that gave matter form; she could see the djinni which served her, flitting through that unworldly terrain.

But not with human vision. The aether had no optical

reality, no colors, no shade nor line. Her angel eyes were translators, making the language of aether into that of light. Like any translator, they must use words already in existence, and so Adrienne saw those beings and that insubstance as if they were mathematical diagrams, plates from a book of science—translated, so to speak, into the visual language of science.

Usually.

But the death looked like Death. Scraps of skin like black parchment clung to a white skull swaying on rotting vertebrae. From between yellowed scapulae, raven wings sprouted and spread high apart, each feather surrounding an open human eye. Taloned fingers groped for her.

She sat frozen by the sight for only a heartbeat before lashing out. Once her command of the djinni had been clumsy; but over the years they had developed a shorthand together, and now the aethereal creatures carried out her commands almost as she thought them. Air hardened and quivered with bound lightning around her and Crecy, as a hundred djinni grappled the death, tore at it, sought to unravel the subtle harmonies of which it was made.

It shrugged them off, grinning its skull grin. It waved aside her protections.

"Finally, you come where I can reach you," it said. It spoke in her own voice—as all the djinni spoke to her in her own voice.

Adrienne renewed her attack. It gave back briefly, but then came on again, folding its wings down around her. She caught a last glimpse of Crecy, frantic with alarm. Crecy likely saw none of this, save the air suddenly flashing with light and flame.

Wrapped in the dark pinions, Adrienne knew she was dying. Her heart shuddered in her chest, and her body faded into unreality.

All but her right hand, her *manus oculatus*. It remained real: an anchor, a beacon, her source of power. She had found it years ago, in a dream, and knitted it to the stump where her real hand had once been. Awaking from the dream, she had found it true. The *manus oculatus* was her link to the djinni, the source of her power and unnatural vision. Ultimately, it was what kept the Ezekiel wheel in the air, and her and Crecy breathing.

She reached with it and caught hold of something that hummed like a plucked lute string. No, not a lute string, but a string of figures mathematical, almost forgotten, suddenly complete as they never had been before. She pulled on the thread, and it sang a higher pitch.

The death tore apart like a rotten linen cloth hung in the wind. It was gone.

She came to herself with Crecy kneeling over her, lean frame bowed with tension.

"Adrienne, what happened? Are we still in danger?"

Adrienne took a moment to gather the reports of her surviving servants, then shook her head. "No. But start us back down."

Crecy nodded, and turned the appropriate valves.

"What happened?" she repeated a moment later.

"Shh," Adrienne replied, closing her eyes. Shards of the death blew about the cabin like snow in a crystal globe, settling on her shoulders and skirt, melting into nothingness. She caught at them, searching for some clue as to its nature—what it was, who had sent it. She saw some hint of that—an eye, a voice, a unique vibration. She also saw how she had killed it, though that knowledge was vanishing with equal speed.

She saw instantly that she had a choice. She could either learn something of where the death had come from, or she could retain the knowledge of how to kill it. She could not do both.

It would be more useful to remember how to kill another such creature, wouldn't it? But then she saw something she recognized, and she made the other choice, cupped the fragments and nurtured them, melted them together until she had something whole. It was an image, hanging in the frame of her thoughts like a little oil painting. Just an image, but she almost wept at the intensity of her recognition.

She saw a boy, around twelve, sitting on a raised wooden platform. He was clad in a silk robe of Chinese design, surrounded by men in similar dress. But while the boy was pale of complexion, those surrounding him were suited to the raiment, Oriental. Two others—clad in clothing of rougher weave—reminded her of the Natchez and Huron Indians she had seen at the court of Louis XIV.

"Ah," she finally gasped, and opened her eyes to Crecy's concerned gaze. "I've seen him, Veronique," she whispered, as gravity sucked them down through thickening air. "After ten years, I've seen my son."

They watched the Earth grow larger for a space. Crecy, long used to Adrienne's moods, waited for her to continue.

"Don't speak of this," Adrienne finally told her friend, "neither the attack nor what I just told you. I need to think upon it."

Crecy nodded. "But what sort of attack was it? I saw some of your defenses. I sensed more, but with each passing year I am less able to see the malakim. It was one of them, wasn't it? One of the *malfaiteurs*?"

"I don't know. It was different from any djinn I have ever known."

"But no match for your own guardians."

"No. It was more than a match for my djinni. I don't know how I survived, or even what I did."

"But—*it* brought you a vision of *Nicolas*?"

"Yes."

"How do you know it was him?"

"I know. He has his father's face, and—" She paused, considering. "—I just know."

"We will find him, then," Crecy vowed.

"Yes, we will," Adrienne agreed.

A long silence seeped into the cabin.

"Congratulations, by the way," Crecy added after a time. "Your wheel seems to be a success."

"I suppose it is," Adrienne replied.

"You don't sound pleased. Did you hope to fail?"

"No, of course not. But this device is nothing very new, really. The same sort of articulator, a somewhat different variety of djinni, nothing more. Indeed, in some ways it is not as impressive as the winged flying machines Swedenborg invented five years ago."

"Nevertheless, I'm sure the tsar will be pleased by yet another sort of flying engine."

"I suppose. If he ever returns," Adrienne replied. "He has not been heard of for three months, since he left Peking."

"Little point in worrying about it."

"It may be time to *do* something about it."

The great wheels surrounding their suspended carriage slowed as they neared the ground.

"Right back to the square," Crecy noticed. "How did we manage that, with the Earth spinning beneath us?"

"The djinni know their way home. It is a simple matter," Adrienne replied. Something had been bothering her all day, even before the attack; and that statement seemed to sum it up without actually revealing it to her. For ten years she had commanded the malakim, and the number of her servants had grown. She had built devices—like the one they rode in now—that she could only have dreamed of as a younger woman. What then seemed so pale about it all?

They emerged into the square before the Saint Petersburg Academy of Sciences, greeted by cheering and applause from hundreds of voices and hands. Peasant and aristocrat alike crowded near to see the angelic device and its creator.

The tsar's lieutenant, Prince Menshikov, met them as they stepped from the carriage. Dressed jauntily in a sanguine and gold coat and waistcoat, he swept his plumed tricorn from his head and bowed deeply.

"Ladies, how was your voyage? We followed you until even telescopes could show us nothing."

Adrienne smiled diplomatically. "Our journey went well. Perhaps next time you would care to ride in it yourself, sir."

Menshikov's return grin was tight. She knew he did not like flying machines, even the proven—if ponderous—airships of early design. "It would by my honor, lady," he replied. Whatever Menshikov was, he was no coward. Together they walked back to the academy, accompanied by the jubilant crowds.

"Still no word from the tsar?" Adrienne asked Menshikov. There was no chance that they would be overheard amongst the tumult.

"No. I rather hoped you would see him from up there." He paused. "I'm joking, of course."

"Of course. But with the wheel we can at least mount fast expeditions, faster by far than the old airships."

"How quickly before one could cross Siberia to North America?"

"I thought he vanished in Peking."

"We now have reliable intelligence that he left there—headed, we presume, toward the American settlements. I wonder, as one crosses the demarcation, if somehow aetherschreibers are rendered useless?"

"It's possible," Adrienne replied. "I shall send servants to investigate. But the wheel could close even that distance in mere days."

"Very good," Menshikov said. "Perhaps we could discuss this more fully later—in private?"

After two or three beats, when she did not respond, he patted her on the shoulder. "I'm joking, of course!"

"Of course," Adrienne said. She did not particularly like Menshikov, with his sly suggestion of a leer, but he was the tsar's closest friend and, for the moment, ruler of Russia. There was no point in insulting him.

"I've prepared something of a celebration," Menshikov went on.

"My lady is somewhat taxed —" Crecy began, but Adrienne lay a hand on her shoulder.

"Nonsense," she said. "If the prince has prepared an entertainment for us, Veronique, we shall not refuse him."

"You won't regret it." Menshikov beamed.

It was more than a small entertainment, but a lavish feast and ball. Menshikov was very free with the treasury—so free that much of it ended in his own pocket. Each time the tsar left his best friend in charge, he returned furious with Menshikov's avarice, but each time forgave him.

If the tsar did not return, Russia would be bankrupt in a few years.

If Menshikov meant to impress Adrienne, his efforts were wasted. She did not taste the food or thrill at the gown he provided her. Instead, she went over the attack and her vision again and again, trying to recall more of what she lost. What had she "pulled" to make the death dissolve?

"Won't you dance, Mademoiselle?" a voice said near her ear.

She looked up and smiled into a pretty young face. "Hello, Elizavet. Your French is improving."

"Thank you," the young woman said, flopping unceremoniously onto the chaise. "I'm quite exhausted from dancing. Aren't you going to take a turn?" She signaled for a servant.

"I'm a bit tired."

"Oh, but there are so many handsome men here tonight!" she replied. "I hardly see how you can resist. They ask questions about you, you know. I don't know what to tell them. You aren't my father's mistress, are you?"

Adrienne's smile broadened. "The tsar and I are friends and confidants, nothing more," she replied.

"So it's only that d'Argenson fellow? Really, I don't see how anyone can make do with only one, unless she is so ugly that she has no choice. And you, Mademoiselle, are far from ugly—"

Adrienne held a finger to Elizavet's lips. "Hush," she said, "or I'll be forced to double your studies tomorrow."

Elizavet's eyes widened. "Surely Mademoiselle does not expect me to come to tutorial the day after a ball?"

"On the contrary. If your father finds I have neglected your education while he is away, he will have me beaten."

The servant arrived, bearing a tray of wineglasses.

"What is this stuff?" Elizavet asked, sniffing at the wine. "Bring me some vodka."

"Yes, Tsarevna."

Elizavet lay back, smiled, and closed her eyes. She was a fetching young creature, a tall, dark beauty. Though less than a decade younger than Adrienne—the tsarevna was twenty-three—somehow the gap seemed centuries. Had Adrienne ever been so carefree?

No, she reflected, of course she hadn't.

"I do hope Father returns soon. I'm sure he will bring something very special from China." She looked seriously at Adrienne. "I hope you will ask God to bring him home safe."

"I have little influence with God, I fear," Adrienne replied.

"How can that be? It is clear that God loves you. Even the patriarch says so. Everyone believes it. Some say you are a saint." Her vodka came, and she took a satisfied gulp.

"You don't believe that," Adrienne accused.

"Well, to only have one lover you must suffer from *some* religious affliction." Elizavet grinned. She finished the vodka. "Well, there." She sighed. "If you will not dance with these poor fellows, my own duty is clear, despite my fatigue." She got up and adjusted her bodice so as to dip it lower, showing her snowy bosom to better advantage.

"But I will see you at your lesson tomorrow," Adrienne warned.

"Yes, of course." She bent to place a kiss on each of Adrienne's cheeks, and then returned to the festivities.

* * *

Adrienne rose from her bed a bit after midnight and went to the window. She parted the curtains and placed her palms and forehead against the thick glass, gazing down at the lights of Saint Petersburg.

Under the moon, it was a fairy city, ice and luminescence, slender towers with peaks like swollen but still-closed tulips, awaiting the kiss of spring to bloom, the Neva River a lambent walkway for snow sprites to caper upon. It was beautiful, cold, and distant. It had been her home for ten years.

The glass was thick and scientific, and yet still the chill worked through, pricked gentle goose bumps on her naked skin. Her human hand, flush against the pane, felt the cold keenly; her angel hand felt it not at all. She wondered if she stood there long enough, letting her blood slowly chill, if she might herself became a thing of snow: a crystal in woman's form, ageless, forever watching, doing nothing, thinking nothing. She would like that.

Bedclothes rustled behind her, but she did not turn, even when Hercule spoke, in sleep-torpid tones.

"Adrienne?" he asked.

"Go back to sleep, Hercule."

"I would that you would join me."

"There is more to the world than what you would have, Hercule."

There was a significant pause, during which the covers rustled a bit more. She did not need to turn to see him, with his thoughtful eyes and broken nose, his thick brown hair in disarray. She did not need to see, for the thousandth time, him trying to puzzle her, to understand what he had done to upset her.

"How beautiful you look, standing there," he said quietly, real admiration in his voice. "You are the most beautiful woman I know."

Adrienne wondered privately what that had to do with anything. Why did men say such things?

"Go back to sleep, Hercule," she repeated, trying to be gentle.

"I cannot, when you cannot. I know that something happened on your sky ship. And yet you say nothing."

"I have nothing to say, Hercule."

She heard his feet hit the floor then and held up her hand, still staring out at the city. "Please, stay there," she said.

"What have I done to you?" he asked. "Are you angry with me?"

"Hercule, this has nothing to do with you."

"I *love* you. If it has to do with you, it has to do with me."

She did turn, then, leaving the curtains open behind her, and brushing her thick dark hair from her face.

"Is it because of Irena?" he continued.

"Your wife has even less to do with this than you, Hercule."

"I would have married *you*, Adrienne. A hundred times I asked you—"

"Hercule," she said, softly, "I do not care to repeat myself. My thoughts do not concern you, your wife, your children, or some marriage to you that I never wanted."

"I do not understand you at all."

"Perhaps you should go, then."

"You were happy enough to have me here earlier."

"I wanted you then, or thought I did." Her voice softened. "I needed a friend, Hercule, a true friend, and I do not have many—only you and Crecy."

"Small wonder, when you treat us so. Why is this friendship only on your terms? Why is it that when you want me in your bed, I am always there, but when I want you in mine—"

"I think Irena is not so broadminded," Adrienne said, attempting a smile.

"You know what I mean."

She gazed at him for a moment. "Have I done so badly by you, Hercule? What did you want when we met? A powerful prince to serve, one suited to the new order of things. A secure position. Have I not provided those? Isn't the tsar the sort of patron you were searching for?"

"I cannot deny it. But—"

"But what? Love was never part of our bargain. You only love me still because you cannot possess me. If we had married, you would now be with some other woman, and it would be me—not Irena—lonely in her bed tonight."

"That is untrue. I never loved Irena. But I needed connections here, and she is the daughter of a boyar. And what man does not want sons?"

"Yes," Adrienne said bitterly. "What *man* does not."

He reacted as if he had been slapped. "I'm sorry, love. I know you miss Nico. I forget sometimes—"

She almost told him, then, about her vision. She wanted to, but some indefinable fear stopped her.

"You see, Hercule? I can never forget. I work in my laboratory, I make weapons and toys for the tsar, I tutor my students, I try to avoid the intrigues of my enemies—and yet, I never forget. I never cease wondering where he is, where he was taken. Whether he is even alive. And yet now—" She stopped, realizing that Hercule had somehow coaxed her farther than she meant to go.

"Now what? Have you had some news?"

"It is nothing. Listen to me, Hercule. This is what is important for you to know. Someone tried to kill me. I suspect that this person has something to do with Nico and his disappearance."

"Someone here or abroad?"

"I am best known here. The question is whether the attack was instigated by a human enemy or one less tangible."

"You suspect the *malfaiteurs*? The evil angels? Surely none here serves them."

"Crecy once did."

"You don't suspect Crecy."

"No. My point is that they are devious and well practiced at keeping their servants secret."

"It's good that you tell me this. I will inform our spies."

"Only those you trust the most. Whoever this sorcerer is, he has at his command something very dangerous, very ugly. It might change everything."

"But you won't tell me what."

"Not yet."

"Because you do not trust me."

"I trust you, Hercule, as much as I trust any living creature."

"Which means you do not trust me very far."

She walked near where he sat on the edge of the bed, and she bent to kiss his forehead. "I cannot help that, Hercule. I have been betrayed too often."

Hercule puffed out a breath. "You carry too much, and love too little. It makes you hard. I love you, but you are not the woman I met, there in the fields of Lorraine."

"No," she quietly replied. "No, I am better than she. Stronger. Now go back to sleep."

"I think, rather, that I should leave."

She shrugged. "As you wish."

He set about gathering up his clothes. When he was dressed, he turned back to her, and she saw a tear glisten in his eye. "I do not think I shall be back here," he said.

"Hercule—"

"I am loyal to you. I will die to protect you, and I will root out your enemies and crush them. But I cannot bear to be your lover anymore. It wounds too deep."

Adrienne felt only the faintest of catches in her throat when she replied, "As you wish."

When he was gone, she turned back to the window, and the scene outside seemed inexplicably blurred, as if she, too, were weeping. She knew that could not be true, for in all her years in Saint Petersburg she had never wept. She had used every last tear she had when her son was stolen.

And so she banished thoughts of Hercule d'Argenson; and in the fog of light and shadow, she saw instead the image of Nicolas. She wondered how she dared hope again. It seemed a dangerous thing to do—to feel, to hope. To love.

Tomorrow she would learn what she could of China.

An hour or so later her eyelids finally drooped shut, but she could not have been long asleep when her djinni servants awoke her. She sat up in bed, the alarm still buzzing in her skull.

In the distance she heard the faint reports of gunfire. And there was someone in her room.

3.

Flint Shouting

"Tell me again about all of the bee-yoo-tee-ful women we're goin' t' see out here in Witchy-taw country," Tug demanded, shading his eyes with one massive hand, staring off mournfully at the distant horizon. It *was* distant, too, the gently undulating terrain and scattered, dwarfish trees doing little to shorten the vastness of the world.

Behind him, one of the horses snorted, and Tug's mount tossed its head. Red Shoes ran his gaze over the lot. Of their original ten beasts, eight remained, but they didn't look well. They needed a long rest.

"We need fresh mounts," Red Shoes observed.

"Id'n that what I just said?" Tug grunted. "How far to the Witchity-taw villages?"

"I'm not sure," Red Shoes told him. "I'm not certain this is Wichita country."

"Y' mean y'r lost?" Tug asked incredulously. "How can an In'yun get lost?"

"How can a sailor get lost at sea, Tug? Water is the same, yes?"

Tug screwed his face into a scowl. "It han't comparable."

"Of course it is. I have never been west of the Great Water Road before. Why should I know my way around?"

"You seem awful certain about where we're goin', seein' you've never been here."

"Going, yes. I have a sort of arrow pointing in my head. It's where we *are* that I'm not so certain of."

"We han't nowhere, is where," Tug grumbled. Then he shrugged. "Kind o' fetchin', though. Does remind me o' the sea, after all."

"You miss sailing?"

"Not a damn bit. Miserable life, the sea. Half the men I've known died o' scurvy, t' other half o' brawlin' f 'r rum, t' other half from the pox. I've gone and lived twice as long as any pirate ever, I think. Nah, I complain, but I'd rather be out here in the In'yun country. Or wherever we are." He slapped Red Shoes on the back so hard the Choctaw felt as if he might cough up a rib. " 'S long as you find me a woman somewhere."

They continued on, through land that looked much the same.

The next day, about midday, they heard someone singing. Curious, they cautiously followed the sound, finally cresting the edge of a small gorge to see a man lying at the bottom of it, naked, staked out spread-eagle. He stopped singing when he saw them.

"Nakidiwa! Nakidiwa!" he shouted.

Red Shoes didn't know the language, so he didn't answer. Instead, he gazed carefully around. "Watch out, Tug," he whispered. "Whoever did this to him might still be near."

"I getcha, Cap'n."

"Eespanolee?" the fellow shouted. *"Fa-lenchee? Enkalisha? Anompa o?"*

Red Shoes raised his brows in surprise. That last was in Choctaw, or maybe Mobilian, the trade language based on Choctaw. He guessed Mobilian, and spoke in that tongue. "You speak this?" he asked.

"As if born speaking it," the fellow answered, with an accent so thick it was nearly incomprehensible.

"What about English?"

"A few words."

"French?"

"I speak French good," he replied, in French. It was better than his Mobilian.

"Hey!" Tug said. "That In'yun is speakin' French!"

"You speak French, yes, Tug?"

"Good enough t' buy rum and tell lies t' a whore." To prove it, he switched to the language. "Hey, you, what the hell you doin' tied up so?"

"Improving my character," the man answered cheerfully.

"Then you wouldn't have us cuttin' y' loose?"

"I'm of the opinion that my character is improved by now."

"Who did this?" Red Shoes asked.

"People who didn't think much of my character. Will you free me?"

"Should I? Did enemies do this or your own people?"

"How should I know? It was dark."

"Good-bye," Red Shoes said. "I wish you luck with your character." He started off.

"Wait!" the fellow called. "Not that it's your business, but it was a simple misunderstanding involving a woman."

"Woman?" Tug perked up.

"Yes. The wife of a chief, if you must know. A family matter—the chief is a cousin of mine."

"Ah. Why didn't they cut your nose off?" That was the usual punishment for adultery.

"They might in another day or so. Come, release me and I can be useful to you. You're a long way from home, yes? You could use fresh horses—some food maybe?"

Red Shoes shrugged. "Horses, yes. And we could use a guide, someone who knows the languages of the plains."

"I'm the perfect guide. I was a tracker for the Frenchmen that came this way a few years ago. I speak a little of every language."

Red Shoes considered, noticing as he did that the fellow's eyelids were tattooed blue. It made him look like a raccoon when he blinked. Hadn't he heard the Wichita were marked like that?

Red Shoes nodded at Tug. "Cut his bonds."

The one-time sailor did so. The young man sat up, rubbing his wrists and ankles. "Thank you," he said. "As the French say, I am at your service. Now, where do you need guided to?"

Red Shoes pointed.

"Northwest. Good. But where?"

"I'm not sure. A great distance. Maybe another few weeks travel. Maybe more."

"You're looking for someone, or something?"

"I don't know."

The fellow blinked, and a wary expression came over him. "Is this shaman business?"

"Yes."

"Wonderful." He rolled his eyes.

"You're still willing to guide us?"

"Will it give me something good to talk about? Will it make a good story?"

"Almost certainly."

"Well, then. It's probably best I'm not seen around here for a while anyway." He considered again. "My name is Tahanitsiaskase," he told them.

"An' my name is Abakabakadakabar," Tug retorted. "I can't say that."

"Ah—in French, 'Flint Shouting,' " the Wichita said.

"When will you be ready to leave, Flint Shouting?" Red Shoes asked.

The fellow looked at the sun, then glanced a little nervously southward. "The sooner, the better," he replied.

As they moved north, Flint Shouting shed his nervousness like a snake rubbing out of a skin.

"They should have known better!" he said. "I can't be caught, and when I am caught, I always escape."

"It may be that Tug and I are due some credit," Red Shoes said dryly.

"The Dreams love me," Flint Shouting said. "If they hadn't sent you to release me, they would have sent someone else."

"Dreams?" Tug grunted.

"The Frenchman I guided didn't know about dreams either. Do none of the white people know about the Dreams?"

Red Shoes shrugged noncommittally. He didn't know much about the Wichita, and though he suspected he knew what Flint Shouting was talking about, he wasn't sure.

"They have their own names for things," he said, "and some pretty strange ideas about the world. Why don't you educate him?"

"Naw," Tug said. " 'S okay."

Flint Shouting ignored the ex-pirate. "Dreams are all around us," he said, waving his hands at the earth and sky. "There are the *Itskasanakatadiwaha*, the Dreams-That-Are-Above—like the Sun, the Thunderbird or the Owner-of-Black-and-White-Knives. Then there are the *Howwitsnets-kasade*, the Dreams-Down-Here, which can be divided into the Dreams-in-the-Water and the Dreams-Closest-to-Man."

"Huh. Angels is the first, maybe—the Dreams above? An' the second maybe divils an'—say! Dreams-in-the-Water? You mean like a mermaid?"

Flint Shouting only looked puzzled at these comparisons, so Red Shoes replied. "There are many dreams in the water—the serpent with horns, the white panther, and the pale people. The pale people are what you call mermaids, Tug, but you would not want to meet them, no matter how much you want a woman. They are not really of flesh, and they are soul stealers."

"Like that thing you say you fought in Venice—the one as took Rev'rend Mather's soul?"

"Exactly."

"So you *are* a shaman," Flint Shouting said. "How did you come by your power?"

"When I was very young, Kwanakasha, the little man,

called my name at night. He spoke to me, sleeping and waking, though no one could see him but me. Being a child, I did not think it strange—I thought everyone had a voice like mine, a kwanakasha. I did not know my danger, did not know that I was slowly being made into an accursed being, a sorcerer, a danger to my people. A servant of the Dreams-in-the-Water, as you call them. But my elders noticed him. They helped me lay a trap for the little man. We caught him and made him my servant. Now I fight them."

"You have Dream enemies?" Flint Shouting asked.

"Every Dream is my enemy. The powers of the other world have decided that we must die, and I will not allow it."

"*Who* must die? You two?"

"Human beings. All of the tribes and nations on Earth."

Flint Shouting swore something in his own language.

"What?" Red Shoes asked.

"You an enemy of the Dreams, and me guiding you to the very heart of Dreams-Closest-to-Man. Maybe my luck *has* run out."

"It surely has if you don't find us those horses you promised, and soon," Red Shoes said.

"Tomorrow we'll come to a village where they still like me. I think."

They camped that night by a clear, shallow stream racing out of the low mountains crouching on the southern horizon. Cottonwoods, elms, and willows whispered in a dry breeze. Tug and Flint Shouting built a fire, Tug doing most of the work while Flint Shouting directed.

Red Shoes climbed the nearby hill to stand first lookout. From there the earth spun away, turning the color of a strong bruise at the edges. Far, far east he saw tiny lights that might be fires. A village? A hunting party?

More than a day's ride, whatever it was, and not in the direction they were going.

He smoked a little tobacco and tried to think, but his mind was tired. He found himself instead listening idly to Tug and Flint Shouting—by some trick of sound and the hollow below, he could hear them quite clearly.

". . . used t' be a pirate," Tug was saying. "Sailed with Edward Teach, Blackbeard, when he took Charles Town, an' later when he sailed out t' the Roman sea and Venice an' all. Aye, that 'uz an adventure."

"Then how is it you ended up here, with a Choctaw?"

"Huh. Red Shoes was on that last trip. Ten years gone, that. See, some wondrous terrible thing had happened, but nobody knew what. God-rotted big waves wrecked our harbors and boats, and in all America we hadn't a flotilla unless we combined English, French, and pirate. But we did it, and we sailed back to mother England to see what was th' matter."

"What *was*?"

"Don't you know?"

"England is where you white people come from?"

"Damn, but y'r more ignorant than me. Yeah, it's where th' best o' us're from, anyhow. An' what was wrong was a big damn hole where London once were. Some French magicians had brung down a piece o' the sky, we found out later."

Red Shoes could hear the strain in the brief silence that followed. The Englishmen—even those, like Tug, born far from England—still took the loss of their mother country hard.

"It's well known that the French and English have been enemies, but both are enemies of the Spanish," Flint Shouting offered.

"Not no more. H'ant no England, no France, no Spain. Just us as call ourselves English or Spanish or whatnot. An' how true is it now? I don't know, nor hardly care anymore."

"That still hasn't explained—"

"Well, Red Shoes 'uz on the expedition, y' see. He saved my life, an' then we were together at the battle of Venice, where our captain Blackbeard made his last stand. Well, after that, I'd about had enough o' the sea, though I stayed on in Charles Town f'r six years. But a while back I took up the trading with the Choctaw, seein' as I had a friend there in Red Shoes."

Another pause. "And I'll tell ya this," Tug went on. "I h'ant never had a better friend. I'm a big man—people have been known to piss 'emselves just lookin' at me. Fear I've had, and respect, but true friends few. That In'yun up there is one of 'em. You durst hurt or betray 'im, and ol' Tug'll make you wish to y'r dreamy gods you hadn't."

"Understood," Flint Shouting answered.

Red Shoes smiled briefly. If Tug knew he had just heard him, he would be mortified. He usually had to be good and drunk to get so sentimental.

The big man, for all his wicked ways, had nothing crooked in his heart. And whether he knew it or not, he was Red Shoes' best friend, too. His own people had always feared him just a little too much to really like him. Even among family he felt set apart. But Tug—Tug had no questions, no reservations. Tug was his brother in a way no Choctaw had ever been or could be.

It was nice, from time to time, to know the big man felt the same way.

"Look like haystacks," Tug said, regarding the village.

Having seen haystacks in Pennsylvania and Europe, Red Shoes had to agree. The Wichita houses were tall, rather conical frameworks of cedar and willow laths covered with bundles of grass. Each had two doors, one facing east, the other west. To Red Shoes, this made them more resemble beehives like the ones the Italians brought with them to South Carolina.

There were only twelve such houses, but each was large enough to hold a small family. There were also a number of open-sided ramadas—summer houses consisting of a roof to keep the noonday sun out and not much more. Even from this vantage, he could see the women moving about in those, cooking, pounding corn, weaving mats and baskets.

Except for the odd shape of the houses, it could almost be a Choctaw village. Strings of white, red, and yellow corn, their shucks plaited in long ropes, hung drying in the eaves of the ramadas, along with strips of pumpkin and other sorts of squash. The sight of that and the smell of woodsmoke mixed with the scent of roasting meat made his mouth water. For weeks he and Tug had eaten mostly "cold meal," parched cornmeal mixed with a little water. Sustaining but hardly appetizing.

Real food would be a welcome break.

He tried not to get his hopes up. *These aren't my people,* he reminded himself. *They owe me nothing.* They might do anything to him, so far from the retribution of his own kin. It was said that there were cannibals under this western sky. And worse.

Five thickset, dark men on horses rode out to meet them. Each had eyes tattooed like Flint Shouting's, and each had a number of small star tattoos picked out here and there. They wore loincloths and rode Spanish ponies, smaller than the sturdy Chickasaw horses in Red Shoes' train.

One of the men called something to Flint Shouting in a challenging voice. Flint Shouting replied. Red Shoes didn't know what he said, but in the next instant the leader of the men facing them brandished his ball-headed war club and kneed his horse toward Flint Shouting.

"Hey!" Tug snarled, reaching for his pistol.

Red Shoes restrained him with a hand. The other men were sitting their horses, grinning, and Flint Shouting was whooping in a way that didn't sound angry or frightened. He and the other man rode in circles, waving their clubs playfully, and then both dismounted and began slapping each other around, the way boys might. Both began laughing.

"This is my cousin, Headbreaker," Flint Shouting explained. "He'll trade your tired horses for fresh—they like the look of them, think they'll be good for the blood of their herd. Anyhow, they just raided the Kapaha and have plenty to spare."

"That's good."

"And a feast, tonight, to celebrate my coming. See? I told you they liked me up here."

"Keep your eyes open, Tug," Red Shoes murmured.

"Don't trust him?"

"Not even a little."

"These Witchy-taw. Are they enemies of the Choctaw?"

"Not that I know of. That is, I can't remember any tales of war between us. They live a long way from the Choctaw country, and there are plenty enough foes in the space between. Why bother coming all the way out here when we have Chickasaw, Kapaha, and Wazhazhe so much nearer at hand? The same with them, of course."

"But yer thinkin' it might occur to one o' these fellas that he don't own a single Choctaw scalp, an' why not get it while it's right in his hands?"

"They don't see many white people out this way, either," Red Shoes pointed out mildly.

"Oh. Yeah." Tug cast longing looks at the women surrounding them. Some were passing pretty. Like the men, they were tattooed—concentric circles on their breasts with nipples in the very center, and straight lines that went down their foreheads, over their noses, and across their lips to their chins. "I wish they had some rum or sumpin'."

Night pressed the sky into a purple band on the horizon. Whippoorwills called from somewhere, and bats fluttered about like crazy leaves. Red Shoes wondered where they lived, the bats—caves? There were few trees around.

The Wichita didn't seem dangerous. It was mostly women and children around them now, curious, asking questions they couldn't understand. Flint Shouting was nearby, waxing poetic about something—probably explaining how he had saved Red Shoes and Tug from some terrible fate.

They were brought food—boiled meat and parched corn, and corn bread steamed in shucks. It was good, and not that different from the fare Red Shoes was used to. He ate until his belly was no longer light, but he was still too wary to bloat himself.

As the night wore on, Red Shoes began to relax a little. Flint Shouting came and flopped beside him.

"They've heard things about where we're headed," he said, without introduction.

"What sort of things?"

"Some men went that way months ago to trade—they haven't come back. Strangers have passed through our country, fleeing something they won't or can't talk about, though one mentioned the Iron People. No one has ever heard of such a tribe. Also, certain dreams came to a few men here, telling them to go in that direction. They went and have not returned. What do you know about this?"

"Not much. There is a shadow there I cannot see into. I think that the greatest of dreams is moving there."

Flint Shouting nodded. "Some of the old men think that the fourth age is upon us, the Time-When-Things-Run-Down. Do you think that's what you see?"

"I don't know."

"They say a four-faced giant will be involved."

Red Shoes spread his hands, feeling slightly annoyed. "I don't know," he repeated. "That's why I'm going to find out."

"But you'll stay here a few days, rest."

"No. We're leaving in the morning. You, too, remember?"

"Of course. I gave my word. In the morning, then."

But in the morning, Flint Shouting, the scoundrel, was nowhere to be found. The other Wichita were as good as their pledges, however. They exchanged horses, and for a little powder and shot and one trade ax, they threw in two more. Red Shoes hated to give up the ammunition, but he had the distinct feeling that where they were going, a few extra shots from a musket would not make much difference.

4.

A Ghost

It was twenty past three in the afternoon when Franklin answered a knock at the door of his laboratory and came face-to-face with a grinning ghost.

He knew the hour because the knock interrupted an experiment he had been at all morning, one that required careful notation of the time. He had already been distracted two hours earlier by the frantic pealing of bells all over the city—not on the hour or even half past it, as one might expect, but at precisely twelve after one. Irritated, he had done his best to ignore the hubbub—which probably signified some inconsequential holiday or anniversary he had forgotten. He had managed to get back to work, and after an hour or so the city-wide cacophony had ceased.

But now this knock at the door.

His impulse was to shout at the offender to go away—he wasn't having a good day and had no time for anything he hadn't planned. The matter of the captive warlock weighed heavily on him—he had wanted to question the fellow immediately, but it would put them on the wrong terms if Franklin seemed too eager. So he had resolved to keep him sequestered for the night and better part of the day, to perform the experiment he had already planned, then go out to Nairne's plantation in the evening.

He didn't need another interruption.

But people generally did not knock at his door without

good cause. And so, rising, he cracked his knuckles, straightened his back, and strode toward the door, encouraged by the warm breeze that stole in through the open window. A part of him distantly noted the odd silence outside. No conversation rode the zephyr in, no rattle of carts or thudding of hooves. Another curiosity, for on a Tuesday the street ought to be busy.

He opened the door and found the ghost, leering at him. A tallish, lean ghost with flashing, perpetually amused eyes, a narrow face to suit his frame, lips oiled by merry sarcasm.

"Mr. Janus," the ghost exclaimed, bowing slightly, "how good of you to still be alive!"

Franklin was aware that he was gaping, and that gaping was an impediment to speech. It was not until the figure had grasped him in a hard embrace, favored him with a Gallic kiss on each cheek, and thrust him back with both arms that he was able to stammer anything.

"V-Voltaire?"

"Your memory is nearly perfect!" his visitor rejoiced. "But I am not this 'Vuhvoltaire'—merely 'Voltaire'!"

"You're alive!"

"But how unfair! I accused you of that first! And not only alive, but sprung rather tall! Though your hair beats an early retreat from your forehead."

"How did you—" Franklin had no idea what to ask first. "How did you find me?"

"Inhospitable, I must say, as you have not yet offered me a brandy."

"Of course! It's just that I am so stunned."

"Not as stunned as I hope to be soon, I assure you, sir. The brandy?"

Franklin nodded vigorously, crossed the room quickly to the cabinet where he kept his spirits, chose a likely decanter and two small glasses, and returned to where the impossible Frenchman stood admiring the apparatus littering his tables. He poured the both of them a healthy drink. Voltaire tossed his down immediately, then—on second filling—held his glass at eye level.

"And now I forget myself, sir. Let us drink to the Newtonians."

"The Newtonians," Franklin murmured, and as their glasses clinked and sun glanced through the amber fluid, he saw them all in an instant, gathered around that table in the Grecian Coffeehouse in London. Voltaire the caustic wit; Maclauren the ever-serious Scot; the dour Heath; the traitor Stirling; Vasilisa Karevna, his first love—and himself, a boy of no more than fourteen years, a mote orbiting with planets about the obscure sun of Sir Isaac Newton. The brandy touched his tongue, and he tasted again Vasilisa's lips and alabaster skin, the hope and fear of extreme youth—the emotions of a giant straining in a pygmy frame. He remembered wonder and joy.

He remembered loss, failure, and despair. Maclauren dead, Stirling turned against them, Vasilisa's sudden cruel change from lover to captor—and London, blasted to ash and memory, more lost than Atlantis.

He swallowed and poured himself another, too.

"Delightful stuff, brandy," Voltaire observed, his eyes lidded.

"Please," Franklin said, his trance breaking somewhat. "For God's sake, tell me what you've been up to these twelve years."

"Yes, what I've been up to." Voltaire sighed, a hint of weariness creeping into his voice. As he folded himself down into the armchair indicated, Franklin noticed that time had indeed passed for the Frenchman. The mind had a way of tricking one with faces, of noticing the familiar first. But now he could see the marks of the calendar on Voltaire. Always skeletal, now his face seemed little more than paper drawn tightly over a skull. He was dressed in a fashionable brown coat and waistcoat, but if he had been wearing battered and dusty riding clothes he would not have looked more road weary.

"How long have you been in Charles Town?" Franklin asked.

"I arrived just after noon, in your splendid harbor down there." He took some more brandy, this time with a little more patience. "I needed only to mention your name to find my way. You've earned some bit of fame here, I see, as you did in Venice."

"You heard about that? Did you sail from Venice?"

Voltaire flashed his old, diabolical smile. "No, but I sailed from Cologne, where the magistrate had me thrown bodily out the gate. Some twenty feet I sailed."

Though impatient for a real answer, Franklin could not repress his own smile. "No doubt he had seen your mainmast full-sheeted and assumed you were ready to depart. His wife?"

"Sir! You have known me of old. Would I breach the holy institution of marriage?"

"I do know you of old, and think that you would breach whomever you took a fancy to."

Voltaire dabbed the lacy end of his steinkirk daintily against his upper lip. "How offensive. In any event, his wife—while I'm certain she had a sweet disposition—was, alas, not endowed by our creator with more *figurative* virtues. No, it was a misunderstanding about a certain mistress which set me upon the road from Cologne."

"From Cologne to Venice, then, and thence to here?"

"Oh, heavens. No, from Cologne to Krakow."

"For the love of God, Voltaire, start at the beginning. And no quoting from Genesis!"

Voltaire waved his hand languidly. "Benjamin, I would dearly love to trade our stories, and I promise you we will. But indulge me first, I beg you. You speak to me, for I am weary and must replenish my strength. Be a kind host."

Franklin forced himself to sit. "Very well," he said. "I shall try to be a good host. But please—tell me first if Mr. Heath survived London as well."

A shadow crossed the handsome features. "No, Benjamin, he did not. Please—I am happy now, seeing you here, alive, prospering. Keep me happy, if only for a little while. Do not make me speak of the crowd of skeletons walking behind me."

That was something Franklin could understand well enough. "What will make you happy, dear Voltaire?"

"What makes us all happy? A lie or two, I should think. Tell me that after all of my wanderings I have found a place to rest—an El Dorado, an American paradise, an oasis from war."

"Perhaps I need not lie," Franklin replied seriously. "It is no paradise. Many did not understand how reliant on Mother England we were. There have been plagues and famine aplenty, and shortages of all goods. And yet we have come through it all with a greater strength. I have been about, too. In Venice, as you know, and two years in Bohemia. America is no utopia, but it is a better place to be than those."

"War?"

"That is where we have been lucky, I think. Europe is torn by petty and great wars alike. Here, our wars have all been petty. Our Spanish and French neighbors were poorer than we, and it was best we all cooperate in some measure for each to survive. Since we opened the trade with Venice, we've had to ally to keep that route open and free of pirates. In all, it has been a test to measure the best in us."

"But there has been fighting?"

"The French in the north are half-crazed with hunger and cold, as are their Indian allies. They have raided our northern colonies and our Iroquois friends. As you might guess, we've had to make much tighter alliance with the Indians, since no army can come from England to quiet them should they become 'grieved against us.

"Within the colonies there has been dissent, too, argument over the land held absentee by lords in England who will never claim it, and over the proper method of government."

"And how did you settle that last?"

Franklin leaned forward, suddenly feeling flushed with brandy and not a little pride.

"Losing England was a harsh blow. And yet some good has come of it."

"I have heard the rumors—that you colonies have become a democratic republic."

"That goes too far," Franklin replied, shaking his head. "But it may be one day. When we knew England and England's king were lost to us, we made do as best we could. Each colony was already in some measure self-governing. What was needed was only an o'erarching body to settle questions of the common good. There was a strong Tory sentiment to find a king, but none was to be had. King George and all the Hanover line are dead or remain lost in the Germanies someplace, probably under Muscovite rule. We have never heard a word of them. And the blue blood here in America is all so distant—and thin of royal corpuscles—that no one gentleman would concede to bow before another. And so we assembled a Continental parliament—makeshift I'll admit, so much so that I myself sit in the Commons."

"Congratulations. And this works?"

"It is a crudely forged thing, but in time I think it can be perfected, if we survive our enemies."

Voltaire leaned forward, suddenly very intense. "And of kings?"

"We have no need of one. We have become quite Whiggish here. I think we have escaped kings at last. We see we have no need of them."

"So you say."

"What do you mean? When I first met you, you had been imprisoned and then exiled by the king of France. You had nothing but disdain for the institution of the monarchy, as I remember you."

Voltaire shrugged. "The question is not what you or I might want, is it? No king has ever governed without that his people let him do it. People, it seems, are mightily fond of being told what to do and of having someone to blame for the sorry state of their lives."

"This may be true of some nations, but Englishmen have a natural inclination to liberty, I think, and the Colonials most of all."

"Think you so?" Voltaire asked, almost sharply. "Well, in keeping with Newton's method, I believe we shall see that tested."

Before Franklin could ask what he meant, there came a rap at the door.

"Aye?" Franklin called.

"It's me," a woman's voice answered. Pushing the already open door a bit wider, Lenka Franklin entered. She brushed back a lock of dark brown hair, which had escaped her lace bonnet and draped winsomely over one eye. Her blue eyes—the most intelligent sapphires that had ever been—lit on Voltaire.

"Lenka!" Franklin said. "Please, come in, meet an old friend of mine. Monsieur Voltaire, may I have the honor of presenting to you my wife, Lenka?"

"Oh, *enchanté,* Madame," Voltaire said, bowing deeply, and before she could react, stepping to her quickly and planting a kiss on her lips. Then she did step back, her face reddening. "I greet you in the English fashion," Voltaire explained, "I find it preferable to the French kissing of hands."

"I do not, sir," Lenka replied, regaining her composure. "It is not a fashion I am acquainted or comfortable with."

"Oh, dear, my pardon," Voltaire said, grinning wolfishly. "Allow me then—" He reached for her hand.

"Now I see where you learned your manners with women, Benjamin," Lenka said, deftly withdrawing her fingers from reach. She turned back to Voltaire. "Sir, I must say you did your pupil proud. Benjamin treated me thus when we met the first time. It was a miracle that we met a second."

"Again, your pardon, Madame, for I detect from your melodic accent you are neither English nor French."

"Lenka is Bohemian, Voltaire. We met at the court of Karl VI."

"That was a lucky court for you, then. I had no imagining that Holy Roman soil could bring forth such lovely roses."

"You may stop seducing my wife, Monsieur," Franklin cautioned.

"I am sorry," Voltaire said, touching his fingers to his breast. "But what tragedy to be instantly smitten by the wife of a dear friend—"

"What tragedy," Lenka interrupted in her lilting accent, "that I must be drowned in honey. Stop it, I beg you."

Franklin thought he detected the faintest hint of disingenuousness in her protest.

"Beside the fact," Lenka went on, "I have come to tell Benjamin that he is wanted down at the statehouse."

"For what purpose?"

Her eyes widened slightly. "Then you have not heard?"

"Heard what?"

"Ah!" Voltaire said, holding up a finger. "The thing I was about to tell you."

"Well?" Franklin asked impatiently, looking from the Frenchman to his wife and back.

"Did you did not hear the great clamor a while ago?" Voltaire asked.

"I heard it. Did they ring the bells for you, Voltaire, when you stepped ashore? Am I to be present at a ceremony celebrating French wits?"

"Not for me those bells and horns, but for a fellow passenger. James Francis Edward Stuart."

"James—the Pretender?"

Voltaire nodded. "It seems," he drawled, "you have a king again."

5.

Snares

"Stand up," Adrienne said, her voice harsh even in her own ears. "Identify yourself or die."

An unsteady shadow rose. "It is me, Mademoiselle," a female voice whispered. "Please do not strike me down. I knew not where else to come."

Adrienne uncovered the lanthorn near her bed, and light papered the room.

"Elizavet?" That made sense. She had a key, and the guards would not stop her.

The young woman collapsed to the floor. She still wore the red velvet gown from the ball, but it was stained, torn, and wet. Her black hair tumbled in disarray, her face was streaked with the tracks of tears.

"My God, girl, what brought you here? Without a coat, in that state? It must be almost a league to the palace."

"I ran, lady. I could not—they will kill me or put me in a convent! Please, you must protect me!"

Adrienne rose and shrugged into the silk dressing gown that lay puddled near her bed. She knelt by the tsarevna. "Be calm," she whispered. "Be calm, and tell me what has happened."

Before Elizavet could answer, someone hammered on the door. "Adrienne, it's Veronique. I must see you, now."

"Are you alone?" Adrienne called.

"Yes. Though I may not be for long."

"Come in, then."

The door swung open and Crecy stepped in. She, too, still

wore her ball gown, but had thrown a sword belt over it. She carried a *kraftpistole* in one hand. She took in the two of them and the room with a single glance, shut the door, and barred it.

"What in the name of God is going on?" Adrienne demanded.

"A coup," Crecy said, simply. "Princess, are you well? Did they hurt you?"

"No. I mean, I'm well," Elizavet said. She was still shaking, however, and Adrienne feared the girl had caught a chill.

"It's the Dolgorukys and the Golitsyns," Crecy explained. "They've taken the palace."

"Menshikov?"

"Made prisoner. They waited until everyone was drunk. There was some fighting, but not much. Much of Menshikov's guard was in on it." She shook her head. "This isn't good at all. I knew nothing of this, nor did Hercule. Nor any of our spies." She nodded at Elizavet. "And they're looking everywhere for *her*."

"You've woken my guard, I presume?"

"Of course. They've already taken their positions. Hercule is on his way."

"What can we expect from this?"

Crecy lifted her hands in an I-don't-know gesture.

"Thank you, Veronique," Adrienne said. "Go do what you must. I'll join you soon."

Crecy nodded and left.

When she was gone, Adrienne rang for her maid. The girl appeared a moment later, rubbing sleep from her eyes. They widened wakefully, however, when she saw Elizavet.

"Anna, fetch the tsarevna some clothes. I think mine will fit her—get one of my hunting dresses. And bring hot water." The air in the room was already warming, as the djinni excited the atmosphere at her command. "And bring my black gown, too."

* * *

She stood with Crecy, watching the line of men falling into ranks around the house. The sky had lightened to gray.

"Those are the old Strelitzi uniforms," Crecy remarked, "the ones the tsar banned." She touched the glass. "You are certain of this window?"

"A cannon could not breach it," Adrienne assured her.

Crecy rested her hand on the hilt of her broadsword. She had donned her own uniform—full-skirted coat, waistcoat, and breeches of Adrienne's Lorraine guard. Her copper hair, unbound, flowed from beneath a black tricorn, and a cravat was wrapped tightly about her neck.

"Hercule seemed upset," Crecy ventured. "And not about the coup."

"He broke with me last night," Adrienne told her.

"Really? What prompted that, after all this time?" Her voice rang with its accustomed mockery, but when Adrienne didn't immediately answer, her tone softened. "Are *you* upset?"

"I—should not be," Adrienne concluded.

"Well, no, not in a logical world. After all, you could have married him." She cocked her head quizzically. "Why didn't you—marry him? You never said."

Adrienne wrinkled her brow. "Because I was not *done*."

"What do you mean?"

The troops were shifting below, and both women watched carefully. Adrienne preferred that—she did not need to make eye contact.

"I think you know very well what I mean. A woman may accomplish something, if she does not marry. We two have proved that, haven't we? With no false modesty, I can count myself the foremost female scholar in Russia—perhaps in Europe, given its sorry state. I have a personal guard, a fine house, students, things of my own. And you—how many openly female officers command troops? Marriage robs a woman of that. To marry is to become the appendage of a man, yes? *His* wife, the mother of *his* children. Veronique, I fought too hard and sacrificed too much—and in the end, gained too much—to throw it away on marriage."

From the corner of her eye, she saw Crecy shrug. "Some would argue a married woman might achieve *something*."

"Elizabeth of England. Christina of Sweden. Ninon de Lenclos. None of them married, and for good reason."

"Christina wed."

"Yes. After giving up her throne, and all her power, and her volition. She proves my point, you see?" Adrienne bit her lip. "When I was affianced to King Louis—when I was his mistress—Crecy, I cannot tell you how much I hated that, hated being so completely in his power. I swore it would not happen again."

"Surely Hercule—"

"Is one of the best men I have ever known," Adrienne replied. "But it is not just him—it is the world. Once I have the mark of Eve upon me, nothing will be the same, no matter how tolerant Hercule makes himself. And as much as I trust Hercule, I do not trust him *that* much—not with all my property and everything that I am." She smiled thinly at Crecy. "Remember, my dear? We are of Lilith, not of Eve."

Crecy chuckled. "I am a poor devil's advocate."

"But not a bad devil," Adrienne observed, forcing a smile.

"So now you need a new lover, I think," Crecy said lightly. "Shall I pick one out for you?"

"I think I shall go dry for a time. Even lovers can be tiresome, it seems."

Crecy made a disgusted sound. "Do not play that with me," she said very softly. "You may fool others—you may even fool Hercule—but you do not fool me. Marriage or not, you love him. You wept for three days when he married. I suspect you wept last night."

"Nonsense. Look—is that Prince Golitsyn?" Adrienne

pointed to a man on horseback, approaching the front entrance.

"It is," Crecy replied.

Adrienne pursed her lips. "Admit him. No one else. He may remain armed."

She went to her reception hall and waited.

She did not have long to wait. Two of her Lorraine guards showed Golitsyn into the room. He bowed stiffly, fingered his thick, graying mustache, and cleared his throat.

"Milady," he said.

"How is it with you, Prince Golitsyn?" Adrienne asked, remaining in her armchair. She did not offer the prince a seat.

"As you must know by now, it has been a busy night."

Adrienne nodded. "It's early to pay a call on me, however, and with so many uninvited friends."

"I wanted to personally explain matters, milady, so that you would not worry unduly."

"How very kind of you, Prince Golitsyn. Do go on."

"It is quite simple, really. When Tsar Peter left, almost a year ago, he only intended to be absent for a few months. He surely could not have meant for Menshikov to remain regent for this long. We waited patiently, hoping the tsar would return before Menshikov embezzled the entire treasury, but now we can wait no longer. Serious matters are afoot overseas, and the empire is threatened from within and from without. Moreover, we now have intelligence that the tsar is dead, and all his people with him."

"Menshikov said nothing of this to me."

"Menshikov has tried to hush it up. Perhaps he even had something to do with it. He intended to hold on to the throne and perhaps name himself tsar. So, we have taken steps to prevent this. I am happy to say that there was little bloodshed."

"And who have you named heir?"

"Anna, the duchess of Courland, of course, is the natural choice."

"Anna is the tsar's niece. Elizavet is his daughter. What of her?"

A troubled look passed across Golitsyn's brow. "The tsarevna, as you know, is a bit—ephemeral. She has little interest in governing and probably little talent for it."

"What shall become of her, then?"

Golitsyn cocked his head. "Is she here?" he asked.

"Who is and is not in my house is not your business, no matter how many soldiers you bring with you. Please be so good as to answer my question."

"For her own good, we thought to place her in a quiet place, away from all of this commotion, where she might receive the moral instruction she direly needs."

"A convent," Adrienne clarified.

"Yes, milady."

She steepled her fingers beneath her chin. "What do you want of me? What will become of the Academy of Sciences?"

"Why, nothing, milady. That is what I came to reassure you of. Nothing shall change for you or for the academy, not as long as you wish it to remain as it is."

"In other words, you wish my support of this coup."

"That would be best, of course," Golitsyn replied. "You are highly regarded by everyone."

"But not so highly regarded as to be consulted before shots were fired."

"If more people had known about this, lady, more shots would have been fired, I assure you. And if we failed, I did not want to see you implicated."

"I never knew how thoughtful you were, Prince. This is truly a revelation." She picked up a fan and toyed with it for a moment. "I have no love for Menshikov," she admitted, "and Anna is a suitable choice for empress. But Elizavet will remain in Saint Petersburg, under my eye. I am her tutor, and I know what the tsar wants for her."

"Mademoiselle—"

"I can cause you much trouble, sir, and am prepared to. Or I can cause you none at all."

He colored, smoothed his mustache once again, and nodded briefly. "You will come to the coronation?"

"In my best gown."

"Very well, then, milady. May I wish you good day?"

"If it *were* day."

She watched him go. A few moments later, Crecy and Hercule joined her.

"I want Elizavet's things moved here," Adrienne said. "I do not trust them."

"And about the rest? About the academy?" Crecy asked.

"Why shouldn't that be true?"

Hercule cleared his throat. He could not seem to meet her eyes. "Things are not as simple as the prince made them out to be, of course. The tsar's reforms have never been popular, most especially with the old aristocracy like the Golitsyns. They are part and parcel with the Old Believers. If the tsar does not return, they will begin dismantling the tsar's progress, you may be certain. Already the Strelitzi are back, many wearing beards, which the tsar outlawed. The academy may follow."

"You forget," Adrienne said, "the Academy of Sciences has become a holy pursuit. We have quite convinced the church that our science is that of the angels and the saints. How can they go against that?"

Hercule stared at his hands. "Do not underestimate the Old Believers, or think that you understand them. Most especially do not underestimate their hatred of the tsar. So many of their heads have rolled in the snow—even saints and angels are not proof against hatred. And if they ever discover how you and the tsar have deceived them—"

"Perhaps they already have," Crecy interrupted.

"What can you mean?"

"I say, what if they have? If they know that for ten years you have had your djinni masquerading as saints, appearing in chapels, working miracles—there are many in the academy who might let such a thing slip."

"Then why have they taken no action—Ah!"

"Yes. Can it be a coincidence that you were attacked on the very day of the coup? Someone feared you would support Menshikov. They fear you still, for the tales of what you can do are exaggerated even beyond what you are capable of, which is much. They certainly would not come for you here, in your own house with all of its protections and soldiers."

"You think they seek to lull me."

"I say we must consider it, that is all."

Adrienne nodded. "One thing puzzles me, however. If the attack on me yesterday was part of the coup, why did the malakus carry an image of my son, far away, in China?"

"What is this?" Hercule erupted.

"I will explain it to you soon, Hercule."

"I think I see an explanation," Crecy said. "The tsar has been in China, yes? And Vasilisa Karevna with him. You well know how jealous she has become of you. Suppose that the coup, the sending, the disappearance of the tsar are all connected to her?"

"You have a suspicious, devious mind, Veronique. You really think Karevna would betray another Korai?"

"The Korai is a sisterhood, Adrienne, and sisters can be the most bitter rivals of all. I think this all a trap. If the malakus failed to kill you, then Golitsyn lulls you into a false sense of security until he murders you here. Or you run off to China, in search of your long-lost son, and they catch you there."

"You should have told me all of this," Hercule hissed. "How can I captain your spies if—" He stopped, too angry to continue.

Adrienne got up and crossed back to the window. "I think Veronique is right," she said, after a moment. "I think this is all an elaborate trap of some sort. But set by whom? I think it beyond Karevna, frankly."

"More important," Crecy said, "what will you do about it?"

Adrienne looked at them both and smiled fiercely. "Why, walk into it, of course."

6.

The Scalped Man

Red Shoes prowled to the edge of the valley. The ghost country had long since swallowed the moon, but to his owl eyes the stars burned brightly enough to let him see each leaf on the scraggly trees along the ridge. Below, there were no trees—only endless waves of tall grass, rolling hills fading silver, then gray, becoming stars again at the horizon.

He strained, listening for sounds few men could hear, and that none could perceive with their ears. A faint call, or the memory of a call, lingered in the still air.

A chill breath of wind sighed across the grass, and Red Shoes shivered. He was far, far from home—two weeks past the Wichita village, almost two months from the village of his birth.

It might be best to return to camp, and Tug. But something was out here. . . .

Across the prairie, the something stood up from the grass, the shape of a man. In all that vastness, it seemed both tiny and gigantic.

"You do not belong here," the shape told him. At such a distance, even a loud shout would have gone unheard, but this was a whisper, carried by the winds behind the world.

"Nevertheless, I have come," Red Shoes replied.

"For what purpose? To die far from your kind?"

"My purposes are not yours to ask after," Red Shoes replied. He was aware of his shadowchildren, gathering near in his defense.

"Walk back over your footsteps," the creature said, "or I shall walk over them. I shall walk over your soul."

Red Shoes laughed. "Better you walk on fire, on the spine of a lightning bolt."

The shape said nothing more. It vanished back into the grass. The wind stilled. Red Shoes waited.

His shadowchildren warned him, as the thing came up at his back. He turned to find it hurtling toward him.

It looked like a Wazhazhe warrior, eyes circled with black, the arc of a tomahawk gleaming above his head, cleaving toward Red Shoes. The warrior's eyes burned like hot coals, and his lip was twisted into a sneer. He had been scalped, and his bald head was mottled with scars. Red Shoes dodged nimbly aside, drawing his own ax. He was fast enough to avoid the stranger's weapon, but the two of them still crashed together. It felt like running full force into a tree. He caught hold of the man's weapon arm and tried to swing his own around and lay open the back of his enemy's head, but his own wrist was caught. They strained there for a moment, muscles taut as wires. Then, slowly, he began to feel his own strength give way. The scalped man was very strong.

Red Shoes pushed forward and then jerked back, kicking his foot up into the scalped man's groin. Falling backward, he threw his antagonist over, then scrambled up, ax at the ready.

The scalped man was faster, a panther leaping. Red Shoes knew instinctively he would never be able to meet the savage attack. But something struck the scalped man suddenly, sent him snarling and tumbling aside. Red Shoes understood an instant later, when he saw an arrow standing in the scalped man's arm. Despite this, his foe laughed as he landed, rolled, and bounded to his feet. Then he leapt again, the height of two men.

Red Shoes drew his *kraftpistole* and fired. A serrated white tongue licked at the air, but tasted no flesh. When the flash faded, he saw the scalped man bounding off through the grass like an antelope.

"I have scented you now," the voice came. "Next time I will devour you."

Red Shoes repressed the urge to follow, dropping instead into the cover of the grass, wondering where the arrow had come from. The enemy of his enemy was not necessarily his friend.

"Hey! It's me!"

The thickly accented French was familiar. Red Shoes stood slowly. Loping toward him, bow slung over his shoulder, was Flint Shouting.

"I got to thinking I was really going to miss something," the Wichita explained. "I was halfway to the western hunting lands when I turned back and found your trail. Just in time, it seems. A scalped man! You were right—you have enemies of consequence. And now they are my enemies, too, I suppose. Ah, well. My fame will be great, though I live a short life. Who can ask for more, yes?"

"Tell me about them," Red Shoes said, ignoring some obvious jibes at that. "These scalped men. We don't have them in the Choctaw country."

"They don't live in villages. They sneak about. Some say they are good, others bad—but they are always alone. Driven out." He twisted his mouth. "I have never known one to be good." He grinned. "Yes, this makes me happy. How often does a man get to kill a legend? A scalped man? Bring him to me!"

"Brave talk from a man who turned tail once already," Tug grumbled.

"Not from cowardice!" Flint Shouting said. He sounded genuinely outraged. "Why should I help you, who are not my kin or even of my nation? No reason I could think of."

"We saved you! Y' gave y'r word."

"Hah. Such words only count with real human beings—Wichita—which you two are not. But now you have more than words. You have my heart. This interests me, now."

"Well, we are fortunate then," Red Shoes said, not entirely sarcastically. After all, the Wichita had saved his life. "Can you tell us anything else about these scalped men?"

Flint Shouting shook his head. "Not much. They are not just men who have been scalped. They are—Dreams. Dreams-Closest-to-Men."

"Huh. Like a warlock? So what's this fellah want?" Tug asked.

Red Shoes pointed with his jaw. "He wanted to keep us out of the valley up ahead. He's guarding it. I think he's done a good job, up until now. Those Kapaha we met two days ago went all the way around it—I found their tracks and a dead man. They just left him."

Tug lifted his brows in surprise. "Them Kapaha are pretty fierce. This one fellah put 'em off?"

"It would seem so. But they were warriors. Warriors prefer to fight flesh and blood. It's what they understand."

"I'm with 'em, then," Tug replied. "So now what?"

"You sleep. Tomorrow we go down there."

"All three of us," Flint Shouting clarified.

Red Shoes gave him a long look. "All three of us," he said at last.

"Looks like a whale carcass," Tug remarked as they drew near the thing.

Red Shoes didn't answer. He was concentrating on his shadowchildren. The night before, his spirits had been unable to come here, challenged by fiercer ones. Today there was no sign of the aethereal enemy or of the scalped man.

Flint Shouting noticed it, too. "Where is the coward?"

Red Shoes answered reluctantly. "I think he knows I'm too strong to beat when I'm alert, especially when I've got you two helping. And he's injured, thanks to you. But he's out there somewhere, waiting for me to relax."

The "whale carcass" had vanished for a moment, hidden by a small rise. Now it came into sight again.

"Holy Mother," Tug swore. "It's a *ship*."

It was. Red Shoes and Tug had met on board a frigate—the *Queen Anne's Revenge*—and Red Shoes had thought it a large vessel. This ship had been twice the size, before she shattered, before her nose plowed into the prairie and her spine snapped.

"An airship," Tug went on, "like we fought at Venice."

"Indeed," Red Shoes replied.

"You mean it flew through the air?" Flint Shouting asked. Now *he* sounded skeptical.

"I've seen it myself," Red Shoes confirmed. "The Russians have such ships."

"Russians?"

"Europeans, but as different from the English as the Spanish are." As he spoke, they rode into the shadow of the dead ship. Near it was a pile of casks and crates. "These were dragged out and opened," he said. "Either someone survived, or the ruin was looted."

"Where are the corpses, I wonder?" Tug grunted.

When they reached the other side of the ship, they saw. A low tumulus of earth had been raised, perhaps fifteen paces in diameter. Nearby was a cook fire and signs of eating. Scattered about like broken puppets were fifteen corpses. The three of them dismounted, letting the horses wander to graze.

They were Europeans, very pale in death. All had been scalped. They wore dark green knee breeches and blood-stained white shirts, but no coats. A few waistcoats lay here and there, but the buttons had been cut from them.

Red Shoes, Tug, and Flint Shouting walked carefully around, taking turns keeping watch.

"Well, Tug, what do you think?" Red Shoes asked, after a time.

The big man pushed his broad-brimmed hat back and scratched his head.

"They wrecked here. The livin' buried the dead. Then somebody come along an' killed the livin', took their guns and things. In'yuns, I guess." He grinned, proud of his newfound tracking ability.

Flint Shouting was still examining the bodies. "Most died from gunshot. Very strange, this far away from places to trade for bullets. Just one arrow." He turned the shaft this way and that. "I don't recognize the tribe. Not Awahi, not Kapaha, not Wazhazhe—not Throat-Cutters, either. Someone from far away."

Red Shoes said, "I trust you to judge. But if *you* don't know who they are, they must be from very far away indeed."

Tug had returned to looking at the ship. "Muscovados," he mumbled. "We came all the way out here t' find Muscovados. An' what now?"

Red Shoes pointed to hoofprints, leading away. "We keep following them. Some of them may have been taken captive. Besides, I want to see these Iron People."

"West, looks like."

"Northwest."

Tug sighed and shrugged. "Further on, then? Well, I always did want t' see the Parcific from this side."

7.

Pretender

"Oh, merciful heavens," Franklin said, when he saw the statehouse.

It had always been a gaudy affair. Built by Edward Teach—better known as Blackbeard—during his rule of the city, it was a Rococo nightmare, laced with gilded arabesques and iridescent pastel murals of Blackbeard doing various noble deeds. There had long been talk of painting over the latter, but in the days since Blackbeard's heroic death, his legend had grown; and over the ten years he had been transformed, in the minds of the people, into a sort of benevolent monarch who had saved the city from chaos.

"Blackbeard would have been proud of this," Franklin murmured.

It wasn't a compliment. As garish as it might normally be, today the center of South Carolina's government was positively florid. Banners of the Stuart coat of arms draped every available surface—pennants, ribbons, and scarves waved everywhere. Guards in velvet and gold patrolled the crowd with comically useless halberds.

And the crowd! More than a thousand strong—singing, shouting, beating drums and jangling bells, sprawling out from Teach Square into New Market and the old Church Yard. Children pranced about, clad in Stuart red and white. Women wore flashy, low-cut gowns that had been out of fashion in the colonies for ten years. The guards had herded them into a sort of double line flanking Broad Street, the approach to the docks on the Cooper River.

"This is unbelievable," Franklin said, staring. "Don't they remember that this is the king they exiled? Have they forgotten that little more than a decade ago they hated him for being Catholic?"

"Which I seem t' remember y' thought silly," Robert reminded him.

"I did. They put an idiot in his place who hated England and could not even speak English, all to have a Protestant on the throne. If you must have an English king, best that he be English and love his country."

"Then what is your objection?"

"I wasn't objecting," Franklin protested. "I was only commenting on the fickleness of men, is all."

Voltaire placed his hand on Ben's shoulder. "Mr. Franklin was just bragging to me that your country no longer has need of kings."

"Nor do we," Franklin affirmed.

"The people seem to think otherwise."

"So they do," Franklin admitted. "Some of them, anyway. But what of the Puritans, the Quakers, the Anabaptists, the French and Dutch Protestants? Not to mention the Negroes—"

"If I don't mistake m'self," Robert said, "I see some of each in the crowd. Catholic or not, I reckon most people believe that any king is better than no."

"You mentioned Negroes," Voltaire commented. "The town looks to be more than half of that African complexion. But they are slaves, are they not? You speak as if they have some say."

"Half right," Franklin said. "When Blackbeard ruled here, he freed the slaves to undermine the rich planters and landgraves who opposed his rule—armed and formed militia of them, even. They remain free, but few have the right to vote, for few own enough property. They threatened to rebel some five years ago, however, and won the right of one representative in the Assembly."

"Bravo," Voltaire said.

"Agreed. And you note that few of them are here cheering. Under British rule, they were slaves and they know many in this colony would see them so again."

"Here's my uncle," Robert interrupted, waving at an approaching figure. "Hello there, Governor."

"Good day, gentlemen," the fellow replied. "Quite a spectacle, eh?"

"Did you know of this, Governor Nairne?"

"Not a bit of it," Nairne replied, doffing his hat to wipe his brow. He was a few years beyond middle age, his hair, unpowdered, the color of iron. "I wish I had, for I might know more what to expect."

"But it is the Pretender?"

"I would use caution with such terms, these days, Mr. Franklin."

Franklin shrugged. "A word to the wise is sufficient," he said.

"If that's so, you'd best say a few more words, Uncle," Robert quipped.

The governor, grinning, turned to regard Voltaire. "I don't believe I've had the pleasure, sir."

"Voltaire, at your service."

"An old friend of mine," Franklin clarified. "He came across with the Pre—with the Stuart."

"Oh, ho. Then perhaps you can enlighten us?"

"I don't know much about it," Voltaire admitted. "I was on a Dutch ship that sailed to Ireland and there mysteriously turned English. 'Tis there we took on our noble passenger. But there was much worry of spies aboard, and I felt that questions might have me swimming for reasons of health, so I curtailed my curiosity."

"Were there other ships or just the one?"

"That's the odd thing. I heard reference to other ships—a

'fleet' I once heard it called—and yet I never saw another sail."

"Hmm." Franklin frowned. "Is Holland still protected by the Muscovy tsar?"

"If that is the word you chose to use. Little is done there without some word from Saint Petersburg. What do you suspect?" Robert asked.

"Nothing certain, Robert, but perhaps you ought to run see who you can get up from the Junto. Use the device we built for the detection of aerial ships, and for aegises, for that matter."

"You think the king has teeth with him?" Robert asked.

"I would not be surprised."

"He hardly seems to need them," the elder Nairne observed.

"He could not know that, though, could he? If he knows anything, he knows that the colonies run Whiggish, what with our more than fair share of dissenters. Perhaps he prepared for a less-than-welcoming reception."

"I'll see to it, I suppose," Robert said. "When you've seen one king, you've seen 'em all; and I've seen more than I wish."

"Well," the governor said, "Mr. Franklin and I don't have such a luxury. I've been asked to gather up the Assembly members to stand at the steps and welcome His Majesty."

"Surely we need not call him *that* yet," Franklin protested. "There's been no vote on the matter."

"Better to be safe. If the vote goes for him, then we don't want to be remembered as having been ungracious."

"Right," Franklin assented. "Voltaire, you will stay at my house, of course?"

"I would be delighted."

"Matters may keep me occupied for a time, but I trust you to entertain yourself." He clapped the Frenchman on the shoulder. "And I *don't* mean with my wife."

At the steps they found all of the members of the South Carolina Assembly; but to Ben's surprise, he noticed six members of the Commonwealth Parliament as well.

"When did *they* arrive?" Franklin asked Nairne. "The Stuart docked today, with no word ahead. How is it that these fellows are here already? There's William Thackery, from Virginia, and Ted Walker from Maryland—James Coleman from New York, for God's sake . . ." His words trailed off as he and Nairne exchanged knowing glances.

"Tory Royalists all," Nairne said.

"And so *someone* knew James was coming, didn't they?"

"I would have to guess so," Nairne allowed reluctantly.

They shuffled into the ranks, and Franklin placed himself across from Thackery, the representative from Virginia.

"How fortunate that you happened to be in town, Mr. Thackery," Franklin ventured.

"I do consider myself fortunate, Mr. Franklin, to welcome the king to American soil."

The man's smug demeanor struck a nerve. Disregarding Nairne's advice, he smiled thinly and said, "I see you've voted for all of us and crowned him already."

"The king is the king," Thackery replied dryly. "Whether you call him so is not to do with voting but with patriotism."

Franklin, keeping his smile glued on, bit his tongue. Literally. *We'll see about that, you dandified, prancing ape,* he thought as, in the distance, trumpets and drums struck up a martial tune.

Up Broad Street marched a procession the like of which the colonies had never seen, and which Franklin had hoped they never would see.

He knew his feelings were not shared, however. Around him, the crowd stirred and rustled, but remained hushed, as the first redcoats appeared, and the banner of the white rose on a red field. And there, in the front, on a white stallion, rode James.

He looked like an equestrian statue, bolt upright in the saddle, shoulders thrown easily back, shining black boots pressing in the stirrups. He wore a hat—not the ubiquitous tricorn, but a broad-brimmed thing cocked on the side, plumed with white feathers, like a cavalier from the last century, like his uncle Charles in the Restoration. His coat was of modern cut, wide-pleated skirts hanging long, and yet baroquely encrusted with gold braid and lace, again recalling earlier days. Next to him, on matching horse and in duplicate clothes, a boy of perhaps twelve years smiled at the crowd—his son, no doubt. Cavalry followed in their train, red-coated infantry, Irish dragoons, and Highlanders in smart, dark, tartan kilts, great basket-hilted claymores nearly dragging the ground. Even to Ben's skeptical eyes, it was a splendid sight.

And someone shouted, "Hurrah for the king!" and the cheers broke like a sudden wave on the rocks, hurling up, churning louder. As James entered the square, the crowd surged in, though smart-looking fellows in snowy coats kept them gently at bay, as white flowers—most made of paper—showered upon him. He smiled—a bright, ivory-toothed smile—and waved, making the crowd roar the louder.

Franklin was mute, but even he felt the tug—a powerful urge to weep, almost, with joy. It was as if, suddenly, the world was as it should be, as if no comet had ever fallen upon London, as if the years of hardship, famine, and war had never been. Almost, he lifted his own hat high. Almost. Instead, he merely put it under his arm.

James pranced his horse right up the statehouse steps, so near that Franklin could have touched him, and there dismounted, raised his hands to embrace the cheers, but eventually beckoned for silence. When a hush settled on the crowd, he spoke in a fine, clear voice.

"People of England!"

There was a fresh chorus of "hurrahs" at that, but James kept his hand up, and they quieted more quickly than before.

"People of England, the English Commonwealth in America, I am touched by your welcome. Many years I have dreamed of this moment, of this day when I might offer up my life to you, to reunite us all, all of us happy Englishmen once again beneath a single banner. I cannot tell you how filled with admiration I am at what you have accomplished here, these past years as I have struggled elsewhere. You have been a credit to our lost mother, and to all of our fathers, and to the God almighty who made us, every one! Bereft, you have made for yourself a government, as legitimate as ever one was, in the absence of a true king, and done it peacefully. And so I do not come here because you are without governance or sense—for being good Englishmen you have both. And I do not come here to claim anything. I come here only to offer you something: the blood of the Stuarts, and my heart and my soul, and everything of me that is England! And if you will have me—and I say only if you will have me, by the vote of your own excellent parliament—I will sit on the throne that has been given you by God to fill as you choose!"

And the air split with a nearly deafening cheer, and once again Franklin felt an insidious, unwanted joy. James looked so handsome and clean, so promising. He *felt* like a king, by damn, and the soldiers around him looked like soldiers, neat as pins. It was hard not to be glad.

Franklin expected more speech, but to his surprise, the address was over. James waved a bit more, and then—at Nairne's invitation—stepped inside the statehouse. As the crowd cheered on, page boys in white coats passed among the representatives, giving each what turned out to be an invitation; and to the delight of the crowd, handfuls of these were also passed amongst them.

A tall, redheaded man in rich garb stepped up to where James had stood a moment before and raised his hat—a cavalier's hat, much like James'. "If y' please!" he shouted, in a thick but intelligible Scotch accent. "While His Majesty regrets that there is no room for ye all t' dine with 'im, he much wished to convey his thanks for this warm reception. An' so I wish ye all a merry evening!"

As he said this, three wagons drew up in the square, and burly men began unloading huge pipes of beer and rum, sides of beef and mutton, and sweets.

In very short order the square became a carnival. Franklin shook his head in reluctant admiration. James Stuart certainly knew ways to the hearts of men.

"There you are, my dear," a soft Bohemian accent whispered in his ear. He turned to discover Lenka next to him, clad in a gown of silk brocade. He blinked in astonishment.

"Wherever in the world did you find that dress?"

"As if you don't know," she said, planting a kiss on his cheek. "Don't you think I look good in it?"

Franklin smiled. "Why, my dear, you would look good even without a dress. *Especially* without a dress. But that gown does, in fact, suit you. Did you borrow it from Mrs. Nairne?"

Lenka's brows knit together. "You mean to say you did not have it sent to me?"

"Indeed I did not."

An I-should-have-known look crossed her face briefly. "Then who?" she asked, voice suddenly cool.

Franklin glanced out over the party. "I've a feeling I know," he said.

The feast in the statehouse was more refined than the one outside, but did not lack for hearty food, which came out, it seemed, by the ton. The first service was birds—grilled partridges brushed generously with butter; duck with a honey glaze and skin so crisp it crackled at the touch; *galantine* of chicken—that is, the whole skin of a chicken enclosing layers of deboned fowl, veal, ham, and truffles. A steaming, fragrant capon pie with leeks.

The second service was heavier. Mince pie, charred racks of lamb, roast beef, suckling pig with a sweet quince sauce, beef with cucumber.

Franklin found himself wondering where all the meat had come from; not from Ireland, that was certain. Had the king's ship reprovisioned elsewhere? That might explain how the representatives from the more northerly states had come to be here. But no, surely he would have heard. The members of his Junto were everywhere, and they would have sent him word instantly via aetherschreiber. Unless they had first gone to the Caribbean . . .

But that made no sense, either. What was most likely was that the king had bought the meat *here*, in Charles Town—or that it had been provided for him. And Lenka's gown? If fit her too well. It had to have been made for her, by a seamstress who already knew her measurements.

He noticed that the wives of some of the other representatives were dressed in new clothes as well. It all seemed mighty elaborate to have happened in a single day. *Someone* in Charles Town had known that James was coming for some time.

And then another, much more worrying thought occurred to him. What chance that the presence of the warlock yesterday was mere coincidence? The way Franklin saw it, no chance at all.

He chewed that thought with his food, raising his glass with the toasts, but more interested by far in who was making them. Governor Nairne made one, but he was, of course, expected to. The others, to a man, were well-known Tories.

"Your pardon, sir, but are you not Mr. Benjamin Franklin?"

Franklin blinked. The fellow speaking to him was straight across the table—one of the king's men, in his colors, a fellow of perhaps thirty-five years, looking faintly silly in his high-piled periwig.

"No need to ask pardon for knowing my name, sir," Franklin replied, "for it flatters me. Unless, of course, you are the king's police agent, and my name appears on your list of troublemakers."

"No, indeed," the fellow replied. "You are written on another list indeed, and a rather short one: perhaps the only student of Sir Isaac Newton's in the colonies. I daresay, from what I have heard, that you are the foremost philosopher in America."

Franklin smiled. "That is not unlike being the foremost man on Mr. Crusoe's island, I'm afraid," Franklin replied, modestly.

"The inhabitants of Venice think otherwise."

"Sir," Franklin said, "your list, however short, appears quite detailed. And still I do not know with whom I am speaking."

"My apologies. My name is Alexander Sterne, and I flatter myself that I have some education in natural philosophy and mathematics. So as you might guess, I have been somewhat anxious to meet you."

"How fortunate for my ego that you were seated near me," Franklin remarked.

"Oh, I shan't insult you by claiming 'twas an accident," Sterne replied. "I requested this seat."

"Well, I'm mighty pleased to meet you, Mr. Sterne. I'm afraid that—like almost everyone here—I'm a bit stupefied by events. It isn't every day that a long-lost monarch returns to us."

"A happy day, I hope."

"Well, sir, I find that happiness is not so much the product of rare occurrences as it is of many small and everyday things." He raised his glass. "To the small things," he said.

Sterne raise his own cup, "The small things," he repeated, a little dubiously.

"And, of course, to the king," Franklin added.

"The king!" Sterne said, more enthusiastically.

"And so, Mr. Sterne, what interest do you have in philosophy?"

"I would much like to discuss particulars of philosophy with you, Mr. Franklin, though perhaps not at the moment, for fear of boring such beautiful ladies." He gestured with his glass toward Lenka and the other women within earshot. "However, I will tell you that my chief interest at the moment is not so much in philosophy as in philosophers. I am, you see, charged by His Majesty with creating a department of philosophy for his court. With the ultimate aim, I might add, of establishing a scientific academy."

"I see," Franklin replied, weighing that.

"I can think of no better man to head such a department than you," Sterne went on. "It would be an immense favor to me—and to His Majesty, I assure you—if you would consider the position. I promise you, there will be an adequate pension involved."

Franklin sipped a bit of his wine, a tart vintage, perhaps Portuguese.

The third service seemed to have begun—scalloped veal, roast hen and rabbit, two sorts of salad. Just the sight of them made Franklin a bit sick.

"I'm afraid," he said, "that the colonies are my home, Mr. Sterne, and I do not wish to go abroad. But it is a flattering offer."

"But, Mr. Franklin—surely you are aware that His Majesty wishes to make his court here, in Charles Town."

It seemed to Franklin that the entire world dislocated somewhat. "I see," he managed.

"And so there would be no need for any immigration."

Franklin took a bigger sip of the wine. "It is a most tempting offer," he replied, "one which I would much like to discuss the particulars of—but perhaps not at the moment, at this table, for fear, as you say, of boring the ladies."

Sterne smiled and raised his glass. "Touché, Mr. Franklin. But I will hold you to that discussion."

Franklin nodded and glanced back up the table to where James sat. *So you will move England entire,* he thought dryly.

Already agitated, he then saw something that sent a midwinter chill right to his bone. Beyond Sterne stood the king, and speaking to him was a tall, dapper man in a dark suit, the black ringlets of his periwig falling to his shoulders. He was laughing at some joke of the king's, and for an instant Franklin thought he saw the man's eyes flash red, and the air thicken and coil at his back. Slowly, Franklin reached into his pocket, grasping for the cool, flat round of his malakim compass. He glanced down at it as he might a watch.

The needle pointed dead straight at the man.

"I make it only five o'clock," Sterne said, apparently noticing his motions. "Is that a late hour in the colonies?"

"Passing so," Franklin murmured.

He should never have put off questioning his captive. It might be a late hour for the colonies indeed.

8.

Taxonomy

The air in the Royal Botanical garden was humid and hot, gravid with the perfume of the orchids and acrid scent of decaying soil, tanged with exotic hints of India, Tahiti, mysterious Africa, and Madagascar.

Adrienne hardly noticed it. Determined to go on as if nothing was amiss, she walked through the gardens with her students, as she had planned. Her only visible concession to the danger she suspected were two of her Lorraine guards, but unseen forces followed her in a swarm. To the outward seeming, then, she preserved her air of nonchalance, of business as usual. Within—she remembered her son, Nico. As an infant clinging to her chest in war-torn France, as toddler with the army of Lorraine—as a strange image in Far Eastern raiment. As an absence, a cavity in her heart.

She tried to distract herself by observing her students, to be amused by their innocent enthusiasm and occasional knowing glances at one another.

"What fascinating plants, these orchids," one of them said, a blondish young man named Carl von Linné.

"When I was a student at Saint Cyr," Adrienne remarked, stroking her finger across the purple inner lip of a particularly outlandish blossom, "we were not allowed to see even drawings of orchids. They were said to incite lascivious passions."

"I—I didn't—" Carl floundered, his light Swedish complexion suddenly very pink. "I don't understand," he finished, somewhat unconvincingly. From the corner of her eye, Adrienne could see that her other pupil—a young Frenchwoman named Gabrielle Émilie Le Tonnelier de Breteuil—was likewise blushing.

"Mademoiselle Breteuil, is Monsieur Linné's fascination contagious?"

Breteuil was quick to compose herself. She fixed astonishing, sea-green eyes upon Adrienne. "I am fascinated, as he is, by their subtle variation. I am intrigued that God, not content to make one sort of orchid, made so many."

"Yes," Linné said, after clearing his throat. "That is my interest in these plants, Mademoiselle."

"Then you would be just as fascinated by, say, the varieties of moss?"

"Of course. In fact, I—Émi—I mean Mademoiselle Breteuil and I—wished to speak to you on that subject."

"Do go on."

Linné smiled nervously. He was not bad looking, but neither was he handsome; not too tall, a little shy, slightly pudgy but with a kind, rather seal-like face. "It occurs to me that it might be useful to put the kinds and varieties of plants—and other living things—upon a systematic and scientific basis."

"Why?"

"Why—to see how God has organized his living things. It is the nature of science, is it not?"

She sighed. "It is. But how is it that you come to *me* with this? My interest in the botanical is limited to the aesthetic."

"Yes, we know," Breteuil chimed in. "But—"

"And—as I recall, Mademoiselle—your interest in plants is rather recent. I have always thought you more inclined to mathematics and pneumatology," Adrienne interrupted.

"Yes, my lady. But in this instance, Monsieur Linné and I have joined our interests."

"I suspected as much," Adrienne said a little dryly, and had the pleasure of seeing them blush again. "I will be fascinated to hear how."

"Plants can be classified by their characteristics," Linné interjected. "Grouped by certain likenesses and distinguished by differences. I believe that this is how our Creator made living things—an orchid is a kind of plant, a *palma Christi* a kind of orchid, and so on. And if He made plants in such a way, then surely animals, too. And if animals . . ." he trailed off, a little uncertainly.

"We believe," Breteuil finished for him, "that such a system could comprehend the malakim as well."

Adrienne stopped and looked at the two as if they stood in the light of an entirely new sun. She tended to think of them as very young—they were both twenty-five—but she was only six years their senior. Linné had come to the academy from the university at Uppsala, Breteuil as a penniless refugee from France, under the care of the mathematician Maupertuis. Both were, in her estimation, brilliant but naïve. She tended to underestimate them.

"That's good," she said. "I once contemplated such an endeavor—for the malakim, not plants—but never quite got around to it. But let me ask you this, Mademoiselle. As Monsieur Linné has suggested, plants might be categorized by their morphology. But the malakim, with few exceptions, are invisible to our eyes. What features would you classify them by?"

Breteuil smiled. She was not a beautiful girl, exactly—she was big boned but not fat, and tall and almost masculine. But her smile and bright eyes went far to correct any deficits of figure, as Linné had apparently decided. Or perhaps he was that rarest breed of man—attracted to intellect more than flesh.

"I would classify them by mathematical characteristics, my lady."

"Very good. Well, then, you have my permission to proceed."

"We will certainly need your help, my lady. No one knows more about the malakim than you."

Adrienne acknowledged that with a reluctant nod, and continued her walk, trying to enjoy the garden. She normally did; the world around her languished beneath ice and snow, but here, in this garden heated by scientific arts, lived things from the farthest reaches of the world. Today, she could only wonder which corner of an all-too-large world held her son. And why—very much, *why.*

And who. Who would she make *pay* for this?

She shook her head. Had someone asked her a question? Handsome in his blue uniform, one of her Lorraine guards, looking a bit bored, ambled ahead. Behind her, her two pupils chattered excitedly, discussing their plans.

A small cough from behind drew her attention. Elizavet was following them.

"Pardon, Mademoiselle, but I was of the impression that I had a tutorial today."

Adrienne motioned to Linné and Breteuil. "I will rejoin you shortly," she said. Taking the tsarevna by the arm, she guided her through a stand of date palms to a more private area.

"Elizavet, you should have stayed at my house. I will teach you there tonight."

Elizavet lifted her chin. "I was frightened last night, as you know. But today I remember who I am. I am the daughter of Tsar Peter, and I will not cower."

"Like your father, you sometimes have more pride than sense," Adrienne replied. "Better that you do not remind them that you exist. I cannot protect you, if you do not stay near me."

Seeing that Elizavet still looked determined, she sighed. "Very well. We will go have your lesson, but then you must return to my house."

Adrienne rubbed her eyes, trying to keep her attention focused on the book before her. The notes of a certain Millescu—a Russian ambassador to the Chinese court of more than half a century ago—were by turns fascinating, irritating, and boring. She was in one of the boring spots, now, but she hesitated to skip over any of it, when anywhere she might find some clue that would lead her to her son. The most interesting thing to her seemed to be a strange—bizarre, even—policy of the Chinese court. In the last century, Cossack settlers in disputed areas of Siberia had been captured, taken to the capital of Peking, and detained there indefinitely. The strange thing was with what silken cords these no-doubt rough Cossacks had been bound. The Chinese emperor had given them their own quarter in the city and provided them with homes, positions, and two wives apiece. He had allowed them an Orthodox chapel and even encouraged them to send to Russia for priests. In time, the ban on their travel was lifted. They were free to return to Russia, but few did, for what seemed obvious reasons. Might her son be in some similar straits? Kidnapped, adopted as Chinese, given a place of honor? She knew that slaves of the Turks often rose to become lords of the sultan's inner palace, but she was quite sure that her son was not with the Turks. Since he had been lost during the tsar's ill-fated invasion of Venice, that was naturally her first thought; and for many years she had focused her attention there.

Before she had given up, that is. And she *had* given up, hadn't she, when the grief and frustration became unbearable?

She pushed the guilty thought away. What hope had she had before? She had done what she could.

Anyway, neither was her son a Cossack, who had wandered into Chinese territory. How would such a distant and alien empire even know her son existed, much less desire to kidnap him? She had tried twice that morning to contact the Chinese court by means of magic mirror, and received no answer—whether because the device no longer had a mate in China or because her query was being ignored, she could not know.

But, she reminded herself, it was in truth the *malfaiteurs*—

not the Chinese or any other foreigners—who had taken her son; and even she could not guess their motives. But if he was alive—as she now had reason to think he was—then he must be in some human nation, for the realm of the malakim was of aether and vortice, not a place where a boy could live.

If she only knew why they had taken him . . .

She shook her head to clear it. Distracted again, she had passed over an entire page without understanding any of it. Angry at herself, she turned back to begin again.

At that moment, there came a knock at the door, and she was almost grateful for it.

"Let them in, Anna," she called to her little servant girl, turning to see who it was, hoping it was some of her students. Around them, she almost felt young again.

It was a young man, one she did not know.

"Pardon me, Your Highness—" he began.

She chuckled and held up her hand to stop him. "Please," she said, "I am no highness. How can I help you?"

He blushed a little and nodded. "My name is Mikhail Lomonosov," he explained.

"Oh, yes. I've a note concerning you. I'm to tutor you in calculus—beginning tomorrow, is that right?"

"Yes, Mademoiselle. Except that I've just been informed that that tutorial has been canceled. I thought to ask why."

Adrienne stared at him for a moment. "I have not canceled our tutorial, Monsieur Lomonosov. There must be some mistake."

Lomonosov withdrew a small note from his coat pocket and handed it to her. He cleared his throat uncomfortably. "It says that instead I am to be tutored by Professor Swedenborg in angelic numerology."

Adrienne stared at the sheet for a few moments, then trying to contain herself, looked back up at the concerned young man. "Monsieur Lomonosov, I expect you to report to me, here, tomorrow, for your tutorial. I will clear up this matter."

Lomonosov smiled briefly and bowed. "Thank you," he said. "I'm sorry to have disturbed you."

"You have not disturbed me," she replied. "Not you."

"Well," she remarked, surveying the three men in the director's office, "the three of you together. More than I could have hoped for."

Prince Golitsyn smiled in the most unfriendly way possible. "Good day to you, Mademoiselle. You know Professor Swedenborg, of course—and you have met his grace, the metropolitan of Saint Petersburg?"

Swedenborg nodded greeting and favored her with a friendly smile. He was a plump man in middle age with pleasant but rather unremarkable features. His gaze, however, was memorable: it had the quality of looking through you and studying you in minute detail all at once. It was intense and uncomfortable, and she recognized it. Swedenborg spoke with angels, with great regularity, and without apparent aid of scientific device. That put him in a rather restricted group of people—herself, those strange individuals like Crecy who were tutored and shaped by the malakim from birth, and finally King Louis XIV and Tsar Peter, both of whom acquired their affinity with the aetheric by consuming elixirs of life.

Where Swedenborg's affinity came from, she had no way of knowing; and despite his faultlessly polite and even friendly demeanor, that made him, in her eyes, untrustworthy.

The metropolitan, on the other hand, hated her—for being a woman, for her connection to the "saints" and angels, for reasons even he probably could not articulate. His cold smile, like a slit in a pumpkin, and his bulging eyes confirmed his contempt more eloquently than even his rasping voice.

She held up the paper Lomonosov had brought her so that they might all see it.

"What is this?" she asked.

Golitsyn took it and looked over it carefully. "It appears," he said, "to be a command signed by Professor Swedenborg, our new minister of the sciences."

Swedenborg took the paper and nodded. "Yes, I signed this," he murmured, almost as if to some fourth party.

"When did the minister of sciences begin assigning tutorials?" Adrienne demanded.

"It is not my job," Swedenborg admitted, still dreamily. "But this is a reflection of a most important statute."

"Indeed," the metropolitan added. "You have, of course, received your copy."

"I have not."

"An oversight," Golitsyn said. "I have a copy here. . . ."

He rummaged for a moment through his desk, then produced and handed her a parchment. She took it and examined it for a moment.

"As you can see, it is signed by the empress and the patriarch," Golitsyn said.

"The empress has not yet been installed. This is not yet law."

"True," Golitsyn said. "But it will be, and I thought it better to begin the changes as soon as possible—I assumed there would be no objection. Shall I explain it to you? We were busy, as you can see, but I can, of course, make a moment for Mademoiselle Montchevreuil."

"I would appreciate that, especially as you promised me the academy would remain untouched."

"It is, it will. The academy and your position in it will remain. It was thought best to make a few changes in curricula, to better reflect the modern state of science. As science is now recognized as a godly pursuit, the patriarch and empress wish to devote all of our energies—and the resources of our state—to those sciences most godly."

"But this says that calculus will no longer be studied. Or alchemy! Or biology! Those are important sciences."

The metropolitan cleared his throat. "The patriarch has decreed them ungodly."

"The patriarch doesn't know a fluxion from his bung," Adrienne retorted. "What business has he—"

"Now see here!" the metropolitan exploded. "He is the *patriarch*, chosen by God. You will never speak of him in that manner, or—"

Adrienne held up her hand, let it glow briefly. "Or what, metropolitan? Shall we have a contest? Between you and me? Between the patriarch and me? I think we shall see who is more favored by the angels."

The metropolitan hesitated at that. "You are perhaps too certain of yourself," he said in a quieter voice. "After all, those who command devils are not always readily distinguished from those who speak to angels." But he did not sound confident.

"Monsieur Swedenborg?" she demanded. "What do you have to say of this? Do you agree with this nonsense?"

Swedenborg turned his odd eyes upon her. "It is time for purification," he said. "We are in the very center of the Apocalypse. When it ends, the world will be either heaven or hell. We must listen to the angels, Mademoiselle. We must. Surely you know this, being so close to them yourself."

Adrienne studied Swedenborg. Had he gone mad? What was he talking about?

Golitsyn coughed for attention. "Mademoiselle, yesterday I saw you fly into the heavens on the backs of angels. What mathematical proofs did that require? What anatomical dissection?"

"For that? None, but—"

"The taloi that work our mines and fight alongside our soldiers, the engines that heat and protect our city, the boats that speed across—and beneath—our waters . . . I believe I have kept up with scientific advances these past years, but I cannot recall ever seeing mathematical demonstrations of any of these things."

"But all of them are based in the calculus and alchemy, ultimately, the advances made by Sir Isaac Newton."

"Yes, but now that the angels have come to serve us, we have no need of those rough, dubious pursuits. Moreover, it has been demonstrated that those old sciences were often traps for the soul, seducing the unwary into a godless, mechanical universe. Now we know, without shadow of doubt, that Descartes and his fellows were wrong. Our science comes from God, is of God; and we must not allow the devil a foothold in our academy. Other than the alteration of a few of your tutorials, Mademoiselle, I cannot possibly see how this violates our agreement. You have published fifty papers since you came to us. I have reviewed them, and I have seen very little in the way of either mathematics or alchemy in any of them."

Adrienne could only stare at the three of them, thunderstruck.

He was right. And she had been trapped, in a way more subtle than she could have ever imagined.

9.

Mask of the Sea

Ben's horse clopped from beneath the overhanging oaks into the broad yard of Nairne's plantation. Robert and Shandy Tupman were already there, awaiting him—he could see them by the light of their pipes and the pale, sickle moon.

"Y' left the party early, I see," Shandy called.

"I've a weak stomach, it seems," Franklin replied. "What news?"

Robert tamped out red sparks from the bowl of his pipe, laying a red constellation at his feet. "Up an' down the coast, no sign of more ships. The comestibles f'r the party, y'r wife's dress—all were bought here by various Tories, as y' suspected."

Franklin nodded, wiping sweat from his brow with his shirt cuff. The night air was still warm, and not a little briny. "Any sign of airships?"

"Not by any reckoning. But they might be far enough away to keep our compasses quiet."

Franklin dismounted, and a boy scurried down from the porch to take his horse. "The compasses would detect airships or warlocks for a range of a hundred miles or more," he mused. "Let's go question our prisoner."

"My name," the man said, "is Leonhard Euler."

"And you are a Moscovado?"

"No. I studied there and lived there for many years, but by birth I am Swiss."

"But come recently from Russia. Let's start with that." As

he turned to Robert, Franklin leaned back until the legs of his wooden stool creaked. "We've sentries up the road?"

Robert nodded. "Y' weren't followed here, not by man, not by sprite or warlock."

"Good. Mr. Euler, I'll come to the point, because I have little time to waste with you. Did you come on the ship with James Stuart?"

"I came on one of his ships, yes."

"Is James backed by the tsar?"

"He is."

"Holy mother—" Robert sputtered, but Franklin waved him to silence.

"And is the tsar backed by these malakim overlords—these cherubim—you speak of?"

Euler chuckled. "You do come to the point, sir. The true answer to that is long and complex. The brief answer is yes."

"It is the brief answer I care about, just now. And here, too—is it the tsar's plan, through James, to conquer our colonies?"

"Yes. Either James will be accepted peacefully, or he will take his throne with Russian might."

Franklin rested his chin on his hand and rubbed his jaw, scrutinizing Euler. The warlock's face seemed a bit blurry—it was time for him to get fitted for those eyeglasses he kept putting off.

"Mr. Euler, why do you betray your country—and your demon masters—and tell us these things?"

"Russia is not my country, Mr. Franklin—I thought I explained that. And the malakim are no longer my masters, as I also explained. I have made myself free of them."

"Yes, you did claim that, didn't you. And yet our compasses still found you right quickly. If you have no aetheric accomplice, how do you explain that?"

Euler shrugged. "Some lingering magnetism, I don't doubt. But I don't *know*. Do your best—you will find no familiar about me."

"We will do our best, never doubt it," Franklin promised. "But let us suppose, for argument's sake, that your claims are true. Remind me why you've sought *me* out, in particular?"

"Because, Mr. Franklin, I wish to join you. Study with you. Become part of your cause."

"What do you suppose that cause might be?" Franklin said mildly.

"True science. True liberty."

A smile forced itself on Ben's face. "They certainly know me well, your masters. You make fine bait, Mr. Euler, better than has been dangled before me in many years."

"So much for your promise to give my plea even momentary credence, eh? I did not learn about you from *them*, Mr. Franklin, but from your publications."

Franklin stared at him in surprise for a moment, and a small thrill of guilt ran through him. Was he wronging this man? What if he were telling the truth? He could be an invaluable ally.

"Have you anything to offer us to prove your good faith, Mr. Euler? Anything at all?"

"Oh, I think so. Something quite valuable indeed, I should think."

"Well?"

"Look in your harbor, and you will see the design of your would-be king."

"There are three ships in the harbor," Franklin said, "and I have seen them already."

"Not *upon* the harbor," Euler said. "*Beneath it.*"

Franklin glanced at the equipment on his workbench, reached to tighten a valve that he had already tightened a few times. Where was Robert? He glanced again at the clock. Robert wouldn't be late for another twenty minutes; it was his own impatience telling. But if what Euler said was true, time was something that could catch up with them at any moment.

He went back to his inventions. Since his life depended upon them, there was every reason to be overcautious.

This was especially true of the cone-shaped device he examined next. He had given it the unlikely name *depneumifier*, though Robert referred to it as "exorcister." What it was supposed to do was separate basically aethereal malakim from the scientific devices they operated through—the floating globes, for instance, that held Russian airships aloft. That was what it was *supposed* to do, but long experience had taught Franklin that you could never be sure what any untested device *would* do. Once in Prague, while trying to duplicate Sir Isaac Newton's aegis—a sort of cloak of invisibility—he had accidentally made instead a device that pushed all that was breathable and nourishing in the air far away. It had nearly been the death of him.

Soft footsteps signaled Lenka's entrance. He glanced up to greet her.

"*There* you are," she said. "How did your skulking go?"

"Well enough."

"They suspected something at the party, I think, though I managed to distract your Mr. Sterne for a time. Did you make certain you weren't followed?"

"As certain as I could. Lenka, that was dangerous work, cozening Sterne. I wish you hadn't done it."

She set her face in a little frown. "I am a member of your Junto," she replied, "though you seem to forget it at moments like these."

He rose and took her hands in his. "I almost lost you once, my dear. I do not care even for the thought of losing you again."

Her eyes told him she did not accept that, but she said nothing, instead disengaging and walking toward what he had laid out on the table.

"Why have you pulled out your diving suit?"

"The man we captured, Euler, claims that the Pretender is

backed by underwater craft of some sort. Robin and I will go tonight and see if that is true."

She looked at him coldly. "Were you going to tell me of this?"

"Assuredly. When we were finished. I hoped not to trouble your sleep."

"I find it difficult to sleep without you in our bed, which means I get little sleep indeed," she said, a bit angrily. "We will discuss these matters, you and I, Mr. Franklin. I am not happy at my treatment." She glanced up at the clock as he began searching for some reply. She cut him off by going on, however. "A visitor shall be at our door in one minute. I suggest you greet him."

"A visitor? Who?"

"You seem ill-disposed to tell me things in advance, so I'll take the same liberty. Perhaps 'tis your king come for a bedtime story; perhaps it is Tsar Peter himself. Good night, and if you drown yourself, don't come dripping your corpse on my rugs, you hear?"

He caught her and gave her a gentle kiss. She responded, but when she drew away, her gaze was unrelenting. "We will talk of these things," she repeated, then turned and went up the stairs, skirts whispering good night on the polished wood.

As predicated, a knock came at the door, but despite the warning Franklin nearly jumped out of his skin. Feeling foolish, he tugged the portal open.

"Mr. Nakaso," Franklin said, with some surprise.

Paris Nakaso bowed at the waist, dapper in coat and waistcoat. Nakaso was a black man, born, as Franklin understood him, in the African country of Angola. He had come as a slave to Charles Town, but had served as such for only two years before Blackbeard freed them. He was the single Negro member of the South Carolina Assembly.

"I hope the hour is not too late, Mr. Franklin." Nakaso's English was flawless but touched by a mysterious, almost musical, accent.

"Not at all, Mr. Nakaso. I thought to look you up soon, in any event. Come in and have a seat. May I offer you Madeira?"

"That would be delightful, Mr. Franklin."

Franklin poured them each a glass, and they both settled into seats near the fireplace.

"I did not see you at the grand fete," Franklin remarked carefully.

Nakaso smiled ruefully. "As a member of the Assembly, I tried to attend, but I was prevented."

"Prevented?"

"I could not convince anyone, it seems, that I am indeed in government here. Certain other members of the Assembly were no help to me, I'm afraid."

"I'm sorry to hear that. You should have sought me out."

"Perhaps. I have often considered you a fair man. When I proposed a more generous representation of Negroes in this colony, you were the only one who stood with me. And the work of the Junto has been—most—unexpected."

"You know, I think, my feelings on the matter."

"I do, or think I do." He sighed and set his glass down. "Mr. Franklin, the hour is late, so you will pardon me if I come to the point. My people are afraid of this English king. They think he will put the old landgraves back on their estates and make us property again. Mr. Franklin, I have worn shackles—I do not like them. The next time I wear them, it shall be as a corpse."

"You will not wear shackles again, not if I have anything to do with it."

"Then the Junto is against this king?"

Franklin considered. "I cannot speak for them yet, but I think it safe to say that they *will* be, soon. I certainly am."

"Then you will fight him?"

"If it comes to that. Hopefully our battles will be the sort won without bloodshed."

"But if it comes to bloodshed, you will need my people to shed some. You will need us in arms."

Franklin hesitated slightly. "We will need every man who wishes to be free, that is certain. I was, indeed, going to speak to you on this matter."

"I'll be brief. I can deliver them to you, but there are conditions."

"And what might those be?"

"The first is that they be properly armed."

Franklin frowned. "There is no law that says Negroes may not bear arms."

"Aye, but there are few who will sell to us."

"Well, after the slaughter when you were freed—"

"We were freed in name. To actually gain that freedom, we had to fight. King Teach armed us—"

"Entirely in his own interests. You helped him overthrow the landgraves who would have resisted him."

"I'm aware of that, sir. Even then, many fled to the margravate of Azilia, taking their slaves with them. Here you have a similar situation. If you want our aid in throwing off this Pretender's yoke, we will need ready arms. More than anything, as a sign of trust."

"That trust will be hard to come by, I fear."

"Even so."

"But didn't you just tell me it interests you to fight the Pretender, to keep from being enslaved?"

"Of course. But there are—other options."

"That sounds like a threat."

"It is. I have been in communication with the Maroons, and with certain Indians of similar persuasion. I can deliver them, too—or I can set them against whoever wins here. Teach gave us our freedom—now we seek the means to keep it forever, Mr. Franklin. And for that we will need better representation in government. There are, after all, twice as many of us as there are of you."

Franklin nodded, not missing that second, more subtle,

threat. "I will see what I can do—it is all I can promise. What of your other conditions?"

"Other colonies—and the margravate especially—still keep slaves. Many of us have relatives in bondage. We would have them freed."

"The other colonies have their own laws. I have no voice in their government, as well you know."

Nakaso smiled. "After the coming war, I think the Junto—and thus you—may well be in a position to dictate terms in many places."

"Only if we win. And you overestimate my importance. I can only assure you that my sympathies lie with you. I consider slavery an abomination and I will work to abolish it."

"Not much of a promise."

"I would be untruthful if I offered more. But consider this, sir. If what you say is true, if there *is* to be a war—and, God help us, that remains to be seen—and if the Junto will be a power if it wins—then you would do well to be with us, would you not?"

Nakaso nodded thoughtfully. "I—I must consult with others. I am not potentate."

"Please let me know what you decide. Very soon now, a decision must be made. If I am to cast, I would prefer to know what sort dice I have in my hand."

"I will speak to you again soon. Thank you for the excellent Madeira."

"You are welcome, every bit. Be safe in your journey home."

"I will."

Franklin walked him to the door. When he opened it, it was to Robert's arrival. Robert nodded a greeting, which the black man returned.

"Ready t' go?" Robert asked, when Nakaso was gone.

"More than." Franklin sighed. "Let's us see just how much more complicated matters can be."

* * *

"Dawn in two hours," Franklin said. "We'll have to hurry."

"Y' don't really trust this thing, do y'r?" Robert asked, watching Franklin struggle into the heavy suit.

"I've tested it before."

"Aye. An' nearly drowned when it sprung a leak. Why not let me go? Better I feed sharks then our best scientific."

"I want to see this for myself. Now hush and help me get this helmet on. Besides, turning the pump is the hard part."

The longboat rocked as Robert fitted the round helmet onto the gasket cuff of Franklin's diving suit. The moon had set, and it was cloudy besides. The only lights were those in Charles Town itself, some half a mile away. A lanthorn in their boat would shine across the waters like a beacon, and they could not risk being noticed out here.

Robert started working the pump as soon as the helmet was in place. Franklin listened for the hiss of escaping air. When he heard none, he went over the side of the boat, made certain none of his lines were twisted, and allowed the harbor to have him.

He sank slowly, air tube and lifting harness snaking behind him, patting the haversack to make certain it was at his side. Dreamlike he fell, until his feet touched softly into the mud of the harbor bottom. He figured himself some fifty feet down. The pump chugged reassuringly in his ear.

He turned slowly, seeing nothing. He had a lanthorn, of course, but opening that would be sure idiocy if what Euler suggested was true. Instead, he reached into his haversack and removed a specially treated sheet of glass. Holding it up to his faceplate, he turned again.

Halfway around, he froze in place.

It was the size of a small whale, the ship. He had missed it by thirty feet or so, coming down. It was shaped like a whale, too. The glass did not give him as good an image as he might hope, for it only brightened the atoms of lux passing through it.

Turning further, he saw another, and another. They seemed made of metal. He saw no windows, but certainly whoever was in them had some way of seeing out—perhaps even in the dark. He shivered suddenly, feeling as if he had blundered right into a school of sleeping sharks. If they awakened . . .

He replaced the glass plate in his bag and tugged lightly on the line. A moment later, the harness tightened and he began to rise. The darkness seemed all teeth, and he counted under his breath for something to do, to keep his mind off the sudden feeling of claustrophobia.

When he finally broke the surface and saw blurred stars, he felt like cheering. Instead he scrambled up into the boat as quickly as he could.

Halfway up he felt nausea and mild flashes of cramping pain. He remembered this had happened before, though not as noticeably. He had gone deeper this time. Was there some malady in that? It bore investigation.

Fighting the unpleasant sensation, he uncoupled his helmet, shucked himself from the suit, then dressed in dry clothing as Robert rowed quietly back toward shore. He lay back wearily, explaining to Robert what he had seen.

"Euler said there's forty of 'em," Robert said, his face invisible, but the shape of his head limned by the distant city lights. "Do y' credit it?"

Franklin nodded. "I do. They must fill the harbor and then some—with a hundred or more men in each. And if even a third of the rumors we hear of the Moscovado armaments are true, that stands as bad news indeed for Charles Town."

"And the rest of the colonies. Why this ruse, though? If the Moscovados have such sneak ships and armaments, what need have they of James?"

"I can think of good reasons," Franklin said, taking the second set of oars. "First off, this fleet underneath us must have cost a pretty penny. The hulls must be adamantium or something awfully close. They must breathe by liberating air from the water itself, and compressing it. If the Moscovado intelligence is any good at all—and it must be, for they've been in communication with their Tory friends here—then they know that we are far from defenseless ourselves, and no matter how tough those nuts down there, we'd likely crack a few. But now look where they have us, Robin. James sits in our statehouse, more than a hundred of his soldiers already on shore. More, he has whatever Tory and Jacobite troops there might be already here in the colonies. What if Thackery brought men with him from Virginia, in case things go badly? They've already come inside our defenses, Robin. I'll wager even now, they have agents near each battery, ready to sabotage or commandeer them. No, we're in a much tighter spot than if they hadn't snuck in under the skirts of an English king. Add to that the certainty that under direct Moscovado tyranny, we would do nothing but rebel. As it is—if they can keep the idea of Russia distant or absent from people's minds—they will encounter little resistance."

"But now there's us. And the Junto."

"Yes," Franklin replied tightly. "It's not as if we didn't plan for this sort of thing. I just despise that—"

Robert interrupted him by dropping his oars, yanking his *kraftpistole* from the bottom of the boat, and firing. Heat brushed Franklin as lightning cleft the air two yards from him. He turned to see what his friend had shot at.

Still haloed in yellow flame, it was shaped like a man but larger, a scintillating shadow rushing across the surface of the water.

"Aegis," Franklin snapped. "It's wearing an aegis."

It came on, cooling and disappearing as it did so.

Robert fired again, but this time the thing was so close the phlogiston billowed back at them, and Franklin felt his eyebrows singe as he yanked out the depneumifier and gave it its field test.

Something flared so brilliantly that it shone through Ben's eyelids, which he had the presence of mind to close. He opened them to red spots and a man shape with four arms: two held aloft a glowing red sphere, while the other two reached for him. Its head was a smooth, silvery globe.

"Shoot it, Robin," Franklin shouted, throwing himself back, away from the grasping steel fingers of the monster.

Lightning roared for the third time, but the awful thing came on. Desperately, Franklin pushed the contact on the depneumifier again.

The glowing red orb went out, and the metal man-thing dropped, suddenly inanimate, though red-hot and smoking. The water received it with a scalding hiss.

Gasping, Franklin rose.

"Your exorcister worked, it seems," Robert observed.

"Hurrah," Ben said weakly.

Robert looked down at his compass, uncapping a small lanthorn to see by.

"Uh-oh. There's more out there. Can't say how many."

Franklin glanced at the shore, still far away. He shucked off his wet coat and began unbuttoning his waistcoat.

"What'r y' doin'?" Robert asked.

"We'll have to run. I'm leaving my aegis to draw them." He got the aegis off and inserted its key. It vanished. Franklin paused long enough to pry the boat's plug out of its hole, and then quickly slipped on the Dutch-looking shoes that lay in the bottom of the boat. Robert donned his, and they both stepped from the sinking boat onto the water. The surface dimpled beneath the aquapeds, but it held them up.

Together they skated across the rough waters, casting frequent glances over their shoulders, wondering what invisible doom might be coming behind.

10.

The Iron People

Red Shoes saw the puffs of smoke before he heard the sound of gunfire. His hands twitched on the reins, but he kept steady. Only a sorcerer could hit them at such a range, and now that his shadowchildren were alert to bullets, only a very strong sorcerer.

"Keep still," he told Tug and Flint Shouting. "Show them you aren't afraid."

"I *han't* afraid," Tug grumbled stubbornly.

The gunshots—there had been only two—were not repeated. But when they came much closer to the bend in the river, a few arrows dropped, all far from hitting them. Red Shoes frowned, and then suddenly urged his mount up the hill at a run. Behind him, Flint Shouting gave a loud whoop and followed.

As he crested the hill, a shaft came near, deflected only by the invisible cloak of his shadowchild. He saw the source immediately; a boy fitting another arrow to his string. He noted a second boy in a nearby bush. Two muskets lay on the ground.

Red Shoes regarded the boy quietly. The boy raised the bow, looking determined; but when Flint Shouting and Tug came up behind, he sagged. Red Shoes gestured for the other boy to come from his hiding place.

Flint Shouting snapped something in a language Red Shoes did not know. The boys looked a bit sullen, then replied. A brief conversation followed, while Red Shoes waited impatiently.

Finally, Flint Shouting looked over at him. "The boys are Awahi. They said that a day ago men came and killed many in their village. They survived because they were away hunting rabbits in the hills. By the time they returned, almost everyone was dead and some strange warriors were in the town. They hid until the men went away this morning. Then they saw us coming."

"They are the only survivors?"

"No. There are a few women and one man, who is badly hurt. And another boy, who ran to another village for help."

"Tell him to take us to his village."

The village was just beyond the river bend, on a little rise sheltered by the hill. Only a few cottonwoods rustled their greeting as they followed the boys in past a small field of knee-high corn.

The bodies lay where they had fallen, amongst six mound-shaped earth lodges. Red Shoes counted twenty, only six of them men—mostly older men. Ravens were picking at them.

As they arrived, one old woman, a woman of perhaps twenty, and a girl a few years younger emerged from one of the lodges. The old woman looked at them, at the dead bodies, at the cattails crowding the riverbank. She muttered something, went into the lodge, and came back out with a hoe made from a stick and a buffalo scapula. She started shuffling toward the garden.

Flint Shouting asked her a question. She looked at him as if he were crazy and answered, a single short sentence, and continued toward the corn.

"She says she has work to do," Flint Shouting translated. "I think maybe she's lost her mind."

Red Shoes rode toward the younger women and dismounted. "Ask her who did this," he told Flint Shouting.

The Wichita asked and got an answer. He spoke with the young women and the boys for a few more moments and then straightened in his saddle. "Iron men," he said, "with many muskets and long knives. They were of many tribes. Some were Crow, some Black Shoes, some Snake People, some unknown. Some were white, like Tug. They had captives—three men and a woman, all white." He looked speculatively at Red Shoes. "She said they have heard of these people before. They come from the west, and grow as they come. Her people did not really believe it, but it seems it is so. They took all the food, except a few caches of last year's corn they didn't find. Like the boys, these women were out of the village when it happened."

"I don't understand," Red Shoes said. "These iron men come from the west. Does that mean they've passed already? The party we've been following was going east."

Flint Shouting briefly spoke to the young woman again, then nodded grimly and turned back to Red Shoes.

"She says they are still west. They wintered in a large camp some twelve days' ride from here, gathering strength. They sent out raiding parties from their camp. They may be moving again, but it works the same way—raiders come ahead, then return. Their path is thus cleared." He paused. "She wonders if we can help them."

Red Shoes pursed his lips. "Tell her we can't."

Tug started at that. "Y' mean we're just ridin' on?"

"I feel we have to catch these men, Tug, the ones who raided the ship. It's why we came out here. And I feel our time to do so grows short. We're less than a day behind them. If we stop here—"

"But they'll die."

"They sent a boy to another village. They must have kin there. My feeling is that if we stop here, many more will die." He turned to Flint Shouting. "Tell her no."

"Kaaki ishtatata'uuhak," Flint Shouting said.

The woman snapped something else heatedly.

"What was that?"

"She asked if we could leave her some powder for the muskets, so she can go kill the men who did this."

"We can't spare any powder either."

* * *

They rode the horses carefully at the walk, trot, and canter. They were in a hurry, but of the ten horses they had got from the Wichita and the four Flint Shouting had brought with him, they were now down to seven. They had a long way to go home, and Red Shoes did not want to run the beasts to death.

The stars rained icy light upon them, and he found his eyes drawn to their glow again and again, when he ought to be watching the horizon. The Choctaw didn't talk much about stars, but Flint Shouting's folk—and these other people of the plains—did. Stars were dreams; dreams were stars. Flint Shouting had endless stories about the stars coming to Earth in human form.

He supposed he could see why. This was not the same firmament he knew, this too-vaulted dome. The skies of Venice and Algiers had been closer to the one he grew up with. The only other place where he had known heaven to so threaten to swallow him had been on the open ocean. The stars had been too close there, too.

One of his shadowchildren returned, whispering of something ahead. He tried to understand what it had seen through its eyes, but the image made little sense. Though cut from a piece of his own soul, a shadowchild could only see in the otherworld. It could see the shape of spirit, but not of matter.

Red Shoes searched again for the scalped man, and thought for an instant he sensed him or the empty space that might hide him. Then the sensation vanished.

"Holy God," Tug murmured. It was not an exclamation he used often. In fact, to Red Shoes it sounded more like an invocation than a curse.

A sentiment he could understand. In the valley below, campfires stretched for as far as he could see. His night vision made out tents by the thousands—the conical dwellings common to the folk of the plains, but also odd, squat rounded tents and huge, house-shaped pavilions like those he had seen in Venice and in the lands of the Turk.

Along with these were five Russian airships and three other machines shaped something like giant leaves. But more than that, he saw the glinting eyes of at least a hundred evil spirits, the things his friend Franklin called malakim. And, in all of that, something else, something singular. It shone through the rest like a fire. And though he had not the faintest idea what it was, he knew it was what he had come for. That, and a vaguer thing near it, a thing with the echo of a scream clinging to it.

Both were in the center of the camp, surrounded by perhaps five or six thousand men.

"What's goin' on here?" Tug muttered.

"How much can you see?"

"Just the fires."

"It's an army. A big army, and not just Indians. Europeans, too. Maybe other nations. We can see better in the morning."

"Aye. And they us."

"I should think so. By morning we shall be in their midst."

11.

Seraph

"Good evening, Mademoiselle Breteuil," Adrienne said softly, as the girl entered the observatory.

"I was told I would find you here," the younger woman said.

"And, indeed, here I am," Adrienne answered. "What can I do for you?"

"Ah, my lady," Breteuil burst out, "Monsieur Linné submitted our proposal to the director—"

"And he told you that you must not proceed," Adrienne finished for her.

Breteuil blinked. "Yes, Mademoiselle. But yesterday, you said—"

"I'm aware of what I said," Adrienne assured her. "At the time, I was unaware of certain changes in policy regarding curriculum."

"I don't understand it. What's worse, they said I was not to be allowed to study mathematics at all. Or pneumatology! I must confine myself to the study of herbal remedies!"

"Why do you suppose that is?" Adrienne asked.

"Because I am a woman. Monsieur Swedenborg said the mysteries of science are not for us. And yet you, Mademoiselle, are the foremost philosopher of the academy. When I asked about this, he said you were an exception."

The girl was crying. Adrienne walked over to her, lifted her chin. "Why do you want to study mathematics, my dear? What would be so wrong with doing what the director says?

Or marrying someone, the young Linné—no, do not blush, I have guessed your affections. Why not be a mother and wife?"

"Because I love science, Mademoiselle, I crave it. I do not understand how you, of all people, can misunderstand me."

"I don't misunderstand you, Émilie. May I call you Émilie?"

"Of course, my lady."

"And you must call me Adrienne, but not where the other students can hear."

"Yes—Adrienne."

"Have a seat on that taboret." Émilie did so, and Adrienne pulled up a nearby stool.

"What is the nature of scientific philosophy, Émilie?"

"It is the study of God and his purposes, through the agency of his angels. It is the quest to produce the useful and the godly at once, to learn and to perfect ourselves."

"Where did you learn this? Who told you this?"

"It is how we are tutored, as students."

"Surely Maupertuis never said such a thing."

"No. But his is an older philosophy, an ungodly one. He must be forgiven that."

"Émilie, do you believe what you say? Do you accept that definition of science?"

The girl straightened her back, considering her hands as she crossed them in her lap. "No, Adrienne, I do not."

"Give me your own, then."

She thought barely three seconds. "The nature of scientific philosophy is to discover things."

Adrienne smiled faintly. "Is that so different from what you quoted a moment ago?"

"I think it is, though I cannot say why."

"Let me add a bit, then. It is the discovery of things merely to know them, to see the true beauty of the world revealed, to appreciate the fullness of creation. It does not matter whether something a king, a soldier, or a blacksmith would consider useful is produced. It does not matter whether angels or devils are involved. Do you know why I am here, peering through this telescope?"

"To see something?"

"I am regarding Jupiter. Come look. Tell me what you see."

Émilie rose and put her eye to the ocular. After a moment she said, "I see a small disk with bands of color. I see two small points of light."

Adrienne nodded. "With the aid of the malakim, I have seen much more of Jupiter. I have seen the tides flowing in his great cloud oceans. I have seen those pinpricks as moons."

"I read your monograph on it."

"And yet tonight I come to this poor tube with its curved mirrors. Why do you suppose that is?"

"I cannot guess."

"The method of science is to observe. We observe, we experiment, we record the results. It all has to do with what we see, hear, taste, smell. Do you see my point? Do you see why my monograph upon Jupiter was worthless?"

"No, Mademoiselle—ah, Adrienne. You observed and recorded what you saw, did you not?"

"I did not. When I look through this telescope, only light mediates that observation. My monographs were based upon what the malakim saw and then translated to me. Have you ever played the game in which a phrase is whispered around a circle—into this ear, then that? The object is the amusement of how distorted the phrase becomes. And in *that* game, there is no deliberate attempt to distort."

"Are you saying the angels of God would lie?" The girl wrinkled her brow.

"Émilie, you must promise me you will not repeat this conversation. Not to Linné, not to anyone. Will you swear it to me?"

"Yes, Adrienne."

"Émilie, there is no proof whatever that the malakim have anything to do with God. None. They might, indeed, be angels. They might be devils. They might merely be beings much like us who live in a different state. But that they come from God, we have only their word. Just as I have only their word as to the appearance of Jupiter's moons. This crude telescope gives me truer observation than they ever could. Do you understand?"

"I think so. But I have read all of your work, and—"

"You have read none of my work." Adrienne sighed. "I have wasted ten years of my life, and only now do I know it. Only when I am slapped in the face with it." She lifted a bundle of papers. "Here is my work, or all that is left of it. All done when I was younger than you. I think you will find one of them particularly interesting, for it concerns the mathematical nature of the malakim. It is unfinished, but I wish to finish it. I would like you to help me."

"Me?"

"I think you retain a perspective I have lost. Read it and comment upon it for me. But do not show anyone. Keep it hidden, safe. Keep some half-written paper on cures for the gout handy to cover it with should someone enter the room. This is our secret work."

"And Linné?"

"I shall talk to him as well. If he is willing, the two of you will continue with your project as you proposed it to me. But you must now do so secretly. It is dangerous; if discovered you could be expelled, or perhaps much worse. Think on it."

"I do not have to, Adrienne," Émilie said, her eyes blazing and quite tearless. "I do not have to." She turned to go.

"Wait a moment, Émilie. I would like to tell you something else."

"Yes?"

"That you should hold on to your love of knowledge. It is precious. It is dangerous for a woman, rare, but beyond worth."

"Thank you, Adrienne. I've often wondered how you—I mean, they say—"

"What do they say?"

"When I was a girl, in France, I saw you once. At the king's library."

"I did not know that."

"It gave me hope, Adrienne, to see a woman at such things. It made me think that there might be a way—"

"A third path," Adrienne murmured.

"Mademoiselle?"

"When I was young, at the school of Saint Cyr, I fell in love with philosophy and mathematics. Yet girls there were not allowed to study more than the rudiments of either. But one of the teachers helped me, showed me how to hide my studies; and I began to dream of something . . . different. I decided I did not want to be a wife, nor enter a convent, but that I wanted to be free, at liberty to pursue my own interests. A third path, you see, between the two available to our sex. But I was not bold—I kept my plan hidden, and it nearly undid me."

"Before I left France . . . I heard . . . some said that you were a witch. That you killed the king and thus brought this blight upon the world."

Adrienne laughed bitterly. "Would that I had killed the king. But it was he, Louis XIV, who brought our world to this state. He had embroiled France in a great war with half the world, and he was losing. As England was his chiefest enemy, he directed his philosophers to destroy England. And so they did. I was amanuensis to the philosophers, but their plan was secret even from me; and by the time I had riddled it out, it was too late. I did try to kill the king then, and stop the comet besides. I lost my hand, my true love, everything."

Émilie stared at her. "Your hand?"

Adrienne held up her right hand. "An angel protected the king. It burned my hand away. Somehow they replaced it. It is now a hand, but not a hand. It allows me to view directly the forces and ferments of the aether. The formula you hold—I once thought I understood how my hand was made and what its purpose was. Now, I do not understand it at all. That is why you must help me, Émilie."

"But in the end, you found your third path, yes?"

Adrienne continued regarding her hand. "In the end," she said softly, "I learned not to be timid, and, yes, I found that path. But now I wonder if there might not be a fourth. . . ."

Later, in her room, she sipped a pale wine and wondered why she had told Émilie—a girl she hardly knew—the story of her life. Oh, she had omitted much. Most particularly, she had neglected mention of the Korai, the secret sisterhood that had first nurtured her and then used her to reach the king. Soon enough she would mention the Korai to Émilie, for she seemed a worthy candidate for the cabal. But now, as she had for many years, Adrienne wondered how worthy the Korai were. Those in Saint Petersburg were a contentious lot: mystical, more interested in the formalities of meetings and the recitation of old wisdoms than in accomplishing anything new.

Of course, she now realized that she had fit in rather well. Ten years of research wasted.

Not wasted, a voice said, humming through her hand. *You are a queen of angels.*

Adrienne looked up and regarded a seraph.

She had seen exactly two seraphim in her life up until then. The first had been the guardian of King Louis, and perhaps driven him mad. It had attacked her and burned off her hand. The second guarded the tsar, and she had seen it more often.

This was a third one, different from the other two somehow, though she could not qualify how. Like them, it had six dark wings quilted with eyes, like the tail of a peacock, and eyes on the joints of its fingers and in the palm of its hand. It seemed made of shadow, its human face obscure save for the lamps of its eyes. It was sexless, and reminded her more of a giant moth than of a man or a bird.

"Who are you?"

"Name me what you want. You know what I am."

"I have suffered because of your kind."

"And benefited. I gave you your hand. It was once a part of me."

It held up one of its arms, and with a tingle up her spine she saw that it terminated in a stump.

"And yet—" She had to stop, and start again. Her hand suddenly felt—repulsive. "And yet, in all these years, you have not come for thanks?"

"You have not needed me, and I was needed elsewhere. Do not fear me, Adrienne. The one who took your hand was my enemy. I gave it back."

"I do not fear you," she lied.

"You should not. You command me, as you command my own servants."

"The djinni are yours?"

"Yes. I left them to serve you. I am pleased; you have done well with them."

"And why, after all this time, do you come to me now?"

"There are new motions in the world. Our enemies are abroad, and there are many of them. And my—our—servants believe you are . . . upset."

"Perhaps because I am."

"Can you explain?"

"You seem to read my thoughts. You tell me."

"I cannot hear all your thoughts—only those with the force of spoken words. Only those you let trickle through your hand."

"You tricked me."

"How so?"

She sipped the wine. "I make miracles. I make them every day. And through these miracles I have gained all this around me—wealth, power, prestige, followers. And yet it's all a lie, isn't it?"

"How can it be a lic?"

"Because tomorrow, if you will it so, the miracles stop, and I am without power."

"That need never happen."

She smiled ruefully. "First, I doubt that, and the fact that I must be content to trust you is the very thing I've sought to avoid in life. I avoided marrying so I would not have to trust a man, and now I find I *have* married—married the least trustworthy bridegroom of all. Second, power aside, I wanted knowledge—and my knowledge of science remains what it was when first this hand became mine."

"I hardly see how that is *my* fault," the seraph said. "I offered you a gift. You took it. There was never a condition that you had to use it, that you should cease doing your sums or whatever you think you have neglected. And did you really not want the power it brought? Would you give up that power now?"

Adrienne quirked her lips, thinking of all she had lost. Her first love, Nicolas. Her son. Hercule. "No," she replied. "No, the power suits me. But as I said—I no longer trust its source. What are you up to, you creatures?"

"What do you want?"

"An answer to that last question."

"Not just yet. What else do you want?"

"I want my son back, first. Your kind took him, and I want him back. Second, I want knowledge and, yes, I suppose, power—but power that I do not owe to you."

The seraph flexed its wings. "You keep saying that. What matter that you owe it to me? I owe *my* power to God, as do you ultimately. Do you revile that debt, too? Do you believe things can begin and end with you, that *you* can be the alpha and the omega? What a conceited race yours is—what an o'erblown example of it *you* are."

"What did you come here for?" she asked, trying to pretend his words had no effect on her, that they did not strike bone and leave her breath uncertain in her chest.

"I am your ally, Adrienne; and if you care for your race, you need such an ally. The *malfaiteurs*, as you call them, have begun the final phase of their program. They believe that they have found the solution to their problem."

"I am not clear as to what their problem is, exactly. Perhaps you can explain."

"They wish to eradicate humanity, as I think you know."

"Why?"

"Because they are jealous and you are troublesome."

"That is not sufficient explanation."

"He whom you call God made us first. He made the world, but since He is unlimited and the world is, by definition, limited, it was necessary to create a place where He was not. If God reaches into the world, He will destroy it. He called upon us, the malakim, to come into this world and build it as He commanded. But once here, some among us understood that they were as free to defy the will of God as to follow it. They created mankind as directed, but then proceeded to play at being gods themselves. This displeased God, but He could do nothing to remedy matters short of destroying the world—or so we thought. But the world is made of harmonies, of law. From outside, there were certain minor things He could change, and He did. He changed the law just enough to rob my brethren and me of much of our potence. We became shadows in the world of matter.

"This angered those who would be gods, but over time most were reconciled to the new way of things. Then human philosophers began affecting the aether with their experiments and inventions. For the *malfaiteurs*, this was insult added to injury; imagine how you would react if upstart children began wandering through your rooms beating cymbals and blowing horns, farting, leaving their excrement on the floor. And so the *malfaiteurs* acted, using what power remained to them. They killed individual philosophers, fomented wars. At first it was easy—philosophers of sense were few, and once those were killed, it took centuries for them to be replaced. Now there are too many of you, and the *malfaiteurs* see that keeping you in check is like trying to hold back the tide. So they have decided to drain the ocean."

"I have heard this fable from human lips," Adrienne remarked, "but none of you malakim have seen fit to speak so to me."

"Those who serve you are not capable of doing so, any more than a mean and uneducated peasant can discuss calculus. I am different; among my kind, you might say I am a philosopher." It paused. "Do you doubt what I have told you?"

She shrugged. "I doubt assertions without proof, and I am doubly skeptical these days. But let us say, provisionally, that I accept your explanations. What have the *malfaiteurs* discovered that changes the conflict?"

"They discovered nothing themselves—they merely guided you. Newton mastered the articulation, which allowed us to more readily act in your world. You improved it. Now your colleague Swedenborg has created the dark engines."

"What is this? I have heard of no such engines."

"Only a few of your kind know of them. They allow our kind to exert our full might in the world. They remain to be perfected; but once they are, it is the end of your kind, unless my faction triumphs. The chances of that are not good, for we are much outnumbered."

"And what of 'your faction'? Why are you not annoyed by us children, banging and shitting in your houses?"

"We are. But God made this world for you, not for us. If we aid you, we hope He will forgive us, liberate us into the infinite world beyond the universe, where we were born, and belong."

"Rather to serve in Heaven than reign in Hell, eh?"

"Yes," the seraph said, with no trace of irony.

"I suppose English poetry is no more fit for angels than for the French," she replied.

"I don't understand you."

"Never mind. These dark engines. What do they do? How do they work?"

"I am not certain. The only thing that I am certain of is that they involve your son. He is the key."

12.

Assembly

Franklin and Robert padded barefoot through the streets of Charles Town, racing against the end of night. The sea in the east had already begun to mist green.

"I think only one is still after us," Robert hissed, staring at his compass. "Will y'r exorcister put it to rest?"

Franklin shook his head. "Its catalyst is all spent." He glanced around, struck by a vivid sense of déjà vu. "Where are we?" The street ended suddenly against the banks of a canal, where a couple of small boats were tied up. Across the way, lights blinked on in a tidy house. Somewhere, a dog was yapping. The air had a peculiar smell—salt, spices, garbage.

"Little Venice," Robert said.

"Oh. By damn."

Across the canal, a door banged open, someone's shadow outlined in it. "*Chi è?* Eh?"

"It's Benjamin Franklin," Robert hissed. "An' he needs your help!"

"Wha's that?" A lanthorn shone suddenly in their faces.

"Robin, I—" The Italians were Catholic, after all. What if they were on James' side?

"Eh. It is! Come over, *signori!*"

There was a pause, and then a board banged down in front of them, like a drawbridge. Robert went without hesitation. Franklin followed with slightly more reserve.

Closer, he made out their benefactor, a man of middle years with a long, dark face and wearing a nightshirt.

"You know me, eh, Mr. Franklin? Paolo Forseti? We fight together at d' battle of Venice."

Franklin peered more closely. "I don't—"

"You don' remember. Is okay—you were busy man. Someone chasing you?"

"Something like that. Robert, give me your *kraftpistole*. Your aegis, too."

"Why?"

"I'm going to put them in one of those boats and shove it off."

"Why? Then we'll be defenseless."

"Yes, but it's our scientific stuff it's scenting. Being armed will do us no good if we're dead."

They hastily stashed all their scientific gear in the boat, and with Paolo's help, cut it loose. It drifted slowly away as they ducked into a small, tidy room.

"Can we shutter that light, sir?" he asked Forseti. "Please?"

"Of course."

The house went dark, and now the small canal and the street beyond were only dimly lit. For a few moments they saw nothing, then Franklin pointed. "Look," he said.

Something like a giant glass lens moved down the road toward them. Paolo mumbled some sort of prayer or curse in his native language.

At the canal it wavered, then went on, following the boat.

After a while Ben realized that he was holding his breath. He let it out, and the other two did as well.

"*Grazie,* Mr. Forseti," he said.

"Wha' was that, Mr. Franklin?" Forseti didn't sound frightened, he sounded angry. "Some ifrit or deevil? That sort of thing I think I leave behind in Europe. Witch and warlock walk free there—'s why I come here. Eight years in America, never see nothing like that. Now what?"

"Our new king brought it with him, I'm afraid, and many more besides."

Paolo's frown deepened. "Wha' we going to do about this?"

Franklin smiled. He liked that "we." It was a fine way of thinking, and it reminded him why he really cared whether there was a king or not. The Italians had come to Charles Town with the Venetian trade. They had settled in the marshes south of town and built a prospering community. In Little Venice, you could forget where you were—you could go a day without hearing English spoken. It was, indeed, like a piece of Italy.

But when the threat came, they were Carolinians.

At least Paolo was. But Franklin would bet his life that most others were as well, whether the invader was Catholic, Presbyter, or Baal worshiper.

"Nothing just yet, Mr. Forseti. I'll be in touch with you, though. Spead the word quietly, if you like, of what you've seen here tonight—but only to those you trust. It won't do for it to get back to King James that I've seen this thing. Do you understand?"

"Clear as ice," the fellow said. "And proud I was to have you in my home."

"Proud I'd be to have you in mine. Come when you will."

"Thank you, sir."

"Thank you, rather. And now we have to go, I'm afraid."

"Go with Allah, then."

Then Franklin did remember where he had seen Paolo, and he remembered something else: all the Italians were not, after all, Catholic—or even Christian.

"Inshallah," Franklin agreed, repeating the word he had long ago learned from this man's captain, the head of a detachment of Janissaries.

As they walked barefoot back toward his house, Franklin turned to Robert. "I'm not happy about this king and his fish ships, Robin. Not one little bit."

* * *

Franklin found Voltaire awake, reading by lanthorn light. The Frenchman's eyebrows leapt up when he saw Ben.

"Good morning, sir," he said.

Franklin eased himself down into a chair and nodded.

"Your new king kept you up passing late, I'd say."

Franklin suppressed a surge of anger at the Frenchman's smugness and simply nodded wearily.

"And you've given him your shoes and the coat off your back. You've convinced me, sir, that Englishmen and Colonials truly love liberty."

Franklin rose and walked over to open a small cabinet. When he turned back to Voltaire, he was holding a *kraftpistole*. The Frenchman first looked amused, but as Franklin returned to his chair, keeping the sharp point of the weapon trained on him, his face clouded.

"See here," Voltaire said, "if you've no taste for my wit, simply say so."

"It's not your wit, Voltaire, though I'll admit I'm in no mood to hear it just now. It's your allegiance I'm worried about. I knew you, long ago, for a brief time. Now I find that I do not trust you."

"Understandable," Voltaire replied. "You were always trusting the wrong people. Vasilisa Karevna, for instance—"

"You trusted her, too."

"Trusted her? No, I merely did us all the disservice of underestimating her. But, yes, she fooled us both. What became of her, anyway?"

"I don't know," Franklin murmured. "You're the one as has been cultivating Moscovado friends. Perhaps you should tell me."

Voltaire sighed. "I told you my story. I heard a ship was to cross the Atlantic, and I wanted to come here, where I heard some sanity still existed. I am no servant of your Jacobite king, nor of the Russian tsar. If you cannot trust my word on that, I sincerely do not know what I can say."

"Tell me you know nothing at all of a Moscovado fleet."

Voltaire held up his hands. "I told you I heard talk of a fleet, but never saw one. I wondered at first why James risked the ocean in a sailing ship, when his sponsors could readily provide him with an airship, but then I can't say for certain James really is sponsored by the tsar. Is there a fleet? Have you discovered it?"

Franklin studied Voltaire for another moment or so and lowered the weapon. "God help you if you are lying to me," he said. "But let me tell you this, for your own information. The governments of Europe are beasts with heads. Cut off the head and the beast dies. America is not so."

"Meaning?"

"Meaning, my old friend, that if you have been sent here to kill me, it will help no cause imaginable. Things will proceed very nicely without me."

"What things?"

Franklin shook his head. "You will see, directly. I'm going to bed now."

He paused at the stair, however. "Voltaire, I want to trust you. You have the edge in that. I want it desperately, and the colonies have need of you—of your wit, of your intellect, of the basic decency I believe you own. But I cannot afford to leave you above suspicion. Please understand it, and if I have wronged you, do not hold it against me."

"What would happen if I chose to leave your house just now?"

"I debated that," Franklin admitted. "I thought to have you followed if you did, so that you might reveal yourself if you are a spy. I have decided that even that is an unacceptable risk."

"I cannot come and go?"

"With an escort of my choosing, or with me. This state of affairs will not last long, I promise you, and then you will be at liberty."

Voltaire regarded him for a long moment and then sighed.

"Liberty and freedom are not one and the same. Which will I have, if I stay at your side?"

"Both—or neither," Franklin replied, and went up the stairs.

To Ben's relief, nothing of note happened the next day. He spent his time in his laboratory and in a secret meeting with members of the Junto. They questioned Euler again, but he claimed to know little more about the fleet than Franklin had discovered.

The next morning he was awakened by a pounding at his door. He rose, gave Lenka a kiss, and put a *kraftpistole* in the inner pocket of his dressing gown.

It was Sterne, in the company of a pair of footmen.

"Oh, dear," he said, when he saw Ben's state. "I hoped not to wake you."

"I was abed rather late," Franklin said. "All the recent excitement, you know. Come in, if you wish, and break your fast with us."

"Thank you, sir, I've already eaten. I only came by to collect whether you have formed an opinion yet."

"As to what?" Franklin asked warily.

"As to whether you are interested in the post of court philosopher."

Franklin nodded. "I believe that I am," he said.

Sterne smiled. "The king will be so pleased. Since that is the case, I wonder if I might impose upon you a bit?"

"In what way? I aim to please, of course."

"In three days' time, your Assembly will debate the matter of accepting His Majesty as sovereign. Of course, as a member of the Commons, you shall already be present. But I had hoped for something further, for next the vote will be before your Commonwealth Parliament. I hear you have invented an aetherschreiber of a superior sort, which conveys not mere written words but image and voice as well. Is this so?"

"Yes, indeed."

"How many of these exist?"

"A handful, sir."

"But could others be instructed so as to build them in the other colonies?"

"You wish for the other colonies to watch and listen to the proceedings here in Charles Town?"

"Indeed. In that way the debate and consequences will be unmarred by hearsay. They will see it as it happens."

"A wonderful idea, sir. However, there is one small flaw in the plan. My devices work well enough—but work best outdoors."

"Oh."

"The weather should be nice, though. Perhaps the assembly could meet in a pavilion on the half moon behind the old Court of Guard? It would be particularly well, if the sunlight holds. The image can be dark and blurry, even in the best of conditions; and I'm certain you wish the king to appear in his best light, as it were."

Sterne nodded thoughtfully. "Not a bad idea. That way, the populace here can look on as well, rather than crowding into the statehouse. A capital suggestion, sir."

"Well, let me get on this then, if we've but three days."

"Thank you most kindly, Mr. Franklin. I think you will find the king's thanks are worth more than gold."

"They already are," Franklin replied.

When Sterne and his men were gone, Franklin turned to find Lenka regarding him with a puzzled expression.

"What was he talking about? Have you invented such a device?"

Franklin smiled. "I had it given out that I have. It got round to Sterne as quickly as I'd hoped."

"What will you say when you cannot produce your crystal ball?"

"Oh," Franklin said, cupping her face in for a kiss, "small worry. I shall have it invented by this afternoon."

* * *

The atmosphere was again carnival three days later, when the Assembly met. Or, rather, it had remained so. The festival that began when James and his court arrived had never really ceased.

The half moon was part of an old bastion, shaped as it sounded, curving out into the Cooper River. Just now it was shaded almost entirely from the glaring noonday sun by a pavilion as grand as the tent of an Ottoman sultan. It was all roof, though, and no walls, so the spectators who clustered around on the landward side had a good view of what was going on.

Brackish winds from the river and the marshes mingled with the scent of cook fires and sausages, baking bread and pipe smoke. The water below cracked the sunlight and tossed its bits about playfully. Almost everything else was more sluggish—it was so hot the air itself seemed to sweat.

Franklin noticed that the number of the king's soldiers had increased. He was unsurprised to realize that some of them were native South Carolinians, dressed in clean new uniforms. James and his people had been busy these past few days. At least half the crowd wore his colors.

James himself was seated in an armchair, as if presiding over the meeting. The legislators sat in rows of pews, which had been removed from one of the churches.

He found Sterne examining a wooden cabinet mounted on rollers. It stood waist high, where a pair of truncated cones emerged from a jumble of tubes and wires, rather like backward horns.

"How does it work?" Sterne asked rather excitedly.

"Much like an aetherschreiber," Franklin replied, tugging at his too-tight steinkirk, already sopping with sweat. "I am calling it an opticon. The brass cone funnels sound into a sheepskin membrane and drum of graphite dust. Its vibrations are translated by a chime into aetheric ones, and in its mates become sound again through the action of a similar membrane. The copper cone, you note, has a lens—like a telescope, it concentrates an image to a small point. A substance of my invention translates the impact of lux atoms into aetheric motion as well. These are reproduced, magnified, and projected much as in a *laterna magica*."

"Ingenious."

"Since it cannot see all at once, my man will stand here and shift the lens from speaker to speaker, as the need arises." He indicated Robert, who made a little bow.

"And each of the other colonies have a receptive device?"

"If they followed my building instructions, and I do not doubt that. And now, if you please, Mr. Sterne, I should join my colleagues."

"Yes, of course."

Franklin took his place and waited for the debate to begin.

It did not take long.

The first to speak was Sir Chapton, speaker for the upper house.

"Friends," he began, "I cannot adequately explain to you how my heart feels at this moment. I was an orphan, and now I have a father again. I was lost in a trackless wilderness, and now I have, at last, a map and landmarks. Every one of you knows the loss I speak of, shares my pain, my worries, my fear. Each of you knows my present joy. England gave us all birth, if not in this generation, in generations past. It was the desire of our fathers to make the world England, and now, at last, England is here!"

He paused for the inevitable cheers. When they had subsided a bit, he continued. "We have before us a choice, but I say it is no choice. Look what has become of us, these ten years alone. We have drifted, my friends, with no firm rudder. How many of you have watched as your neighbors have donned the manner and even the dress of the Indian? How many Latin ways have come to us with the Venetian silks, from our commerce with the Spaniards in Florida and French in Louisiana? In a few generations, all that is England will have left us, and we will have become like the savages who once owned this continent. It is the nature of Englishmen to have a king; the people and the king are inseparable. Without the will of the English people there can be no king, but I say to you without a monarch there can be no people. Each is axis to the other, and one without the other is like half a house."

That got him more cheers, and he went on mixing metaphors in that vein. The next two speakers were Tory as well, and they said much the same; and to Ben's eye most of the crowd seemed pleased.

Finally Theophilus Smith arose, a Whig, and cleared his throat. "I agree with much of what has been said here today. I wish, however, to add this. That the guarantee of English law provides not only for a monarch, but for liberty. We look around us and see many kings but little liberty. Is there liberty under the tsar? I hear not. Does Louisiana have just law under her king? No, indeed. And so I say—"

He was interrupted by a chorus of loud booing, both from the legislators and from the crowd. He set his jaw and continued stubbornly. "Hear me out! I do not object to a king. How could I, for I am English. But I would know that I have an English king, and the liberty that comes with such a king. We have heard of Latin ways, but the Stuarts are Catholic, and thus loyal to the pope; and where was James Stuart raised if not in France and Urbino, Italy, amongst Romish cousins?"

More booing followed, as well as some cheers, but all were silenced when James rose from his armchair.

"Dear friends," he called in a loud, clear voice. "Listen to this man, for he speaks the truth. I see you all do desire a king. This man does, too. His only concern is to know that I will be an English king of an English people, that law and divine right are clasped hand in hand. This is more than reasonable, it is necessary. Do not shout him down for raising the concern which is the duty of you all to consider."

He bowed slightly to Smith, and sat back down.

The crowd went mad for a space of five minutes. When the

cheering died away, all eyes turned to Franklin, whose turn it was. He stood, clasped his hands behind his back, and flashed the whole company a little smile.

"Mr. Smith has just made a very pretty speech about liberty," he said, "and the king has given it his second. I applaud it, I do indeed. But I do not think we can speak of liberty without speaking also of duty, for one does not exist without the other, though some seem to think it. It is said that liberty thrives best in the woods, and those of you here who live on the land and in the woods know that to be true. How often have I heard you say that you are beholden to no one? Have you said it? Or you? Your smugness in your liberty, I say, comes from your lack of duty. What duty is there in the woods? Only to yourself, and there is the problem. That is why some of you do not want to see a king, for you will have duty to him. That is why some of you, in your arrogance, came to these shores—to have liberty and escape duty.

"And you argue you have duty to yourselves, some of you. A man told me yesterday that his duty is only to keep his land, to make a living, to turn a profit if he can, to feed his children and his wife. This is not duty, my friends, but self-interest and not deserving of good remark. You mistake liberty for simple wildness, as the good Sir Chapton has just explained to us. You mistake the savagery of the Indian for liberty.

"I can hear some of you now, already arguing with me. You say you hold a duty to your neighbor, to protect him as he protects you, and that you have done so these past twelve years, and even before that. You prattle that it is your duty to protect the rights of your fellow men, so that they will protect yours. You argue that when the Spanish and Apalachee tried to take the homesteads in the South, the call of duty brought men from every colony to defend that land, and that this duty needed no king to demand or enforce it.

"You are all deceived, and I am—I admit it—angry to see you have deceived yourselves. You should plainly see that duty to yourself, your family, your neighbors, and your countrymen is only the shadow of duty. Real duty—true duty—comes only from servitude to a single man, to a king. Real liberty, true freedom, comes only in being told what to do. So I say, welcome the king! Embrace our long-lost father so that we might become children again. Look at him and look to the harbor, for there your liberty lies!"

He thrust his finger toward the water, and the stunned silence that had settled during his speech continued for a few heartbeats, as people struggled to understand what they saw.

Like a pod of whales coming to surface, long black forms were bobbing up from the deeps.

"There is a tyrant's liberty!" Franklin shouted. "Moscovado warships should you not be blockheads enough to put the yoke on yourselves!"

"They are not Moscovado!" James shouted, leaping to his feet. "Those are my own ships! English ships!"

"Then why hide them, Your Majesty?" Franklin returned over the rising hubbub of the crowd.

"Hush, Benjamin Franklin," Sir Chapton shouted. "Your disloyalty to the Crown is well known. You have no wish but to make America your own dominion, all of us servants to your scientific demons."

"You all know me!" Franklin returned. "You know I am loyal to my country. It is this king and these Tories who are disloyal—to everything we've worked for. Would you be the vassals of the Russian tsar? That is what this man offers you. Ask him to open up those ships. Ask him to have—"

"Benjamin Franklin," roared Chapton, "by order of this legislative body, which you have much abused, I order you to cease this treachery." As he said this, red-coated soldiers suddenly seemed to be everywhere, muskets leveled, not just at Ben but at the crowd and any member of the legislature who had shouted in support of Ben.

"Well, now we see," Franklin said, "as do the other colonies."

"Jesus!" Sterne shouted. He lifted a *kraftpistole* and fired a shot through the opticon. Robert hurled himself aside barely in time. The crowd surged, not so much forward as in all directions as the crackle of the discharge faded.

"I declare martial law," Chapton shouted. "Until we have sorted it out, until we have discovered what sorcerous trick Mr. Franklin has played upon us. I—"

"Enough of this!" James bellowed, drawing his sword and walking out between them. "Enough. I am your king, by God! By divine right I am your king, and you will treat me as such!"

Now there were a few jeers, but as the soldiers packed tighter around them, these subsided.

Panting, James paced and then thrust his blade into the ground. "No more of these parliamentary games. The gall, the absolute gall." He whipped on his master of arms. "Arrest Mr. Franklin. Arrest any known to side with him. Now."

Franklin grinned. "That was not your wisest command, Your Majesty."

"How is it that you think to instruct me?" James asked.

"It's just I count you outnumbered by two to one," Franklin said, pushing his thumbs into his coat pockets.

James looked around, as did the crowd. Encircling the pavilion were upward of a hundred and fifty men; farmers, traders, Indians, militia, Italians, freedmen—all armed to the teeth.

"Now," Franklin said jovially, "I believe my friends and I will walk out of here."

"I have twenty times this number of men," James said. "I have more powerful weapons than you can imagine. Already your forts and munitions are occupied by loyalists."

"Sir, I don't intend to fight you here and now, not unless you force it. But if my friends see those ships unloading, or more troops approaching, they'll open up. We may lose, but I'll die secure knowing you won't sit on any throne save in hell. So let's all take a deep breath and calm ourselves down. I've said what I came here to say, and now it pleases me to leave."

The tension stretched, and for a moment Franklin knew it all rested on James, a man he did not know. Was he more proud than sane? It would determine whether many lived or died.

"Go," James snapped at last. "But go from this city, or I will have you hanged." He raised his voice. "To all the rest of you—lay down your arms now, and I'll offer you not only amnesty but a place in my army. Stay with this man, and you are damned to die, I promise you."

Not a man wavered. Franklin felt a lump of pride rise in his throat. The Junto had done a better job with the militia than ever he imagined they could. Still smiling, he stepped off his bench and strode from the pavilion into the mass of men, who cheered him as he came. Robert stepped out to meet him.

"Is it all ready?" Franklin asked.

"The women and wagons are already on their way," he said.

"Let's go then, as soon as we're off the parade ground. If we haven't cleared the redoubts in half an hour, they'll start cutting us to pieces."

"Brilliant piece of work, Ben."

"I'm just glad the stuff I had you pour in the river made the boats rise."

"Not f'r long. They're already sinking. Same stuff as went on y'r aquapeds?"

"Something like that. I'll explain later. Now it's time to move."

"I'd like to move with you, if you don't mind."

Franklin turned to find Voltaire, grinning like a thief. He paused for a moment, trying to see through the man, wishing he had some invention that could reveal what lay in a heart.

But then, that's what his own heart was for, wasn't it?

"Voltaire, my friend," he said, reaching out his hand, "welcome to the Junto."

13.

Sun Boy

"Some kind o' Chinamen, I think," Tug said, sotto voce, staring at the squat men moving around the tent huts. They looked different from the other plains people, with flatter faces and lighter skins. They wore baggy pants and shirts, and most wore some sort of splinted armor—strips of laquered wood sewn to leather harnesses.

"I don't know as I like this, strollin' amongst 'em as free as y' please," Tug continued.

Red Shoes nodded understandingly. "But no one has challenged us," he observed.

"There are people from ten tribes here, maybe more," Flint Shouting told them. "And these fellows, who are of no tribe I know—and I've seen white people, too. Why should they challenge us? How could they tell we are invaders? We don't stand out any more than anyone else."

"Still—" Tug seemed to be struggling with the idea. "These white men are Russians, by their uniforms—if they try an' talk to me, an' find I'm English . . ."

"You're just a trader, Tug, with us." Red Shoes nodded around him at the vast encampment. "All these different people on the Red Road, the War Road," he observed, "together. This is strange."

They had crept past the sentries and into the camp before dawn—no mean feat, though Red Shoes had been able to ease their way with his arts. What they saw was incredible. The big camp was broken into half a hundred smaller ones: warriors from plains tribes and Europe—and, if Tug was right, China. *They grow as they come,* the woman had told them. *Iron people.*

They had iron and steel in plenty: muskets, breastplates, swords, and cannon. Red Shoes suspected that most of the latter—and probably supplies of food and water—were on the airships. That would explain why they stayed so tightly together, rather than spreading out, foraging. The smaller raids were probably more to spread terror than to obtain supplies.

"They must be aimin' to conquer the colonies," Tug said.

That was evident, Red Shoes thought, but why? And who were "they"?

It had to be the Europeans, and he guessed the Russians. After all, the tsar had conquered all of the west in Europe. He had been frustrated at Venice and against the Turks. If he turned east—but the world was supposed to be a sphere, wasn't it? So east would meet west. Facing west, he faced Russia. . . .

A dizzying thought. Dizzying, probably, even for the English and French colonists in America, who would expect any attack from Russia to come from the ocean they named Atlantic, not across the vastness of earth and water that lay in the other direction.

If that reasoning was right, his own people were in peril, for between this army and Charles Town were the Choctaw villages. Red Shoes suspected that the law of this army was join or die. It appeared that so far most had joined.

They spent the first part of the day wandering around the camp, but by midmorning, it was on the move. The three of them fell in with a band of Wazhazhe, whose language Flint Shouting spoke well and Red Shoes passably.

"Choctaw," the lead warrior said. "Huh. You are far from home, farther even than us. Come here to fight them?"

"Yes," Red Shoes lied.

"Us, too. We heard about the great iron people, the things

they had. The Kapaha and Shawano keep us from French guns and trophies, and English ones, too. But guns, hatchets, and cloth started coming to us from the West, and soon enough stories about the iron people came with them. Thirty of us rode out in war party, thought we would ambush them. Of course, we didn't know then how many there were. Or about their wakanda and the sacred path it takes them on."

"What do you mean?"

"When I was very young, I had a vision, but even the old men could never tell me what it meant. I saw pale men, pale like snow. They touched my people and made them into bone. They touched buffalo and made them bone, too.

"The old men told me that some had dreamed the same vision, long ago, and then a great sickness came, an unknown sickness, and killed many of our people. There were rumors, then, of pale men in the south, but we never saw one."

"My folk did," Flint Shouting said. "They were the Sapani. And sickness followed them, as you say."

"I knew it was true when they told me. It felt right. And since that time, the sickness has come again and again, and many of our people have become bone. Since my grandfather's day, our folk have done nothing but dwindle." He cast a glance at Tug, who, of course, was following none of this.

"Now we know the white people, of course. They bring useful things, pretty things, but we have to go far to get them, through hostile peoples jealous of the trade. Without guns we are easy targets for them, and our women and children for their slave raiders."

"Where did these western white people come from? And what about these short people who are not white?"

"Both are from beyond Where-Water-Swallows-the-Sun. The brown ones are strange, but they know horses very well. They make a good drink from mare's milk. Some of the people who live on that sea have known them for ten years or so. They began coming, in their wakanda clouds, building towns and trading. Then, all of a sudden, they want to go to war. Everyone over there wanted to know why. Then the Sun Boy spoke to them."

"Sun Boy?"

"A boy, a white boy. But he is the son of the Sun. What he says comes true. He says the white people from the east—the English and French—will be our death, and when he says it, we are reminded of our visions. From every tribe, there is at least one who had my vision. The Sun Boy reminds us, and then we know what we have to do."

"I imagine," Red Shoes said dryly, "that you also collect many scalps along the way, of those who don't join you. And I suppose imagining what you will take from the white men in the east is an incentive."

The Wazhazhe war chief grinned. "Yes, of course. But it is stronger than that. Go hear the Sun Boy speak, and you will know."

"But he is a white man. Why trust him?"

"From the west, not the east. White because he is the son of the Sun."

"West is the direction of death and failure."

"Ah, but we are marching east, bringing death *with* us, leaving new life behind. The world has lost its harmony. We will cleanse it and make it whole again. The disease will go away."

"And you will gain much loot."

"Loot, yes, and honor. I will own more horses than my whole village has seen." He shook his head. "You doubt me? Go see the Sun Boy."

"What about your villages, shorn of warriors, helpless against those who do not join you?"

The Wazhazhe quirked his mouth. "Those who do not join us will perhaps raid villages in the ghost country. Not elsewhere, for just that reason."

* * *

In the next two days, they passed several villages, but all had been abandoned. However, several bands of warriors also joined them.

"How do they know?" Red Shoes asked Slapped-in-the-Face.

"The scalped men tell them," the Wazhazhe answered.

That was what Red Shoes had thought, but did not say so.

They camped that day well before evening, as a black monster of a storm scraped across the flat earth to the west. Red Shoes found Flint Shouting watching the distant lightning as if trying to read something in it. Red Shoes joined him. The Wichita had been uncharacteristically silent since they had joined the army.

"They might be right," Flint Shouting said, after a time.

"Right?"

"About the white people. Maybe it is best if we drive them away."

"Maybe, but the white people are behind this army, too. It is a trick, Flint Shouting."

"You have been to their country. You know how they think. What do you say?"

Red Shoes laughed. It felt good, for he had not laughed in some time. "The nations of the white people are numerous. They do not all think the same, no more than the Wichita and Choctaw think the same."

"But you and I think more alike than either of us do like the French. And perhaps these white people from the west are more like us, too."

"Look around you," Red Shoes said. "What do you see? Do you see people behaving in a way you understand? I don't. The Choctaw fight to protect themselves. They fight for glory, for trophies, for revenge, sometimes to help allies. The French, the English, the Spanish—they have been very good at getting us to fight their wars for them, have you noticed? The English Queen Anne waged war on the French and Spanish. But who died? Yamassee, Apalachee, Muskokee, Alabama, Choctaw. A few white men, a handful. A few of the black men they brought with them. Mostly, red men died, killing one another. Why do we do this? Because we think we will gain trade goods. Because they arm us against our enemies, enable us to fight for our own reasons, but better. Because some of our leaders see only the next raid, the next silver gorget to hang on their necks. And now, what do you see here? A handful of white men and thousands of Indians. This goes beyond that, though. How many brawls have you seen in the camp?"

"Two."

"Yes, when the Crow man fought the Throat Slitter and again when the Black Shoe fought the Cheyenne. Hated enemies, people with blood debts going back to the ancient times, and now they all march together with white men as if they are brothers. It is unnatural, Throat Slitters and Crow walking together, and only two fights."

"That might be a good thing."

"It is a European thing, this idea of creating a mob of people—not kin, not even friends, for no purpose other than to fight. I saw it in their own country, and what it leaves behind is terrible. Not a few ghosts, not small blood debts, but such death and emptiness that no one even cares. What you see around you is *not* just a very large war party. It is an *army*, and that is something different. And when they fight, when they come against first the French and then the English—it will be just as I said: Indians fighting a war for white men. And who will they kill? The tribes in the south. My people—"

"And your enemies. Think if you joined your people with these, how your ancient foes, the Chikasha, would fare."

Red Shoes sighed. "Yes, except that the Chikasha would probably join them, too, and then we must pretend to like them."

"And if your enemies join, and the Choctaw do not—" Flint Shouting made a gesture as if slashing his belly.

"Yes," Red Shoes said. "I must reach my people first, so they will have time to deliberate."

"Why not send one of your dream spirits to tell them?"

"I can't do that from within their midst. It would be like dropping a cricket in a pond full of fish. I must be far from here before I try that."

"We're leaving, then?"

"I want to see this Sun Boy, first."

A few days later, Slapped-in-the-Face advised him to fast.

"It is best to prepare to see the Sun Boy," he said, "as for any holy thing."

They fasted and went without sleep for two days, and on the afternoon of the second day, they saw the Sun Boy.

A broad plaza was formed around the airship, and people gathered expectantly. Red Shoes felt the hush, the thinness of the universe. Fasting and denying sleep brought even the most ordinary man nearer to the world-beneath-the-world. As the substance of the body faded, the shadow gained power. For him, always nearer the otherworld than most people, the effect was magnified.

It was as they had been told. He was a white boy of perhaps thirteen, slim as a willow. To Red Shoes' ghost eyes, he flared like a brand, like lightning given form. And crouched all around him, in the air above him like a cloud, Accursed Beings swarmed. *Nishkin Achafa,* with their single eyes of flame, beasts that were panther, bird, snake, and fish all at once. Writhing about the boy like smoke were the forms of two Long Black Beings.

In the nadir of his soul, Red Shoes felt a sudden sympathy, a kinship, something whetted keen like a knife edge. And fear—he felt that, too. Once he had battled a single Long Black Being, and come very near his doom. Here were two. What if they should catch the odor of their brother, whom Red Shoes had swallowed and made a part of himself?

He tried to make himself quiet to the spirit world, to mask his scent. He felt beads of sweat forming on his forehead.

"God Almighty," he heard Tug whisper, and Flint Shouting grunted something similar.

"What do you see, Tug?" Red Shoes managed to whisper.

"Angels," the big man said, "glorious bright."

"Stars," Flint Shouting added. "The Dreams-That-Are-Above walk about him, as they did when the world was young."

As the Sun Boy began to speak, the spirits came among the crowd. The boy spoke a language that Red Shoes had never heard, but the meaning was clear enough in his head, not in words but in the language of dream. He remembered nightmares, and worse than nightmares. He saw the death of his people, smallpox and famine. He saw the white people revealed for what they were, creatures from the muddy waters below the earth, pale, half-formed things with mouths filled with garfish teeth, hungry, always hungry. He saw victory for himself and for his people.

It was not coming from him. It was not him thinking those things, as the boy sang of redemption, of the conquest of death, of a polluted world made clean again.

He had to concentrate, for the spirits were all around him now; and if they scented him, if they knew him, he was doomed.

Trembling, he closed his eyes, but found the disturbing forms there more distracting than vision, and so opened them again.

He saw the scalped man, pacing through the crowd. It was as if no one but Red Shoes noticed him. He walked slowly, examining faces, nodding, grim. He had not seen Red Shoes yet, but he was working his way nearer every moment.

Then the crowd was screaming war whoops, firing muskets, clapping weapons with open palms, and it was over. The spirits sighed away, and Red Shoes slipped out from the crowd and didn't stop walking until he could feel the presence of the scalped man no more.

* * *

Later that night, his strength returned, he cloaked himself in *hoshonti*, the cloud, and went to the great airship. No one—not human or spirit—noticed him climb over the rail or pad across the wooden deck. He moved along, hunting, a panther, an owl.

He could feel the Sun Boy, feel him as he might a raw wound on his own flesh.

He found him on the deck, beneath the night sky. He was seated on a wooden dais, and ten men sat around him. All were speaking together in a language he did not know. The spirits were no longer translating. He crept closer.

Hiding in the shadow of the forecastle, he saw that they were not all men. One was a lovely pale woman with slightly slanting eyes. One of the men wore iron chains. He had a mustache and the beginnings of a beard and wore the green uniform of the dead Russians. When Red Shoes saw him, his dream from the Natchez country came back unaccountably—of a spirit shrieking, of a shadow dying. The vision leaked from the man like smoke through a thatched roof.

This man was from that dream. This man had come from the crashed airship.

Red Shoes listened to the strange speech. It was not French or English or Italian—he did not know Russian.

But near the Sun Boy, crouched in a sense at his feet, was one of the Long Black Beings. If he could touch *its* mind, it might translate, as it had when the boy spoke earlier. But the *risk*—if he were found out . . .

It would be very difficult, perhaps the most difficult thing he had ever done, to touch so lightly.

He had decided to try anyway when the Long Black Being suddenly stirred awake, and all the one-eyes suddenly gathered about the Sun Boy like flies around rotting fruit—or like bees, protecting a queen. Red Shoes bit his teeth together, ready to fight, but then he realized that it was not him they had noticed. *He* was still invisible to them.

Their attention was on a woman, who suddenly stood across the deck from him and fired a musket at the Sun Boy. The sound of the gun roared out into the quiet night, and then all was suddenly motion, as if ants had been kicked from an anthill.

Five pistols barked back at the woman, as she calmly raised a second musket and fired again. One of the strange, squat men fell screaming. The others drew blades and charged after her, and in that instant Red Shoes recognized her as the young woman from the Awahi village. For a powerful instant, he wanted to help her, for no other reason than that she was young and fearless and beautiful. But then he noticed something in the confusion that no one else seemed to. The white man in chains, the one in the Russian uniform—had lurched to the side of the boat and was throwing himself over.

Red Shoes made his decision in an instant. His shadow-children hurled themselves toward the man, wrapped a shroud of wind about him. At the same time, Red Shoes ran as fast as he could, leapt up to the rail and out into space.

He hit the earth about the same moment that the Russian did. Only the intervention of his magic saved the stranger from a broken neck.

Now the spirits were turning their eyes toward him, and the aether filled with keening and animal chittering. They knew him for what he was, knew he was a worse enemy than the crazy woman.

And he suddenly felt the scalped man, too, out in the darkness, a bullet arriving.

He reached the Russian man in a few strides. He was struggling to his feet, chains held in front of him. Red Shoes hadn't realized how tall he was.

"Come with me!" Red Shoes said. In response, the man swung his chains viciously. Red Shoes ducked the attack. *"Viens avec moi, si vous voulez vivre!"* he tried again.

The man's wild eyes cleared somewhat, and then he shook his head. *"Bien,"* he said.

Bullets rained from the ship. And they ran near, beneath the curve of the vessel, to make the shots more difficult.

Coming around the prow, they ran into the woman, with four warriors right behind her. She was just recognizing their presence as the first flash of powder in a striking pan lit them all.

Red Shoes acted without thinking. He boiled the blood of the men chasing her, and they all fell, screaming. The rifle roared, spitting flame at the heavens.

The woman blinked, as Red Shoes shoved his *kraftpistole* into her hand, and then nodded savagely.

Come, he signed in the hand language.

They ran through the camp, men and demons waking all around them. And still coming, near now, the scalped man.

14.

Direction

Adrienne hammered on Crecy's door near midnight.

"I'm not here!!" A voice shouted from within.

"Veronique, it is Adrienne. I'm coming in." She pushed the door open.

Crecy was sitting up in her bed, sheets pulled to her chin, her covers mounded over a suspiciously large bulk.

"A moment, please?" The redhead glared.

"Oh—pardon. But it's important, Veronique."

"No doubt. If you could step out for a few moments—even around the corner?"

Adrienne withdrew as requested, and a few moments later heard steps retreating down the rear staircase. She reentered the room. "I'm sorry about that."

Crecy was shrugging into a dressing gown. It wasn't buttoned, and she made no move to fasten it, but instead poured a glass of wine and flopped into an armchair, resting one slim, pale leg over the arm. "Nothing I can't have again, if I want it. What's the matter?"

"What have our spies to say about our security?"

Crecy frowned slightly. "This could not wait an hour—or, more appropriately, fifteen minutes?"

"Perhaps, perhaps not. It certainly could not wait until morning."

"Our spies equivocate. I think some are no longer trustworthy. The short of it is, I think the usurpers are securing their hold, and when they are secure enough they will arrest you."

"When will that be?"

"Weeks, I think. But in the meantime they nibble at you. Already rumors are circulating that you are Menshikov's lover, and that the two of you conspired to kill the tsar."

"I thought as much. They weaken me at the academy, too. And I do not think they will tolerate Elizavet free for even those few weeks."

Crecy looked apologetic. "There is another thing, one I learned scarcely an hour ago. I would have informed you, but I imagined you were asleep and did not think there was aught you could do."

"What?"

"Your wheel of Ezekiel has been stolen."

"Stolen?"

"Or perhaps 'confiscated' is a better term. Prince Golitsyn, the metropolitan, and Swedenborg took it."

"In what direction did they fly?"

Crecy snorted. "Up."

"Damn," Adrienne swore. "That changes things."

"Do you plan a countercoup?" Crecy asked. "We might just be able to manage it, with Golitsyn gone—though the Dolgorukys are formidable. If we wait—"

"No." Her decisions were emerging like crystals precipitating from a solution—inevitable, a chemical process. "No, Crecy. I am not entirely sure what those three are up to with my wheel, but I am quite sure they must be stopped. Furthermore, I suspect this *and* my son *and* the tsar are somehow all mixed in the same stew. I will neither wait here to be arrested nor wage bloody war to keep a throne I am not heir to. No, my roads all lead away from Saint Petersburg.

"So this is what we will do. Very quietly, we will gather the household—all my guard, the books I select, some equipment. Two nights from now, we will seize three airships and leave this city."

"To go where?"

"To stop Swedenborg and find my son. Hopefully the tsar as well."

"And if you are wrong—if those three lie in different directions?"

"Then we will take things as they present themselves. But I feel certain none of these events are coincidental. The tsar vanishes in the east, I dream of my son in Chinese garb, Golitsyn and the metropolitan seize Saint Petersburg and then immediately set forth, presumably for some distant land, if they needed my ship. These cannot be unconnected events."

"Well argued," Crecy said. "You are certain enough for the both of us. Though more information would be nice, for the sake of logistics. China, for instance, I understand to be rather large."

"I think we can learn more from Menshikov, too. I think he knows more about this than he lets on."

"Menshikov is in prison, if not dead."

"That in a moment. Can you arrange what I ask?"

Crecy nodded thoughtfully. "It will be difficult, making the preparations. We may have to fight for the airships."

"Can we win at low cost?"

"Low enough. Lower than a countercoup, anyway. But we have to get all of our people out, or they will suffer reprisals."

"Yes. And I want some of my students—and Elizavet, of course. And Menshikov."

"You are certain you need him?"

"For more than one reason," Adrienne replied. "I don't like Menshikov, but the tsar will never forgive me if I leave him here to die."

"This will not be easy."

"Easier than staying here, I think."

"What of Hercule?" Crecy asked softly. "He has a wife and children who will suffer if he leaves. Some of the other men in your guard do, too."

"They will be given a choice. Staying here will be dangerous for any of my people, but if they speak ill of me after we're gone they might buy some safety. Speaking ill of me should require no acting on Irena's part. Hercule . . ."

"Hercule will leave his wife to go with you. You know that." Crecy finished her wine and poured another glass. The dim light made Crecy's long, unbound hair the color of blood, and the red wine seemed to match it exactly.

Adrienne rubbed her forehead. "I'm tired." She sighed. "Steal four ships, then. We will take the wives and children of those who wish it. But they must be here, at the hour. I will not wait."

She turned to leave, but stopped at the door. "Make your plan to free Menshikov at the same moment the ships are seized. I will go with those liberating Menshikov, so you may figure me into the plan. Good night, Veronique."

Adrienne felt a certain glee as the stone wall cracked, spalled, and then collapsed like so much sand. The heavy door fell outward, and two of her taloi caught it before it could clatter against the stone of the corridor, the bruise-colored muscles of their arms knotting. They eased it down gently. Stone was difficult to transform, due to its complexity. The door would have been easier to destroy, but would have released lightning—a fine thing to do to an enemy's weapon from far away, not so fine in a crowded corridor.

Menshikov lay in the cell, one eye swollen shut. He still wore his finery, but it had been torn and soiled almost beyond recognition. He managed to turn his head a bit, but gave no other clear sign that he noticed them.

"Carry him," Adrienne snapped to a talos. Obediently, the mechanical creature bent and cradled the prince. The taloi were built on a design discovered in Sir Isaac Newton's Prague workshop. Constructed of metal and an alchemical substance resembling muscle, they translated the will of her djinni into animal spirit, which in turn allowed them to move physically. They looked like caricatures of men, with small, mirrored globes for heads.

Menshikov's good eye opened and focused on her. She could see now that he had been knouted—his entire back was an open, oozing sore, and she realized that the whole rescue might well be for naught. Menshikov might be dying already.

It was too late now. Getting into the cells beneath the Winter Palace had been simple. Getting out would be more of a problem, with or without the prince.

"Adrienne?" Menshikov moaned.

"Never fear," Adrienne told him. "We are leaving this place."

They numbered only six—she, Crecy, and four of her Lorraine guard—plus, of course, the hulking taloi and now Menshikov.

Vague sounds scampered like mice from the corridor ahead. Adrienne sent one of thc taloi to reconnoiter and was rewarded by the crack of gunshot and whine of bullets rebounding from stone. She sighed. "No time for caution or mercy," she murmured, and then, to the others, "stay back."

A moment later, a white glare spilled around the corner accompanied by a chorus of very brief shrieks.

She tried not to gag as they picked their way through blackened bodies that had once been human beings.

Taloi attacked them, but that was even simpler. She merely cut the bonds between malakim and substance, and deprived of animating spirit the taloi dropped like puppets.

Alarms were clanging everywhere as they crossed the Neva, and bullets ticked against ice with almost metronome regularity. Anger knotted up like a fist in Adrienne's belly. Who did they think they were dealing with? She could shatter the Winter Palace if she wanted to, boil the fools in their skins, send white-hot air through every corridor. They certainly could not touch her or her friends with *bullets*. It was only her mercy that saved them, but they were testing her.

"Ahead," Crecy murmured.

Adrienne focused on the ice in front of them. Some twelve yards away, a man sat his horse. Behind him hulked five taloi of the sort designed for war; their arms ended in knives, and heavy armor covered their vulnerable integuments.

"Adrienne de Mornay de Montchevreuil," the man said, "you are under arrest."

"I do not know you, sir, and I certainly do not recognize your right to arrest me. Moreover, I doubt that you have the power to enforce your command. Stand aside or die."

The man was silent for an instant, then said, "Adrienne, you pursue the wrong course. This is unwise, I promise you. Ask your lovely friend Crecy."

"Jesus and Mary," Crecy hissed. "Oliver!"

Adrienne couldn't help but snap a quick look at the redhead. She had never heard her sound so.

"Indeed. Will you not counsel your friend wisely, Nikki? *You* are lost, but she—"

He was interrupted as Crecy's pistol roared. Oliver flinched but otherwise seemed unharmed.

"Nikki, I am hurt and disappointed. I have grown stronger, and you only weaker. Surely you know that."

"We are walking around you or through you, sir," Adrienne warned. Behind them, the river shattered at her command as the first of the pursuing soldiers set foot on it. The ice continued to dissolve until it was only a few yards from them. Near the shore behind them, the water began quietly to boil.

Oliver looked skeptical. Adrienne shrugged and melted the ice beneath his feet.

Or tried to. Her djinni would not obey her. She could not make them attack the man.

Oliver grinned coldly and raised his pistol. He shot one of the guards in the head—Fritz, who had been with her since Lorraine. The poor fellow moaned and pitched back.

"Now," he said, as his taloi started forward.

Crecy howled and leapt. Even now, Adrienne was sometimes amazed at what her friend was capable of. She hurled forward six yards and up, sword drawn and held out like a spear. Oliver had another pistol and fired it, but a spume of ice kicking up proved that he missed his mark. Then Crecy struck him, and the two went over the side of his horse.

Her remaining guards acted instantly, kneeling in front of her and firing *kraftpistoles* at the advancing taloi. Lightning played upon the things, but they kept coming. Adrienne ordered her own talos against them, but like her immaterial servants, it too was insubordinate.

Oliver and Crecy bounced up, swords drawn, and began a peculiar dance. Though both bore heavy military basket-hilt broadswords, they fenced with them as if they were feather-light sabers.

"Go!" Crecy managed. "Go!"

Oliver laughed, but Adrienne thought she detected a hint of disingenuity in his disdain.

"Quick!" he said. "You still have some of that old fury in you."

"I still have all of it, you bastard." She rained a flurry of blows on him then, and he slipped. For an instant his defense was open. Crecy's blade hit something—his arm perhaps—and sudden dark speckles appeared on the ice. In the brief instant, something else slipped. The approaching taloi had just speared a young guard named Alexander in the chest, but now all five machines dropped as Adrienne finally snapped the stuff that kept them animated.

Crecy slashed down for the kill, but Oliver was up, matching each stroke again.

"Run, God damn you," Crecy shrieked at Adrienne.

Stubbornly, Adrienne drew her own *kraftpistole* and shot Oliver. She was not certain what happened; the man's body hurled back into the night and skidded for many yards across the ice. Somehow, she did not think he was dead.

"To the ships, now!" Adrienne shouted. She pulled up her skirts and started running as best she could on the ice, and the rest fell in with her.

All except Crecy, that is, who wiped blood from her ashen face and started toward her fallen enemy.

"No, Crecy," Adrienne shouted. "With me. I mean it."

Crecy hesitated for only an instant, then joined them in flight.

Adrienne glanced back over her shoulder to make certain Crecy was obeying her and saw a man shape rise, and then five more, as the taloi stood again to serve their master.

Adrienne and her group reached the banks of the river and flew through the open fields that lay beyond. Less than a mile away, the red spheres above the airships winked. Behind them, however, Oliver and his automatons were gaining ground.

"Let me go back," Crecy begged.

"No. I need you with me, not dead or captive in Saint Petersburg."

"He'll catch us anyway. You don't know Oliver—"

"But you do. And you'll tell me about him later." Her breath was coming painfully now, ice-cold air cutting at lungs softened by sedentary life. She could fly, if need be, command her djinni to bear her up on thickened air, but she could not do that for Crecy and the rest. Besides, if their attacker could rob her of mastery of her own servants, that might not be safe.

One of her surviving guards stopped, knelt, fired, and ran after them, reloading. Another took his place, and they alternated in that way, a fighting retreat. Adrienne glanced back, saw red eyes like those of a hound, nearing.

They reached a low rise, and Adrienne stumbled in the snow. Crecy could bear it no more. "The hell with your orders," she snapped and turned.

Adrienne opened her mouth to shout at her friend, but in the same moment a horse came hurtling by her, and another. Muskets roared and at least two *kraftpistoles*. She stared up and recognized Hercule and his light horse, pouring over the hill, twenty of them. The night opened to fire.

* * *

Five of the riders took them up, and moments later they passed through the perimeter Hercule had hastily erected around the airships. A few people still scurried around, but for the most part they were ready to fly, soldiers and passengers peering over the rail back toward the city. Exhausted, Adrienne allowed herself to be lifted onto the flagship and made her way to the bridge.

She could not see Hercule and his horsemen in the dark. The shooting seemed to have stopped. But from the city, a swarm of light moved toward them: it looked like a whole regiment. They were downstream, where the river was still frozen.

"It went smoothly here, it seems," Crecy said. "Hercule secured the ships."

"But where is he? They should be back, by now."

"He will return, never fear. We should lift anchor."

Adrienne paused an instant. "We wait," she said, "for Hercule." She sent her djinni out, searching, but no longer trusting them when they found nothing.

"How exciting!" a woman's voice said. It was Elizavet, clad in a splendid velvet riding dress and long marten cape.

"Men are dying," Adrienne said, shortly.

"But I've never seen a real battle, only read about them."

Adrienne looked at the younger woman, then reached over to grip her hand. "This is not a real battle," she said, holding the tsarevna's gaze. "Pray you never see one."

Cheers erupted below. In the space beneath the ships, twelve horsemen pranced, hats raised. One of them was Hercule.

"There!" Crecy said. "I told you! Now!"

Adrienne nodded wearily and gave the order, even as Hercule and his men piled into the large baskets, leaving the horses behind. Already, bullets were humming by from the approaching force. A couple of stragglers arrived, leapt into a second basket, and the flotilla was finally drifting aloft.

As they rose, up and up toward the familiar stars, the sounds of gunfire faded. Saint Petersburg became a mirror, reflecting the heavens, a puddle of light, a faint glow in the distance, nothing.

Adrienne raised her face to the wind, which grew colder by the instant. With her own mortal eyes, she looked out into the ocean of night, toward Siberia, China, North America—distances somehow less imaginable than those between the stars. She closed her eyes and saw only a face, a single face, and felt something—a slight tug of unnamed affinity, as if a hair-thin wire were tied to her heart, as if someone far across the world were pulling on it.

He was out there, across those plains and rivers, beneath these stars.

Her son was there.

Part Two

Cartographies of Darkness

Perhaps the whole frame of Nature may be nothing but various Contextures of some certaine aethereall Spirits or vapours condens'd as it were by praecipitation . . . Thus perhaps all things be originated from aether.

—Sir Isaac Newton,
Hypothesis of Light 1675

At a certain time, the Earth opened in the West, where its mouth is. The earth opened and the Cussitaws came out of its mouth and settled near by. But the earth became angry and ate up their children; therefore, they moved further West.

—Chekilli,
Emperor of the Coweta, 1735

1.

Fort Moore

The sky gathered its strength, the dark furnaces of the clouds burning fitfully violet and crimson. The wind they drove before them was thick and wet, perfumed with bruised leaves and burnt air.

Below Franklin, cornstalks bent like rows of gaunt penitents, and the giant trees of the primeval forest beyond the fields grappled with the sky.

Lightning streamed in the distance.

"We reached this fortification none too soon, it seems," Voltaire remarked. He stood next to Franklin on the narrow wooden battlements of Fort Moore. In Europe, the structure would hardly be considered redoubt—a wooden stockade a hundred or so feet on a side, a motley collection of log buildings within. To Franklin—who had seen the place only on a map until now—it suddenly seemed an insubstantial place from which to plan the liberation of the Commonwealth.

But here they were. Besides the fort itself, the scattered cornfields, and a few houses of Indian construction, they might have been surrounded by a forest from the beginning of the world, before man and woman were cast from paradise.

"Believe it or not," Franklin told the philosopher, "the storm will not last long. If we had been caught in it, it would have been terrible but brief."

"It's hard to credit. It looks like the end of the world arriving."

"Hardly. We've seen a better representation of that, you and I."

A look of pain crossed Voltaire's face. "Too true. Still, some virtue of this weather seems grander even than that, perhaps being natural. . . ." Voltaire hesitated, then cleared his throat. "I wonder if I could impose upon you, Benjamin, to explain what our situation is?"

Franklin gave a laugh, trying to keep any bitterness out of it. "Well," he began, "it's like this. The Junto started as a philosophical club, and that only. Our membership grew, year by year. Very quickly, the topics we discussed took on a practical air—a very American thing, as you shall find. And our greatest, most practical concern was what to do when the European powers took note of us again. We thought on it long and hard."

"A secret government, with Benjamin Franklin as its leader?"

"We work behind the scenes, yes, but I am not the hierarch, as such. We are arranged more republicanly than that, but once we had decided on a course of action we were very selective about those we let in on things. It was clear that the colonies, as such, would not unify politically. Oh, we have the Continental Assembly, but it would never function without the secret movements of the Junto. And you see, come crisis, how the 'legitimate' governors find themselves all split."

"Aye, but this is not the foe you expected, a long-lost king of England."

"No, we *did* consider it. That's why the Junto stands together now, when the Assembly does not. We are more than Whiggish, we are democratic. What else can we be? Voltaire, the Junto is made up of peoples from every nation and religious persuasion. In it there are Negroes and Indians and even Frenchmen and Italians and Spaniards from Louisiana and Florida. Some are landed, but for the most part the colonies are now a land without a gentry or hereditary aristocracy. The Junto aims to keep it that way. That is why we will conspire even against an English king. Especially when that king is the puppet of a foreign tyrant."

For once, to Franklin's surprise, Voltaire's cynicism failed to surface. "It's a noble dream, Ben," he said, his voice actually wistful. "It gives me hope."

"Thank you. It's good to hear that we aren't simply mad. Or that if we are, it's a madness with a contagious quality. But I fear for us."

"And so this flight to the wilderness—it is part of some o'erarching plan?"

"It was one option. We knew we could never build and maintain a standing army like those the tsar commands, and though we have worked to develop new weapons, it was never there that we could divert our greatest resources, not with people starving and so many other troubles to be mediated. And so instead we made this design—it's a loose one, I'll grant you. We spent our time first assuring that for each militia in each colony there was a secret one in communication with us via aetherschreiber. Until now, our main task has been to keep the warlock adepts of the malakim from our shores, and we have done passing well with that. The other was to form mutual protections and aggression pacts. If there was time, and it looked the right thing to do, we might have fought for Charles Town. But it wasn't the right thing to do: their men were already in the town, the harbor was filled with ships, and there was treachery on the part of the Tories. So here is our other option—rather than wasting our strength on battles we cannot win, we conserve it for those we can, and negotiate ourselves time to see the difference. In this case, we put the forest at our backs and fight from it."

"Fight from it how?"

"As we may, I suppose—I'm no general or even man-at-arms. We have other men for that sort of thing. Some will strike as Indians—here, there, and gone again. Others, like myself, will invent ways to deal with diabolic weapons."

"I don't mean to offend you, but the numbers I have seen—"

"As I said, it's not just South Carolina. We have members and militia in every colony. In fact, from latest reports, the ports of Virginia have been successfully defended from the invader, at least for the time being. North Carolina has fallen to the suboceanic navy, but our friends there were swift to move into backcountry—and occupy forts such as these, built for just this purpose. And so on. And there are units of brave men who stayed behind to harry the enemy as he marches after us—there have been casualties in this war already, I hear. However many troops James has at his disposal, they will have to spread themselves thin to search us out, and our attacks and retreats are always designed to draw him away, into the wilderness."

"Still, if they consolidate the cities, they may be hard to push out. And to actually win this, that is what you must one day do."

Franklin cocked his head. "When did you start taking an interest in these military matters, Voltaire?"

The Frenchman uttered a dark laugh. "Ask a fish what interest it has in water. This last decade has seen to my education. But it takes no Marlborough or Vauban to see this—they have their backs to the sea and all of the soldiers and artillery of Russia behind them."

Franklin shrugged. "That's all true, too. But we shall make do."

Voltaire stared at him, openly skeptical. "Do you have allies?"

"Well, that is what we shall see now. In theory, yes—we long ago made a mutual defense pact with Florida and Louisiana. The word has gone out via aetherschreiber—I now await representatives or letters from them. We can only hope that they honor our treaty. It worries me that I have not yet had word back from either."

"What of the Indians?"

Franklin threw up his hands. "The Cherokee in the mountains will support us—they have long been our friends. The

Cowetas have been as standoffish as the French in replying to the invocation of our treaty. The Apalachee have sent representatives but do not say how they will go. Another worry is the margravate of Azilia. They broke from the other colonies even before the fall of the comet, and have strange politics."

"Overseas?"

"The Venetians are our friends, but our word is that they are hemmed into the Mediterranean by the Turk, who has made a pact with Russia to keep them neutral in this endeavor. Charles XII we count our friend, too, and I have sent message to him, but heard nothing."

"The Lion of the North? Has he regained his native Sweden, then?"

"No, Charles remains in Venice, but he commands brave troops—veteran Swedes and Janissaries." Rain began spattering around them. "Best we seek shelter, now. These storms care little what becomes of such as us, my dear Voltaire."

"What storm does?"

"Mr. Franklin!" someone called from below. He looked down to see a tough-looking, sandy-haired fellow of perhaps forty dressed in deerskin leggings, a battered justaucorps, and checked shirt. He had a musket thrown over one shoulder and a tomahawk stuck in his belt.

"Mr. McPherson!" Franklin returned. "How is it with you?" He hurried down the rampart. When they reached the fellow, Franklin offered his hand and had it firmly shaken.

"Voltaire, let me aquaint you with James McPherson, a captain in our Southern Rangers, and a pretty fine fellow."

"Y' can call me Jemmy, like most of 'em," McPherson said, stretching out one of his long, lean arms to shake hands with the Frenchman. His soft, low-country accent had some of England and Scotland in it, but in sum was all Carolina.

Voltaire took the hand. "Good to meet you," he said. "But what, may I ask, is a ranger?"

"Layabouts, most of us," McPherson replied, face deadpan. He scratched the four or five days' worth of beard that roughened his face and smiled.

"They were formed up about ten years ago, to watch our borders," Franklin explained. "You'd look hard to find braver men, or better ones in the woods." He clapped McPherson's shoulder. "It's good to see you here, Captain."

"We almost didn't make it," McPherson said. "The Pretender brought maybe a hundred troops up the Combahee and nearly boxed us in at the Saltcatcher's fort. We weren't fixed to fight them, so we followed th' plan. I left back some good men to harry 'em, though, so I expect 'em to come more slowly now."

"It's the best you could've done," Franklin replied. "What about your wife, Rachel—how is she?"

"We brought the women with us," McPherson said. "She's with the rest of my party, half a day away yet."

"I'm glad to hear that."

McPherson worked his jaw angrily. It looked like he was cracking pecans in his cheeks. "I had a pretty good cow pen there, Mr. Franklin—five hundred acres—and now it's been stolen from me. I don't care for that, nor did I care for running. We will turn and fight, eventually, won't we?"

"When we have the strength," Franklin assured him. "Have you reported to Nairne yet?"

"No—I only just now got in the gates. I will, though." He nodded at Voltaire, then seemed to remember something else. "By the by, I ran across a Maroon on the way to meet up with his fellows. He didn't give us trouble, so we gave him none, but he said he was coming here for a meetin'."

"It's true. I gave out the invitation, through Mr. Nakaso."

"Can't trust 'em," McPherson opined.

"So I'm told," Franklin replied. "But it may be time to set aside such prejudices."

McPherson shrugged. "I won't trust 'em at *my* back. Just lettin' y' know."

"Well, tell Nairne, for I'm no military man," Franklin replied.

"I will. And I shall see you later. Mr. Voltaire, a great pleasure."

"Agreed," Voltaire said.

The fort was a flurry of activity as tarps went up over cook fires and huddles of talking men and women. After marching out of heavily occupied Charles Town with only a few skirmishes, and traveling for ten days on the "great western road"—really nothing more than a muddy path through the wilderness—it was time for some celebration, storm or no. The scent of venison and pan bread mingled with woodsmoke; and a song struck up, accompanied by bagpipe and fiddle. As they passed, men waved at Franklin.

"There's our magus!" one of them cried. "Tell us, Mr. Franklin, what new wonder will drive them tsarcobites back which way they came?"

The question came from a fellow he didn't know, a big man with a bushy beard and a missing front tooth. A score of others raised mugs at the question.

"As much as I'll take credit for my puttering when it's all said and done," Franklin said, "it won't be any new wonder that licks 'em, but plain old colonial guts."

That got a few cheers. Rum and compliments always made for an appreciative audience. He doffed his tricorn and moved on.

"They seem confident enough."

"Aye."

"I wonder, though, if any have much idea of what the reality of war is."

"They've seen their share of mayhem."

"I doubt they've seen anything like what James' troops have known in Europe. Or the Russians. It's been hell and more than hell there for centuries, Ben."

"I know. And I intend to keep the borders of hell secure somewhere out in the Atlantic."

They crossed on to the headquarters. It wasn't a fancy building—dressed logs, solid and serviceable, but not exactly a fine planter's home. At the front of it, they found Euler, seated on a small stool, regarding everything around him with apparent interest. Nearby Shandy Tupman, whom Franklin had assigned to guard the fellow, watched Ben's approach with matching but more singular interest. Franklin nodded.

"We'll take him for a bit, Shandy."

"Good. I thought I'd take a crack at some of those fish in the river, if you don't mind."

"Not a bit," Franklin replied, "though it is raining."

"Not for long, I'll wager."

As Shandy hurried off, Franklin turned to the captive.

"Hello there, Mr. Euler," he said cheerfully. "I heard you've been asking to see me. The march wasn't too hard on you, I hope."

"Not at all," Euler replied pleasantly. "I appreciate being unbound."

"We earn our trust by degrees. You did us a damn good turn, and we appreciate it. *I* appreciate it. If I had listened to you earlier, things might have gone even better for us than they did."

"And so this time you only dally for *half* a day when I ask to speak to you."

"Believe it or not, I'm a busy man," Franklin replied. "But here I am now. You have more to say to me?"

"First, a request," Euler said. "I'd much like pen and paper. I've some calculations I'd like to work on."

"Done, though you'll understand our stores of such things are limited." Franklin cocked his head. "You'll also understand, of course, that we still can't trust you entirely, so we'll be keeping a watch on you."

"Of course. You won't like it, I think—what I have to tell you."

"Go on anyway."

"This flight to the countryside is a mistake. You were better to stay in Charles Town where they might have let you work. You won't win this battle with musket and sword, Mr. Franklin, with a thousand men or ten thousand."

Franklin regarded the fellow for a moment. "You drink rum, Mr. Euler?"

"If you don't have vodka."

"Let's go inside, then."

The rain was falling in sheets, and the illumination was that of a bleak twilight.

A boy brought each of them a plate of venison and corn cakes, and they retired to the makeshift war room they had spent the morning setting up. It was dark, lit by a few tapers and oil lanterns. It smelled of unfinished wood.

He poured each of them a glass of rum and sent the page for Robert.

"There," Franklin said. "This is bound to be more pleasant with some food and drink before us."

"This is quite awful," Voltaire said, sniffing the rum.

"I'm sure you've had worse, or it's had you. Well, Mr. Euler? At your leisure."

"A toast, first, to my hosts," Euler said, holding his cup aloft.

"Indeed," Voltaire agreed.

When Franklin made no move to drink his own health, Euler stopped with his cup near his lips. "In my country, it is the custom to drink one's own health, when it is proposed."

"Ah." Franklin raised his cup, watched as Euler drained his. Holding his breath against the fumes, Franklin finished his own, then poured another round.

"What *is* your country, Mr. Euler?"

"Ah, that is a question, is it not? And not easy for me to answer. Just now I was referring to the customs of Russia, but as I told you, I wasn't born there. I was born in Switzerland, in

Basel. I was—as I told you, and as you recognized me—a creature of the malakim. I knew no others like myself, but in time I came to understand that I was different from other men. I was naturally inclined toward mathematics, however, and I studied it. I was called at a young age to apply for a student scholarship to the Academy of Sciences at Saint Petersburg and, through the agency of a friend, I was appointed there.

"The academy, my friends, was a place of wonders. For me, it was heaven. But it was also through my studies there that I gradually came to understand the full depth of what my masters were planning."

"Well, they mean us no good, that much is obvious."

"True. But what you must understand from the very beginning is that there are, amongst the malakim, factions—just as there are factions amongst the people of Earth. I don't pretend to fully understand the intricacies of their politics—after all, I was raised with the point of view of only one—but I can characterize the two main camps I knew as a child. The one camp—let us call them the Radicals—believe that the only permanent solution to their irritations is the utter obliteration of mankind. Only then will they be at peace, untroubled by our scientific proclivities. It is, I believe, this faction you are most familiar with, as it was they who contrived the fall of the comet upon England."

"Go on," Franklin said, his voice flat with anger.

"There is another faction—let us call them the Liberals—who think it wrong to destroy humanity. They believe a kinship exists between Man and their kind, and they also believe that there is some service we can perform for them, though I have never been certain what that service was."

"I take it you were a Radical."

"Yes."

"I guessed as much."

"The Liberals wish to control and limit mankind's explorations of the sciences. Through the ages, when they perceive advances being made, they make appearance and offer their services, lift the onerous burden of calculation and experimentation from the shoulders of the philosopher. This has the effect, over time—"

"Of killing science in the cradle," Franklin said.

"Yes. They substitute results for method, so that philosophers become confused as to what their endeavor is. With tame genii to do the magic tricks, it seems unnecessary to prove things, devise elaborate demonstrations."

"Sir Isaac understood this long ago," Franklin said.

"Yes," Euler agreed, "and so he was killed. And so would they kill *you* if they could. But I'll return to that. The Liberals, as we agree, create an illusion of science, and when the knowledge of the method is lost, they withdraw their aid. Thus, it is said, did they confound the Greeks, especially Aristotle. They led him to mistake metaphor for reality, kept him from the method of testing and experimentation. Once his knowledge was established, it became a false canon for a thousand years. It happened in other places and times—Hermes Trismegistus, also known as Thoth, was helped to become a magician, and again millennia of alchemy were born. For you see, when after a generation or three the malakim withdraw their aid, they leave empty ritual and nonsensical learning behind them. Man's knowledge of them fades to the status of folklore, and men forget—until the next time. It has worked countless times, since the first at Babel."

"But not this time."

"Oh, they are near. The most powerful centers of learning today are in Saint Petersburg and in Peking of far Khitai, and in both places the malakim have quite subverted the method of science and replaced it with fairy wonder. The underwater ships you saw, like the Russian airships you may remember, owe their motive power and operation to malakim. No, their program goes well, save for two things."

"Those being?"

"The colonies, of course, are one. Here you conduct science according to the method of Newton. You reject the malakim and have in fact managed to bar their presence and conceal your activities from their sight. As you say, you have discovered their plan, refused their seductions. This has happened before, with lone philosophers, but it was a simple matter to kill them. Now it is not so simple. They must kill whole nations."

"I see. So the Liberals and the Radicals can agree, at least, that we Americans must die."

"Precisely."

"And the other thing?"

"Something happened amongst them, something I don't know the details of. Something that transformed their annoyance with mankind to true fear. It has caused some shifting of allegiances, new political alignments. There is now a third group, a coalition of members of the original two, who share a purpose. They mediate between these extremes. They cooperate in a way they could not, ten years ago. The immediate consequence of this is the invasion of your shores. And, I promise you, this only begins it. There are things at the academy . . ." He paused. "You have seen, as I said, only a few of the malakim—those who have some natural proclivity for manipulating matter, and thus those that affect us, become sensible to us. But the greatest among them are the least material—that is, until now."

"What do you mean?"

"You know. Newton's final discoveries were of the animal spirit, the force that joins the material and the immaterial. He found a method of clothing the malakim in matter, of making them presences in our world."

"Indeed." Franklin grunted, remembering the talos, the man of metal, who had ultimately been Sir Isaac's death.

"The Academy at Saint Petersburg found much to work with in Prague. Two philosophers—Emanuel Swedenborg and Adrienne de Mornay de Montchevreuil—have taken these studies to entirely new heights. They have made engines of dark aer and fire, armies of taloi." He looked off into the middle distance. "When I left they were not perfected, all of them. But it will not be long. These soldiers of flesh they send against you—they are a prelude, a first act. Something to keep you busy and away from your laboratory. Your real doom is coming."

Franklin felt very tight. All of what Euler said could be lies, but somehow he didn't think so. It all fit too neatly.

"Why—?" Franklin stopped, tried to focus his thoughts. "Why not bombard us from heaven again? Surely they have the knowledge."

"Oh, aye—but it does not serve their purposes to do so. For one thing, the impact at London—it changed something in the aether. Not much and not greatly, but something, and not to their liking. It was destructive to the world of matter, but caused at least discomfort amongst them. Two, they suspect you colonists have a countermeasure anyway."

"That we do. But I did wonder. What of the airships, such as they used in Prague and Venice?"

"Again, they fear you may have Newton's method of unbinding the angels that keep them in the air. They have developed flying machines not as dependent upon the malakim to stay aloft, though still motivated by angelic power. Why none of them has been seen, I cannot say. Perhaps they are saving them for some future use. You must also remember, Russia has many fronts to defend."

Franklin took that in. "Very well. Tell us of these dark engines then. Why don't they fear we could dissolve them, as we might their airships?"

"Because they are fundamentally—"

At that moment someone pounded on the door.

"Enter," Franklin called.

The door swung open, and Shandy Tupman stood there, face drawn and pale. "I think you'd better come out, Mr. Franklin. An army has just marched up out of the wildwood."

2.

Bargains

The ship rained a fiery liquid from the sky. They watched it spatter against the icy fields far below.

"A pity," Crecy said.

"It's always a pity when good men die because their captain is a fool," Hercule commented.

"Nonsense," Adrienne said softly. "There is no cause for their deaths other than that I willed it. You cannot pretty that up by blaming a captain who was only obeying his orders."

"Adrienne . . ."

"Crecy, it was you who taught me long ago that sometimes one must kill others to survive. Remember? When you and I fled the king's musketeers?"

"I remember. I remember how upset you were, how much it pained you to take a life."

Adrienne shrugged. "That was a lifetime ago. This is not the last trouble we will see. By now Golitsyn, Swedenborg, and the metropolitan know we are following them. They may suspect I know what they are up to and that I can find them, though they travel much faster than we."

"Can you? Follow them?"

"I built the wheel. Some of its affinities are very particular. I can sense its direction. It is headed east, just as we are." She did not mention the other compass needle in her head, the one she believed pointed toward her son—also pointing east. "I can set our course. It may take us to China—it may not." She massaged her brow.

"Hercule—the man who was chasing us. Did you kill him?" Crecy asked.

"No—but we managed to slow him and kill his horse. Then he vanished."

"Damn."

Adrienne rubbed her forehead. "I'm going to my room. I don't want to be disturbed."

She felt their gazes, puzzled and possibly disapproving, follow her belowdecks.

She barely had the door closed before tears began streaming hotly from her eyes. She sat on her bed, clenching and unclenching her hands, trying to cry silently.

"Why do you cry?"

Through a prism of tears, she made out the dark shape of the seraph.

"You lied to me," she snarled. "I did not want to kill them, only disable their ship."

"As you just lied to your friends," the creature riposted.

"Because I took the blame for murder? But it *was* my fault—my fault for trusting you. And I don't want them to know I can't control you."

"Nonsense. I only wish to serve."

"Then why did you kill them?" It came out as something between a shriek and a sob, but with that, her anger eclipsed her grief, and she felt the threat of further tears subsiding.

"Disabling their ship was more difficult and less certain. I chose the certain method, to best serve you."

"You best serve me by following my command. But again you lie—you do not serve me at all."

"Again—of course I do."

She laughed scornfully. "No. Do not insult my intelligence. For more than a decade you creatures have encouraged my lofty self-opinion like a garden of nightshade, but I am not as stupid as all that. You and your vassals are not my servants.

If you werc, you would have aided me against the sorcerer who attacked us in Saint Petersburg."

"He caught us unawares. He . . ." the seraph trailed off, as if uncertain.

"He serves a master more powerful than you? Someone who is possibly your master?"

"In a sense. I could not go against him—not then. It's best that I remain unnoticed until my strength can be used to best advantage, milady."

"Don't call me that. We will not continue this charade that you are my servant, at least not in private. We are at best conspirators."

Another hesitation. "If you wish."

"What are we conspiring at?"

"I thought I was clear in that matter. To destroy the dark engines and the means by which they are made."

"You said my son was key. I will not destroy my son, if that is your implication."

"I will not ask you to."

"No? But what if you and I *do* have a difference of opinion? What then?"

"Let us hope that does not happen."

"But if it does—it is *your* will and not mine that keeps our ships suspended in the air, that prevents our freezing to death, that defends us against our enemies. A will that may prove fickle if I become obstinate against you, yes?"

"Yes."

"Thank you for being honest. But I also see, my good and trusted seraph, that there must be something you need from me, or you would not bother with this whole charade."

"Desire, yes. Require, no. Your cooperation will aid my cause, but not assure it or wither it by its absence."

"We shall see. As you say, at the moment our purposes are one. When they cross, do not expect that I will capitulate to you merely because I fear dying. I do not."

The seraph folded its six wings, and its multitude of eyes blinked like inconstant constellations. "As you say, Adrienne."

She shrugged again. "Are you like your simpler servants—nameless—or do you have a name?"

"Men name us. We do not name ourselves, even those of us who were born uniquc, as I was. If you wish me to have a name, I will accept one."

"Very well. I name you Uriel."

"Uriel," the seraph repeated.

She stayed in her rooms until almost sundown, reading about China, discovering many curiosities but nothing that suggested why her son might have been there—if, in fact, he ever *had* been there, which she was beginning to doubt. The people in her vision might just as well have been some variety of Tartar. Given the fact that Russia had been resettling all manner of such people on the new, western coast of America—and given that the course Swedenborg and Golitsyn seemed to be following drew a line ever farther north of Peking—that seemed a more reasoned guess.

She had been unable to contact any of the Russian outposts on the American continent, nor even those in eastern Siberia, either by aetherschreiber or magic mirror. It suggested—along with the tsar's disappearance and the course set by her stolen Ezekiel wheel—that the colonies were in unfriendly hands, Russian or otherwise.

Which suggested, in turn, that a trip to Peking might be wise, for the Chinese might have some intelligence of the matter.

Of course, the Chinese did not answer her queries, either, though she had brought the magic mirror that was supposed to communicate with them.

Bored with reading, bored with thinking, bored with sulking, she went back on deck.

She found Crecy on the poop deck, fencing with Lomonosov. Their blades gleamed a dull gold in the fading light.

Elizavet, in fur-trimmed cloak of deep red, watched with evident delight. Linné and Breteuil, who might have been watching at some point, were certainly not now, but were instead gazing into each other's eyes.

Adrienne took a seat next to Elizavet.

"What a wonder!" the tsarevna said. "To see a woman do that. And so well."

"There are few who can best her."

"Poor Mikhail cannot," she observed.

Adrienne, who had often seen Crecy fence, could tell that she was barely exerting herself. As they watched, the redhead raised her smallsword and stood *en garde*—sword extended, blunted tip pointed more or less at Lomonosov's heart. She advanced toward him, crabwise yet somehow elegant. Like a dancer.

Lomonosov swooped his blade up at hers and came forward. The steel he meant to beat aside, however, was no longer there. Crecy had twitched her blade in a small circle, and his attempt to control her blade failed utterly. Lomonosov, still coming forward, was in the process of impaling himself on her still-extended weapon. He stopped, blushing furiously, as Crecy's tip tapped him lightly above his heart.

"Always be sure you have my blade before you come," she said. "Always."

"I will try to remember." He set himself back to *en garde*. They danced back and forth a bit, and this time there was a somewhat livelier play.

"So long as Crecy is disposed to give lessons, Elizavet, why not have her instruct you?" Adrienne asked.

"I doubt very much my father would approve of that."

"I doubt it as well. But things have never been quiet between you and him."

"That's true. It might be worth doing merely to make him angry." Her face fell a bit. "If I ever see him again, that is. Do you really think he is dead?"

"I spoke with Menshikov. He admits that he has had no word from the tsar since he left Peking; but, contrary to what Golitsyn claimed, I really don't think Menshikov has had any word of the tsar's death—only of his silence."

"I don't know," Elizavet said. "Menshikov—he likes ruling Russia. Could he—mightn't he have arranged for something to have happened to my father?"

"I do not like Menshikov very well," Adrienne said, "but I know something about him, I think. He loves your father fiercely. I think it impossible that he would turn on him. I think we have far more likely conspirators in Golitsyn and the metropolitan."

"I'm glad you think so," Elizavet said. "I have the same opinion, but I know—yes, I do know, despite what people think—that I am naïve in matters of politics." She huddled a little deeper into her cloak. "How is he? Menshikov?"

"Resting comfortably. Soon he will be up, about, and making trouble. I'm sure that in the end I will regret having saved him."

"Really?"

Adrienne smiled and shook her head, but she was really only half joking. Menshikov still considered himself the tsar's surrogate. He would probably try to seize control of the expedition. It was a battle she would win, one way or the other, but she did not look forward to having to wage it.

Crecy and Lomonosov finished their exercise and saluted each other. "That's plenty for me today," the young man said. "Mademoiselle, I am much in your debt for the lessons. A man of my low station has little chance to study the art, much less at the hands of a master—ah—mistress—" His mouth worked on another word or two but didn't finish. He was blushing again. "Well, I suppose I look foolish enough now," he finally managed. "I think I will bid you all good night."

"A moment," Adrienne interrupted, "while I seem to have you all together. This voyage will be long and at times tedious. I have decided to institute a coffee at midmorning each day, where we will discuss matters scientific. This is in addition to any tutoring you receive."

"Mademoiselle, I think that a most excellent idea," Lomonosov said. "I very much look forward to it."

"Good. Then I want you to be the first to prepare a lecture on some item of interest. For tomorrow."

If Adrienne expected dismay at that, she was disappointed. Lomonosov beamed back at her and nodded enthusiastically. "Very well. I must go and prepare, then. So if the ladies will allow me?" He picked up his hat, bowed to them, and hurried off.

"Mistress, hey?" Elizavet said. "What else have you been teaching the young man, 'mistress' Crecy?"

"Hush, you impudent creature," Crecy replied, though her tone made the remonstration light, "and go find some mischief elsewhere. I need a private word with Adrienne."

"Oh, I see," Elizavet replied. "What a bore. Here am I, a girl in the bloom of youth aboard a ship full of soldiers and sailors, and you expect me to find entertainment easily? Well, I suppose I will make a go at it. . . ."

"No, you'll return to your cabin and study fluxions," Adrienne said. "You have a tutorial in the morning before the coffee. Good night, Elizavet."

"So *you* say. It is not proving itself so to me." She drew herself up and left them alone. Linné and Breteuil had vanished somewhere, as well.

"It's good of you, Crecy, to play the tutor."

"I've been restless. And I need the practice. I very nearly failed you yesterday, Adrienne. I'm sorry."

"Nonsense. You saved us, Veronique. Is this why you wanted to speak to me?"

"In part. You didn't ask me about Oliver."

"So I didn't. I've learned, over the years, that the way to learn your secrets is to *not* ask you about them. It seems I'm correct."

"I would have told you about him long ago, if I thought to

ever see him again. We met when I was very young—fourteen—and parted years before I met you. I supposed him dead."

"He was your lover?"

"My first. He found me—usually our kind work alone, but sometimes we are brought together. He came to teach me—the use of arms, espionage, the pleasures of the body. He taught me very well." She chuckled. "I was so young, so silly, that I even thought he loved me. A foolish thought. We . . . killed a man together, he and I—a mathematician, a musician. He made certain that it was I who struck the death blow, that I was the last thing the man saw. After that, he left. I never saw him again—until now."

"And Oliver—is he with your old faction, the *malfaiteurs*?"

"He was. At least I think he was."

"Hmm. I think the politics of the malakim are considerably more complicated than we thought."

"I wouldn't doubt it," Crecy said. "Theirs is an unseen kingdom, and we can only accept what they tell us. No one understands that better than I. No one is more skeptical of their claims now. Anything and everything they tell us might be lies."

Adrienne smiled. "I once had the same opinion of you."

Crecy did not return the smile. "I was their tool then, and my habits of thought were theirs. I hope that I have improved. I hope that I have become your true friend."

"My truest," Adrienne replied. "Truer than I deserve, I daresay."

"Hercule is also your friend," Crecy hinted.

"I know. I have not used him well, I admit. I will talk to him soon. I think we cannot be lovers again, but we can be friends." Her chest tightened, and her eyes moistened. "I hope I have not gone too far. I don't want to lose him." She moved to the rail. Below was nothing, a sea of dark air. It seemed to welcome her, cajole her, beg to swallow her up.

"I feel as if I've been dreaming," she murmured, "a dream with no pain or joy, a dream in which the loss of Nico did not hurt so much, but in which—" She broke off. "I will not go on like this."

"Perhaps you should," Crecy said, joining her at the rail.

"I will not, but I will make the things right that I can. The things I cannot . . ." She shrugged. "What is most important, above all other things, is that my son is alive. It's as if I've been lost in the woods, and now I see a light through the trees." She gripped Crecy's hand. "But is it right that I've made it your quest and Hercule's?"

Crecy squeezed her fingers. "For my part, I have been happy enough following you through this enchanted forest of yours, but for years I've been rather . . . bored. Philosophy, the adventure of the mind—I don't have the brains for it. Danger, travel, battle, sex—the adventure of the body, that's what I'm made for."

"Well," Adrienne said, "I think you shall have it."

Crecy leaned dangerously over the rail, flirting with the distant, unseen landscape below. "This has been a damn good start," she said, "a good start indeed."

She and Crecy had some wine, and she returned to her quarters in far better spirits than she left them. She fumbled with the latch, realizing that she had perhaps overindulged a bit.

Inside was very dark. The lanthorn was covered—something she did not remember doing. Puzzled, she shuffled toward where she could just make out her desk.

She heard a small sound, one she recognized: the lock of a pistol drawing back.

"Go on to the lamp," a voice whispered. "I want to see your face when I kill you."

3.

A Tale

Red Shoes kicked Tug awake. Flint Shouting was already on his feet, gathering his things.

"What th' devil—?"

"It's time to ride, Tug," he whispered.

For the moment, the very size of the camp hid them, but that would not last long.

"Who the hell're they?" Tug asked, stabbing his finger at the woman and the Russian.

"Later."

Around them was chaos. The sound of gunfire had raced ahead of the news, and here on the fringes of the camp it was clear that the warriors believed themselves under attack. Slapped-in-the-Face and his party were armed, and stared curiously at them.

"The Sun Boy was attacked," Red Shoes explained. "Horsemen—I don't know the tribe—in the center of camp."

"Who is this man?" Slapped-in-the-Face demanded, jerking his chin toward the Russian. "Why does he wear iron ropes?"

Red Shoes said in French, "Close your eyes. Now."

Slapped-in-the-Face, who spoke no French, frowned.

Red Shoes clapped his hands over the Awahi woman's eyes, closed his own, and lit the air more brightly than the sun. The Wazhazhe shrieked.

Red Shoes and Tug helped the Russian onto a horse as Slapped-in-the-Face and his men rolled about on the ground, trying to salve their eyes with their palms. The woman and Flint Shouting leapt upon mounts on their own; and moments later, taking advantage of the renewed pandemonium around them, the five of them rode off.

Both the Russian and the woman seemed at home on horseback, which was good.

They made it almost to the edge of camp before they were challenged by a group of ten horsemen of the short, dark-skinned folk, accompanied by a young man in green Russian uniform. The Russian shouted something, and they all turned toward them. A few of the horsemen produced muskets, but most had wicked-looking bows made of bone.

Red Shoes gathered his shadowchildren to attack them—and a concussion almost knocked him from the saddle. He tasted blood, and his head seemed ringed by a halo of sparks.

His vision cleared just in time to see the scalped man riding toward him, shrieking, ax whirling over his head.

Guns barked and the scene was lit by the flash of a *kraft-pistole*, but Red Shoes had eyes only for the scalped man. A half-dozen one-eye spirits flew before him like flaming bees, tearing into Red Shoes' shadowchildren. One died immediately, ripped to shreds by the one-eyes. It felt like losing a piece of his soul—for the good reason that his shadow-children *were* pieces of his soul. A terrible, unnatural remorse overcame him.

Why live? his sick heart asked. He drew out his ax, blinking blood out of his eyes. Where had the blood come from? It didn't matter.

He ducked the scalped man's vicious stroke, and their horses crashed together. Now anger spun up through the grief. If he was to die, he wouldn't die alone, but take the source of his misery with him. He dug his fingers into his opponent's clothes and swung, felt the blade strike something, but at a bad angle, so that it skidded off.

For an instant they were face-to-face, the scalped man's eyes burning red, his mouth twisted in a sneer. Then their horses wheeled apart. Red Shoes' fingers jerked loose of his foe's shirt, and they hurtled along side by side, leaning in to strike at each other. Blood sprayed as the scalped man struck Red Shoes' upper arm, and he felt the odd thunk of steel against his bone. Around them, otherworld lightnings writhed like burning spiderwebs. Snarling, Red Shoes struck back, and the sharp edge of his weapon hit the scalped man's skull, turned in his hand, and scalped him a second time.

The scalped man drew a pistol, screaming; and screaming as loudly, Red Shoes drew his.

Twin thunders crashed as one. He knew no more.

Red Shoes awoke to pain, a crackling sound, the smell of burned flesh; and before he could master himself, he screamed. Or tried to: a rag had been stuffed in his mouth.

Tug was standing over him, grinning. "That got y'r attention, eh?"

Red Shoes raised his head, looking dizzily at the smoke rising from a puckered black mark in his shoulder. Beneath it, a blood-soaked rag bound the ax wound. With his left hand, he removed the rag.

"What did you do, Tug?" he murmured.

"Burned out the wound with powder. It wuz what this Moscovado fellow said t' do."

Red Shoes grimaced. European medicine seemed more interested in continuing to wound a patient than in curing him.

"Now lie still so's Doct'r Tug can bleed you. I think you've got a fever. We'll get some o' the sick blood outta ye."

"No," Red Shoes said with finality. He sat up, his body feeling like a hollow reed. "What happened?" he asked.

They were on the prairie somewhere, no sign of the camp or warriors. It was perhaps midday.

"While you were a playin' wi' that ugly character, we made work of the other fellahs. Y'r woman here burned more than half with her krafty gun."

"We escaped, then?"

"Nah. We're in a Turkish dungeon. Of course, we escaped, y' nitwit. Y' think anyone was goin' t' follow us after they saw you and that warlock man goin' at it with all the fires o' hell? Not likely. Not right away, anyway. We've got a start on 'em."

"It won't last. We need to ride."

"Well, we agree there."

"I would like to thank you," someone said in French. Red Shoes turned to find the Russian squatting next to him, hand thrust out. "You saved my life."

"You were trying to kill yourself."

"Better than the fate they had in store for me."

Red Shoes gripped the offered hand.

"My name is Peter Alexeyevich," the man said, "and I'm in your debt. You only need ask your reward."

Red Shoes covered his astonishment. "Once we're riding," he said. "I have many questions to ask you. Especially if you can tell me more about this Sun Boy and this army."

"I can tell you about it," Alexeyevich said.

"Good," Red Shoes replied. "And may I say I am honored to meet Your Majesty."

Alexeyevich scowled, but it turned into a wolfish grin. "Even *here* I'm known? Well, I'm pleased to meet you, too," he replied.

Red Shoes found it hard to sit straight in the saddle. His whole side stung with the pain of his wounds, but more than that, he felt sick from the loss of so many shadowchildren. Swallowing the Long Black Being in Venice had made him powerful, perhaps the most powerful *hopaye* in the world. But *hopaye* he was. His servants were not spirits but fragments of his own spirit, and each loss left him slighter of soul. When he cast no shadow, when it was all gone, he would be worse than dead. His body would live but with nothing in it—or worse, with something very bad and not at all human inside the skin.

"How did you come here?" he asked Peter, to keep his

mind from his suffering. "Was that your ship we came across?"

"Yes."

"Very far from Russia."

"First you know who I am, then you know where my country is. What sort of red man are you?"

Red Shoes sighed. "Tsar, I was at Venice, when your fleet was destroyed. I fought for your enemies."

The tsar's face darkened, but then, after a moment, he chuckled dryly. "Well. I felt the whole world was arrayed against me in Venice. Now I know it. A coincidence that we meet so, yes?"

"No coincidence," Red Shoes said. "I felt the Sun Boy from far away, and came to see. I felt something else—something to do with you."

The tsar regarded him with brooding eyes for a moment. "I once had a creature who accompanied me, spoke to me—a sort of ifrit. It saved my life more than once."

"But it turned on you."

The tsar nodded and cast his gaze out to the vast horizon. "I see why the Mongols like it here," he said, "and the Cossacks."

"Mongols? Cossacks?"

"Horsemen from the steppes. It is a long story."

"We have a long time," Red Shoes observed.

"Pursuit," Flint Shouting interrupted, looking back over his shoulder. A cloud of dust smudged the horizon.

"I know," Red Shoes replied, "but for the time being, I can keep us ahead of them. And we can't run the horses too much." A thought occurred to him. "Did I kill the scalped man?"

Flint Shouting shrugged. "I did not stop to check his breath. He was still, but so were you."

"Well," Red Shoes muttered. "In any event, Tsar—"

"Please, call me Peter. I am not tsar here."

"Peter, please tell me your story. I believe it is of importance."

Peter nodded. "It may be." He shifted in the saddle,

stretched, then settled back into his beast's rhythm. "For years, my empire has expanded, not just west and south but east. Before the world turned upside down, I wanted trade with Europe, to get ships and goods and scientific things. But we had little the proud merchants of the West wanted—except furs. Siberia is rich in furs, so our trappers and settlers went east into Siberia, Mongolia—finally China. The Chinese would not negotiate with us for long years. We fought minor battles with them; they captured many of our people. Still they would not recognize us or make treaties. It was only after the strange times came that we found the key to open them."

"To conquer them, you mean?"

"Conquer? No. There has been enough war. I wanted trade with them. In fact, our key to trading with them was in *preventing* a war. At first, they treated us like barbarians, no better than the savages native to Siberia. But then we discovered the Mongols. The Mongols have conquered China before—Russia, too, for that matter, if only briefly. The Manchus, who rule China now, were like Mongols themselves a few generations ago; and though they now pretend to be like the Chinese they rule, they know very well that if they could take China from the Chinese, the Mongols could take it from them.

"You know of the fall of the comet upon England?"

"I saw the hole with my own eyes," Red Shoes replied.

The tsar arched his brows. "I shall beg your story from you, then. My agents have seen the crater, of course, but how a native of America came to England and Venice should be a tale worth hearing."

"I will tell you," Red Shoes promised.

"In any event, the French king struck England with a comet, but in so doing he wounded the whole world. My philosophers tell me that the comet brought with it a subtle atmosphere, one which acted to cool that of our own. Whatever the cause, winters were long and hard those first five years, and are still much worse than ever they were before—especially in Siberia and Mongolia."

"Oh."

"Yes. Whatever cost was involved in conquering China, the Mongols—and my own Cossacks, for that matter—saw that it was either that or freeze to death. Our spies learned that the Manchus had strife in the South as well, from other causes. And so, in return for their trade and goodwill, we solved their problem."

"How?"

"Ten years ago, my captain Bering took an airship across Siberia and found the west coast of America. He claimed much land for me, and in the next year we started small colonies. I offered to resettle the Mongols there, if they would accept Russian protection and if Peking would bear most of the cost. They had no choice but to agree, despite their Oriental pride. Altogether, it seemed a good thing—trade with China, new frontiers for Russia, peace with the Mongols."

"Something went wrong."

"Yes. Something always goes wrong, unless I am there myself. I have always known this, but I suppose in my old age I grew too trusting.

"I have always loved to sail, whether on the sea or in the air. I am not content, like some kings, to sit in my palace. I like to go, to see, to do. I nearly died of illness, rotting in my palace, and I swore I would be idle no longer. So I provisioned a ship to come here, to see my colonies, to explore this new land." His eyes blazed. "But what I discovered was treachery. My lieutenants had been killed or turned against me, and all had gathered around this boy, this Sun Boy. The Old Believers were at the heart of it, from the priests on down. They had won the Mongols, and the Indians, too.

"They tried to capture me and destroy my ship; and when we escaped, they pursued. We could not find a clear way back to Russia. We were forced farther and farther inland, and at last I determined to sail around the world. It would have been the first time such a thing was done in an airship. But then my own guardian angel turned against me. It told me to go back, to join these rebels, to lead them as tsar in conquering all."

He stopped, then, and Red Shoes did not prod him. Men spoke when their words were ready to be released.

"My Catherine was with me." Peter sighed, at last, and Red Shoes noticed tears beneath his hard eyes. "She was always willing to come with me. Once, in Persia, she cut off all her beautiful hair because of the heat, but she stayed by my side. . . ." He trailed off, began again. "I buried her. If you saw the ship, you saw the grave. When I refused my angel, you see, I learned who the master was. They play at being servants—great tsar this, great tsar that—but we are *their* servants, made so by our stupidity. I should have known, when they helped me win the Old Believers. They never planned to help us, only to use us." He turned to Red Shoes. "When I refused it, the angel tried to kill me. But one of my philosophers had given me a gift, for she never trusted them, not entirely. And so I killed it—or was rid of it, anyway—but it got its revenge. It freed those ifrit that kept my ship aloft, and we fell." His tears were still flowing, but his voice did not catch. "Ah, how we fell. . . . But I lived, more's the pity, and then they captured me, made me a pet. The pet tsar." He snorted bitterly.

"I will show them they were foolish not to kill me. I have dealt with many revolts. The heads of the Strelitzi rolled like so many stones, and their blood soaked the ground. Now the rivers of America will run like opened veins."

Red Shoes grinned wryly. "With your army of five and only one spare horse?"

For a moment, the tsar's face burned as red as a torch, and then he bellowed out a laugh so loud and painful that the others turned in alarm. "Yes, yes. A minor setback, I should think," he managed. But then he sobered again. "It is more than just my pride, this thing," he said. "My poor dead son, he was right—bless his soul and damn mine. These creatures are devils, and I know their plan. They plan to kill us all: Russian, Frenchman, and Indian alike. They set us against one another to bring the Apocalypse, and, Lord save me, I was long their tool. We are on the brink of the end of everything, my friend, and God has turned away his eyes."

Red Shoes clenched his teeth against a spasm of pain, and then looked steadily at the tsar. "That's what I think, too. It's what I expected to find out here—a great death walking."

"Let me congratulate you then," the tsar said, "for you have found it."

4.

The Margrave

The worst of the thunderstorm had slackened, but Franklin and Voltaire were still drenched by the time they reached the stockade. Robert was already on the wall, gazing down at some fifty men arranged in formation below. Out in front of them, a tall, slim fellow—he looked to be in his late thirties—sat on a Chickasaw pony and gazed impassively up at them through the water sheeting from his hat. All wore coats of a dark umber.

The fellow on the horse took his hat off.

"The margravate of Azilia answers the call for parley," he said in a high, penetrating voice.

Robert whistled, low. "That's Margrave Oglethorpe himself."

"I know. What do you think?"

"I think he's Jacobite to the core."

"He's also a man of honor," another voice said. Franklin turned to see Thomas Nairne. "If he says he came here to parley, he came here to parley."

"Well, it's your decision, Governor," Franklin said.

"Is it?" Nairne replied, perhaps a bit bitterly. "I'm sure it's been declared by now that I'm no governor of South Carolina. The Junto is our government now, and in the Junto one of *your* words is worth five of anyone else's."

Franklin sighed. "We should settle this now, Governor. What you say may be true, and I'll not murk the water with false modesty—I've much popular support in all the colonies. But if I won't shy from that, I'll not shy from the other side—I don't have the political and military experience to make proper use of that popularity in this situation. You are the governor of South Carolina. You are also, until better comes along, the supreme commander of Junto troops in the Carolinas and backcountry. You act that role, and leave me to worry about those things I'm best equipped for."

Nairne gazed at him steadily for a moment, and then seemed to both grow in stature and bow with a certain extra weight at the same moment. "Very well," he said. "I hope I'm equal to the task. My training in military strategy leaves much to be desired, but I'll allow I have more than you do." He nodded toward the men outside the stockade. "And Oglethorpe more than any other here." He sighed. "Oglethorpe, whom we can't yet count friend. But we can't let them stand there in the rain, can we? Let them in." He turned to the ladder, to go down and greet them. Franklin followed.

Oglethorpe bowed stiffly—not to Franklin but to Nairne, despite the older man's assessment of his position. "My men will remain outside your gates, Governor," the margrave said.

"They are welcome within," Nairne assured him.

Oglethorpe smiled thinly. "I shan't waste time before saying this, Governor Nairne. I am not at all convinced that our mutual protection pact binds me in this instance. It may be that when I leave these gates again it will only be to turn and storm them. Given that, it would be ungallant of me to accept your hospitality—for myself or for my men. Indeed, I won't come in myself, other than to inquire when the meeting is."

Nairne cleared his throat carefully. "You are the first to arrive. We're still waiting for the Spanish, the French, the Creek, the Cherokee, the Maroons—"

Oglethorpe frowned sharply at that last. "The Maroons? That rabble has no pact with any of us. Just turn your back on them once, Governor Nairne, and they'll cut your throat for certain."

"A risk we'll take," Franklin interjected, "especially if those we thought bound allies are to defect from our agreement."

Oglethorpe's sharp face grew even more dour. "I do not mean to discuss this at length before the meeting, but surely you see that our pact was against foreign aggression and to keep power balanced in our own nations, not to protect us from our own rightful sovereign."

"Tsar Peter, you mean?" Franklin said heatedly. "For that's who you place on the invisible throne behind James. You—"

"Enough, sir," Oglethorpe said. "We will all have our say at the meeting, will we not? You included?"

"He's right, Ben," Nairne said. "If we cannot convince you to share a drink with us, Margrave . . ."

"I must decline, but thank you for the offer."

He bowed, then turned to where his troops were erecting their tents, back near the trees.

"Well," Franklin observed glumly, "I wonder how many unfriendly armies we're going to have camped at our doorstep before the day is done?" So far, things had not gone as he had optimistically planned.

The Cherokee delegation arrived that night. They had the look of having traveled hard and fast, and they made no effort whatsoever to spurn Carolina hospitality, but came straightaway within the walls. Franklin, not wishing to get entangled in what could conceivably be a long, ceremonial business, watched from a distance as Nairne greeted them. Nairne would handle it best—before being governor, before being Blackbeard's aide, he had been the Indian agent of South Carolina, and he knew the peoples of the interior as well as any white man could. Still, Franklin, naturally curious, could not help but observe for a moment.

There were seven of the Cherokee, men ranging in age from perhaps sixteen to perhaps fifty. They wore motley clothing; matchcoats of deerskin or military justaucorps, loincloths but for two who sported faded knee breeches. They were ornamented with earrings and gorgets, and their hair was cut or plucked in various strange ways. They carried muskets and wicked-looking tomahawks. One of them seemed, to Franklin, extraordinarily pale. He guessed the fellow to be the son of a deerskin trader, not an unusual thing in the backcountry.

He knew something of the Cherokee, of course, and had spoken with those representatives that came to the Charles Town Assembly and to certain more-secret meetings of the Junto. The nation was powerful and had been a valued ally in both the Flanders War—known as Queen Anne's War in these parts—and the Spanish incursion. Nairne had expressed a good deal of optimism about their allegiance, and Franklin trusted his opinion.

He spent the rest of the day drafting the various letters he needed to schreibe—to Louisiana, Florida, the Choctaw, the Natchez Nation, the Chickasaw, the commanders of the various Junto divisions, the governors of the colonies. . . . Night crept on him, then midnight, and he was still only a tenth done when Lenka came and laid a hand on his shoulder.

"Come to bed, Ben. You'll accomplish nothing by not sleeping."

"Not true. I'll accomplish what I must before I sleep."

She tapped the letter he was working on. "My English isn't all it could be," she said—though after ten years her English was nearly flawless—"but it seems to me that this last sentence makes no sense at all."

He blinked and read the line. She was right.

"Maybe just a nap," he allowed.

"You need a secretary," she said. She tilted his head back and planted a kiss on his nose.

"Oh, well, if *that's* the sort of secretary you mean, I've an idea who might fill the job. . . ."

She put on a look of mock surprise—though one with some small measure of what might be real bitterness. "Is that how it is?" she said softly. "To get you in our marriage bed, I must pretend to be someone else, an employee?"

"Lenka—no. I'm busy, that is all. What can you expect?"

"Nothing," she said.

"Huh." He reached around her waist and drew her down into his lap. She felt supple and warm through her nightdress. "I have neglected you?"

"Yes." Then she sighed. "It's more than that, Benjamin. I've nothing to do in this whole matter. I'm just a camp follower."

"If that's all there is, I'm sure there's work enough to be found. My back, for instance, has developed an awful, tight pain. . . ."

She kissed him again, this time on the lips. "This feeling of being swept along as by a wave—I don't like it."

"Neither do I, my dear. Not in the least. Even less do I like doing the paperwork for Armageddon, but there it is." He gestured at the letters scattered about his desk.

"Is it really so necessary to write a different letter to each faction?" Lenka asked. "Why not some general declaration?"

"I've thought of it, but each must be convinced by a different logic. The Tory governors will not be swayed by the republican sentiments of the Junto, nor will the French king in Louisiana. The Indian nations care not what form of government we English have, so long as trade continues and their sovereign domains remain secure."

"It seems, still, that you might sum up in some general statement. Some declaration that the nations of the Continent have no business here in the Americas. It seems to me that would suit everyone."

Franklin rubbed his eyes. "That's not a bad idea," he allowed. "We would leave the matter of the Pretender unstated and ambiguous—let the Tories imagine our reference is to the Russians. It would make Louisiana happy, as King Philippe would then have grounds to defend himself against other claimants to the French throne. The Indians would see it as a declaration of their own sovereign rights. . . ." He broke off, thinking. "It would have to be worded very carefully."

"Aye. Something you can't do just now. Come to bed."

"How was it I found such a brilliant and beautiful wife?"

"Well God loves fools and Americans, I've heard it said," she replied, "and God provides."

"Let's see what he has provided underneath this nightgown," Franklin said, leering.

"This from a fellow too tired to write a sentence straight?"

"I can get other things straight enough, as you'll see," Franklin replied.

"What a disgusting man you are," Lenka said, and kissed him again.

Despite Lenka's efforts and some pleasant physical exertion, Franklin was able to snatch only a few moments of sleep. His brain was too activated and agitated by Lenka's suggestion.

Voltaire rose up from his covers when Franklin shook him, a cadaver returning to unholy life. He sounded the part as well.

"Pray tell, Lord Satan, what you want of me at this hour of the morning?" the Frenchman moaned.

"You've been asking what you can do to help. I've hit upon it."

"My head is what you hit upon," Voltaire complained. "Each word like the forging hammer on the anvil."

"I need your help in writing something," Franklin said.

"What?"

"Something that needs written! A declaration that the continent of America and all its several nations are hereby independent from their European parents. A declaration that the meddling of Russia or any other foreign country won't be tolerated here."

Voltaire rubbed his eyes. "I thought you had such a proviso. Your mutual protection pact."

"No. That's too weak, too provisional—as we have clearly

seen, most are reluctant to commit to our cause. It lacks—it lacks a *philosophy*, a raison d'être—a skeleton to hold the flesh up. It says only that we will not war with one another; after that, it becomes vague. It does not protect the French colonies from France, or the English colonies from England. You see?"

"I think so." Voltaire, despite his apparent hangover, was starting to look interested. "But why do you need my help?"

"I am a philosopher of science. It is what I have concentrated on. My skills as a social philosopher are not so highly developed. And I am not as eloquent as you."

"Whatever eloquence I have is at your command," Voltaire said, starting to look a bit more alert. "I fear it will not be enough. Still, it's an exciting idea. And if you've no one better . . ."

"I doubt that I do."

"Very well. I will jot down some ideas and speak of them to you. How soon will you need it?"

"As soon as possible, I should think."

"Not before this meeting with the margrave and the Indians?"

Franklin rubbed his jaw. "If possible—something. If there is to be grand meeting of all the native powers of the colonies, it will be no time soon. Despite prompting, I've heard nothing still from Louisiana, Florida, or the Coweta. The margrave, on the other hand, is here—our most immediate threat and ally. We will convince him soon or fight him soon."

Voltaire nodded. "I see. 'Alacrity' will be my watchword, then."

"It should be one," said Ben, "but let 'liberty' be another."

Thomas Nairne was already up, too, shuffling through communications from the aetherschreiber. He glanced a bit feverishly at Ben.

"Can you build more of those opticon things?" he asked.

"With the right supplies and tools, yes, of course. I don't have those things here yet."

"But you could build it quickly?"

"Certainly. It was no huge task the first time."

"It would be a great help. Those in the other colonies seem to have worked, judging by what we've heard."

"Yes. What use did you have in mind for them?"

"I wish each of our field commanders to have one. Communications would be faster."

"They are too large to be practical," Franklin said, "though I might be able to make one that carried only the voice, which would be more manageable."

"With what you have here?"

"No."

"How is it you didn't invent these things earlier?"

"I didn't see the need. Aetherschreibers are quite fast enough."

"For war, the faster the better."

Franklin nodded understanding. "I know little of strategy and tactics. Design a straightforward weapon, yes, that I can do—"

"And have done admirably well at."

"Thank you, though I find nothing especially admirable about things made to kill. And supply trains were explained to me, so we have portable manna machines. But as to communications—"

"That's most vital of all, and last thought of," Nairne replied. "But it never occurred to me that the aetherschreiber could be made to carry voice and image. If it had, I would have urged you to make many of them long ago."

"What brings this up?"

"Van Duyn. He's fighting on the run. He scarcely finds time to scribble even a quick note to me, and rarely gets any of mine. I have to send four, five letters to get a single response."

"How are they doing?"

"They've been harrying a force of some five hundred or so.

Five hundred human men, that is. Besides that, they have at least twenty of the automatons and a flying boat for their resupply."

"Ah-hah. So they do have airships with them—but they keep them away from the battle. That means that even if they haven't managed to build a smaller manna machine, as we have, they can still carry an unlimited food supply with them."

"Yes, a problem for us. It means they can move quickly into the backcountry." He clasped his hands together. "What do you need, Ben, if you're to keep us supplied with scientifical weapons?"

"Lots of things. Some are cached here, in various places. Others—well, we have to have allies in one of the big towns and a clear route to them."

"That, in your opinion, is our first priority? A friendly city and right-of-way to it?"

"Yes."

"Very well, Benjamin. This is what I think you ought to do. You've already admitted that you've no skill in military things, and you've said I should take up that burden. Here's the one I think you ought to take up—now, whilst we don't need you to run the fancy guns and such you've invented for us. We need you as ambassador to those nations keeping clear of our cause. We need you to get us that city and that clear path to it, and more men and guns besides."

"I'm no diplomat, Governor—you're the one who has been ambassador to the Indians, not me."

"Ambassador? I was a *spy* against the French. They still don't think well of me down there, the late governor Bienville aside. We need someone who can shake both the Coweta and the French out of this reluctance of theirs. Maybe you are no diplomat. I'm no general, but I'm closer to one than you are. You've treated with two kings and the Venetian Divan before your twentieth birthday, and have conspired and built alliances all over this new world, and are thus closer to a real diplomat than anyone handy. I well trust you may not *like* diplomacy, but I must humbly request that you *do* it, for, of all the things that need to be done right now, this is the one that suits you best. And you know it. If you do not accede to my request, I may be forced to order you and then to remind you of the power you yourself so recently reserved to me."

Franklin chewed on that for a moment. What Nairne said made a good deal of sense, but that didn't mean he had to like it.

"You'll conduct the meeting with the margrave and the others who come here?"

"I'll be present, as will you."

"And you'll instruct me on Indian diplomacy?"

"As well as I can. I can show you my earlier journals, which I have used before as instruction."

"Don't I recall that you were put to torture once and nearly slain by the Yamassee?"

"Well, no diplomatic career is without its little bumps, is it?" Nairne smiled, but it fled from his face nearly as it formed. "What's that sound?"

Franklin heard it, too, a growl like distant thunder but constant—and approaching.

Nairne took up his *kraftpistole* from the table, shoved it into his belt, and ran outside. Franklin checked his own weapons and followed.

The noise was a bit louder out in the open, but though a number of people were gazing up at the sky, none seemed to have discovered the source of the racket. Franklin and Nairne hurried to the stockade for a better view.

Franklin noticed that the margrave's men, outside and below, were also warily surveying curdled-cream clouds; so whatever the sound represented, it was not something the Azilians were familiar with. Franklin found the tower's spyglass, but with nothing clear to aim it at, soon put it back down.

Then, with a faint chill, he remembered Euler's words, and produced the compass he had made for the detection of malakim. The needle quivered oddly. He moved—the needle did not.

"Northwest," Franklin said, "look northwest."

The noise, which had receded a bit, now grew louder again. Suddenly, something damn strange came into view. It seemed at first a pure geometric form, an oval or ellipse gliding through the air perhaps sixty feet above the ground. Gliding like a bird but lacking head, tail, wings—well, perhaps not much like a bird at all. But more like a bird than any flying machine Franklin had yet seen.

It was flying straight toward Franklin and Nairne; and suddenly, in the fort yard, a fountain of flame and earth erupted, carrying maybe six men and women up with it. Or pieces of them, anyway.

Nairne jerked out his *kraftpistole*, but the little knot of Cherokee, who had been watching along with everyone else, reacted even faster. Their muskets roared so close to the explosion in the yard that the only way Franklin knew they had fired was by the black trees growing from their weapons. A few seconds later, though, he heard their shouts. *Tlanuwa! Tlanuwa!* Something in their own tongue, he guessed. Maybe they had seen one of these things before, though he much doubted it. It had to be a Moscovado contrivance. Hadn't Euler spoken of new sorts of flying craft?

Franklin saw sparks of bullets striking the thing, and then it had flown over him. He made out four legs, like the legs of a table, set toward the center. He had an incongruous moment when he almost laughed—it looked like a badly designed card table, but flying. He also noticed now that its structure was ribbed, put together very much like some kites he had seen.

Now guns were thrown up everywhere, but it was over the wall. Oglethorpe's men looked on in puzzlement as the machine slowed almost to a hover above them. Because of the stockade, they had not seen the explosion, though they had surely heard it.

"Watch out!" Franklin called down.

But Oglethorpe was yelling something at them, and they held their fire and their ranks.

The *tlanuwa* did not respect their truce. This time, Franklin saw something drop through an aperture in the middle of the thing. He wished he could see the upper surface. Were there passengers, or was this another sort of talos, a mechanical thing to give the insubstantial malakim working substance?

To many of Oglethorpe's men, the answer would never matter—they perished in a bloom of flame that curled over them. The rest broke formation and retreated, though more than one had the presence of mind to fire at the thing.

"Man the damn murder guns!" Nairne shouted. "Stop staring and shoot!" He fired his own *kraftpistole*, and a jagged line of phlogistan writhed—apparently harmlessly—against the machine as it began once again to move, turning in the sky—again, somehow in the manner of a large bird—and started back toward them.

5.

Irena

Adrienne uncovered the light, but she had already recognized the voice.

"Hello, Irena," she said.

Hercule's wife was an alabaster carving, her hair and skin of the same white, almost silvery, cast. Her eyes were droplets of blue so near black her pupils were scarcely distinguishable. Hercule complained sometimes—in his least charming moments—of Irena's too-thick waist and squarish features, swearing that she suffered much in comparison to Adrienne. It might be so, but her striking coloring drew the eye and often held it.

Now what held Adrienne's attention was the old-fashioned pistol aimed at her heart. The lock, as she had heard, was drawn back, and the pan seemed to be primed. Irena knew how to use the gun, then.

"Do not move," Irena said. "Make no signs with that devil hand of yours, nor mutter any strange curse."

"Why should I obey you, if you mean to kill me whatever I do?"

"I *do* mean to kill you. But I would have you confess to me first. Confess your affair with my husband."

Adrienne arched her eyebrows in genuine surprise. "Must I? I suppose I thought you'd always known."

Irena's finger twitched then, and a flash of utter hatred moved across her face, but she managed herself. "Yes, of course I knew. And you knew I knew. And the whole court. But I want to hear you say it, here, now, to my face."

"Very well. Since long before you married Hercule, I was sleeping with him. After you were married, he continued to come to my bed. I did not turn him away."

Tears sparkled in Irena's eyes. She blinked them clear. "Thank you. Now I can send you to hell."

This time, she did pull the trigger. The powder flashed, and the next instant, the cabin rang with a deafening explosion.

The smoke stung Adrienne's eyes and filled her nostrils with, at least, the brimstone Irena had promised. But the lack of pain—and a brief examination of her chest—proved that Adrienne was still in the world of the living. It appeared that her djinni still honored their obligation to protect her.

Peering through the serpentine coils of smoke winding and slithering in the lanthorn light, she saw Irena collapse against the bulkhead, clutching at her thigh. The pistol lay on the floor, forgotten.

Adrienne hesitated a moment, then approached her.

When the other woman saw Adrienne was alive, she closed her eyes wearily. When Adrienne lifted the Russian's skirts, she did not object.

A deep red stain spread on Irena's white hose. The bullet, turned from striking Adrienne, must have ricocheted to return to its mistress.

At that moment the door was nearly ripped off its hinges. Crecy towered over them, naked save for her sword, her fiery hair unbound. It took her only a few seconds to utter a low laugh.

"Well, well," she said. "The girl has some claws."

"Hush, Veronique. And for heaven's sake, don't stand there naked. The last thing we need right now is *more* attention."

"Oh—yes," Crecy said, as if realizing for the first time her state of undress. "You'll pardon me if I didn't stop to think—"

"I much appreciate it, Veronique. It's good, as always, to know you are watching out for me."

"I'll throw on a dressing gown and return, if you have the situation in hand."

"I have it in hand—and there's no need for you to return. If, instead, you could deflect any others who come to investigate with a tale of a misfired weapon?"

"Of course." She gave a little bow and started toward her own quarters, flicking the door shut behind her.

Adrienne turned her attention to Irena's wound. It was not bleeding as much as she'd first thought.

Irena was watching Adrienne, not the hole in her leg. She was obviously in pain—and just as obviously trying not to cry out.

"Will you let me dress this?"

"I would rather bleed to death."

"Very well. Would you like me to call someone else?"

Irena bit her lip, then shook her head. "Why?" she asked huskily.

"Why what?"

"Why did you send her away?"

"She was naked."

"That's not what I meant. I meant to kill you. I tried to kill you."

"Yes, and in a perfectly just world, you would have succeeded. In your place I might well have done the same thing."

"You never thought that I would, then—is that your meaning? You flaunted your liaison with my husband because you thought I would accept it forever?"

"You stood it for seven years. I suppose I thought you might stand it forever, yes." She paused. "You *do* know that Hercule ended our affair?"

Irena's eyes widened. "What?"

"Last week. Which, I suppose, makes me wonder why you chose now, of all times, to try and solve the problem of Adrienne." She glanced back down at the wound. "Come. Let me bandage this."

Irena hesitated again, but her eyes showed her confusion. "All right."

Adrienne went to her cabinet and found some linen bandages and ointment. She probed for the bullet in Irena's leg while Irena sucked in gasps of pain.

"It's been a long while since I doctored a bullet wound," Adrienne mused, "ten years, when I was riding with the army of Lorraine."

"Where you met Hercule."

"Yes. He rescued me from a gang of brigands. He was kind to me. We became friends."

"You became lovers."

"Eventually. Friends—comrades in arms—first." She wiped away more blood, and Irena gasped again. "I don't think the bullet is in there," she observed.

"He is my husband now. He married me because you would not marry him."

"You knew this when you married him?"

"Yes. I thought he would come to love me. He didn't."

"Ah," Adrienne said. The bullet was on the floor. "See?" she said, holding up the deformed lump. "It was already spent when it found you."

Irena laughed, bitterness tinged with hysteria. "Much like Hercule, yes? When he found me then, and when he troubles to find me now."

Adrienne wiped blood from the wound and put some ointment on it, and Irena's laugh became a moan. Adrienne began wrapping the linen around the other woman's thigh. "Do you love him at all, Irena, or is it just your pride that's hurt?"

"How can you ask that?"

"The timing of this. All those years in Saint Petersburg, you made no protest. After all, in the court all men have affairs, and most women. Didn't you?"

"Yes, now and then," Irena murmured, "to try and get back at him. It was pointless, though."

Adrienne nodded. "And if Hercule knew of it, he pretended

he didn't. If he hadn't, he might have been forced to a duel, or some other unpleasant act. And so with you—you pretended to not know what was going on, so as to avoid expressing the proper public outrage, yes? But here on the ship, you weren't going to be able to keep such a pretense up without appearing unbelievably stupid."

"Oh, I am already considered that, believe me. And you—" She stuttered off into another moan as Adrienne tightened the bandage. "Yes, damn you, people at court have affairs. It is the way of things—I know that. But you made no effort to hide it! You were not even passing discreet. The contempt you showed me! It was unbearable, unthinkable. And now, he—*he* abandons everything and forces me to leave our house, my friends, my life—all to follow you, *his* one true love, to the ends of the earth. And he doesn't have the good grace to at least discard me! Better a pitied, wronged wife in Saint Petersburg than . . ." Her sentence collapsed into hard breathing, as she searched for the words to express exactly what she thought her situation was.

"Then it *is* pride."

"What if it is?" Irena snapped. "You think I'm entitled to no dignity, no self-respect? What did I ever do to you that I don't deserve that? What about my children? What will they think of me when they are old enough to understand?" She drew her leg away and pushed her skirts down. "So what if it is my pride? But it is more than that, God damn you. It is—it is because I *do* love him, I *do*, and everything he does only proves that *he* loves *you*. And you love him. And I am only a sort of—of impediment, a fixture in *your* love story. Hercule is not my *husband*, for all that he managed to father two children. He is *your* husband and my—my—breeding stallion. You make me feel that *I* am the whore!"

Adrienne placed her hand on Irena's cheek. She expected the other woman to flinch, but she did not. "I do not love Hercule," she whispered. "If I did, I would have married him when he asked. I do not love him, not as husband. He is my companion, my brother in arms. He is very dear to me—but I do not love him." It was like an incantation, saying it, but one that had the opposite effect. She suddenly knew she loved Hercule after all.

"But you—"

Adrienne paused, almost ready to repent her last statement. But she had begun this, hadn't she? She would finish it. "My body is used to him," she said. "It knows him. And I did not want to hurt him."

"That's it? Your body is *used* to him? This makes no sense! For that you have made my life miserable these last seven years?"

"I did not think of you, Irena, not much. You never brought it to my attention. You never complained. I suppose I honestly thought you did not care." She considered her own words for a moment. "No, that is a lie. I knew you cared, but I suppose I convinced myself that you did not care very much and that . . . Irena, do not mistake me for a good woman."

Irena looked down at her bandaged leg. "I would not. I do not."

"But I will not bed him again. If you had asked me not to seven years ago, I would have complied even then. It did not require a gun."

"I should not have had to ask. I should not have had to beg you like this."

Now Adrienne laughed. "You consider this *begging*? What a fierce woman you are. How did you hide it so well?"

"If you were a normal woman, you would know that hiding is what we do."

Adrienne felt a sudden anger for the first time in the entire confrontation. "Irena, I was raised in the school of Saint Cyr, where we were punished for whispering—for the mere suspicion that we might be telling secrets. It only made us better at them. I went to the French court. I ate lies and drank them; I wore them. I hid every single true thing about myself, because the truest things about me were unseemly in a woman. Because of this, I lost everything I hold dear. I lost my virginity to a mad, ancient, disgusting king. I lost my true love, my—" She shut her mouth, took a deep breath to try and calm herself, and started again. "I'm sorry, Irena, sorry for your sake. I apologize for my long affair with Hercule. I do not apologize for not bothering to hide it. I no longer hide who I am. I will not. Do you understand me?"

Irena struggled to stand. "Yes. I think I do."

"Sit on my bed. You aren't able to walk yet—"

"I am."

"You aren't." She watched as the other shakily sat on the bed. Adrienne went back to her cabinet and produced some brandy.

"Take some of this," she said. Irena did so, downing the first glass quickly, and the second, too.

Adrienne decided to have some herself. The two of them sat there in silence for a few moments.

"We have had an awkward moment here, you and I," Adrienne said after a few moments. "I hope—I hope we can put it behind us."

"You are truly done with Hercule?"

"Yes."

Irena nodded. "Good. It will not make him love me more, I know. But it will make me hate you less. I think—I think I should *like* to hate you less."

Adrienne poured them each another drink. "Here's to hating less," she said, and they drank together.

She answered the rap on her door, still wiping the sleep grit from her eyes, and found Crecy there, smiling cheerily.

"Well, at least you're decent this morning," Adrienne noticed.

Crecy frowned. "I haven't said anything nasty about *you*—why do you feel the need to insult *me*?"

"Just from habit."

"Ah. Well, better to have a habit than to wear one, I suppose. And speaking of habits, Madame d'Argenson seems to have developed a new one. A limp . . ."

"Yes. She tried to kill me and wounded herself instead. What of it?"

Crecy raised one eyebrow. "There is curiosity about it."

"In all quarters, or just in the redheaded one?"

"You can start by satisfying my curiosity, thank you."

"It's simple—no baroque intriguing here. She was finally tired of being made a fool of."

"And you have resolved all this?"

"I think so. She does not call me sister, but I do not think she will try to perforate me again."

"No, perhaps she has learned her lesson. She will use poison next time."

"Nonsense."

"I'm serious. Having worked up the nerve once—and having received no punishment—she will find her courage twice as easily next time."

"Veronique, there is no need. My liaison with Hercule is ended."

"She is in the habit of believing you sleep with him. She will continue in that habit."

"I'm the one who spoke with her. I believe otherwise." She beckoned Crecy into the room and began pushing through the gowns in the small chest. "Besides, what would you have me do? Throw her overboard?"

"Nothing so drastic. Move her and Hercule to one of the other ships."

"I would rather not. I would rather keep him here, that I might protect him."

"He is more than grown. If you are going to relinquish your hold on him—"

"As lover, not as cherished friend!"

Crecy rolled her eyes. "And now we are back to the reasons

that Irena will never believe you and he have given up your afternoon wine and cheese."

"Which gown, Veronique?"

"The blue one. Are you listening to me?"

"About the dress? Yes. As to the rest—thank you for the advice. I love you dearly and this particular conversation is over."

"Very well." Crecy shrugged. "You are a grown-up, too. You've your tutorial with Elizavet now?"

"Yes, and then the coffee with the students. Anything exciting happening today?"

"No attacks or intimations of them. Actually, Hercule wants to land at least one of the ships this afternoon."

"For what reason?"

"We left light on provisions. They hope to acquire more."

"We have the manna machines—"

"Yes, but no one wants to eat that stuff. I certainly don't."

"I'm wary of towns. Golitsyn could easily arrange a trap."

"The idea was to find a herd of something or other and kill some, or find some Tartar tribesmen who will trade a goat or two."

"Oh. Well, that's entirely different. Tell them to go ahead, if they wish. In fact—Where are we, anyway?"

"We've crossed the Urals."

"Perhaps—if it's safe—we can even arrange a collecting expedition for the students."

"Collecting?"

"Yes. Plants, rocks, that sort of thing. Natural history."

"How exciting. It's too bad I'll be doing the boring work of hunting and fighting off the wild Tartars."

"Philistine. Help me put this on."

"You didn't bring a maid? Or am I that, too?"

"You haven't been a maid in twenty years, nor would anyone mistake you for one, you old jade."

Crecy made a point of pulling the corset laces a bit too tight.

* * *

Lomonosov stood, an expression of mixed apprehension and excitement on his young face. The others looked on respectfully, sipping their chocolate.

"These ideas of mine are not fully formed," he began, "but I believe they will provoke some thought. I would hesitate to offer them in a formal discussion as something proven, as a fait accompli—"

"Informal is the nature of these meetings," Adrienne remarked. "Imagine this a coffeehouse—such as philosophers once frequented in London or Paris—rather than liken it to a lecture hall in a college. We are here to promote open and free discussion and debate amongst friends."

Lomonosov smiled gratefully and nodded. "Let me begin with what we all accept, I think, with three propositions we find in the works of Newton. The first proposition is that matter is composed of various proportions and arrangements of four sorts of atoms—damnatum, lux, phlegm, and gas. The second proposition is that these atoms are given shape by ferments, the arrangements of immaterial forces—attractions, repulsions, and harmonies that conspire to collect the appropriate atoms to form a given matter. The first cause of these ferments is considered to be God, who, at the moment of creation, made a finite number of ferments and placed them into the world. The third proposition is that the forces of affinity and harmony upon which existence is predicated are of two sorts: limited and absolute. Now, to be provocative, I would like to say from the outset that I consider each of these propositions to be flawed in some way."

"Are you saying Newton was wrong—that in effect all modern science is wrong?" Linné asked.

"Let us take care," Adrienne cautioned, "not to make of Newton a new Aristotle. Science stagnated for hundreds of years because the assertions of Aristotle were not considered questionable. For science, everything is questionable."

Lomonosov nodded in relief at her agreement. "Thank

you, Mademoiselle. To be more clear, let me explain that I do not say that Newton was wrong so much as incomplete. Let me begin with the last proposition first, if I may—the difference between limited and absolute affinities.

"Magnetism and gravity are perfect examples of imperfect affinities, the former more limited than the latter. Magnetism is an affinity only between like substances—certain metals—and its effect diminishes with distance in proportion to the square of the distance from the source. Gravity is more general and catholic—affecting all matter equally—and yet still obeys the inverse-square law. The perfect, or absolute, affinities we know best are the harmonies. The harmony that connects two aetherschreibers, for instance, is said to not diminish with distance and, as well, propagates instantaneously."

"Doesn't gravity propagate instantaneously?" Breteuil asked.

"I question it," Lomonosov said. "By an experiment I have shown magnetism does not—it travels at the same speed as light—and that to me suggests that gravity behaves in a like manner, because they are similar affinities—both imperfect."

"Will you describe your experiment to us?"

Lomonosov hesitated. "It would be a lengthy explanation," he said, "and not quite to the topic. . ."

"A presentation for another time, then," Adrienne inserted. "We will accept the premise for the moment."

Again Lomonosov looked relieved, and he continued. "Since we are met informally, I will be brief. As I suggested, up until now, it has been considered that there were two sorts of forces—those that diminish in inverse proportion to the square of the distance and those that do not. Those that do—like gravity—are considered to be those created by God most necessary for maintaining the finite aspect of the material universe. After all, if gravity did not diminish with distance, all matter in the universe would quickly end stuck together in a single mass. In contrast, *absolute* affinities are considered to be operations of an *infinite* God—since God is all seeing and all knowing, it follows that he cannot depend upon the limited affinities for his existence and information. What I mean is that if God depended, let us say, on light to conduct information from that part of himself which occupies Jupiter to that part resident here on Earth, he cannot be considered to have perfect knowledge of everything at once—and this we know he has. Likewise, the malakim—and, indeed, the animal spirit and the soul—are considered to be composed of absolute affinities, being nearer God than matter."

"But you disagree with this?" Linné interjected.

"Yes, in two related ways. First, none of the affinities we know are in truth absolute. Even the affinity of aetherschreibers diminish incrementally with distance. Truly absolute affinities remain hypothetical, not demonstrated. The related notion is that there are actually a variety of affinities which fall between absolute and limited. Some, for instance, diminish arithmetically with distance rather than geometrically—these are the forces that mediate between the so-called limited and infinite."

"Like philosopher's mercury?" Adrienne asked.

"Just so. I think—"

He was interrupted by an odd little yelp from Breteuil.

"Émilie?" Adrienne acknowledged.

"I am sorry, Mademoiselle. It is just that . . ." She glanced at Linné, who nodded what looked like approval. "As you know," Breteuil continued, "Monsieur Linné and I have been working on a taxonomy of the malakim—"

"I would have said you were dabbling in anatomy," Elizavet remarked, a bit languidly.

"Elizavet!" Adrienne said sternly. The tsarevna smiled, looking thoroughly unreproved.

"Go on, Émilie," Adrienne said.

Émilie blushed furiously, but go on she did. "We were examining copies of Newton's notebooks—the ones from Prague—and there were notations in the margins on his observations on the animal spirit. The passage itself, of course, was the key to godly science. It was the equation that allowed devices to enable the malakim to operate in matter. But the notes—they might have to do with this." She nodded at Lomonosov. "Forgive me, Monsieur Lomonosov. I don't mean to interrupt you—but it seems your hypothesis explains those notations rather neatly. I think—it suggests to me a key to mathematically describing the malakim. And, Mademoiselle, your own notes—"

She broke off, suddenly worried that she had revealed something she shouldn't. But Adrienne was remembering suddenly—remembering the equations she had begun long years ago, the ones she had once seen nearly entire that promised to explain the nature of her strange hand, the dwellers in the aether, of many things hidden and unseen.

It was all coming together again—her old notes, Newton's experiments, Lomonosov's insights. In a rush she felt intuitively where it was going—back to those thoughts she had lost so long ago, back to her hand, back to the nature of God and the world.

And she felt a sudden, almost hideous fear—not merely for herself but for everyone at that table. She had begun this journey before, alone, and she had been stopped. Subtly, by deceit and corruption, but she had been stopped cold.

Surely they would be stopped again. This time, perhaps, in a more assuredly final manner. She had told the seraph that she would not relent because of fear of death—but could she take it upon herself to doom the others?

She watched them, detached, as they began to excitedly discuss the sudden conjuncture of ideas, and wished she had a good answer to that.

6.

Ambassador

The explosion rattled the tower, and for a moment Franklin thought it was broken, that it would collapse and take Nairne and him with it. It also finally rattled some sense into his brain. Guns and cannon were firing all around now—they might bring the flying thing down, but they might well not. He knew something that would do it for sure, and he should have been going for it this whole time.

They went down the ladder quickly, jumping the last ten feet, and pounded off through the chaos raging around them. The flying machine was presently out of sight. Its attack might even be over, but Franklin fervently hoped not. Though it seemed intent on doing some damage, its primary purpose was undoubtedly reconnaissance. The job might already be done—if the pilot had some form of aetherschreiber or its demonic equivalent—but it might not be. In any case, if a human flew the thing, he might be intimidated enough to fly whence he came. Franklin didn't want that. If there was any chance of keeping information from reaching the forces of the Pretender, it was worth taking.

But people kept getting in his way. The Cherokee were still firing into the air, reloading, firing again, screaming at the tops of their lungs. The Colonials weren't doing much different. Franklin wondered briefly how many of them would be killed by the hail of their own bullets coming back to earth.

He pushed on through, finally reaching the wains, which as

yet were not completely unloaded. Cursing, he began searching through the crates and bundles.

God slapped him, slapped him good, and for a few moments he became one kinetic object amongst many, lifting, falling, colliding. Then he was shaking his head, the bright smell of blood in his nose, wondering if his skull or some other vital part was cracked and had not yet gotten around to informing him that he was dying.

Of course. Destroy the supplies. He had run to the very spot their aerial attacker was most interested in. Why hadn't they unloaded the wagons and put their contents under cover? Yes, they wanted to be able to move at moment's notice, but they knew the Moscovados had airships. . . .

Stop thinking, you idiot, and look!

The wain had been blown onto its side, its contents strewn about. Another few feet, and he would have been made confetti along with everything else. As it was, the spilled cargo was easier to search through. Grimly, Franklin tried to keep his gaze on its task and away from the sky, but it was no easy thing, knowing he might as well have an archer's bull's-eye on the top of his head.

He flinched at another explosion, and the wagon only a dozen paces from him turned into flaming splinters. He was shielded from the blast by the overturned carcass of the wagon he was hunting through, but he still stumbled. Well, at least bull's-eyes were not so easy to hit as all that. Still, when your arrow was so large . . .

It took him a second to remember what he was doing, and a few more to understand that he had fallen onto exactly what he was looking for. Frantically, he set to unwrapping it from its canvas. Above him, bullets cracked steadily against adamantium. The thing must be hovering, steadying its aim, but he could not spare the time to look.

Then he had it unlimbered, an odd-looking device shaped much like a large tuning fork, his new and improved depneumifier. He set it into operation by the twist of a key and pointed it upward.

Perhaps the flier—or the devil that powered the thing—sensed something amiss; perhaps the fellow had decided he had overstayed his welcome or run short of grenades. In either case, the strange machine had started off again, gaining speed quickly. Franklin aimed the depneumifier, feeling a bit silly, since it made no obvious emission. But it hummed, not a bad sign.

The flying machine did not, as he hoped, suddenly plunge powerless to earth. He remembered, with terrible clarity, what Euler had told them: that the Moscovados had perfected flight that did not depend wholly on the malakim for motivation.

But then, like a bird whose wings have seized, the machine stalled. It continued to glide, but heavily, wiggling frantically, almost as if trying to flap.

It passed beyond sight of the wall, and Franklin heard hoarse cheers go up all around him. He realized that he was trembling so violently he could barely hold his invention. Feeling quite faint, he slowly, carefully placed it on the ground.

He did the same with his body.

Robert reached him a few moments later.

"You did it, Ben—or I suppose it was you. It's smashed itself into the trees at the edge of the forest. The margrave's men are galloping toward it full tilt, and Uncle Thomas sent some men, too. Hurry up. Let's go see it!"

"I think I can survive at seeing it second- or thirdhand," Franklin muttered, sitting on a crate and trying to shake the ringing from his ears.

His friend looked suddenly concerned. "Are y' all right? Y' weren't broken up by the grenado, were y'r?"

"No. Leastways I don't think so. But I'm—I'm not cut out for this sort of adventure, Robin. I'd hoped I was done with it."

His friend clasped his hand tightly. "So y' say. But I've never noticed you hate telling stories of our exploits abroad. Y' won't flinch from enjoying these either, I reckon."

"Maybe not—thirty years from now, when I'm a fat old man surrounded by grandchildren. For now I'd be just as happy to make up lies as live the damned truth."

"We'll sit here a minute. I reckon they might go to fightin'—Oglethorpe's men and ours—so it may be best that we leave them to work it out. And who knows, the thing may still have teeth. But they'll handle it, now as you've clipped its god-rotted wings."

"You go, if you wish, Robin."

"Nay. I'll stay with you whilst you tell me what y' did."

Franklin took a deep breath, and then another. For an instant, he felt as if he were fourteen years old again, proudly displaying his first scientific invention to his old friend, John Collins. Things had seemed so simple then, the future so bright. He was to be famous, a great scientific man, with the whole world at his feet.

Well, he had gotten that wish, but twisted up, the way the genii in the Arabian stories might do it, for spite at being bottled so long. Famous he was, but the world at his feet—the world he himself had brought to pass—would have been better off stillborn and himself happier as a printer back in Boston. Now Boston was all but abandoned, his father dead of a distemper in Virginia, his mother a widow there, living with his sister—a sister who would not speak to him, much less write. And John Collins—whatever had become of him? Dead, most likely. He had feared him killed by Bracewell, but he had heard reports since that John had lived, to become best friend with the bottle and finally to vanish in the insanity of the battles against New France. He was, most likely, dead after all.

"Well?" Robert repeated.

He looked at Robert, a better friend than he deserved. "Ah. 'Tis an improved version of my depneumifier."

"Your exorcister? But you never explained how that worked."

"You remember that Sir Isaac first designed the flying globes that keep aloft the Moscovado airships."

"I've a short memory, but not that short."

"Then you know at the battle of Venice he showed he had the art of unmaking them as well."

"I thought his talos monster did that, somehow."

"It did. The globes are structured of certain harmonies—both cages for the malakim and engines that work on their energies. At Venice he had his talos dissolve them."

"And then it killed him. You swore never to dabble in such stuff."

"And I never did. But anything that can be contrived through the use of those devils can be contrived through honest means as well—'tis just more work to do it, more thought entailed. I've had ten years to make a device which would perform that same function. I wasn't certain it would."

"Maybe it didn't. There was no globe in that thing—it was flying like a bird, not like Sir Isaac's old boat at all."

"I think the prison engine was inside, somewhere. I think you're right. Most of the time, when it's moving fast, that machine gets its buoyance from natural action of the atmosphere. Even without its motivation, it did fly somewhat, you noticed. But even a bird must have a heart, and if you stop that, it must fall, however prettily. Thank God they haven't perfected some undevilish engine. . . ." He trailed off, suddenly, staring into space.

"Where'd you go, Ben?" But then Robert himself made a funny sound and started again excitedly. "Y'r own invention—the flying box—"

"Exactly, Robin. By heavens! What we couldn't do with the two of them together!" He stood up so quickly he almost got faint again. "I do want to see this thing, Robin. I want to see it right this instant!"

* * *

By the time they reached the machine, a crowd of nearly a hundred had gathered to poke and prod it. As Franklin had suspected, it was made of some alchemical alloy—not adamantium but something very similar, harder than steel but lighter, almost, than wood. One soldier proved this by tilting the whole machine by himself.

To Franklin's relief, all the gawkers seemed to be peaceful, Oglethorpe's dragoons and the men of the Junto side by side.

He could better see the machine's structure from the ground. It *was* like a kite: one great wing, elliptical in cross section. In the center were several movable panels that he supposed must steer it. There was also a small cabin of alchemical glass enclosing a chair, and below it, as he had suspected, a now-vacant globe that had once housed a malakus.

"Ingenious," he admitted, with mixed admiration and dread. What other things had the Moscovado sorcerers invented?

They might get answer to that, in part, for they had captured the pilot. He seemed stunned but otherwise not badly wounded. In fact, many of his wounds might be accounted for by the pummeling the margrave's dragoons had given him when first they reached him. More than one of their fellows had been blasted to bits by the airman's grenades, and they were probably not in a forgiving mood.

"Who is he?" Franklin asked, eyeing the fellow. He was a small man, knobby, balding. A regular kobold, as the German settlers might say.

"We're not sure," Nairne said. "It seems he only speaks Moscovado."

"Well, well. Imagine that," Franklin said, glancing sidewise at Oglethorpe. The margrave got the point, all right. His face reddened. Franklin decided to say no more and let it sink in—a word to the wise ought to be sufficient. He now must hope that Oglethorpe was wise.

"It's quite a strange thing," Voltaire remarked in his ear. Franklin hadn't noticed the Frenchman arriving.

"There is a noble mind at work here," Franklin said,

"though not a noble purpose. I would like to meet the inventor of this in better days. I wonder if we would still be enemies?"

"I wouldn't wish for things like that, if I were you," Voltaire remarked. "You might just get your wish—and an answer to your question that you might not like at all. There are many clever hands with no good at all behind them."

Franklin nodded. "True. Though in the end, the most harm seems to be done by those with clever hands and those intentions that pave the road to hell."

He meant, as always, himself.

He continued inspecting the machine, marveling at it, explaining to Voltaire how he thought it operated. He noticed that the Cherokee were studying it as well. After a moment, one of them separated from the rest and came toward Franklin and the Frenchman.

It was the pale one, the one Franklin had wondered about earlier. As he drew close, Franklin suddenly understood that he was no Cherokee at all, but a white man dressed as one of them and with his hair cut in the Cherokee fashion.

"I'm told you are Benjamin Franklin, the magus of Charles Town."

"That's me."

"I am pleased to make your acquaintance. My name is Christian Gottlieb Priber. I've read a number of your papers."

"Have you?" The fellow spoke English pretty well but with an unmistakable German accent.

"Indeed. Not so much your scientific ones but your dissertations on natural liberty."

"I wrote those long ago. I'm surprised that you've seen them."

"They were passed along to me when I still lived on the Continent. Before I managed my way here and began working at my great purpose."

"Was your great purpose to become a Cherokee, sir? For, if so, it would seem you are well on your way."

"Clothes do not make the man, sir, but they do situate him,

so to speak. No, my purpose is a simple one, and one I wish to speak to you on, if you've a moment."

"I'm somewhat busy, Mr. Priber."

"I understand that, Mr. Franklin. But I am given to understand that you English are quite sure of Cherokee aid in your present civil war. I've come to tell you that isn't so and explain why. I've also been given, you see, to understand that you are the foreign ambassador of your—" he smiled indulgently "—nation. I would have spoken to you immediately, but you were not with the delegation that welcomed me and my Cherokee brothers into town."

"I do apologize," Franklin said, wondering what in the hell was going on, "but I had not received my appointment as ambassador at that time. And Governor Nairne has said nothing of this to me—"

"As I have said nothing to him. To be frank, I do not trust him—he served as spy amongst the Indians and kowtowed to Blackbeard. Your tracts on liberty lead me to believe I might be able to trust you, however. If you will not make time to talk—before the meeting—I might withdraw that opinion."

"You want to talk now, I suppose, sir?"

"If possible. I understand that the Apalachee and Maroon delegations are within shouting distance, and there is little time to lose."

"Very well. Let me be sure that someone is appointed to deal with these things, and I will meet you in one quarter hour's time in the hall. Will that do?"

"Indeed it will. And thank you, sir."

He started off. Franklin watched him go, thinking how silly he looked with most of his pale arse showing around his loincloth. The Cherokee did not look half so silly.

What next? Franklin asked himself, a silent groan.

He found Thomas Nairne, who was making plans to secure the airship in case it should take a mind to fly off again.

"Do you know of this Priber fellow?" he asked wearily.

"I've heard some rumors about him. I wondered if that

was him, but he never spoke when the Cherokee made their entrance."

"He seems to think the Cherokee are not our friends."

Nairne frowned. "I've heard nothing like that. Unwanequa seems to be the headman of this little bunch, and he tells me that the Cherokee are with us."

"This Oowa—ah—this other fellow, he's a real Indian? A chief?"

"Not a powerful chief—as I said, he's a young fellow. But he's had the power to speak for his superiors before, and I imagine he has it now. I don't know what this German fellow is about." He grinned. "But I suppose you ought to speak to him, Mr. Ambassador."

"I suppose I should. Do we have anyone who speaks Russian to interrogate the prisoner?"

"Well, there's our *other* prisoner."

"Euler? Yes—but can we trust him to translate? We should try and find someone else. Maybe even have him listen while we have Euler talk for us."

"Ah. To test him. You've a devious mind, Mr. Franklin."

"I know. I can't say as I like having it, either," he replied glumly.

He noticed that Voltaire still stood near. "Come with me," he told the philosopher. "I've a feeling I'll need a second in this matter."

Priber was a small man, almost as koboldlike as the pilot of the airship. Inside, his Indian garb made him look even sillier, like a courtier dressed up for some lavish costume ball.

"What's on your mind, Mr. Priber?"

"Utopia, Mr. Franklin."

"An interesting condition," Voltaire quipped. "I've a cousin with a blemish on her face that bears passing resemblance to the map of Peru, but to have a whole country—" He stopped and peered at Priber's partially shaved head. "So that's what it looks like, eh?"

Priber blinked at Voltaire, and his eyebrows puckered in annoyance. "I don't think I've had the pleasure, sir."

"Ah. Voltaire, at your service."

"The author of *Oedipe*?"

"If someone must take blame for it, I will do as well as any other."

"Utopia, Mr. Priber," Franklin said mildly, wondering if it had been a mistake to include Voltaire after all.

"Ah, yes. You will both admit, I think, that the Old World has made a mess of itself?"

"It's looked better," Franklin allowed.

"I have long believed—no, dreamed, even—that a more perfect society could exist. I know that you have—both of you, now that I know who you are, Monsieur—likewise pondered on how the human condition might be improved. I sought in my own country and those near, and I found that the people in the countryside—simple, honest people living in the ways of their forefathers—were more nearly perfect than the jaundiced society of court and city. Still, in those countries—even now, with all changed—the weight of history is too heavy. It is spoilt, I think perhaps beyond redemption."

Franklin shrugged. "I've had similar thoughts."

"And I think you agree that it's in this New World, so bright with promise, that we might at last create a country—an empire—that is entirely good, sane, just. But we will not find it by bringing the woeful ways of Europe with us. We will find it, I believe—and have believed since I first read of them—amongst the people native to this world, who have never felt a tyrant's yoke, have not the habit of oppressing or of being oppressed."

Franklin nodded, beginning to warm to the little man a bit. "I've often thought there is much sensible in the government of our Indian neighbors."

"Sensible, yes. Perfect, no. *Perfectible*—yes!" He said this last with considerable triumph.

"And how would you perfect them, Mr. Priber?" Franklin asked, suddenly cautious.

"First, I am a man of action. When the time of calamities began in Europe, I knew that the time had come. I might have delayed longer, if things had been more ordinary, but the atrocities and stupidities of those in governance in Saxony, where I lived at the time, convinced me. It was no easy thing, coming here, for ships were scarce. But some three years ago I managed it, working as a sailor."

"A fascinating account. You left in search of El Dorado, yes?"

Franklin caught the sarcasm in Voltaire's question. Priber did not. "El Dorado? It was long sought, but for the wrong reason—greed for gold. No, El Dorado will be made, not found. Still, I was drawn by the tales of the New Andalusia, of Chicora, which the earliest explorers found here, in these climes. And that fabulous place was nothing more than the lands of the Cherokee, magnified by the natural longing of Man for the society I propose. In any event, come here I did, and dwelt with the Indians, seeing what was good and what was bad. I had things to teach them—of a practical sort—and they valued me. But when I began speaking to them of a better way of life, they were intrigued. To make it all short, gentlemen, the great chief at Tellico has made me his prime minister and given me the charge of helping to create as near to paradise on Earth as any of us can imagine."

"Imagine this paradise for me, if you will, Mr. Priber. In a few words."

"A few words will not do it justice. Indeed, I am writing a plan in book form which will help to lay it all out."

"But, as you said, time is short."

"It's true, so I will explain some first principles. The foremost is that all men should be admitted equally to the nation—Cherokee, Muskogee, German, French, English—all nations and all hues will be dissolved in paradise and become one."

"Laudable enough," Voltaire replied, sounding interested but still skeptical.

"All things shall be held in common," Priber went on. "No one man will own a single thing that is not shared with every other man. You see the reason of that, don't you? It's the great divide of power and wealth that destroyed the Old World. Paris fell apart like a rotten cloth because the burden on the poor to support the ridiculous excesses of the wealthy could no longer be borne. Eliminate the possibility of wealth and you eliminate the possibility of poverty." He hunched over as his enthusiasm grew. His fingers tapped the table like ten little gavels. "Even women will be shared. No man may claim a single woman as wife. And the children shall be raised by all, in common, and so count the entire nation as their parents."

Franklin glanced at Voltaire, wondering how a diplomat was supposed to respond. He cleared his throat and attempted a smile. "Mr. Priber, I do agree with you in some measure—avarice and happiness are often not acquainted with each other, and wealth is more often the possessor than the possessed. Your notions of equality are likewise laudable, and I account many of the world's troubles have their root in the mildewed soil of aristocracy and privilege."

Priber nodded enthusiastically.

"But—what would become of industry, of thrift, of hard toil to better oneself—if there was no bettering to be had? If the sluggard benefited much from the sweat of the industrious, and the hard-working from the slothful not at all? And as for your idea of sharing women—I have shared a few in my time, and it never even *promised* a happy end."

"I notice, too," Voltaire remarked, "that as you are prime minister of an empire, this equality seems not to extend to the ruling classes—or do you intend to open your office to election?"

Priber frowned. "You will note that in nature, certain beasts in a herd are better able to lead than others. So it is with men.

In the society I propose, those more able to lead would naturally come forward and be recognized."

"And they would take on this added responsibility, despite that they would obtain no more or less in the way of goods and things than those who, for instance, carry the slop buckets for the hogs?" Voltaire asked.

"Just so."

"That is an optimistic vision, I think."

"Do you?" Priber asked coldly. "And Mr. Franklin?"

"Just what is it you want of me, sir? My endorsement? Your system will either work or it will not."

"I know you seek for a unified country, Mr. Franklin, one that encompasses all the peoples of this continent. How did you put it? A single arrow may be easily broken—a bundle of arrows proves stronger. My paradise is a single arrow. I wish to add to the bundle."

"You wish for the colonies to join your utopia?"

"Yes, of course. But I know that such a desire is not entirely realistic. Still, I am secure that, given time, my nation will convert others by its example, if it is allowed to flourish. I want firm promises to *that* effect, sir."

"I can't guarantee that, of course."

"But you can endorse it, and that would go far."

"The best endorsement you can give is to aid in the fight for the freedom of us all," Franklin told him. "Surely you don't think the Pretender will grant your philosophic principles substance, if he is triumphant here."

"No. But I do think my people might profitably benefit from watching the two big dogs in the yard fight until one is dead and the other much tired and wounded. Then my little nation might give the remaining cur a swift kick and a bon voyage."

"Profitably benefit? I thought there was to be no profit in your utopia."

"Profit always for all, sir, and never for one."

"Sir, as witnessed by the airship you saw today, it is not two big dogs fighting, but a mastiff worrying at a terrier."

Priber set his jaw stubbornly. "Do I have your endorsement?"

"I cannot give it. I find too much about your scheme impracticable and in some instances as detestable as what you would replace."

Priber drew himself back, eyes blazing. "In that case, sir, I must advise my emperor to withhold his support from your cause. If my choice is between two evils, I will choose neither." He stood, bowed stiffly, and exited.

"Well," Franklin said dryly after he was gone, "there went the one ally we were sure of. How much better can we fare with the rest? My career as ambassador is off to an auspicious start."

7.

Siberian Vision

The forest had a funereal quality.

Boughs should not be green, not when snow lay on the ground. It was as if they were dead but had preserved their color, their semblance of life: flowers at the graveside. And the silence! A green forest should be alive with trilling birds, scampering squirrels, the startled scuttling of a rabbit in the brush.

Even after years in northern climes, when Adrienne ventured into these forests, heavy with their pitchy perfumes, she felt a sense of dread totally unrelated to the wonder she had known in the forests about Montchevreuil when she was a little girl.

She wasn't alone in her dislike. The Russians didn't like their forests either, populating them with cold, lonely phantasms, the ghosts of drowned maidens, and much less human things. Things which, given what she knew, might well have some basis in fact.

But, no, to the malakim and their kin one human country was very like the next. Climate and the color of trees did not enter into their nature or choice of habitation, so far as she could tell.

"How very like the forests about Saint Petersburg," Émilie commented, as they walked along, reflecting her thoughts. Adrienne felt reasonably safe. Their airship and one other rested on a marshy meadow within sight, the other two stationed above as sentinels. Hunters and patrols had ridden off in all directions—and still, though she did not entirely trust them, she had her djinni.

And Crecy, of course, came armed with musket, pistol, and sword.

"Why should they be different?" Elizavet asked. "A forest is a forest, yes?"

"Begging the tsarevna's pardon," Linné said, "but no. The forests of Tahiti, for instance, or Guinea or Peru, are quite different from these."

"Even in France they are different," Adrienne commented. "There are more sorts of trees. Here they are all of a kind."

"Most," Linné corrected apologetically. "I've noted many here which are subtly different from those in our native forests."

"It must be a very subtle difference," Elizavet sniffed, "for I see none at all. Which puzzles me more, actually. We have traveled a long way, yes? As far as Tahiti?"

"Perhaps not so far," Linné said, "but a long way."

"Well, I do remark now the strange and wondrous plants in my father's hothouse. I suppose I imagined them only as curiosities, and thought that otherwise the forests at the far edges of the Earth were much like our own. But you seem to suggest that the farther one goes, the stranger the plants become. Yet surely we have gone farther than France, which mademoiselle our teacher claims is indeed different . . ." She trailed off, perhaps unsure of the point she meant to make.

Linné saw a point in it, though, and nodded enthusiastically.

"I don't think it has to do with distance but with climate. Traveling eastward as we are, at similar latitude to Saint Petersburg, we encounter climate similar to what we left. Traveling south, toward the equator, finds warmer environs. I have noticed that food left out too long in a warm room encourages all manner and varieties of mold to form; but in cooler weather, there may be little or none. I hypothesize that the heat in tropical lands stimulates a greater variety—and stranger sorts—of flora and fauna."

Elizavet frowned. "You speak as if these things come about of their own accord. But surely God made all varieties of things. Why would he so impoverish Russian forests?"

Linné nodded vigorously. "You catch the imprecision of my speech, Princess. You have a keen mind. What I meant, of course, is that God created those forms which benefit best from their climate. You see? In India and Africa, elephants are very nearly bald, but in these Siberian lands we find the remains of elephants altogether as shaggy as bears. Both are elephants, but God fitted the ones in the North with hair, to match them to their climate."

An amused smile played on Elizavet's lips. "You are from Sweden, are you not, Monsieur Linné? That is farther north than Saint Petersburg, if I remember my geography. Do you then have more hair than other men, beneath your garments?" She eyed him speculatively.

Linné looked mortified.

"And I, being French, must be substantially less hairy than *you*, a Russian," Émilie said, her tone somewhat caustic.

"Less hardy, maybe," Elizavet demurred. "Perhaps, for hairiness, we could propose a comparison. As Monsieur Linné is our naturalist, perhaps he would agree to judge."

Émilie flamed scarlet. Linné seemed to have something caught in his throat.

Émilie recovered before Linné. "Monsieur Linné—weren't you planning on collecting examples of the local flora?" she asked rather pointedly.

"Ah—yes, I was planning that. I would be glad of help—"

"That sounds delightful," Elizavet said tranquilly.

"Oh, I should think that would be dreadfully boring for you," Émilie responded quickly.

"I can judge that," Elizavet haughtily replied.

"I thought the two of us might take in some target practice, Tsarevna," Crecy interjected.

"Your pardon?"

"You expressed an urge to hunt."

"So I did," Elizavet said, tapping her chin. She looked up innocently. "I thought that was what we were doing."

Crecy beckoned with crooked finger. Elizavet shrugged and started after her.

"Do you mind, Adrienne?" Crecy asked. "I promised."

"Not at all. I've a mind to walk alone for a bit."

"I would rather you didn't."

"I will stay within sight and protection of the ships," she promised.

Crecy nodded. She and Elizavet went back toward the ships, while Linné and Émilie went off along the edge of the forest.

"Don't get lost, you two."

"We won't," Linné promised. He did not sound altogether happy. He probably guessed—as Adrienne did—that he was going to receive an upbraiding from Émilie for his part in the exchange of a moment before.

In a few moments, Adrienne was alone, in the mausoleum of the trees; the train of her hunting dress brushing fir needles made almost the only sound. She heard the occasional call in the distance, the report of a musket, and wondered if the hunters would find anything. Apparently Hercule counted not so much on actually hunting game as on locating native tribesmen who would sell it. There were many, hereabouts, she had heard—strange dark peoples with tongue-twisting names, as primitive and wild as the natives of America. They had spied an encampment and landed some distance from it, to avoid frightening them. Hercule had taken a detachment and a supply of trade goods.

Which was why, just a few moments later, she thought she was hallucinating when she made him out, on horseback, moving through the trees at some pace, head turning this way and that, as if searching for something.

It struck her that he was probably looking for her. She had carefully avoided him since Irena's murder attempt. He must want to talk about it—and it was a conversation they must have, someday—but today she could not bear it, nor did she wish to inflame Irena. Especially not here, in the forest, where all kinds of suspicions might be aroused. She stepped behind the massive trunk of a tree, gathering her skirts so that they did not bell out, and waited for him to pass.

When she looked again, he was nowhere to be seen.

"Why do you hide?"

She spun on her heel, startled. A woman was watching her.

She was clad in skins and furs—not rudely thrown on, but cleverly cut and sewn, embellished with bits of ivory and painted designs. Her complexion was dark, her eyes narrow, almond-shaped. Familiar.

"Karevna?"

"Not my name."

Adrienne looked closer. The resemblance was strong, but at second glance, it was certainly not Vasilisa Karevna. The nose was wider, the eyes a shade browner than black—and Vasilisa's skin was almost as pale as Irena's, where this woman was tanned leather. And her Russian, though comprehensible, was very thickly accented.

"Your pardon. I thought I knew you."

"Perhaps we have met in the world of spirits. They are strong about you, I see."

A little chill ran up Adrienne's spine. "You see them?"

"As mist."

"You have some scientific means?"

"I don't know that word. If you mean is my hand like yours, no. I have never seen the like of it. It drew me here."

Suspicion bit Adrienne like an adder. She opened the eyes of her *manus oculatus*, no longer content to rely on the warnings of her djinni.

There were things with the woman, three of them. They were unlike any of the malakim she had ever known before, which usually appeared as certain geometric shapes to her aetheric sight. The seraphs and the death which had attacked her above Saint Petersburg were the only exceptions. Here were more. They were shadowed, unclear, with strong lines of force drawn between them and the woman, who appeared much as they did.

"What are you?" she whispered.

"An ordinary shaman, not very different from a hundred others. The real question is what are *you*?" With sudden astonishment, Adrienne realized that the woman was on the verge of fleeing. Her voice trembled, as did her limbs. She was terrified. "When I was young, I was lured to deep water by the *kul* which lived there. He spoke kindly to me, made as if to be my friend, but all the while he was drowning me, taking my soul. My uncle saw what was happening, and he called an old shaman, who cut the *kul* up and fed it to me. I was very weak. Almost I died, but then I was strong again. And I could still see *them*, as through a veil. I learned to shamanize, to make their substance into my own. Spirits serve me, as you see."

Her voice dropped lower still. "But they are not like those that serve you. They are not like your hand, which is no hand at all."

"What do you see, when you look at my hand?"

The woman stepped forward, eyes rolling. She reached out to touch Adrienne's false fingers, and the Frenchwoman let her.

"It is a tree." She sighed. "It is *the* tree that holds up the world. It is the pole of the house, the smoke hole, the North Star."

"I don't know what you mean."

"I have seen the other tree," she murmured. "It flew high above—like you were flying, carried by spirits of the air. But it did not fly so high that I did not know it. When it passed over, it twisted everything in me. Not much, for it did not intend to. If it had *tried* to twist me, I would have been lost like a flicker of flame in a storm. No, what I felt was just the long smoke of its fire, burning my eyes. Just the surge of its sap, pulling at my blood . . ." She stopped. She stopped trembling as well. "I came here to kill you," she said.

"Why?"

"Because you can shiver the tree, perhaps even break it. Because you are a mad thing that should not be in the world. But now I see I cannot kill you. My strength would be wasted for nothing, and my people will need me when your time comes. And there is still the other tree, the tree with a thousand birds in its branches, with its roots beneath the waters where the *kul* dwell, with its topmost limbs beyond the heavens. It is more dangerous than you—you may be the best hope against it. You are most dangerous together, however, which is why I meant to kill you." She backed away a step. "Let me go back to my people."

"Wait. This other . . . tree. How long ago did it fly over?"

"I was a girl. Ten summers and more have passed. It drew spirits after it like geese, a skyful of black stars. I am going now."

"No. Wait. Talk to me more."

"I won't. There is something with you that wants my soul. It is coming. If I remain, I will not be able to resist it. I will die; my life will have been as nothing." She hesitated as if to say something else, and then she turned and ran like a deer.

In the same instant, Uriel appeared, stretching himself out toward the fleeing woman.

"No!" Adrienne shouted.

"This is not your concern," the seraph replied. "She is an enemy, an abomination."

"I said *no*."

"You remember our previous conversation, I think."

"I remember it well. If you still want my help, leave her be."

"I will chance your ire," Uriel said, and was gone.

So was the woman. "Go after them," Adrienne commanded her servants. "Prevent him from harming her."

"We cannot, lady. He is our lord, too."

Adrienne dismissed them viciously. Where was the power

the Tartar woman had so feared? She had none! She had none. She never had.

Despairing, she sank to earth, feeling mired in the scent of resin, an insect in rarefied amber. Defeated.

She tired of defeat rather quickly. If her illusion of control over the malakim was gone, she still controlled her own mind at least. Since it was the best thing she had, she must force herself to use it.

What had the Tartar woman said, in sum? Her son was dangerous. *Adrienne* was dangerous. Together they were *very* dangerous.

Why? How? What did it mean? Obviously her talk of trees was metaphorical. When Adrienne looked into the aether, she saw scientific diagrams—the result of her education, of her predispositions. What did the Tartar woman see? And if *she* saw a tree, what would Adrienne see, how would *she* understand it?

She summoned a djinn. "Show me myself," she demanded.

"I don't understand," the djinn replied.

"Myself. What do I look like in the aether?"

The djinn—a top-shaped creature—spun, flattened, became a surface like a mirror.

In it, she saw herself, pretty much as she had last seen herself in earthly reflection.

"You cannot see yourself," a voice said. "You know yourself too well." It was Uriel, a cloud of eyes amongst the trees.

"Did you kill her?" Adrienne asked angrily.

"No. She was crafty. She planned her flight well, and her abominable use of our kind—" He broke off.

"She tricks you somehow, doesn't she? Uses your nature against you?"

The seraph didn't answer.

"Very well. But you will tell me this, or we will part company, I swear to you—"

"An empty threat."

"Do *not* test me. I wrenched apart one of your kind, one in the shape of a death. I think I can do the same to you." That *was* an empty threat. The knowledge of how she had destroyed the death was gone, and none of her efforts could recover it. She could make a device such as she had once given the tsar, but that would not kill Uriel, only break her connection to him.

"Ask your question." Uriel hummed through her hand. "If it pleases me, I will answer."

"That woman spoke of my hand as a tree. What did that mean?"

"I do not know."

"She spoke of another, like me, but stronger. She meant my son, didn't she?"

"Probably."

"What does she allude to when she says we are most dangerous together?"

"I do not know."

"You lie!"

"If I do, you will have to be content with it."

And she wished then, wished more than anything, that she *could* tear this creature apart, reduce it to blind ferments bereft of glib speech and insinuation. Perhaps sensing this—or perhaps not wanting to be questioned any longer—the seraph receded.

Nearly shaking with rage, Adrienne turned back toward where the ships ought to be, and suddenly realized that they were no longer within sight. Still angry, she began trying to retrace her steps, but she couldn't see prints on the prickly needle mold. More annoyed, she changed direction. If worse came to worst, she could call on Crecy for aid, but she didn't want to do that. She could use her djinni, but at the moment she didn't want to do that either.

She was very near doing so anyway, when she spied a bright blue, a color that could not be natural here. She turned toward that. A little nearer, she made out a woman in riding costume, reclining.

A little nearer yet, and she stopped, recognizing Irena. And yet there was something strange about her, something very strange. She seemed to be staring at something, and she wore a ruby-bright necklace. . . .

It snapped into focus. Irena's throat had been cut, ear to ear.

In the instant of realization, there came a rustle in the bush and then an exclamation.

"Dear God." She turned to see Crecy, regarding the corpse. Crecy turned wide eyes upon her.

"Well, my dear," Crecy whispered, a little incredulously. "It would seem you took my advice to heart."

8.

A Box of Snakes

To Franklin, the council chamber felt like a box full of rattlesnakes.

In a cloud of suffocating tobacco smoke, ebon-faced Maroons glared at flint-eyed rangers, fingers toying with tomahawks and dirks. The rangers scowled back, keeping it clear that they, too, remembered the blood debts between them. Apalachee and Yamacraw and Cherokee sneered over hooked noses at one another; Carolina regulars and margravate dragoons bayoneted one another with angry stares.

How had he ever imagined these people would work together? The various hatreds in this room could never be matched by theoretical concerns like freedom or liberty.

He had imagined himself brave when he spoke in Charles Town, defying James and his court. But in Charles Town he had been assured of the support of the Junto—it had been prearranged. Despite appearances, he had always known he had the upper hand. Here, he felt decidedly outnumbered and deeply uncertain and . . . surrounded. Even familiar faces, like Paris Nakaso's, seemed threatening. Despite that he had lived among the black men and women of Charles Town for nearly ten years, he understood, suddenly, that he did not *know* them.

Much less so the Maroons. They were Negroes who had taken their freedom before Blackbeard granted it, tough men and women who lived like Indians in the backwoods and isolated coves, often as not raiding and thieving for their livelihood. Many of them were slaves who had escaped in the first months of their captivity, and so they were very African, often to the point of speaking little or no English. They were an entirely unknown quantity; and by their wild hair, motley clothing, and numerous weapons they were no easy bunch. Nor would others be easy about trusting *them*, as McPherson—and others—had made plain.

And Indians had never seemed particularly threatening when he had seen them in Boston or Charles Town. Interesting, yes; curious, of course. Plenty of the Junto's members were Indians, but pretty civilized ones, the ones who had adopted European ways. Some could not even tell you what tribe they were from, being well mixed from many tribes, with white and Negro blood as well. Again, though he passed them on the streets daily, he knew little of them. He counted none as close friends, save possibly Red Shoes the Choctaw—who was not here. Those who were here looked wild—like the old chief of the Yamacraw at Oglethorpe's right hand, a fellow named Tomochichi. He wore no shirt, so as to show to best advantage the tattooed wings that unfolded upon his chest. Add to all of them the now-ominous Cherokee and the newly arrived Apalachee, and he felt as uncomfortably at sea as he had when he spoke at the Turkish Divan.

Why shouldn't they turn on us, given all the grief they've suffered from the English? Franklin wondered.

He hoped he had an answer for them.

Nairne opened the discussion, detailing the invasion of the English colonies, taking pains to point out the known backing of the Russians. He spoke with fair eloquence, but Franklin could read absolutely nothing in the faces of those around him to hint at how his words were received.

When Nairne finished, the room was still, save for various translators finishing the job of making his words into other tongues. Then, as if at some silent signal, everyone began shouting, declaring, arguing at once.

Nairne waved for order, but it was Oglethorpe's reedy, strident, patrician voice that brought some measure of attention.

"It's no secret," Oglethorpe began, "that I support the Jacobite king. He is, in my opinion, the true sovereign of all Englishmen." His face pinched with displeasure at the hubbub that followed that, but he held out his hand for silence, and again—surprisingly—got it.

"If the choice were *mine*," he went on, "I might abandon my will to his. My will, however, is no longer my own. I represent a nation; and many—nay, most, in fact—are not English. They are Yamacraw and German, French and Spanish—aye, and Englishmen of every religion and stripe, not just Catholic. We of the margravate have forged our own way for many years. England could not support us, our sister English colonies *would* not aid us, and we were forced to make our own policies and alliances. We have fought for our existence, and won it, and I will not lightly give that up, nor would my people let me—most especially to a puppet king of the Muscovy tsar, whatever name or title he is possessed of, whatever I might personally think of his cause."

Franklin realized he had been holding his breath. Now he slowly let it out. If they had lost the Cherokee, it seemed they had gained Azilia.

But Oglethorpe wasn't finished. "That's on one hand. On the other is this alliance Mr. Nairne and Mr. Franklin would have us join. Not only has the Commonwealth not been our friend in time of need, they have been our active enemy. We have suffered at the hands of the Carolinians most particularly. In the last war they took our port at Savannah, and keep us cut off from the Venice trade to this day. We must buy more expensive goods from Carolina traders and from the much poorer Spanish trade. As well, our Spanish and French allies are suspicious of this alliance, and I believe with reason. This is an English war—and we are no longer English, in any sense of the word. I therefore hold forth that it is in the right best interest of my country to hold aloof."

"They will not let you alone," Nairne warned. "They will not see it in that light."

"On the contrary—I have had communication with the Pretender, and he did, indeed, see it that way. He proposes that the margravate remain independent."

That blew around the room in murmurs for a moment, and it was easy to see what direction that wind was taking. *Maybe all he wants is the English colonies,* they were all thinking.

It was time Franklin said something. "He says so," Franklin shouted over the growing din, "and yet look at the treachery he practiced on us in Charles Town. You cannot trust his word, I fear. He is not his own man."

"As to the matter of Savannah," Nairne added, "it has been discussed, and we will relinquish it to you, as a sign of good faith."

Oglethorpe laughed bitterly. "You return it to me, now that it is no longer yours to give? Very nice. What when I asked for it scarcely a year ago?"

"I could not bring the Assembly around to it," Nairne admitted. "There was much anger when you—an English colony by charter—allied with the Spanish in their incursion against us."

"We had no choice," Oglethorpe snapped, "nor do I apologize for it."

"You were in a hard place, and, as I said, I tried to bring the Assembly around to it. Now it is done."

Oglethorpe made a face. "There are other matters."

"Yes," said a fellow with skin as dark and rich as teak.

"Stand and be recognized, sir."

He did. "I am t'et one t'ey call Unoka," the fellow said, standing. "I t'at one accounted leader ah t'e free Maroons. T'e margrave is afraid you'll make him free our brot'ers in bondage, if you win. The damn English hab promised not t' inte'fere."

"The internal affairs of the margravate are its own," Nairne explained.

"S'at so? Well, some of us has bret'rn in t'e margravate, wearin' shackles and workin' t'e rice fields. If 'n y' expect us to fight for you, somet'in' has to be done about t'at, don' ya t'ink?"

"Impossible," Oglethorpe stated flatly. "Absolutely impossible. Oh, I sympathize—as you well may know, when I accepted the margravate from Sir Thomas, I did indeed try to manumit the slaves. The colony was chartered originally to *have* none, and I own none myself. But many a landgrave fled Carolina to the margravate when Blackbeard ruled, and the law was changed. I am accountable to those who own property. I do not have the authority to take it from them. They would not have it."

"An ne'er 'll we hab it," Unoka snapped, with some heat. Behind him, his lieutenants and bodyguards, a fierce-looking bunch, brandished fists in agreement.

"And we," another voice said. Franklin looked to see Paris Nakaso stand up.

"Sir?" Nairne asked.

"This seems as good a time as any to discuss several things," Nakaso said. "For one, we are in perfect agreement with Mr. Unoka—"

"Who is *we*, Mr. Nakaso?" Nairne asked. "You are a member of the Charles Town Assembly and a sworn member of the Junto."

"Elected to speak for the Negroes of our colony," he reminded them. "And, as such, I have several things to say."

Nairne, looking troubled, nodded reluctantly.

"If we fight, we must know what we are fighting for. We are free men, Governor, but we are not equal men. We would have that change. We want the same vote as white men get. We want the same opportunity to hold property. Moreover, as Captain Unoka says, we want our relatives who are still held in bondage in the margravate, Virginia, Maryland, Pennsylvania—all the colonies—freed."

Nairne was red in the face. He hadn't expected this, despite Ben's mention of it to him on the overland march.

"Perhaps we should take this one step at a time," Nairne

said. "You know that if James wins, you all will return to bondage—"

"No damn chance ah t'at," Unoka shouted.

Nairne sighed. "If you have to fight to retain your freedom, we are your allies—"

"Your pardon," Franklin interjected, "but they are right."

That had the desired effect. It stopped the conversation in the room as surely as death stops a heart. Nairne gave Franklin a warning glance, but Franklin plunged on anyway.

"Margrave Oglethorpe put it very nicely," Franklin said, "though I think he did not mean it as I heard it. This is not a fight for Carolina or for the liberty of Englishmen. This is a fight for the freedom and liberty of us all. I say that if the Maroons and free black men of Carolina fight for this cause, they must be rewarded for it, and any among you with sense will wonder why they do not simply *take* what is due them. Margrave, I feel for your plight—and by God I swear we need your help, for I have seen what the Pretender is bringing against us. But if there is any man here who doubts that what is at stake is every last one of us, and our very lives and destinies, then I say the hell with you. Here we are, begging you to take the inoculation that will spare you the plague, and yet all of you fret fearfully at the vaccine. 'Let *them* fight,' each says, 'let *them* die. It's not *our* fight. We will reap the rewards later.' Gentleman, there *is* no later. This is not a government we fight, nor a tyrant, nor even the emperor of Russia. Russia is behind James, true enough, but behind Russia there is a race of devils. And these devils do not want our homes, our plantations, our lands, or our goods. The single thing they want of us, gentlemen, is that we die. That we die without heirs, without hope, leaving no future and nary a footprint in the sand to ever say we were here. They do not prefer white, black, or red skin. They think Protestant no fitter for life and liberty than Catholic or Mussulman. What comes is not an army, but death, and then silence, the end of all our days and of every generation unborn.

"Many of you know this. Many of you have fought with the Junto against these devils—have hunted the warlocks they send to our shores. What you have seen—the flying machine that deviled us yesterday, the undersea ships in Charles Town harbor—these are the smallest of breezes from the hurricane that is almost upon us. And, damn me, but all any of *you* can do is make petty intrigues and scheme to see which of you will be last exterminated!

"If we do not throw these back across the sea, now, while we can, we will never do it, ever. And none of us shall enjoy freedom or property or anything like it. We shall all hang together, gentlemen, or all hang separately. That is the way of it. It will be hard medicine for some of you. That's too bad. It's just too bad. I've spent long years of my life working to protect us from this enemy. Now I begin to regret it. I wonder if any of you are worth it, worth the price of the men and women who have paid with their lives so that you might live another day, month, week. If there is no more greatness in the human soul than you folks display, then more speed to our foes, and may they end us all with merciful quickness. I, for one, applaud the destruction of our race, if it be as petty and mean as you all make it seem."

He finished, feeling like a tower of fury, no longer in the least afraid of anyone in the room. They suddenly looked like children to him, every one.

Silent children. He had managed to shut them up.

The silence stretched close to half a minute, when one man began chuckling. As everyone in the room turned to stare at him, his humor migrated to his belly, and he fairly roared his laughter.

"Sir? Have I amused you?" Franklin snapped.

The fellow took the floor, sweeping an oversized tricorn of some glossy fur from his head. In hue and features he looked an Indian, his dress a curious mixture of Spanish and native. A weapon, something between a smallsword and rapier in length, dangled at his waist. Yet in his hand, he carried something like an Indian war club, with what looked suspiciously like a human scalp depending from it.

"Amuse me?" the fellow said, in an English nearly drowned in Latin accents. "No indeed, Señor. It is this roomful of women who amuse me. *You* have heart! *You* look through all of the black-painted words here and see the real enemy they cover up!" He straightened, made a stiff Spanish bow. "I am Don Pedro de Salazar de Ivitachuca, Nikowatka of the kingdom of the Apalachee. I and my warriors are at your disposal, with no questions or remarks, no feigned indifference, no mewling. You battle no less than the forces of Satan himself, and it is not a fight that any warrior of the Apalachee would ever shirk from. The heads and scalps of a hundred demons shall adorn our council house, I swear it, and perhaps the horned one himself, should he come within my grasp!"

The Apalachee thrust the scalp contemptuously at Oglethorpe and then at the Maroons. "And you, you with your bare scalp poles, with your guns hidden under your beds—and yourselves under there with them—you may count yourselves poor in our eyes for a hundred generations!" He brandished the war club and shouted in a most unSpanish way, a long ululating call that was taken up within and without of the room by others of his tribe.

That was surprising enough, but the Cherokee suddenly took up the shouting as well—which fact caused Priber to blush furiously. Tomochichi and those with him joined next, and no less than half the Maroons. Guns thudded and blew chips of wood from the ceiling. The room went almost opaque with the smoke.

Franklin was sure that the battle was already joined, right under his nose. It took him several stunned seconds to understand that this was a good sign, not a bad one.

Only Oglethorpe and Nairne looked bewildered. Everyone else had taken up the call.

There had been a vote, and the vote was for war. Suddenly jubilant, Franklin added his own voice to the howling mob.

Franklin gulped down a cup of the hot cassina and made a face. It was strong and bitter, like badly brewed coffee with a handful of dirt thrown in. Still, it kept one awake, and in a world where coffee and tea were worth twice their weight in gold, something of a necessity. Especially when it was near sunrise, no sleep had or promised, and plenty yet to do.

"I won't do it," Oglethorpe was saying. "I am the margrave. My first responsibility is to my nation, as I have made plain."

"Sir," Franklin said wearily, "you have agreed, albeit reluctantly, to our enterprise—"

"On my terms. I will not lead Maroons, nor do I feel comfortable with Southern Rangers. I want nothing to do with this Continental Army."

"Then you want nothing to do with winning this fight," Franklin said, "for it is only as a continent that we can fight it. We must have a military plan of action, and it must be unified. Surely you know that, sir. Who else among us trained under the prince of Savoy himself? I knew Prince Eugène personally, and, though I know little of warfare, I can guess he would dearly love to come against an army that had no head or common leader."

Oglethorpe rubbed his eyes. "Yes, I see your point. I have seen it for hours. But what can I do with such men? When should I train them?"

"Do you train your Yamacraw troops?"

"No, of course not. I use them as scouts, as sneak thieves and assassins."

"There's your answer, then. The Maroons live like Indians. Use them so."

"They are *not* Indians. The Yamacraw fight for honor and scalps. Maroons fight for plunder."

"You must find some use for them."

"Me? Why must it be me?"

"Because," Thomas Nairne interjected, "you are the only real general we have. We need you to command."

"If the margravate comes into danger, I must come to her aid. Don't you see this will make me a poor commander for a mixed force?"

"No," Nairne said, "for everything you do out here will keep them away from the margravate. If they come under danger, it will be because you have failed. Besides, if you command our troops, that frees more of *your* men for the defense of the margravate itself, an idea you surely must like better than us marching troops in."

"Is that a threat, sir?"

"Good heavens, no! By God, man, whence comes this intractable temper of yours?" Nairne exploded.

Oglethorpe glowered, then softened. "My people have suffered," he murmured, "more, I think, than you understand. And whilst once they were a motley collection, and I a man of high birth, I *do* consider them my people now. Their safety is a charge I take *most* seriously. I was once much taken with notions of equality and charity. I have opposed slavery, for I think it weakens the slaver as much as it wrongs the slave. But I have learned to think very small, gentlemen. The common good has become, to me, the good of my own, and no others."

"I urge you to think larger again," Franklin said. "You have come to love, as you called them, your 'motley' people. Well, that is the Commonwealth in a nutshell. Without us, you perish. Without you, we perish. Very simple, very much in the logic you have just explained. You are an honest man, Margrave Oglethorpe, a hard man, and brassy one. Be our general."

Oglethorpe pounded the table hard with his fist but said nothing. His knuckles turned pink, then welled red; he had split the skin.

Then he tapped the table much less forcefully.

"I will do it," he said at last. "God save us all, but I will do it."

* * *

Two days later, Franklin rose to watch the first of the Continental Army march. Led by Oglethorpe, they numbered two hundred—mixed companies of rangers, Carolina regulars, Margravate dragoons, Yamacraw, and Maroons. He watched them go with pride and trepidation. He had helped make that strange union of men, and if they met with defeat, he would own part of that, too.

When they were gone, he remained outside the fort, waiting. It was his turn next.

A small figure appeared at the gate of the fort, paused, then made a straight line for him.

"Good morning, my dear," he said, as his wife came close. "Come to see me off?"

"I'm going with you."

The morning air was still, the grass of the prairie wet with dew. The forest in the middle distance seemed heavy, a deep green ocean still dark with night. Against it danced sudden green flashes, exactly like schools of fish upon the surface of the deep.

"Parakeets," Franklin said, pointing. "Did you see them?"

"I've seen them often enough in our garden, stealing our corn," Lenka replied. "Do not change the subject."

"I've been through this with you before, my dear. Once before I put you in harm's way. I won't do it again."

"You leave me in a wooden fort, as a war begins, and think that I am not in harm's way?"

"I leave you with people I trust, people who are capable. The Pretender's army may well find its way here, but they will find only scorched earth. Governor Nairne will see to you. Out there—" he gestured westward "—out there, I am a fish on dry land. It will be the most I can do to worry about my own life, without you thrown into the bargain. The Coweta may greet us with open arms or they may put us on frames and burn us slowly. The French may do no better. I will not have you with me, Lenka. It will be distracting."

"Thoroughly selfish, you are. I can make my way."

"Yes? Can you light a fire, hunt game, contrive to cross a deep river, parley in Shawano if we encounter a murderous band of them?"

"You can't do those things."

"Yes, and so I'm a dead weight to those who can. But with my scientific supplies destroyed by the airship grenades, I am of little use here, and Governor Nairne has ordered me on this mission. The same is not true of you."

"He did not order that I stay."

"But I do."

A dark look crossed her face, but her words were soft. "When has it ever been that you could order me about, Ben? We are partners in this life, as you have said many times, and with equal shares. Why then do you decide who carries what burden?"

"In this case because I do, and for no other reason," he said, a little sharply.

"Benjamin—don't do it. If you do, take me with you."

He took her hands. "Lenka, why do you persist? You know that I would have you with me if I could."

"I do not know it at all," she replied. "I think rather that you have become bored with me. We met in excitement, in adventure. It will renew us to live so again."

"Lenka, we do not need renewal. I am content with our marriage."

"Content? Yes, 'content' is a good word. I did not marry you to be content, Benjamin. I married you because you promised me more than contentment."

"And I married you because I love you. And I remember, if you do not, the sight of you bleeding out your life because I had no more sense than to take you where you should not have been."

"It was my choice," she said softly. "Mine. My fate. Do you think in marrying you I have cast off choice?" When he didn't answer, she nodded briskly. "I see that you do."

"Lenka—"

"No. Let it stand. Perhaps I was mistaken in you, Benjamin Franklin."

"Lenka, not now. Please, let us not come to blows now, just before I go. Let us part friends."

She snorted. "Very well—friend. Fare you well. But do not expect to find that I have gone with the rest of your luggage and furniture when you return. If you think I have relinquished my will, you will find yourself much surprised."

"Lenka . . ."

"Adieu." She turned very abruptly and strode off.

He pinched his face, kicked at the grass. Damn her! Didn't he already have enough to worry about? Why spring this on him so suddenly, when the whole world was tumbling?

Almost he followed, to try and make amends, but at that moment, more of his party emerged from the gates of the fort.

Let her have the last word, then. He would make it better when he could, when he had time to breathe. She would calm, given time.

"Ready?" Robert asked.

"As ever I will be." He looked over the rest of his escort. They were all Southern Rangers—not neat, as soldiers went. They were roughly shaven, their faded coats worn over checked shirts of various colors tucked indifferently or not at all into knee breeches. Some wore leggings, like Indians—in fact, two of them *were* Indians. They wore throwing axes at their belts and carried carbine muskets, and each had two pistols in holsters on their saddles.

Most wore battered, plain hats, only their captain affecting a tricorn. Franklin recognized him gladly.

"Captain McPherson," Franklin said, taking the calloused hand.

"Damn fine speech the other day, Mr. Franklin, I must say. And I'm proud to be your guide into the deserts of America."

He gestured at a stocky brown mare. "This here is Lizzie, and she'll be your mount, if that be agreeable."

"I'm not much of a horseman," Franklin allowed. In fact, he avoided horses when he could. His first real experience with the beasts had been traumatic, a nightmare ride with Charles XII of Sweden. On the way to Fort Moore he had stayed mostly on foot or in a wagon.

"Not t' worry. Lizzie's gentle enough. And if y'r ready, Mr. Ambassador, it's best we put some miles behind us before sundown."

Franklin nodded, went over to Lizzie and patted her a few times, then tried a foot in a stirrup. She didn't complain, and a moment later he was mounted.

"I'll introduce y' to the rest as we ride," McPherson said. "You'll find 'em all good. Here, what's that?"

He followed McPherson's chin jerk. Five more men were riding toward them from Fort Moore. Franklin recognized Priber and three Cherokee. Voltaire was with them.

"Wait for them," Franklin said. "Let's see what they have to say."

Priber smiled as they came within speaking range. "Well met, Mr. Franklin. I was hoping that you would allow me and my men to ride with you."

"May I ask for what purpose, Mr. Priber?"

He shrugged his shoulders. "My fellows have been convinced to join your cause. I must admit, your speech moved me as well. I would like to help, if I can. I speak French, Spanish, Latin, Greek, and Cherokee all passing well, and have some acquaintance with the Muskogee tongue of Coweta. I can be of great help to you, I think. And, I will admit, I hope to speak to you further on matters philosophical."

Franklin considered for a moment. "And you, Voltaire? You want to brave the wilderness?"

"Me? It's not unappealing, but no, I merely came to bid you farewell. I have my task laid out for me, as you know."

Franklin nodded, cogs suddenly engaging in his head. He

most assuredly did not want Priber along with him—he was still not sure he could trust the man, for one thing, and he did not wish to hear endless arguments about communalistic utopias for another—but he also did not want to alienate him. "Mr. Priber, if you really want to help, I've a better use for you, I think, one you will enjoy."

"Sir?"

"Mr. Voltaire here is in the process of drafting a resolution, a declaration to affirm the independence of this New World from the Old. It must contain principles agreeable to all parties—Indians, freedmen, the French, Spanish, English; Catholics, Quakers, Anabaptists, and pagans. I should think with your background and inclination you should be most admirably suited to that task."

Priber frowned for an instant, then brightened. "My ideas will get a hearing?"

"Of course. I put it in Voltaire's hands to be arbitrator, but he will hear all you have to say." He almost smiled at the dismay and then friendly promise of revenge that crossed the Frenchman's face, only to vanish behind his usual smile.

Priber looked to Voltaire. "We can be agreed in this?"

"In this as in nothing else," Voltaire said impishly, doffing his hat to the German.

"Well, then, I accept," Priber replied. "I accept most enthusiastically. You will not be disappointed, I think."

Oddly, Franklin believed him. Voltaire needed some genuinely idealistic impulse to temper his natural skepticism. He also needed a broader viewpoint. Franklin had already arranged for the Frenchman to meet with Nakaso and the Maroons, but he needed the Indian point of view. Priber, for all his faults, could probably serve as translator for that.

"Now we need to get moving," McPherson reminded them.

"Yes. Godspeed," Voltaire said, waving his hat. "I hope it will not be another twelve years before we meet again, Benjamin."

"Me, too. Or even twelve months. Voltaire—" He paused,

and the philosopher gave him a questioning look. "Not to set a fox to watch the henhouse, but—could you look after Lenka?"

"I would certainly be pleased to look *at* her, Benjamin—yes of course, my friend. I shall guard her with my life."

"Thank you."

He turned then and, with Robert, followed McPherson and his men into the trees.

9.

Mongols

"The easiest thing would be for us to just kill them," Flint Shouting muttered, gazing across the ridge at the line of horsemen. Red Shoes counted twenty of them, but there could have been more.

"And what would you consider the *hardest* thing for us to do?"

"Wait, like cowards, as they close the distance, as we have waited for ten days. Wait for our horses to drop dead so they can catch us on foot."

"How long before we reach Wichita country?"

"Too long by a few days. We need fresh horses—even if we have to steal some of those ugly little ponies."

"Ugly, maybe, but they look sturdy. What's your plan for getting them?"

Flint Shouting looked at him as if he was crazy. "I just told you. Kill all of them and take their horses."

"The two of us?"

"Yes. Call lightning down from the sky, as you did a few days ago or boil their blood—something like that. I'll kill whatever your medicine doesn't."

"Every time I send one of my shadowchildren to attack them, I lose at least one. I've already spent my strongest and it's left me . . . weak."

More than weak, actually. The loss of a shadowchild was the loss of a piece of his own shadow, the half of his soul from which he drew his power. The resulting depression was terrible, had always been, but this time was different. He was starting to feel . . . angry. Not anger as he knew it, but anger like a wasp sting, like the hot peppers white men sometimes ate. A kind of hatred. Not at anything in particular, but at everything, each grain of dust.

Though he was also getting irritated with his companions, who seemed to expect him to do everything for them, spend his soul to save their lives.

So maybe this anger had nothing to do with the loss of his shadowchildren. Anyway, it was better than the heart-wrenching grief he usually felt. Much better.

"You're afraid the scalped man will catch you weak? Don't worry. If he returns, I will kill him for you."

"Of course you will," Red Shoes said, unable to keep sarcasm from his voice.

"Are you calling me a liar?" Flint Shouting's voice suddenly had an unaccustomed edge.

"No. I'm saying you can't beat the scalped man, any more than the two of us can charge over that ridge and kill all of the Monkolas. You aren't a liar, you're just stupid."

Flint Shouting's face worked through astonishment into fury. Red Shoes felt his own blood rise. Who did Flint Shouting think he was? It wasn't as if they were kin. And the Wichita would never know what had happened to him if he died here, days from their territory—if they even cared, which they probably didn't. He was, after all, an adulterer, a thief, and a liar. No one would care if he . . .

No.

"I'm sorry," Red Shoes managed. "I'm tired. I'm not angry at you, Flint Shouting. I shouldn't have called you stupid."

The younger man's lips stayed tight for a moment and then he uttered a crippled little chuckle.

"You aren't the first to say it, or the first to be right." He broke the gaze. The white people were the only people in the world who considered it polite to stare into someone's eyes when talking to them. With most people, it was a challenge. They were no longer challenging each other.

"So how do we get their horses?"

"I have some ideas. We can—"

"Hsst! The leaf canoe!"

Red Shoes immediately intensified the obscurement that kept him and Flint Shouting from the eyes of spirits. They were still visible to eye and telescope, however, so they crouched lower, watching the thing come.

"I thought you destroyed it, back when you called the lightning."

"I did. This is another."

"How many do they have?"

"They have a lot. Peter says he thinks the main body of airships will arrive in the east when the army does. The ones accompanying the army are just to supply food and carry the leaders."

"And hunt us."

"Yes. It's how they find us, when we fool their trackers." It was a small ship, oddly shaped—very thin, seen from the edge, and shaped like the leaf of the cassina plant—hence Flint Shouting's name for it. It flew more like a bird gliding than the big ships—it had no red globes carrying it aloft. Its engine was a spirit, though, of some sort. It could move fast, very fast—in fact, it seemed to prefer to. But it could slow and hover as well.

"I'm glad they sent another one," Red Shoes murmured. "It's given me an idea."

They worked their way down the other side of the hills, switchback. Despite appearances, their mounted pursuers were still hours behind them; they would have to find the same ford in the river that Red Shoes and his companions had, and it would likely take them some time to pick up the trail on the other side.

They were back in the country of low trees—few were

more than twice as tall as Red Shoes. It made him feel like a giant trying to hide in a landscape he dwarfed, especially with the leaf canoe searching for them. It was better—many times better—than the grass, but he would not feel comfortable again until he was home in an honest wood, where the sky was pushed up where it belonged.

The others awaited them in a clump of scrubby oak. The woman—who called herself simply Grief—tracked them in at arrowpoint. They had exhausted their powder on a group of Snakes who managed to catch up with them. The Snakes had used all their powder in the battle, too, but they had been armed with bows.

Tug looked as if he was asleep. Tsar Peter was scraping awkwardly at his own face with a knife. There was a fair amount of blood; he had knicked himself more than once. Red Shoes wondered if it was some sort of ritual of kingship, this cutting of the beard. He plucked his own fine hairs out by the root. "Well?" the tsar asked.

"Some twenty of them, pretty near. I think they have a Kansa guiding them. The rest look like those people you called Monkolas."

"Mongols. Were there any Russian uniforms amongst them?"

"Two, I think. Also, they've sent a new airship. This one looks different, and it's faster."

"Shaped like this, and flat?" The tsar traced an oval in the dirt.

"Yes."

"A Swedenborg."

Red Shoes shrugged to indicate that meant nothing to him. The tsar did not elaborate.

"The horses 're near dead, han't they?" Tug sat up, rubbing his eyes.

"Yes."

Peter directed his finger at Flint Shouting. "I thought

you said we could reach your people before they caught up with us."

"I was wrong," Flint Shouting said simply. Red Shoes knew the Wichita didn't like the tsar very much. He thought he talked too much and smelled bad.

"No fresh horses, no powder, no shot—and no allies. That's the situation?"

"Yes."

"We can get *all* those things," Flint Shouting said. "If we are brave and strong and swift, we can get them."

"He means to fight for them?" Peter asked.

Red Shoes nodded. "And he's right. That's exactly what we'll have to do. And we'll do it tonight. For the moment, though, we need to make a little more distance south."

They rode, and the big sky dimmed and darkened.

Tsar Peter came alongside him. He was a large man, the tsar, and he looked uncomfortable on the pony that sagged beneath him.

"Our chances are bad, aren't they?"

"They could be better."

"May I ask you a question?"

Red Shoes wondered why white men said such things. Why did one need permission to ask a question? One either knew whether asking a question was appropriate or not. Asking permission to ask it would not make it any more or less so.

But he had spent a lot of time with the white people. "Of course," he said.

"Why are you helping me?"

That surprised Red Shoes, but it shouldn't have. He thought for a moment, to formulate his answer. There was another thing about white people—they didn't like pauses in conversation. They didn't want you to have time to mull something over. If you didn't answer right away, they imagined that they had somehow not framed the question clearly.

So the tsar started again. "You say you fought against me

once. There are many men who can make that claim. Few would be disposed to aid me against my enemies. Nor am I foolish enough to think that the prerogatives of royalty mean anything to a savage. Oh, I'm sure you're loyal enough to your own king—"

"We don't really have a king, as such."

"No ruler?"

"We have a *minko*, but his power is mostly the power to explain to the people why they ought to do what they already *want* to do." He suddenly felt the anger again, stirring in his belly like a bad meal. "You ask why I help you. I don't know the answer to that. You are an important man, part of huge movements in the world. At this moment I cannot say whether it would be better—for my people, myself, the world at large—to kill you or save you."

"But you chose to save me."

Red Shoes smiled. "I can always kill you later. I cannot raise you from the dead."

The tsar smiled somewhat wolfishly. "Considering the things I've seen you do, I wonder about that. But I think I understand you now. Good. And I think . . . I think you will find my goals to your liking."

"What are your goals?"

"To frustrate these creatures who style themselves angels, to take my empire back from their puppets, to repair my people and keep them from war, on this or any other continent." He paused, ducked a low branch. "All I have ever wanted was what was best for Russia. To make it equal to the nations of the West. I strove at that for years. Then, one day, we were *more* than equal—not because Russia had become such a fine place, but because the world had gone mad and the great nations of the West had fallen. I once admired those countries—I saw so much good in them, so much that my own people needed. It was intolerable that it should all slip away just as it was in my grasp. And the world, being mad, began to make my nation colder. So, my mission changed. I extended my empire, that I might preserve what I could of Holland, France, England—and so that I could have the fertile fields of Poland, Bohemia, and Hungary to feed my people with."

"And, as I understand it, you attained most of those things years ago."

"Yes. And then I was determined to turn my eye inward. And yet always I was drawn into another war, and another. I see now that I was manipulated by my evil councilors, that I fought battles that there was never any need for. When I discovered some of my generals plotting to invade this continent—the English, French, and Spanish colonies, that is—I put an end to it. I had one of them beheaded. I thought the matter settled.

"But, as we see, it is not. They *do* invade, and Russia cannot bear it."

"They seem well armed. Why do you think they cannot win?"

"Win? What does that mean? We have many weapons I hoped never to use, things which have not been seen since the days of the Old Testament. Oh, we have the might to conquer this place, I think, to crush any armies here. But it's so big—we could never hold it! And think what taxes they must have levied, in my absence, what they will continue to bring to pay for this! And, all the while, as our might and blood is poured on this ground, the Turk waits at our south, and a hundred barbarian tribes to the east, and still Charles XII plots against me from Venice. No, this is a plan calculated for the downfall of all nations, Russia included."

Red Shoes nodded. "The spirits mean to end us all. I have seen it."

"An apocalypse? But an apocalypse without God," the tsar murmured. His face twitched ferociously. "In any event, I am in your debt. By extension, I am in the debt of your people. I do not forget my debts."

Red Shoes just nodded, and they rode on, each to his own thoughts, until near sundown.

The leaf canoe flitted here and there on the horizon, but he was certain that it hadn't found them yet. That was good.

He drew his horse out of the line. "The rest of you continue on, as we've been going. I have something I have to do—a false trail to lay."

"I'll help," Tug offered.

"No, this is the sort of trail only I can lay."

"You'll rejoin us?"

"Yes. After sundown. No matter what you do, stay hidden from the airship. Don't let it see you."

"Got y'."

He rode off at right angles, trying to imagine the lay of the land. The Mongols seemed to be good trackers, and they had a Kansa scout, but he and the rest had lost them countless times. It was the airship that always found them again. He hoped this had made the Mongols lazy. Up until now he had done his best to avoid the airship. Why should they expect he would reveal himself to it?

He hunted for the right sort of spot, knowing he did not have a lot of time. He found it by moonlight, a well-sheltered campsite in a hollow, with good prospects for sentinels and a clean stream for drinking.

Now he let *hoshonti* slip, let the scent of his shadow-children waft up. Distantly, he felt the cautious triumph of the spirits in the searching ship.

Now he cloaked himself again, to make it seem a momentary omission.

It was dark, but the moon would be good for another few hours, and it was full and silver. His plan counted on several things, now. It counted on the Mongols continuing until the moon set and the accuracy with which the ship could guide them to this spot.

Now he went to work. He produced what remained of his shot: eight lead balls. He had kept them back from the others, anticipating this. They were out of powder, anyway.

He moved quickly, pressing them into hiding places in the

dead interiors of bushes, in the thatch beneath the grass. The vegetation was brittle; it had been a dry winter and a dry spring.

Then he remounted and rode back to where he reckoned the others to be. He found them easily. They hadn't gone much farther than where he had left them.

Peter and Tug clapped their weapons when he entered the campsite, but Flint Shouting chuckled and stepped from the low forest, arrow fitted to his stolen Mongol bow. It was an odd weapon, made of laminated horn and wood, powerful, better suited for firing from horseback even than those of the plains folks.

"Are we ready?"

"Yes," Red Shoes said. "This is what we will do. I will use my shadowchildren to start some fires around their camp. Flint Shouting and I will try to slip in and cut the tethers of some of their horses. The fire will drive the horses downwind, and that's where the rest of you will be."

"Ah—won't the fire drive the Mongols downwind as well?" Tug asked.

"Yes. But horses run faster than men. Catch a horse or two and go. Flint Shouting and I will try to get some at the source. The fire will be causing some confusion by then—they'll think we're out in the woods, setting it."

"This is a risky plan. I'm not sure that I know much about catching horses," Peter said.

"It's no great thing, Majesty," Tug said. "I'll be there to help."

"*I* cut tether."

All heads swung toward the woman. Flint Shouting had been trying to teach her their lingua franca—which was, fittingly enough, French—but it had been unclear whether she had really been paying attention. Now, however, she spoke in understandable, though heavily accented, French.

"Have you done this before?"

"Yes."

Was she lying? She had shown herself both fierce and competent back on the Russian airship.

"Very well," Red Shoes said.

"What happens if all three of you get killed?" Peter asked. "I certainly don't know my way in this land. Do you, Tug?"

"Not hardly."

"Good point. Flint Shouting, you stay with them."

"No!"

"Yes." He switched to Mobilian. "I need you with them, Flint Shouting. Two white men, alone out here? They won't even be able to *find* the rest of us. And neither of them has the faintest idea how to use a bow. It's important, Flint Shouting, more important than your honor."

"I want to kill one of those Monkolas," Flint Shouting complained. "What if I never get the chance to kill another one?"

"All the more reason you should not go. This is not a raid for scalps, just horse stealing. Anyway, I have a feeling that you'll have more than ample opportunity to kill a Mongol, my friend. But if we don't do things my way, you may never get to brag of it, and that's the important part."

"I can always brag to my ancestors."

"Not as much fun as bragging to the pretty girls on a summer afternoon," Red Shoes said.

"Huh. That's not a bad point."

"*Achukma okeh?* It is good?"

"*Okeh.*"

"Let's go, then. The moon is set."

The Mongols weren't trying to be quiet, so he knew that they had taken the bait long before he reached them. They had camped just where he hoped.

They separated, Flint Shouting, the tsar, and Tug remaining back and downwind. He and Grief crept closer.

He summoned *hoshonti*, bending what dim light there was

around Grief and himself. The most sharp-eyed might notice a distortion in the air, nothing more.

They crept nearer and nearer, until they could see the light of the fire through the trees, then the faces around the fire. And the horses, beyond the circle of light.

Red Shoes closed his eyes, wishing he could smoke Ancient Tobacco to strengthen himself. That might give him away, so he made do without it, sending off his only other remaining shadowchild—a little spirit who had but a single ability, an affinity with the ferment of lead. He commanded the little spirit to find lead and break it apart, release the fire inside it. It started off. Red Shoes hoped it survived long enough to accomplish its task, before the spirits accompanying the Mongols discovered and destroyed it. If that happened, then even *this* slimmest of hopes was gone.

10.

Suspicions and Ribs

They buried Irena that same day in the cold Siberian soil. They could not dig very deep, for the earth was frozen, and so they piled a cairn of stones to keep the wild beasts away. Father Dimitrov—the single priest Adrienne had reluctantly included in the expedition—conducted the services. His words and motions seemed senseless, beneath those cold skies. His God—the god of miter and vestments, who listened to prayer in ornate, close, safe churches—Adrienne could not imagine him here, in this wild place. Liturgy here should sound more like the call of a hunting bird, the moan of the wind.

Adrienne wondered if the Tartar woman was watching and, if she watched, what she thought. How would she bury a murder victim, that the corpse would not rise to trouble the living again?

Hercule held himself as straight as an ash, the expression on his face as impenetrable as a figure carved of the same wood.

Other than the priest, no one said much of anything. Afterward, they boarded the airships and continued on their way.

She had to seek Hercule out, and found him on the bridge, watching the land unfold beneath them.

He noticed her approaching from the corner of his eye. He still wore the funeral black. He looked like a Puritan preacher, a strange and unbecoming fashion on him.

"Hercule, I—"

"I gave it out that she was killed by Tartars," he said, quietly. "No one else knows."

For an instant she was so furious she couldn't talk. "Why, Hercule? She did not deserve to die."

The face he turned to her then was so incredulous he looked like some sort of ape, pretending to human emotion.

"What?"

"I *saw* you, Hercule—in that quarter of the forest, when you were supposed to be hunting—"

"You think *I* killed her?"

"I—" She hesitated.

"*Par dieu,* you *do*!" he exploded. That was loud enough that the helmsman turned his head. "Lash that and leave," Hercule shouted at him. "Now."

When the fellow was gone, he faced her again. She noticed his eyes were red. "Understand me," he said, his voice as low and dangerous as she had ever heard it. "I did not love Irena as I love you, but I was not without feeling for her. She was the mother of my children. She cared for me when your heart was cold. If you think for one second—"

"I'm sorry, it's just that I saw you riding in the direction I found her—"

"So naturally you assume I murdered her. What, because then the way would be clear to you? Holy hosts, but don't you think I know you would never marry me, Irena or no Irena? Haven't you made that perfectly known to me? You think I would murder my own wife and leave my children motherless all because of *you*?"

His anger made her feel small suddenly, like a little girl being chastised—like a little girl who deserved it.

"I'm sorry, Hercule."

"You really don't know who killed Irena?" he snapped. "Or is this some vast pretense to keep me from my duty?"

"What are you talking about?"

"To anyone not blinded by your sympathies—" He struggled for control and found it. "Crecy murdered her," he said.

"Crecy?"

"Good God, Adrienne, it's no secret that Crecy loves you, that she would do anything to protect you. It's also no great secret that Irena made an attempt on your life. Crecy acted to make certain my poor wife would never threaten you again."

"No," Adrienne said, "I don't believe it. She was as surprised as I."

The look he gave her was an old one to them both. *This is Crecy,* it said. Indeed, in the past Crecy had proven quite adept at deception. In the present, as well, when the target of her lies was their enemies.

"I still don't believe it. I saw a Tartar woman—"

"Now you invent monsters in the wood to excuse her? No. It must have been Crecy."

"Hercule, do not be hasty."

He laughed bitterly. "This from the woman who came to accuse me of murdering my own wife?"

"I've apologized for that. It was just strange to see you, riding there, and then to find her so."

"I *was* looking for her. We had argued earlier, and I wished to press an apology. The guards said they had seen her walking into the forest in that direction."

"I thought you did it. You think Crecy did it. Crecy thinks I did it."

"One of us is lying, and if I had to wager on it, I damn sure know who I'd pick."

"What will you do?"

"A duel seems appropriate, I think?"

"No. Hercule, she would kill you."

"I've always been touched by your faith in me."

"And if she doesn't, you will kill her. Neither prospect pleases me. Give me some time, Hercule."

"For what?"

"It may be that none of us is lying. Someone else on these ships may have had cause to kill Irena."

"Impossible. She was the most mild, inoffensive—"

"Hercule, she *shot* at me. I think you did not know her as well as you thought."

His head tilted away from her. "Perhaps not," he admitted.

"Go console your children. Give me time, so that you do not rashly deprive them of a father as well."

He nodded, then suddenly pressed his face into his hands. "I haven't even told them yet," he said. His voice quavered. "I don't know what to tell them."

Adrienne wanted to comfort him. She wanted to help him.

She had not the faintest idea of how to go about it, and so left him there, weeping into his hands.

Menshikov raised himself on one elbow and regarded her. "Rumor says *you* did it," he said, "or commanded your demons to. It seems reasonable to me."

She frowned, and he laughed. "I'm joking, of course."

"How would you know what everyone says, lying abed?" Adrienne demanded.

Menshikov coughed and sat up, wincing. "I know you think ill of me. I deserve it, I suppose—I was, after all, as drunk as a churchman when the usurpers took the throne I guarded. But consider—all these years I have survived where others have not. I have endured the tsar's fits of rage, a hundred efforts to supplant me as his favorite, more than one knife aimed at my back. All this despite the fact that I am not nearly as clever as I think I am. It is because I always keep words in my ear. I cultivate friendships where I must. I have an instinct for it."

"Do you think I killed her?"

"I do not care. She was no friend of mine, nor was her father. What I do care about is finding my tsar."

"How do you imagine the two are related?"

He snorted. "These people were content to follow you to the ends of the Earth when they thought you a saint. And yet, turn a saint upside down and you get a devil, yes? You are dangerously near having your feet in the air. No one hates so much as one who once loved, that is a fact. Are there hardships ahead of us? Yes. Will these people face them for you? I begin to doubt it."

Adrienne pressed her hands into her lap, a demure habit still with her from childhood. "You imagine yourself a better leader, Prince Menshikov?"

"I am the leader the tsar intended, am I not? I thank you for rescuing me, of course—"

"It was an afterthought," Adrienne told him. "Such was not my primary aim."

"Nevertheless, you knew it was politic to do it, and you did."

"I'm beginning to regret it, nevertheless."

"Well. I suppose you could kill me, too." He spread his hands and smiled. "I'm joking, of course."

She smiled coldly. "If you really think me a murderess, that is an extraordinarily stupid suggestion to put in my ear."

"I said I was joking. I don't think you killed Irena. Assassination is not your style."

She allowed herself an ironic smile at that. She had, after all, tried to assassinate Louis XIV, the greatest king the world had yet known. Still, Menshikov was right: she had failed because she didn't have murder in her.

Then.

She leaned close. "Here is the plain truth," she breathed. "I seek the tsar, yes. But that is not my most pressing goal. I am searching for something much more dear to me and much more dangerous to the world. So let me tell you without embellishment, Prince Menshikov, that while I did not kill Irena, I will not hesitate to kill *you* if you place yourself in my way. I rescued you as a favor to the tsar. But the tsar may or may not still be alive, and I would much rather live with his displeasure than surrender my command. Furthermore, once the tsar learns of your graft and incompetence, he may well demand your execution or exile himself—you know Peter. All that presupposes, of course, that the throne of Russia is ever regained, something even the tsar will not likely do without my aid. In brief, dear sir, I am more valuable to him than you, and should he be forced to turn a blind eye to the fact that you expired in my care—wounded and sick as you are—I *do* think he will manage it. Are we—" she reached out and tapped his forehead "—is this getting in there?"

Menshikov's face twisted into a sour grimace. "You will need my aid," he said. "You will need a leader the people trust."

She uttered a bright, false laugh. "Well, who do we have like that? No one." She patted his arm. "I'm joking, of course!" But she leaned in again. "You understood all I said?"

"I know when I'm being threatened."

"Oh, *very* good. Then I shan't have to repeat myself, as I might to a dull-witted child."

He shrugged as if indifferent, but his face betrayed his fury. The prince was not a subtle man.

"Now, if you will excuse me, I think I will retire. Sweet dreams."

His only answer was to lie back down.

Coffee with the students offered her some relief, though she thought she caught worried and speculative glances even from them.

Linné and Émilie advanced the preliminaries of their work, and Adrienne was interested enough in it that her cares were, for a short time, forgotten.

"In classifying the malakim," Linné began, "we are presented with the problem of criteria, as they are mostly unseen, and their characteristics are unseen as well. We started by classifying their effects—that is, we know from mademoiselle our teacher that some mediate between affinities. Others have connection with the elements of matter, and manipulate that matter in small ways. Still others, such as those that move this ship, repel against gravity.

"The most interesting thing about this is that each sort is

capable of contacting or repelling a single kind of affinity or matter—except in the case of the mediators, which blindly create links between elements they can *not* effect in any way singly. This means that the malakim differ from creatures of matter in being even narrower in their design. God had made each for a *single* purpose."

"You mean as he made men?" Elizavet asked.

"And some not even good for *that*," Crecy quipped.

"No, no!" Elizavet said. "I was not joking! I mean that some men are designed by God to be kings, others to be peasants, others to work at the docks—"

"Don't forget," Adrienne broke in, "that while your father is tsar, he has also labored at the docks, built ships with his own hands."

"Oh."

"In theory, any man could be a king," Émilie said. "And in history it has happened that a man of less than royal birth rose to lead his country. Cromwell in England, for instance."

"Who?" Elizavet asked.

"Continue, Linné," Adrienne said, shaking her head.

"Yes, well—but the tsarevna gives us an analogy to work with. Imagine the ranks of men, from emperor to peasant. Imagine that, by design, one *cannot* do the job of another. Suppose, too, that God designs the kings and tsars of the malakim, the kings and tsars in turn create the dukes and archdukes, those in turn design and produce the counts. . . ."

"Or better," Émilie put in, "God designs a workman, and the workman designs his tools. The tools, in turn, design the tools necessary to reproduce themselves—"

"This becomes very confusing," Elizavet opined. "Now we have shovels making the spade with two backs? I don't understand."

Adrienne did, however. "I've never—That's very, very interesting, if true. On what do you base this?"

"On Newton's notes and on your own. The malakim are made of patterns of affinities, which can be observed. The lesser sort are simpler, but their affinities are to the greater sort—as if, well, as in the Bible story, where Eve was made from Adam's rib. As if the more powerful malakim, the greater ones, pull pieces of themselves to fashion lesser—and more specifically natured—ones."

Adrienne had a sudden, vivid memory of the forest woman, of the spirits that were like appendages of her self. What had she said? About learning to use her own substance and the substance of spirits?

"I want to see your notes on this," Adrienne said, "all of them. I want you to walk me through it, step by step. If this is true, it is the most significant discovery regarding the malakim ever made."

"It is hypothesis only," Linné cautioned, "based on too little data. What we really need is what Newton had. We need to reproduce his experiments but take them further than he did."

"Tell me what you need, and we will see what we can come up with. Perhaps we can use parts of one of the taloi, as Newton did. . . ."

She stopped, almost out of breath. It was unbelievable. Her heart was pounding, and in her belly, already, she knew they were right. How had she missed this so completely?

Because she hadn't looked, of course. She had let her brain be charmed to sleep by lullabies of power.

That night she dreamed again of walking through the crumbling ruins of Versailles. Light fell through huge gaps in the ceiling, and pools of stagnant water collected on the marble floor, grimy mirrors that let her see herself. She wore the *grand habit* Louis XIV had given her, and her hair was caught up in an elaborate tower.

"Hello, my love."

A soft voice, a rustic accent. A man, stepping from the shadows, lean and lanky, beautiful to her eyes.

"Nicolas?"

"Yes."

"Where have you been?"

"Waiting. I wait still."

She moved to clasp him, but he backed away.

"Nicolas, will you not hold me?"

"I cannot. It is not to be—not yet. But walk with me."

"Very well." They began walking, beyond the rotting palace into the gardens. The gardens had once been a marvel of the world, their precise geometries laid out by as remorseless a logic as any equation. Now thorns entangled statues, clumps of yellowed grass sprouted through the stone pavements.

"Remember when first we walked here?" she asked him.

"Of course. You explained the gardens to me."

"You wondered why something so beautiful from a distance could be so painful to walk in."

"But now I understand," he told her, his eyes dark and sad. "I understand that they were a product of reason."

"What?"

"Look again."

She did, and suddenly all was transformed. The returning wild was beautiful, the false symmetries it destroyed were the ugliness.

"Thus grow things when only God shapes them," Nicolas murmured. "Don't you see? You and your kind—Newton, the rest—they pretended that reason was the way to know God. It is not. It is the antithesis of God, a weapon aimed at him. It is an addiction, for it seems to offer the chance to be *as* God. You know this, in your heart, but deny it, build elaborate pretensions that you are doing *his* work."

"You aren't Nicolas."

"No."

"But you aren't Uriel either."

"No. Uriel is my servant."

"You claim, then, to be God?"

The thing in the shape of Nicolas laughed gently. "I do not.

I will tell you the truth, Mademoiselle, I am no more certain that there is a God than you are."

"I do not doubt God."

"Of course you do. For years you have seen the angels, commanded them, worked through them. You have looked upon our world, the real world, which lies behind the cloak of gross matter. And yet where have you ever seen God?"

"Uriel told me that God is outside the world."

"So we believe, for it is convenient. After all, that would explain why *we* can't see him either."

She lifted her chin, challenging. "Why do you tell me this? Do you plan to kill me?" A sudden thought. "Did you kill Irena?"

The image of Nicolas shook its head. "Your students are right: the more powerful we are, the more removed we are from the finite, from matter. Our humblest and most lowly servants are those most effective in your world. I command legions of my kind but cannot personally stir a single atom. Does that seem strange to you?"

"It begs the question. You have human servants."

"Yes, of course. I did not bring about the death of Irena. I do not care about such things."

"What do you care about?"

"I want you to find your son."

"Why?"

"Because I cannot find him myself. Because he is in the hands of my enemies, and yours as well. Because they will use him to ignite the fires in the dark engines."

"I should think you would want that," she said. "The death of reason, the end of our influence in your realm."

"No. To destroy you is wrong. You are our children, in a way."

"In what way?"

"I don't care to explain that, nor do you need to know it. I want you quiet, not dead. Like this garden, you are most beautiful when you let nature rule."

Now Adrienne laughed. "It would seem that to defy nature *is* our nature," she said. "For time and again, you must stop us."

"You may be right. That is why we fear you so."

"Who are you?"

"I have had many names." The form shifted, clouded, and refigured itself. Now it was Crecy. "You might call me Lilith or Sophia or Mother. It does not matter what you call me. All that matters is this: of all of my kind that exist, of all of the princes of the air—only I remain loyal to your race. All of the others have fallen away."

"Why? Why now?"

"Largely because of you. More because of your son." Crecy stepped into the shadows.

"Wait. I've been told before that my son is dangerous. But I've also been told that the greatest danger is if we are together."

"True. But that is also our greatest hope. Much more I cannot say, just this: it *may* be in your power to save your race. But be assured, you *certainly* hold the power to destroy it."

Part Three

Dark Engines

The changing of bodies into light, and light into bodies, is very conformable to the course of Nature, which seems delighted with transmutations.

—Sir Isaac Newton,
Optics 1717

"I am going to die, so it makes no difference to me whether the sickness or a man kills me. I know I am a bad man for having so long a time concealed, in order to preserve my life, what I am going to tell you. I am the cause of the death of my nation, therefore, I merit death, but let me not be eaten by dogs."

—Words of a Natchez temple guardian who polluted the Sacred Fire, related in 1725

And there came two angels to Sodom at even . . .

—Genesis 19:1

1.

First Blood

James Oglethorpe held up his hand to halt the company, and put a finger to his lips for silence. His hawklike gaze picked across the Indian fields to the woods beyond.

"Hear that?" he asked the Indian next to him in a voice just louder than a breath.

Tomochichi, the chief of the Yamacraw, shrugged his ancient shoulders. "I'm getting old," he murmured, "too many muskets fired too close to my ears. What do you hear?"

"A horse, I think, running."

"One of the scouts?"

"Perhaps. But one of ours or one of theirs?"

Tomochichi stared at the woods, until his eyes almost seemed to glaze over.

"Spirits out there," he said, "walking through the woods on thin black legs."

"Do they know we are here?"

"Not yet. I can hide us for a little while."

There had been a time when Oglethorpe thought the old chief was—however admirable in other ways—a superstitious savage. He had left that time years in the past. The red men had always known what philosophers like Franklin had only just recently proven through the methods of science: that terrible things walked in the world. When Tomochichi said something about spirits, it was best to listen. Oglethorpe drew his pistol and lay it across his lap, narrowing his eyes at the middle-distant trees.

An instant later, a rider broke into the clearing, riding as if the devil were nipping at his mount's tail. It was a Maroon, his face an inky dot at that distance.

A few moments later his features, shiny with sweat, resolved. It was Unoka.

"T'ey over t' next hill." The black man grunted.

"How many?"

"March in column, t'ree deep, maybe two arrow shot long. Four hundred, maybe. T'ey hab t'ose metal men you talk about, about t'irty, I say."

"Artillery? Flying ships?"

"I seen no o' t'at," Unoka replied, perhaps a bit skeptically.

"Coming behind, then. This lot is just to soften us up. 'Tis clear they mean to take Fort Moore. Very well, fellows, let's soften *them* up. Captain Unoka, take about thirty of your men and drop down in the tall grass on the right side of the trail."

"Out in t' open?" Unoka frowned. "You tryin' t' kill us all so no worries about us later?"

Oglethorpe locked gazes with the Maroon. He had known the fellow would be trouble. His people were less given to taking orders even than the Indians.

"You're under my orders; you'll do what I say."

"T'ey *my* men."

"Listen, you stinking, insolent—"

"The Yamacraw will take that task," Tomochichi interrupted.

Oglethorpe bit back a comment to the Indian to mind his own business. He wanted the Unoka to pay attention to him, damnit all, not have someone else step up for them.

On the other hand, they didn't have time for a protracted argument.

"Very well, Captain Unoka. Withdraw your men to the rear, if you wish, and the Yamacraw will take your position." He turned to his aide, Jack Jones. "Tell Mr. Parmenter to deploy some rangers, as well—fifteen should do."

He had *told* Franklin this would be useless.

He mopped his head with a dirty kerchief and took a deep

breath. *Get ahold of yourself. You need your wits about you, now.* This was America, after all, where trust was earned rather than given freely. As irritating as it was, there was no particular reason for the Negro to trust him. After all, Unoka had been taken like an animal from his native country and brought here to work to death, hadn't he?

It would be hard to trust, after that.

Unoka drove that point home. "Where you goin' t' be, Lord English, while t'ey out t'ere wit'out no cover?" He gestured at the Yamacraw entering the field.

Oglethorpe flashed him a contemptuous smile. "If you're man enough to find out, stay here by my side," he retorted.

"Is so, t'en," Unoka said. "First I move my men back."

"Do that. Perhaps you can find a nursery for them, somewhere in the rear."

The rest of the scouts returned. About half were Indians, the other half Maroons. It perplexed him that the Negroes were brave and willing to ride alone toward the enemy but not to stand and fight. Trust, again, he supposed. As scouts they made their own decisions. If death caught up with them, it was their own fault, not the fault of a commander they didn't know.

It was different with the Yamacraw. He had earned their trust over the years. He even fancied they thought of him as a kindred spirit, and he watched them take their positions with a certain pride. From this raised prospect, he could just make them out as they lay on their bellies in the grass. The Pretender's men, coming from lower ground, shouldn't be able to see them at all.

"Go back and get the devil gun," he told Jack Jones. The young man—just a boy really, fair haired and blue eyed—nodded vigorously and rode to get the scientifical weapon Franklin had given them.

Then there was just the waiting, which in his experience was the better nine tenths of any battle. He checked his weapons and listened.

They heard the Pretender's forces long before they saw them. They were making no particular effort at silence, chattering in ranks as they marched.

He would see that they soon learned to watch that. This wasn't Europe, and they weren't fighting a European war.

The column appeared, led by two Indians—Cusabo?—and several mounted men in bloodred coats. Behind them was a small company of light horse—maybe forty men—and behind them the taloi. Unoka could count pretty well—there were thirty of the automatons. Watching their unnatural gait sent an unaccustomed thrill of fear up his spine. Men he knew how to fight, but he hadn't seen these things battling the Turks and the French with Prince Eugène. While Franklin had explained them, the young philosopher knew no better than anyone else how they would figure in a skirmish. How many bullets would it take to stop one? He hoped Franklin's depneumifier—the devil gun—would do its work. Where was Jones, anyway?

The redcoats were halfway across the field—within shouting distance—before they saw Oglethorpe and his horsemen, square on the trail, just inside the noonday shadow of the woods.

An officer in front shouted, and the drums beat a halt. The column came to good order; these men were well trained.

"Good day to you, sirs," Oglethorpe called. "I am General James Oglethorpe. Welcome to America."

"I am General McMinn," one of the redcoats returned, "and I demand your surrender in the name of His Majesty James III."

McMinn. He had served with a McMinn in Europe. Too bad he couldn't make out the fellow's face from this distance.

"I can't oblige you, sir. This is the sovereign territory of the Commonwealth Province of South Carolina, and it is under my protection. You may retreat or you may die. These are the choices I give you."

"The rightful king of England and her colonies recognize no such state," McMinn shouted back. "If you will not surrender, we shall be forced to take your surrender with the sword."

"As you wish, sir," Oglethorpe replied. He kicked his horse, hard, drew his pistol, and charged down the trail, the rest of his cavalry spreading behind him like a raptor's wings.

He almost laughed at the enemy's reaction. The horse wheeled, trying to form to meet a charge they should have expected but hadn't. Did they really think he would parley? Probably. The column of foot, meanwhile, was for an instant paralyzed before they scrambled forward into firing lines.

The first volley roared out, just plain old guns blowing blue-gray clouds and lead balls. Most of these last thudded into trees behind them, though one of his men let out an unholy shriek. If anyone else was hit, they took it more quietly.

He could make out enemy faces now—some frightened, some determined, most both. Their cavalry had finally gotten moving, and he aimed his weapon very carefully at the lead man.

As he pulled the trigger, the Yamacraw and rangers rose out of the grass at either side and lit powder, so that the field was suddenly an alley, bounded by two walls of smoke and fire and ended by forest. Men screamed and fell, and the forming lines milled once more into disarray.

He didn't have time to take any more of that in. His Fahrenheit gun roared, spewing a mist of red-hot silver into the first rank of horsemen. The jagged bolt of a *kraftpistole* missed him by a few hairs, and he whispered a quick thanks to God almighty as he drew his basket-hilted broadsword and cut down the first redcoat to reach him.

The Pretender's cavalry crumpled at the first charge, parting as if by magic. The first line of infantry was still trying to fix their plug bayonets when he swept into them, too, laying about with a sword that was already gory to the hilt. He had another glimpse of the column stretching back into the woods, trying desperately to find targets in the smoke and grass. They fell, and they fell, and they fell.

After that, there were no more bullets in the front lines. The battle went to bayonet, hanger, and broadsword. He noticed Unoka, laying about with a pair of tomahawks. The savage wasn't afraid to fight, at least.

When they reached the taloi, things changed. Jets of flame suddenly cut through the Colonial horse; the air filled with the stench of burning hair and flesh. Some of it was his own—he felt his eyebrows singe from a near miss—and he suddenly understood something he should have guessed before.

McMinn had artillery, all right. It marched with him. The *taloi* were the artillery.

"The devil gun," he bellowed, wheeling his mount. "Fire the Goddamned devil gun!"

He saw Jones, wide-eyed, swinging the awkward forklike weapon up, then saw the young face and most of his head vanish as a *kraftpistole* bolt jagged through him. Cursing, he fought his steed that way, butchering an infantryman to get past him. If he did not reach the weapon, they were certainly done.

Unoka was faster. The black man pounced out of his saddle, clubbing an opponent in the face with the flat of his ax, and in two quick steps had the device. He spent no time at all figuring at it, but raised it up and slid the trigger—he must have been watching when Franklin demonstrated.

The taloi dropped in their tracks, every last one of them.

At that point, the army of the Pretender, which outnumbered them more than two to one, turned and simply ran.

"Let them go!" James shouted. "Do not—" But here came the Yamacraw and another bunch of Indians—Kiawahs—from up the hill, shrieking into the woods in pursuit. For an instant, he almost charged after them, for the sheer love of carnage. The Indians fought not from the head but from the heart. Territory, goods, and national sentiment meant very little to them. Covering themselves in glory, bringing the scalps of their enemies back to adorn their villages—that's what they fought for.

As well try to stop the tide as stop them going after a fleeing enemy.

He sympathized. He also felt the pulse of savagery in his veins. Unfortunately, he knew something that they didn't. An army this well trained would not flee for long. They had surprised McMinn's forces with a quick, vicious charge, but in time they would form up again. However many losses they had taken, they still outnumbered his own forces considerably. But the Indians weren't stupid either. When that happened, they could run as well as anyone, and better than most.

But he couldn't risk himself and his horsemen in a foolhardy chase that might suddenly find them enclosed. He reined his men back and surveyed the field.

Perhaps fifty of the redcoats lay dead or dying, and a good fifteen of his own. Plus the taloi, damn their eyeless faces. If it weren't for them, the battle would have gone much more his way.

"Cut those damned things up," he told Philamon Parmenter, the captain of his rangers, "in case they take a notion to come back to life. Salvage any weapon that looks like we might be able to use. Then fall back to the hill."

"Are we gonna hold it?" Parmenter wiped blood from his bulldoglike face with the back of his sleeve.

"No. We'll pick at 'em. Teach 'em what Indian fighting is all about."

"I hope they don't learn too quick," the ranger replied.

Oglethorpe nodded, trying to see who he had lost.

Jack, of course, poor lad. By chance he had fallen next to McMinn, who had been shot through the throat. Oglethorpe rolled the corpse over with the toe of his black riding boot and saw, with some relief, that it was not the same man he had fought with in Flanders—he was far too young for that, scarcely older than Jack. But seeing him lying there, in his sash with its white rose emblem, he felt a sudden grief. In his heart, he had always believed the Stuarts were the true kings of England. It would have taken so little for him to be fighting with these men, instead of against them. If he had stayed in Europe, instead of taking a tour of the margravate, if the great comet had not destroyed London, stranding him here . . .

No, too many ifs. These people were his enemies, Jacobites or not. Watching the rangers as they hacked apart the tough stuff of the automatons, he knew that for a fact. Any friend of the devil was no friend of his.

He caught Unoka watching him.

"Yes, sir?" he asked.

"You a damn crazy fellow," the African opined. "T'e gen'ral go in back o' t'e army, not chargin' in t'e cannon!"

"So I've heard," James replied. "Mr. Unoka, from here on out, I expect you to obey my orders and have your men obey them, too. Otherwise, we can bloody well do without you."

Unoka shrugged. "Ma'be it be so."

"Not maybe, sir. Next time, you fight as part of this army, or we part company." He hesitated. He ought to praise the Maroon for his own work just now, but that might weaken his admonition. He turned, saying nothing.

The light pattering of gunfire in the woods suddenly took on a new character—orderly volleys, many muskets firing in unison.

"That's it," Oglethorpe shouted. "Start the retreat."

"Retreat?" Unoka grunted. "T'ey are on t'e run."

"Not anymore, they aren't," James replied. "Crazy fellow or not, I say it's time to go. We won't win this fight in a day."

On the way back up the hill, estimating the considerable remains of the Pretender's forces, he privately wondered if they could win it at all. Whatever the case, he much doubted he would catch them asleep again.

2.

A Question of China

"The magic mirror has a Chinese ambassador on it," Crecy said.

Adrienne put her book down and looked up at the redhead. "They finally deigned to answer?"

"So it would appear."

"Good." She rose and turned toward the door.

"Are you joking?" Crecy asked. "Surely you don't intend to be seen like that?"

"Like what?"

"Your hair is a rat's nest. You've had that same gown on for days, and it has stains on it—here, and here."

"What matter what I look like? Veronique, I have greater cares than that."

"Well, for one thing, you've begun to scare the crew, and more seriously, people are whispering doubts about your sanity. For five days you've left your cabin only to meet with your students, and then you have a certain feverish air about you that does nothing to allay fears. Now you finally have a chance to speak with the Chinese—who I hear are among the most fastidious people in the world—and you intend to address them so? I will not allow it. Change that dress and let me do something about your hair. You are thought of as a sort of queen, Adrienne, and we depend upon that illusion. You may not let it slip. Besides, if you do not make the ambassador wait at least half an hour, he will not think you worthy."

Adrienne resisted an irate riposte. She knew when Crecy

was intractable; and besides, she was right. It seemed nonsense to worry about her appearance when the apocalypse was gathering, but that was the way of things, wasn't it?

"Irena had a lover," Crecy remarked, as she began combing Adrienne's hair.

"She told me."

"Did she tell you who it was?"

"She said she had taken several in the past—to get back at Hercule or to find some solace."

"No, I mean she had a lover on one of these ships, perhaps this one. I found a note she was writing to him, hidden in her quarters."

"You searched her quarters?"

"Someone had to. Everyone seems to think everyone else killed her, but no one knows. Entirely too many people think one or both of *us* did it, which is no good at all. There is considerable grumbling about, favoring installing Menshikov as leader of this little outing. Some of that probably comes from Menshikov himself, through agents, though I've no absolute proof of it. Some of it rises from the ranks, however. It would be nice if we could find someone to hang for this murder. You make no move to solve this problem, so naturally I assume you want me to do it. It's the sort of thing I do for you, after all."

"Do you resent it, Veronique?"

"Resent what?"

"Doing these 'things'?"

"It's what I've always done, since I was a little girl. Spying. Lying. Killing. I don't know what else I *would* do."

"Get married. Have children."

Crecy's laugh bubbled in her throat. "Who are we talking about now, my dear? I no more want those things than you do."

"Sometimes I want them."

"Not often. Not for long. I am not a stranger to you, my friend."

"I have a son," Adrienne said softly.

"Yes. But you did not wish for him. I . . . I know you loved him—love him. I do, too, for that matter. But it was not something you planned."

"Maybe that's why I loved him so—because he wasn't planned. Or because he was the only good thing that came from those terrible days. . . ."

"You loved him because he was your son. Because he was little Nico."

"Yes? Then why did you love him?"

"Because he was your son. Because he was your little Nico." Crecy paused—to Adrienne it sounded as if her throat had gone too tight to speak. "Because—he made us a family, of sorts," Crecy went on. "And I've never had a family. Without him, we—" Now Crecy did break off.

"We what?"

"Nothing."

"No, say what you have to say."

"We grew close, in those days. We were like sisters, at the very least, and maybe something more. I have never been so close to any human being as I was to you, Adrienne. Yet when Nico was stolen, you blamed me—"

"I did not!"

"You did. Think back. You blamed me, and I think you continue to."

"Why on earth would you think that?" She looked up at the other woman, and was amazed to see the glint of tears in Crecy's eyes.

"Because you said so. Because in the years since then, you have never said otherwise—and because you *should* blame me. He was in my charge. I let him go. And after that . . . you became distant."

"Crecy, you are my dear friend."

"Yes, as dear a friend as you have, to be sure. Nevertheless you drifted away after that. Rather than becoming closer, we drew further apart; and time has only served to make that . . .

comfortable, in a way. We are not *better* friends than we were ten years ago, only more worn and familiar ones. So, too, with Hercule. You kept that distance—"

"I explained. After losing Nicolas, the thought of being too close was intolerable."

"I know, but in my case it is more. You still blame me. You think I may have *given* him to them."

"Nonsense."

"Listen to yourself. Listen how unconvincingly that word is pressed to service."

"Hush, Crecy. Just hush. You don't know what you're talking about. Besides, how he was lost is no longer important. Reclaiming him is. And yet the closer we get, the more I fear it. The more I do not want to find him, in a way."

"Truly? Why?"

"My heart says to find him, always. But my heart has never been my brightest organ. I dream things—my malakim tell me things about him. Bad things. What if I have to choose between him and the world? I have been told to expect such a choice."

"Told by the malakim? They are liars, of course."

"I know. And yet—what if it is true?"

"What if it isn't? Don't you trust yourself to know, when we get there?" She tugged on Adrienne's hair a final time, then patted her head. "That's as much of the tangle as I can get out. Hold still just a few more moments, while I put it up. Perhaps I should use the Chinese comb, eh?"

"That's fine," Adrienne murmured. "Veronique . . . could you kill me?"

She could feel her friend freeze behind her.

"What sort of question is that?"

"A practical one. If it became necessary, could you take my life?"

"How could such a thing ever be necessary?"

"The malakim warn that my son may bring the end of the

world. But they also warn that I might do the same thing, or that the two of us together might."

"More lies," Crecy said as she fastened dark clouds of hair with a lacquered comb. It felt for all the world as if her hands were trembling.

"Veronique, what do you know? I did not surprise you just now, did I?"

Crecy stopped again, and this time she came and knelt in front of her friend, and took her hand.

"They are *liars*, Adrienne. I do not mean as you are, or as I am. Lying is their *science*. They cannot *do* things in the world without us. And so while our sciences are alchemical and physical and natural—about the things of matter and how to change them—theirs are about *us*. Their sciences are aimed at getting *us* to do what they want. They have done this for thousands of years, keeping careful notes, I assure you. There was no fall of Rome for them, no sacking of Greece. Everything they have ever learned from the beginning of time they still know. And about mankind, they know much. They know about our hearts, the circulation of our blood, the reason we sweat. Think how they were able to cure King Louis, once agency was introduced into him by the Persian elixir. Think how they did the same for the tsar! How they made my own body stronger and faster as I grew. They learned all this by experimenting with such as myself, we unlucky few that are born to their touch. Now imagine that they know a thousand times as much about the ways in which we think, feel, understand. They have equations for hatred and desire, theorems of love and passion. They tell you things to make you *do* things. Do not credit them—believing them can only bring disaster."

"But sometimes it must be the truth—not a lie—which obtains the desired reaction," Adrienne replied.

"Sometimes," the redhead admitted grudgingly.

"And if *this* is the truth—*can you kill me?*"

"Adrienne, I would see the world burn to ash before I did you harm."

"That's not what I want of you."

"Nor do I care. I love you, which is not the same as being obedient."

Adrienne searched for a response, but none was there. She looked at her reflection in the mirror as Crecy finished, wondering what she saw there. Of all of the things she could look at, name, dissect, understand—what she saw in the mirror remained beyond her comprehension.

Coiffed, powdered, and in a fresh gown, she settled in front of the magic mirror. It was another invention of Swedenborg's, and like most of his inventions, useful. She did not like it or trust it, because like all Swedenborg's devices, it was angelic. A single malakus connected her mirror with the Chinese one. It seemed obvious, now, that a similar, nonangelic device could be built—one that operated like the aetherschreiber but transmitting sound and light instead of the motions of a pen.

No one, least of all herself, had bothered to give it thought. Swedenborg's device was simple if expensive to make, already present, and, of course, sanctioned by the church. Its only defect was that the image was blurry to those who had no affinities to the malakim. Swedenborg, Tsar Peter, herself, and a few others could see through it clearly.

By his look, the Chinese official was not such a one. His gaze was never exactly on hers, his eyes squinting and somewhat unfocused. All that work on her hair, and she probably looked like a wet painting smeared by a mischievous child.

He looked less . . . *Chinese,* somehow . . . than she had imagined. His head was shaved except for a long, plaited queue, but put that and his outlandish clothing aside and he could easily be a darkly colored Russian.

When he spoke, however, she understood not a single word.

"Do you speak Russian," she asked, "or French?"

"Of course," came the reply in oddly clipped Russian. "Who does this humble person have the honor of addressing?"

"I am Adrienne de Mornay de Montchevreuil."

"A woman?"

"Yes."

"I was told I would be speaking to the commander of the aerial fleet encroaching on our border."

"I am she."

A long pause, during which time she took notice of the background. The ambassador had placed himself strategically in front of a window, so that she could see the sweep of Peking beyond. It was a city of low buildings: few towers, no sky-challenging, multitiered structures. But for all of that, it was fantastic, with its curling, gilt roofs. And it went on forever. There seemed no end to it, though this prospect was raised. She felt a sudden, odd thrill. It could—it must—be the largest city in the world.

After years of trade with China, they still knew almost nothing about it. Travelers from Russia were allowed only at markets on the border and in certain parts of Peking, never anywhere else. It was strictly illegal for a Russian to purchase Chinese maps or geographies, or anything of the sort.

What might such a vast place hide? What secrets, sciences, demons?

The ambassador finally decided he would speak to her, though he was clearly reluctant.

"This person is Sa-Fin Yakao, of the Bordered Yellow Banner, sixth grade official of the Li-Fan Yuan. This person may also be named Yakov Savin, if it is pleasing to you."

"You are Russian?"

"This person is of the Bordered Yellow Banner, the Russian company. He was born in Peking of Russian parents."

"But you are an official of China?"

"Of the Li-Fan Yuan, yes. The Siberian Department."

From her reading, Adrienne remembered that it really

meant something more like "department for barbarian control" or some similar and equally insulting thing.

"We are searching for news of our tsar."

"The *O-lo-ssu Khan*—your pardon—the *tsar* was in Peking four months ago. He has been gone for almost as long. Your governor—Menshikov?—was informed of this some time ago."

"The tsar has vanished. We would like to come to Peking, to learn what we might of his destination. Do you know where he stayed, to whom he spoke? We would like to interview them."

"He and his people stayed in the O-lo-ssu Kuan, east of the Jade Canal, which is set apart for Russians. He met with the emperor Yung-cheng, an honor the like of which there is no other, and whom you certainly may not interview. Two days later, he left."

"Yes, but certainly he spoke to some of our Russian merchants. They stay also in the Russian house, yes? Or to some geographers, perhaps one of the Jesuits in the city, concerning his route to America?"

Sa-Fin Yakao shook his head. His queue swung behind like a pendulum. "You will not be allowed in the imperial city. Indeed, our reports put you perilously near our border. The peril, I might add, is yours, not ours. This person's intent is to warn you that if you cross it, you will be met with great force."

"I wish to negotiate on this matter."

"I am not authorized to do so."

"Pass me on to someone who is, then."

Did he smile slightly? "Your request for a conversation with this unworthy person was registered two weeks ago. I received authorization today, only because your ships cause us to worry you will trouble the emperor's serenity. You may approach no closer. You may wait for authorization to speak to a higher official, but it will take time."

"How much time?"

"Much more than the two weeks it took for you to reach this unworthy person."

Adrienne tried to keep her face and voice neutral. "Can you tell me anything at all about the tsar?"

"It is a matter of record that he took his airship east, toward the O-lo-ssu and Zunghar settlements across the sea. That is all I am permitted to say."

I bet it's all you know, Adrienne thought grimly.

She tried one more direction. "Three men passed this way not long ago: Prince Golitsyn, a philosopher named Swedenborg, and the metropolitan of Saint Petersburg. Did you receive them?"

"This humble person knows nothing of that."

"Would you know if they came there?"

"For Russians, there is no gate to China save the Li-Fan Yuan. I assure you, this person would know if they were received in any circle." For an instant, the official's voice and face became a bit more candid, almost conspiratorial. "This person earnestly suggests you seek in the east. Much is moving there. You are aware that vast numbers of Siberians—Russian, Zunghar, Mongol—have immigrated there?"

"In the past, yes. We helped resettle Tartars that were causing you some . . . concern where they were."

"Many more have gone recently, however, for lands have been discovered much to the liking of the horse barbarians. Surely you know the activities of your own government?"

She almost answered but didn't, for she detected a certain slyness in the question and suddenly suspected that the whole shift in demeanor was an attempt to learn exactly what was going on in Russia. The Chinese must have some inkling that there was unrest, but they didn't know the extent of it. Looking beyond that ambassador to that enormous city, she suddenly felt the less the Chinese knew, the better.

"You can be of no more help to me?"

"I am miserable, because that is the extent of my knowledge."

"Very well. We will do as you suggest."

"Commendable." He smiled, and the mirror blanked.

"Isn't the sea magnificent?" Elizavet sighed. "It looks dressed in scales."

"I was just thinking the same thing," Adrienne remarked, gazing down at the mixed ice and ocean.

"You, thinking the same thing as me? You make fun of me, Mademoiselle."

"What? Why would you say that?"

"It's no secret that I am the stupidest woman on the ship. How could your mind work in the same fashion as that of someone so stupid?"

"Elizavet, you are not stupid—you are lazy. There is a great difference. And, of late, you have been more industrious than I have ever known you to be."

Elizavet opened her mouth, almost as if to protest. Instead she inclined her head, once. "Thank you Mademoiselle. I *have* been trying. I have a sense that I am among greats, people who will be remembered for all time."

"You are a tsarevna. Surely there will be a place in history for you."

"Not if we don't find my father. Maybe even if we do." She shrugged. "What sea is it?"

"The charts call it Bering, after the man who discovered it, a captain in your father's aerial navy."

"Surely those who live near it discovered it first. How could they not know it was there?"

"Yes, of course," Adrienne remarked. "Yet I saw no cities or roads in those lands we crossed last, so perhaps no one lives there."

"And what will we find in America?"

"I very much wish I knew. Some Russians, some Cossacks. Tartars of various sorts. But what have they been doing? I don't know. We will find out."

* * *

The next day they reached a mountainous, cloud-shrouded coast, and, looking at their charts, Adrienne understood that this was her first glimpse of the New World. On the charts, the coastline was all that was represented. Past the mountains was nothing, a vast blankness beyond which, somewhere, lay the English, French, and Spanish colonies. Knowing the size of the Earth, knowing the latitude, it was possible to calculate exactly how vast that blank spot on the map was, but it in no way helped to fill it up or make it in the least more comforting.

They rose above the mountains, still following her compass. The charts showed an inlet, and then another range, and their eyes showed them the same thing, despite the filmy bedcloth of clouds that lay upon it all. They could not, however, see the other feature the map named, a dot marked "New Moscow."

But a little later they were able to infer its approximate location, as red globes began emerging from the mists, dragging after them a fleet of airships.

3.

Coweta

Franklin flinched as muskets snapped at the sky. Across the stream, a dense cloud of iron-gray smoke billowed and then hung motionless in the hot, still air. Earsplitting war cries sounded from the forest.

"Easy, Robin," McPherson said. "They're shootin' in the air, not at us."

"Or are damn poor shots," Robert commented, reluctantly putting his pistol back in the case on his saddle.

Franklin noticed most of the rangers seemed unconcerned. Like Robert, he had trouble mustering that same level of indifference.

But a few moments seemed to prove McPherson right as, across the ford, a number of Indians assembled on the bank in plain sight, as if waiting for them. No more shots were fired.

"Okay, fellahs," McPherson said, motioning forward. "Let's go. Keep brave faces."

Two at a time, McPherson and Franklin first, they sloshed into the stream. Franklin wiped his salty brow. The temperature had been climbing all day, and now it was a steam bath. His horse's neck was weltered with sores and bright beads of blood from the fierce, often huge flies. Ben's own exposed flesh wasn't much better off.

The Indians watched them come. Under their scrutiny Franklin felt like a shooting target, with a great red circle over his heart. His pulse beat in his temple, and his throat was dry.

He concentrated on studying the Indians. Like those he had

seen before, they were dark, copper tinged, most of them naked save for loincloths. They were tattooed with wavy lines, suns, animals, and fabulous monsters. Most had thick, squarish features, though the leader was somewhat foxy faced.

Like the Cherokee, they did odd things with their hair, plucking most of it out to leave long locks in strange places. Some wore earrings or gorgets made of shell or silver. Most had visible scars. They shifted restlessly on the bank, as if being motionless was a chore.

"Are they Cowetas?" Franklin asked, sotto voce.

"Oconees, I'd say," McPherson replied.

"Are they part of the Coweta empire?"

McPherson chuckled.

"What?"

"Only somebody as has never been amongst 'em would call what the Coweta have an empire."

"You mean it's not?"

"If it's an empire, I don't know who the emperor would be. The fellow we're headin' t' see, Chekilli—he's the *mikko*, which some folks might call a king, of sorts. But he ain't, really. He's more a demagogue—he tells his people what to do. They do it or ignore 'im as they please." The ranger swatted absently at a horsefly. "Likewise these so-called provinces—like this Oconee we're comin' up on. They've got their own separate chief and government an' all, but they cozy up to the Coweta an' mostly do what they say, because the Coweta are *strong* and this is dangerous country. A little tribe doesn't have much of a chance on its own, not with war parties everywhere and everyone out for what they can grab."

"So it's more an alliance, then? And these Oconee are part of it?"

"Yes."

"Good. Then they have the idea of a confederation between sovereign states for the purposes of mutual protection. We're proposing nothing more than that."

"It's nay *that* simple. It's nay a strange idea to them, no. But these Cowetas are an arrogant lot. For thirty years they've clobbered everyone has come against 'em, but good; and the English and French colonies have practically kowtowed to 'em to have 'em on their side. Don't let 'em fool you. These are sharp customers, and they're used to lookin' for the best deal."

"Well, I hope I can offer them one. So this bunch—these Oconees—are they a welcome party?"

McPherson twitched a grin at him. "Looks like a war party to me, but this greetin' says they'll parley. Otherwise, they'd of just stayed at distance until they could attack us to best advantage."

"You mean, for instance, while we're crossing a stream?" Franklin asked nervously. He was close enough to see their features well, now, which seemed to him to express mostly a sort of haughty anger mixed with disdain.

"Yes, I'd thought of that. I have a feelin' about it, though, and out here that's sometimes all y' get."

They made it across; and the foxy-faced fellow—who was sitting a pony not much bigger than he was—came up, rasping and trilling in his own language.

McPherson replied in the same tongue, a bit more tentatively. After that they spoke—or maybe argued—for a few moments. Finally, McPherson gestured for one of his men, who brought a pistol and a silver, crescent-shaped gorget from his saddle packs. McPherson presented them to foxy face, pointing now and then to Ben. Franklin blinked, smiled, tried to look important. After a few moments, the ranger turned back to him.

"This fellow's named Fixco, and he's a war leader of the Oconees, as I thought. He says he will take us to Coweta."

"How much further is that?" Robert asked.

"From what he says, I'd guess about forty miles, so we'll overnight between here an' there. He also said they were told to keep an eye out for you."

"For me by *name*?"

McPherson turned and posed the question. Fixco replied; and Franklin heard his name in the answer—or guessed he did—though from Fixco's mouth it came out "Falakkan."

McPherson confirmed his suspicion.

"Who told him?"

"His chief, who got a message from Coweta."

Ben frowned. "I did schreibe that I was coming, but had no reply from them. I assumed their aetherschreiber was broken. I guess it isn't."

"Like I said, they're something arrogant, the Cowetas."

"I dunno," Robert mused. "That's odd—not answering a schreibed message, but sending out this party."

McPherson shrugged. He didn't seem particularly worried.

They started back along the trail. Most of the Oconees—there seemed to be five or six of them—vanished, slipping into the woods. Franklin was used to that. It was how the rangers rode normally: spread out, hunting and foraging as they went, often not together again until time came to camp.

But by contrast, the rangers were pulled together now, almost in formation. It made Franklin nervous. McPherson's words said everything was fine—his actions suggested they were in danger.

Nevertheless, at first opportunity, Franklin lagged back with Robert. McPherson and the other rangers were chattering.

"I don't like this, this not knowing what's going on," Franklin confided.

"That's the two of us, then. You think McPherson ain't bein' straight with us?"

"I think he doesn't want to worry us."

"That's probably the nub of it. Of course—" He lowered his voice even further. "Of course, he's a Scot, ain't he? They tend toward the Jacobite."

"Your uncle trusts him."

"Aye. He trusts me, too, my uncle, and see how foolish he is there?"

"Well, we can only keep our eyes open."

"And hope what we see makes sense afore it kills us. Aye."

The landscape, at least, was kinder than it had been. In the week since leaving Fort Moore, they had crossed a series of high, rocky ridges cut up by fast-flowing, difficult-to-ford streams. Now the land was pretty level, varying from wolds of huge-boled trees to open savanna and to vast, murmuring forests of cane. Of course, this lower country brought with it the troublesome flies and greater heat, but nothing was perfect, Franklin supposed.

They passed through a cornfield, planted in the Indian fashion. Franklin had seen a few of these near Charles Town, and noted it seemed a practical way of doing things. The earth was hilled into mounds about every yard or so, and from each mound grew two or three stalks of corn. Beans twined around the corn stalks for support. Scattered rather aimlessly were other plants—sunflowers, melons, pumpkins of various sorts. It looked rather messy, and was certainly weedy. Indians didn't seem to care much what their gardens *looked* like, so long as they produced food.

They passed a house a moment later. It was essentially a cube with walls of wattle and daub, though so well plastered it might have been Spanish adobe. A roof of overlapping cypress-bark shingles was pitched steeply to shed the rain of fierce southern storms. Next to it was a summer house—a roof and two walls and not much more. An old woman and some children sat under that, shucking green corn. One of the Oconee warriors hollered something at the old woman, and she laughed.

The houses and fields grew closer together, and in time they came upon a town, nestled in the curve of a river significantly larger than any they had crossed since Fort Moore.

It was a pleasant enough place for a town, shaded by sprawling oaks, sky-reaching elm, and hickory. The black earth between the houses was trampled smooth and bare as a ballroom floor by the people, dogs, chickens, hogs, and cows, all of which seemed to wander at will. He wondered what kept the cows and pigs out of the gardens.

Part of the town had a palisade of logs about it. There was no gate as such, but two sections of wall overlapped to form a narrow entrance. They passed through that and came to about twenty cabins arranged about a rectangular plaza. Bordering the plaza itself were a series of long sheds with covered porches and one larger, round building at the far end. The buildings were all plastered white and many of them were painted with hieroglyphic beasts. Some were recognizable—panthers and bears and such. But others were chimerical—combinations of snake, bird, cat, man, and who knew what else. Other figures were purely geometric—circles and zigzags. It struck Franklin that he had seen most of the devices before, tattooed on their guides. He wondered if it wasn't some primitive form of heraldry.

In the center a tall pole towered some thirty feet over the piazza. Some boys were tossing a ball at it with odd game sticks, a bit like tennis rackets with very small heads. Each held two, one in each hand; and he was amazed at the dexterity with which they caught the little ball in the air, launched it to strike what looked like a bear skull on top of the pole, then caught the ricocheted sphere once more.

Fixco dismounted and spoke a few words to an old man sitting on one of the porches. Franklin wondered if he was a chief or some such, but he wore no badges of rank that Franklin could make out, unless the blue-black tattoos all over his body counted.

After talking quietly for a moment, Fixco remounted, and they started off again.

They forded the river of Oconee and traveled on west. The land beyond, if anything, was richer than before; and Franklin couldn't help but imagine how productive it would be if it were all put to use. It was beautiful, of course, but it seemed something of a waste that all the rich black soil underfoot should grow nothing edible—not with the hundreds in the northern colonies going hungry. The Carolinas were fed, at least—though Franklin was heartily sick of rice, which was the most part of what they grew. This land here could probably produce wheat, vast tons of it, and he had already seen that the canebrakes made for fat horses and cattle.

He wondered, should the alliance succeed, if the Coweta might be convinced to keep bigger herds. They could drive them to market along the very trails he had traveled from Charles Town, and fetch a handsome price, benefiting everyone. McPherson had said they were sharp, with a sort of keen business eye—why not?

And so he spent the rest of the day dreaming of a world united and plentiful, imagining inventions that might help to make it so. He scribbled much in his notebook, something he had learned to do quite well on horseback by now.

They camped near sundown, and Franklin rose early to help catch the horses. He was eager to see the capital of this empire.

Rounding up the horses always took longer than he liked. They were hobbled and allowed to forage during the night, and wore bells so they could be located the next day. Still, some could wander a considerable distance, even so constrained.

The next day's riding was much like the first. The sky through the trees was fiercely blue and pressed on them like a hot iron smoothing linen when they passed through one of the frequent open savannas.

Toward evening, crossing one of these, Franklin noticed something odd: a large hill, too perfectly formed to be natural. It was flat on top and four-sided. It reminded him of a depiction he had once seen of the tower of Babel and also of Egyptian pyramids.

"What's that?" he asked McPherson.

"One o' them old towns you see now and then." He spoke a few words to their guide, who replied at length.

"That's the place where the Coweta and the Kashita first

settled when they came here from the west, Fixco says. A very old place, but no one lives there anymore."

"Why?"

"He says people went bad, there. Some of 'em started consorting with—I guess you'd say witches or demons or somethin'. He says you can still hear their ghosts in there sometimes at night, beatin' drums and dancin'."

Fixco said something else, and laughed nervously, spurring his mount to a slightly faster walk.

"He don't want to be here at night," McPherson explained. "He says hurry up."

They passed more of the mounds, some of them of impressive size. It was a little hard to credit, from what he had seen of Indians thus far. He had never heard of them building such monuments.

Of course, what he didn't know about Indians could fill several books. And those Indians down in Mexico were supposed to have built some pretty amazing things. Maybe they were building them again—word from Mexico was that the Indian slaves and peasants had risen up and conquered their Spanish masters. Yet another warning to the white people of the colonies, outnumbered as they were ten to one by Negroes and Indians. The day for playing the pale sovereign was gone, he was convinced of it. English colonists would accommodate themselves to that or die.

Or the malakim would have their way, and everyone would die, maybe. *One step at a time, Ben,* he told himself.

"You said something about Kashita?"

"Another tribe, but them an' the Coweta went in together a long time ago. Coweta is the red town, Kashita the white. That is—Coweta is where they make war from and the other is where they make peace. They have a chief for each, see—one in charge when they're at war, the other in charge when they ain't."

"Why do we go to Coweta, then?"

"Well, these days they're mostly at war, I reckon."

It was nearly dark when they finally reached Coweta.

It was the largest Indian town Franklin had yet seen. Homesteads and fields sprawled around it for miles, and the heavy-timbered walls enclosed perhaps a hundred houses. The plaza was commensurately larger and more grand than the one in Oconee. The pole in this square was covered, top to bottom, with what he first thought were horse tails, until, with a bright tingle of horror, he understood the truth—that he was looking at upward of a hundred human scalps.

Children were running alongside them, brandishing toy weapons—at least he hoped they were toys—and shouting what sounded like threats. Adults stopped what they were doing to watch the procession arrive. Most were dressed in little more than what God had given them at birth—the women in particular seemed to have no truck with shirts, though some men wore chemises of Venetian or Carolina cloth.

He tried not to stare at the women, but some were more than passing attractive, and after a moment he realized that they probably did not think him rude to look, undress being their natural state.

The large round building here was *very* large, a virtual amphitheater. It looked as if it could hold two hundred people. In front of it were assembled maybe two score Indians, ranging in age from perhaps twenty-five to one old gent who might be a hundred.

"We'd better dismount here," McPherson said. "Those fellahs assembled over near the round house are the ones we want to talk to. I hope you can hold your tobacco—there's always a damn lot of that smoked in these parleys. And we'd best get our gifts out."

"What's the chief's name again, and which one is he?"

"That's Chekilli—that fellah with the feather cape. That fellah next to him is probably the Kashita chief—I don't know him. The others are likely clan headmen and chiefs of some of the smaller tribes—like the Oconee."

"Well enough."

"And don't walk straight through that square. Walk sunrise around it. It's a superstition of theirs."

"Those are human scalps on the pole?" Franklin asked, just wanting to be sure.

"Yes, indeed. Delightful custom, eh?"

"It makes one stop and think," Franklin replied dryly.

He collected himself, trying to remember the greetings Nairne had taught him. They froze in his throat, however, before he reached the chiefs, along with much of the hope in his heart.

Emerging from the round house were a number of quite un-Indian men in bright red coats and black tricorns trimmed with the white rose cockade. With them were four taloi, gleaming like dull, blue-gray beetles in the fierce sun.

Franklin recognized the leader at once.

"Sterne!"

The rangers were quick to react. Even before Franklin had named the Pretender's man, their carbines leapt to their shoulders. McPherson had both his pistols out in the same heartbeat.

About that time some forty Coweta warriors emerged from the cabins surrounding the square, muskets primed and cocked.

"Mr. Franklin!" Sterne called. "Delightful to see you again! I do hope you have given the matter we discussed earlier some thought."

"Idiot," Franklin snarled. He did not mean Sterne—he meant himself. He raised his voice, addressing the old man in the feather cloak. "Chief Chekilli, I am Benjamin Franklin, the ambassador appointed by the true government of South Carolina to speak to you on their behalf. I come also with the authority to speak for the Cherokee, the kingdom of the Apalachee, the margravate of Azilia, and the true governments of all the English colonies. I hope you will see your way clcar to treat us as ambassadors in your territory, not subject to the intimidations of our foes." McPherson translated that, and Sterne simply smiled as he did.

Chekilli seemed to deliberate for a long time. Then he spoke, and McPherson in turn made it English.

"He says he didn't ask you to come. He says he has come to an agreement with the English king. He says the English are free with their giving of guns and other weapons, as the colonies have not been. He has no desire to treat with you or any other representative of those who are advancing on their land, and especially has no love for anyone allied to the Apalachee or the Spanish, who have spilled much Coweta blood."

"What of our earlier agreement?" Franklin asked. "What of the treaty with Emperor Brims?"

"He was another man, whose name you should not speak, for he has traveled to the ghost country. The council has met since. The English king will arm us against our foes. You have been stingy with us—for fear of us, perhaps, but it is no matter. This is the result."

"This man has lied to you. He represents—" He struggled to remember the words Red Shoes had used. "—*Hattak Okpolhusi.* Evil spirits."

"That's Choctaw, not Muskokee," McPherson said in a low voice. "I'll render your meaning."

Another pause. Franklin was beginning to understand that the appearance of deliberation was just that—a form and manner of speaking, a pace of argument—not a sign of indecision. The answer seemed to bear out his hypothesis.

"I have said what I'm going to say on the matter. The council hears all of this, and they can reconsider if they want."

"Let us go, then. These men have no right to kill us or make us prisoner."

Chekilli shrugged and said something.

"Sterne claims blood debt against us," McPherson said. "So do the Coweta."

"What? What have I ever done to them?"

"You? Nothin'. That don't matter. In their view, any Carolinian can pay the blood debt of any other."

Franklin drew himself as tall as he could. "We came here in good faith. To attack or detain us is base treachery."

"Lay down your weapons, or die this moment," translated McPherson. He turned aside to Franklin. "They'll kill us anyway."

Franklin tightened his lips, looking around. He counted upward of fifty guns aimed at them now, not to mention the taloi. "If we live, there's hope." He sighed, at last. "Dead, we have none at all. Lay down your weapons, boys."

4.

Sinti Lapitta

He heard a sharp crack in the distance, as one of the lead balls turned into an expanding sphere of flame. Instants later, another.

The reaction from the camp was instantaneous: the Mongols swarmed like hornets whose dwelling had been shaken by boys. He heard commands in a strange language and the hiss of arrows into the underbrush. If the men had any guns or sorcerous weapons, they were saving them for a foe they could see.

He and Grief began cutting tethers. The horses raised a fuss, of course, but the scent of smoke already had them nervous, and the general hubbub of the camp would cover the noise.

Cutting tethers was quick work. Some of the horses were hobbled, too, and he cut them free, careful about the stamping hooves. Grief did her own work well and quickly.

They were almost finished when Red Shoes turned to find that someone had discovered them—or, rather, discovered the freed horses. The Mongol, a short, bandy-legged fellow, was staring right through Red Shoes, who was still hidden by *hoshonti*. The Mongol began to yell, but was interrupted when Red Shoes buried his throwing ax in his windpipe. The Mongol gurgled and dropped.

"Let's go," he told Grief. He grabbed one of the horses by its peculiar bridle and heaved himself up.

Fire was visible in the woods now, and more of the Mongols were thinking of their horses. Red Shoes swatted several of the beasts within reach with the flat of his ax, but they didn't need a lot of encouragement: the scent of the fire was doing its work.

On the other hand, it was dark, the land cluttered with undergrowth, and the beasts first panicked aimlessly, unable to decide on a direction, stamping in circles, crashing into each other. The Mongols, whatever else they knew, knew horses; and despite the confusion, more men arrived with each heartbeat. Red Shoes kneed his stolen beast repeatedly, feeling as if he sat in the eddying shallows of a swift-flowing stream, able to see the waters that could take him away from his enemies but unable to reach them.

One-eyes were swarming now—not powerful spirits in and of themselves but dangerous in numbers. Worse, they could herald the coming of the something truly powerful. A *na lusa falaya*, such as he had battled in Venice, or the scalped man.

Even as he thought that, he felt something large move in the distance, a giant waking.

It was not the scalped man. It did not have the feel of a Long Black Being. What it was, he did not want to know.

Another Mongol came near, reaching for the horse Grief was on, though she herself was still invisible.

Red Shoes threw his ax. It hit badly, with its blunt end—but it struck the man in the head, and he staggered to his knees. By the time he got back up, screaming and looking about wildly, Red Shoes and Grief were out of the grove, tearing through thinner brush. Now, at last, the horses had their heads and clear terrain to run on, though the smoke from the burning hillside was so dense it seared the lungs. The ponies dug in to run as fast as they could. Branches slashed at Red Shoes, raking his face and bare upper body. A couple were heavy enough to raise bruises, and one low branch nearly unhorsed him. To his left, he could sense but not see his companion.

"Let them go where they want," he called to Grief. "We want—"

He felt it coming only instants before it arrived, a deadly purpose with no form or shape. It hit Grief first, where his power was weakest, pulling apart the cloud that bent light around her, and then, like a dog following a scent, it moved from her to him. Grief was visible now but alive and well; her own shadow was safe and tight within her. Those with no power in the otherworld were only barely susceptible to it.

Red Shoes was another story. It could not harm his body, but it could grasp the frayed strands of his spirit and pull it apart like a poorly made cloth, leaving him soulless but alive.

Or worse, hollow him out and wear his skin.

Which was exactly what it tried to do. It seemed to slit his skin open in seven places, tried to flow into him like black water into a cracked pot.

He couldn't fight it in the middle world, the world of Man. He had to go beneath, to the chaos where his enemy—whatever it was—lived. He forced his hands to grip the horse's mane and then left them there, hoping desperately that they would not forget their task when he forgot his body.

His spirit tore loose of the clay it lived in and plunged into the underworld. It was cold and dark, like a deep pool. It was the place that had been before time, and lay behind time. It was the darkness over which all bright things were but a thin skin of paint.

At the crossing was disjuncture, a moment like a drop of water forming on the edge of a leaf, not yet swollen enough to fall. It was oddly peaceful, and in that protracted moment—as if looking through the curved glass of a sailor's telescope—he saw the Ancient Times, when the middle world did not exist, when the water of the underworld met the sky and the four directions unhindered. The lords of the deep and air moved like great waves, like tornadoes and hurricanes, joyful in their freedom, incomprehensible in their size and power.

And then Hashtali, whose eye is the sun, plunged great hands beneath the waters, found the mud and clay far below, and pulled it up, spread it upon the waters, baked it into dry land—sealing the lords of the waters in the dark and cold, far from the sky. Then, perhaps to complete the injury, he took children of the newly formed underworld, clothed them in clay, and brought them above to live on his new, flat world between.

And below, anger became hatred and festered into venom. The lords of beneath swore vengeance, prowling up through holes in the earth, doing harm, always plotting against the upstarts that Hashtali made to walk upon their heads. Through springs and caves, deep lakes, they came, and through the darkest, widest holes of all—those in the minds of men.

The drop fell, the moment passed, and Red Shoes was there before his enemy, seeing him for the first time.

Nothing one saw in the beneath was true, any more than a word that described a thing was actually the thing. But what he saw helped him understand and fight.

And what he saw was terrible.

His foe glittered, a thousand obsidian scales in coils that went into nowhere and everywhere. It had wings like those of a bat; but each long, webbed finger was a snake, and the edges of the great wings were thus fringed with hissing rattles. The wings opened above him, a vast canopy of serpents, and rearing above the wings was the head of the greater body, the deep-ridged eyes of a rattlesnake, slitted eyes yellow-green as venom, and like a third eye in the middle of its skull burned a Sabia stone, bright as a small sun. With it came the sharp scent of musk, the smell of burning hair, and a scent only a maggot could love.

"I have you, thief," it said, a thousand cicadas chirping the words in unison. "You have stolen my servants; you have taunted my kind. You think to thwart our designs. You are strange and strong, but we know you. And now we make an end of you."

It did not await an answer. The light from the actinic Sabia stone between its eyes increased; and Red Shoes felt the flesh of his face crawl, then strain, trying to flay itself from his bones.

It was the strongest enemy he had ever known. The *na lusa falaya* had stalked him for months before daring to attack him, waiting for his weakest moment. This thing did not care. It was older, darker, more bitter than even the most powerful of the Long Black Beings.

But still he resisted it. "You take liberties," Red Shoes managed. "You take the form of Sinti Lapitta, the snake who makes pools and rivers, the most powerful of all who dwell in the underworld. You are strong, but I doubt you own *that* strength."

"You see me as you wish to see me," it answered. "I have no part in that. If you see me as the most powerful there is, it is perhaps because I am the most powerful you have ever faced—that you ever *will* face."

"I devoured one of your relatives," Red Shoes said defiantly, "a *kwanakasha*. He warned me of the 'great ones' and summoned a Long Black Being. I devoured him, too, and *he* warned me of worse to come. You spirits keep coming, and I keep defeating you, and you keep telling me the one who will finally beat me is coming along. I begin to become bored. Are you the one they keep promising me? Are you a great one, he-in-the-form-of-Sinti-Lapitta? Are you more powerful than your defeated cousins? I doubt it!" It was a lie, but it sounded good.

The snake spoke with talking wind and raindrops hissing on fire. "Assume what you wish. I am your doom, that is all. It is good enough." The light increased, and coils dropped down around Red Shoes, tightening. The creature's nauseating stench filled his lungs like a liquor made of rotten eggs, and for an instant he began to unclench. Why fight? Why continue this show of bravado? He was beaten. Sinti Lapitta would devour his soul and shadow and step into his skin; and if anything remained it would be a ghost, barking in the night like a sick fox, lost, stupid, and alone.

But no. He had known this day would come. He had a steel thing, coiled in his belly. A razor. A bullet. His weapon of last resort—one he did not, could not, hesitate to use. He did not know if it would work, of course, but he was a dead man if it didn't.

Devouring the Long Black Being, he had taken its shadow and made it a part of his own. But there had been a part—a single, dark thing—that he had kept from himself out of fear, out of loathing: a thing he did not believe he could digest at all. But he had kept it, forged it the way Europeans forged metal. Each year he had added something to it, some subtle variation on its original power.

He released it now and felt his shadow shatter and re-form, felt a glory and a power more satisfying than any pleasure, more vicious than anything he had ever conceived.

He walked through the great one. He ate through it. Scales filled his mind, heavy as iron. He swallowed the glowing Sabia stone. His blood became iron. His flesh became stone. His shadow became fire.

He awoke to grayness and confusion. The world had a sharp smell, as if to compensate for its lack of color. The faint odor of burning lingered, reminding him in part of what had happened on the other side of—nothing. Closer, he smelled sour, centipede earth and leaf mold, the sweat scent of another person.

His eyes began to focus, and the gray resolved itself into the interior of a cave. The entrance was not visible, but the pale light leaking in was.

Grief sat near him, her eyes closed.

He remained motionless for a long moment, wondering what had happened. They had stolen horses from the Mongols, he remembered, and then—well, after that he didn't remember anything at all. With a sigh, he straightened his sore body.

Grief's eyes snapped open, and the exhausted *kraftpistole*

resting in her lap jerked up to aim at him. Her eyes glittered with the determination he was coming to expect from her.

"It's only me," he murmured.

The weapon didn't waver.

"Could you tell me where we are?"

"You led here," she said simply.

"I did?"

She nodded guardedly. "Enemies all around. You bring us here."

"I don't remember."

"You crazy. Like—" She furrowed her brow and said a few words he didn't understand. She looked frustrated for a moment. "Not—ah—soo-veh-nee?"

"*Je ne souviens pas. Soo-vyehn.* No, I don't remember."

"Ne soo-vyehn," she repeated, more or less correctly this time.

What had happened? He must have battled with some spirit. He closed his eyes, trying to sense his shadowchildren. He had none. The last of them was gone.

But that was odd, because he felt none of the sense of loss he usually did. He was a little sore but otherwise fine. His shadow felt strong, capable.

"I'm going out for a look around," he told her. She shrugged as if she didn't care what he did. Probably she didn't.

She was an odd one, Grief. He had helped her because he admired her bravery and respected her need for revenge—and because she could fight; and when they fled from the army they needed anything like a warrior they could get their hands on. But he hadn't really expected her to stay with them—after all, she did have some relatives left alive back at her village. Or did she? Maybe not. Maybe all her own kin had been killed, and there was no one left in her village to protect her or for her to protect.

Even now that they had a language in common—well, reasonably so, anyway—she did not seem to feel the need to explain herself. It would be rude to question her too closely.

He could tell one thing: she was afraid of him now, as she had not been before. She covered it well, but he had seen it in the way she held the useless weapon, in her eyes. She was not a woman who was easy to frighten. What had she seen?

The cave entrance was narrow—though not too narrow for the two Mongol ponies that stood tethered within—and opened onto the familiar small-treed landscape. The light was gray outside, too, not a morning light but an overcast sky. To his peculiarly heightened sense of smell, the scent of rain was as rich and powerful as the sea.

Very faintly he could smell men and horses.

He quietly and cautiously worked his way to the top of the hill. It wasn't the highest around, but it was high enough for him to see that he and Grief were the only human beings within several miles, at least. The riders he smelled must have passed through long before.

Where were Tug, Flint Shouting, the tsar? If all had gone well, they had horses now and would presumably continue on toward the villages of the Wichita, where they might get help from Flint Shouting's people. If all hadn't gone well . . .

There was no way to know. He might make shadowchildren and send them out to search, but they weren't much good for such things. Their eyes did not work well in the middle world. They could see the substance of creation, the beneath, but the *created* remained a mystery to them.

But he would make shadowchildren. It was dangerous and would almost certainly attract attention, but he had an opportunity to do it now, and, furthermore, however unlikely it seemed, he had the strength. As much as he disliked it, the most important thing right now was not finding his friends. If their days were broken, there was nothing he could do about it. If they were captured again—well, there was nothing he could do about that, either. It had been a dream to think they could outrace an army of men and spirits in this strange country—it was time to admit that now. That being the case, his duty was to the Choctaw. He would make a messenger and send it to speak in the dreams of the chiefs. He would rather be there himself, so that he could argue whether they should join the marching iron monster, resist it, or flee it. But, in a way, he was glad he wasn't. It was too great a decision.

With a sigh, he started gathering the things he needed, wishing once again he had tobacco, which made all things easier.

He found Grief as he had left her.

"I have to do something now," he told her. "I have to make a magic. When I have done, I will be too weak to defend us. Do you understand?"

"Yes. I defend—defend? Defend you."

"You would be better off leaving. What I do will attract our foes."

"Then why do?"

"Because I must. My people must know what is coming for them."

She regarded him for a few moments, and for an instant he saw beyond the stone she had dressed herself in. To a woman who might have once laughed, smiled—who might one day have raised a family, been a grandmother.

"I had kin, and people," she said. "Now I have only revenge. Having people is—better. You have. Do, and I will watch."

He looked into the fire, the eye of the world above. "Thank you," he said. He handed her his pistol. "If my soul does not return, you must kill me. Do you understand?"

"I understand."

"Good."

And he began to chant.

5.

Lines of Supply

"General Oglethorpe?"

Oglethorpe opened his weary eyes a crack. The voice with the thick upcountry accent belonged to Lieutenant Smalls.

"Yes?"

"I've finally gotten word from Governor Nairne on the aetherschreiber. He congratulates you on four successful engagements."

Privately, Oglethorpe wasn't sure he ought to be congratulated. They had scarcely slowed the redcoats, and their own casualties were mounting. Oh, the Colonials took two or three of the enemy for every one they lost—and had brought down one flying ship that came too close—but the redcoats were getting wilier. Slowly but surely, the Continental Army was being forced back toward Fort Moore. In two days, they would be there, and what then?

Maybe Nairne knew. Oglethorpe took the communiqué from Smalls.

As he expected, they weren't going to try to defend the fort. Nairne was marching what remained of their forces south into the margravate, as he had promised. That was a relief, anyway—he didn't like leaving his own people defenseless.

The rest of the letter was harder medicine. He rubbed the grit from his eyes and stood. His feet were sore in their boots, his back hurt, his face was burned red by the fierce heat. Like Tomochichi, he was getting old.

The climate, as unpleasant as it was, was their friend. The Pretender's forces, many of them Scots, were unused to the blistering weather, whereas the rangers, Indians, and Maroons had been living with it for most of their lives. Each time they engaged the enemy, fewer and fewer wore their coats, or even shirts, and at least a few had dropped from heatstroke.

Still, the redcoats came on, and on, and he suspected that they weren't the only army in the field.

"Go find Parmenter, Unoka, and Tomochichi," he told the aide. "We have matters to discuss."

Oglethorpe poked a stick into the embers of the campfire, wasting a second or two to marvel. Who could imagine that a piece of wood had so much flame locked inside it, such heat? One would never think it, gripping a hickory branch, and yet there it was, unlocked by the simplest alchemy. Why should the occult forces lurking in iron, in the very air, surprise him?

There must have been a first time when a man saw fire. Adam, almost certainly, after being cast out of Eden. Had he thought that first flame as strange, as impossible as Oglethorpe considered aetherschreibers, *kraftpistoles,* and airships?

Probably. But fire, however magical, was not his problem just now.

"The problem—our very chiefest problem—is their airships," he told the other leaders.

"Nah," Parmenter said. "That devil gun does a good job of bringin' 'em down when they try and come close."

"I don' t'ink he mean as weapons," Unoka said.

"I don't. It's that they don't need a supply train. Think—if they were hauling their food and drink in wagons, what an easy time we would have. We could fell trees it would take them days to clear, dig trenches in their path—that sort of thing. As it is, they can travel almost as fast as we can." He poked angrily at the fire again.

"So we have to bring down the ships," Parmenter said. "All

that need's doin' is for a few of us to get close enough to use the devil gun on 'em."

"Exactly right. High marks for Mr. Parmenter." Oglethorpe didn't try to keep the acid from his tone.

Parmenter blushed angrily but did not reply.

"What I need *now*," Oglethorpe went on, "is some plan to get us that close."

"We do it," Unoka said without looking up.

"Sir?"

"I said, we do it. Or are you goin' deaf?"

"You'll watch your tone, Mr. Unoka. And, no, I heard you—but 'we do it' is not a strategy I remember having studied. I'll need more than that from you."

Unoka rolled his eyes. "We hides in t'e woods. T'e army, she come past, an we wait—t'en up we creep, little mice, and t'e ship, down t'ey come."

"Are you suggesting I lend you our only depneumifier, our only defense against these flying craft?"

"No, we bring t'e ships down wit' sling rocks," Unoka said sarcastically. "O' *course* we need t'e debil gun. Y' said it y'self."

"Sir," Parmenter interjected, "I can take ten rangers—"

"No," Oglethorpe said. "Mr. Unoka is right. This is Maroon work. I need the disciplined fighting troops up here." *Though it sits ill, sending the gun with them. What if they should run off with it?*

He quashed the thought. No matter who dropped back, odds were they would all be killed before coming near enough to the airships to do any good. Better to lose the Maroons than troops he could make other use of.

Still, to send them out, unchaperoned, with the depneumifier . . .

"It's a brave offer," Oglethorpe said, "and an honorable one—but maybe each company should send a few men, to keep things fair."

"You don' trust me wit' your debil gun?" Unoka asked slyly, showing his white teeth.

"It's not that," Oglethorpe lied.

"T'en we go. Tonight, eben."

Oglethorpe shrugged. "Very well, Mr. Unoka. Make your plans."

Unoka was as good as his word. By morning, he and his Maroons were gone. James stepped up the level of sniping, to keep the redcoats worried about what was in front of them and give them less chance to wonder what might be behind. He did this simply by putting a bounty on Jacobite scalps, to be paid when possible. He had made good on such promises before, and the Indians remembered.

And they pressed on, back toward Fort Moore, with all speed.

"Seems a nuisance, just riding back the way we came," Philamon Parmenter commented.

"That was always the plan, one way or the other," Oglethorpe told him. "We meant to use the frontier forts as places of refuge. We never dreamed they would mount such a large expedition so fast."

"We ain't goin' to hold Fort Moore?"

"No. We'll resupply and then burn her to the ground."

"Nairne has already cleared out?"

"He left a small force to guard it against Cowetas or come who might, but yes. Another Jacobite army has been sighted approaching the margravate."

"Oh." The ranger was silent for a few moments. "Don't you itch to go down there? That's your country."

Oglethorpe set his jaw. "I've been encouraged to think of all the colonies as my country. I'll see my way to do so. Once we've finished off this army, then we'll go fight alongside Nairne, if needed." He sighed. "I'll admit I don't like retreating, but the extra raids the Yamacraw and Kiawah are making will cover that for a time. The trick is for the redcoats to think we're just over the next hill, so they'll come cautiously."

"An' when they do ken we've hightailed it?"

"Then they will think they have us on the run."

"Don't they?"

Oglethorpe rubbed the hilt of his saber. "Not as they think. There is a method to it—at least I like to hope so."

Parmenter grinned. "We'll send a few more Jacobites to hell then, sir?"

Oglethorpe frowned. "To my mind, Mr. Parmenter, the Jacobite cause was a just one. I kept that to myself for many years, but now, with the Hanover line well dead, I don't think it much matters anymore. I will say I dislike naming our foe in that manner—it does not describe them. Howsoever many of those redcoats think themselves fighting for the Stuarts, in fact they do not. They fight for the tsar, and next for the devil himself so far as my poor, simple mind can tell. True Jacobites ought to be our brothers in arms, and it's a great pity that they aren't. We're killing good men bent to an evil cause."

"Yes, sir. I meant no offense, sir. I never thought much of King George, myself. They say he never even learned English."

"Not much, and not well, and he kept his mistresses German, too. Even the whores of Britannia were too low for him, I think." He shook his head. "That's past, Mr. Parmenter, all dead history. We have to fight for what we have now, for this place we have made our home."

"Well said, sir."

Two days later they reached Fort Moore. As expected, Nairne and his troops were gone, leaving ten men to defend her. Once they arrived, James set his troops to packing up what supplies they could carry and destroying the rest. Reluctantly, he ordered the few remaining cannon spiked and the spring filled in.

There had been no word from Unoka and his Maroons. He reported to Nairne via aetherschreiber and got a terse, "marching" rcply that stressed the weakness of Nairne's position on the overland journey—after all, the majority of the women, infantry, and artillery were with him, and they must travel slowly over poor trails.

Oglethorpe understood the unstated part of the message: his task had changed. Where before he had been the vanguard, carrying the fight to the enemy, stinging it like a hornet and retreating to sting another day, now he was rearguard for the rest of the Colonial forces.

He called his officers together in the war room to explain their new situation.

"What it means, gentlemen," he said, by way of summing up, "is we either stop them cold here, every mother's son of them, or we lead them astray."

"We might hold them here," a young fellow named Barton ventured. "Not for long, maybe—"

"Not for long at all, I think. A few days, and then we die and the southern colonies lose a third of their army. They want the North, or they wouldn't have sent an army to Fort Moore. Well, we're the only force in the North. Without us, they have it. With us still on the loose, they have to deal with us before consolidating and turning south."

"You think we should go farther north, sir? Toward our Cherokee allies?"

"Allies, mine arse!" Parmenter snapped. "If they're our allies, I say where are they?"

"That's a good question," Oglethorpe said. "I don't know the answer. Mr. Priber seemed to think thcy had troubles of their own, and maybe they do. But that isn't where I thought to go anyway. I thought to go west."

"West? Into Coweta territory? Have you heard from Franklin or McPherson? Do we have alliance with them?"

"I have not, and so assume we do not."

"General, that'll catch us between two rocks, if you get my meanin'."

"Consider: we are resupplied. Assuming Unoka and his men were successful—"

"If you pardon me, sir, that's a hell of an assumption. The Maroons are by nature thieves and cowards. They're probably halfway to Jamaica with that devil gun by now—if not to Charles Town, selling it to the foe."

"That'll be enough of that," Oglethorpe snapped, "quite enough." Never mind that he had the same fears himself—he could not allow talk along those lines. They needed the hope that the ships would come down, even if it was a false one. "Now, as I was saying, assuming the Maroons succeed in their task, the redcoat army will be without supplies. If we march through Coweta territory, where do you suppose they will get those supplies?"

They all looked puzzled for a moment, all but Tomochichi. He nodded and said something to one of his braves in their own tongue.

Parmenter got it next. "From the Cowetas. But that's a dangerous trick, General. Suppose the Indians blame us?"

"Who will they blame, Chief?" James asked Tomochichi.

The old man didn't think about it for more than a second. "The redcoats," he replied.

"Exactly. Indians will fight for revenge, glory, and gifts—in that order. The redcoats loot their farmsteads, the redcoats will pay. It might not be much help, but it might sway the Coweta to our cause."

"Or it might wreck the negotiations Franklin was to work at."

"Those have done well or failed by now," Oglethorpe said.

"The Coweta are fickle. Us goin' onto their land might anger 'em."

"A chance we'll take."

"There's another thing, sir," Lieutenant Smalls said. "If we get pushed way out there in the west, aren't we goin' to get cut off from the margravate and the rest of the army? How are we goin' to get back?"

"Well, gentlemen," Oglethorpe said, solemnly, "getting back isn't our job. Keeping this redcoat army out of the South *is*. For a time. When we decide to go home, it'll have to be straight through them, I'm afraid."

6.

New Moscow

The governor of New Moscow was a nervous little man with a full beard, a balding head, and the formidable name of Rimsky-Korsakov. He kept gnawing at his lip.

"I must insist that you surrender," he repeated for the third time, his voice a bit quavery through the magic mirror.

"That will never happen," Adrienne told him. "Once you understand that, this discussion can move on to more productive ground. The men you take orders from are traitors and usurpers. We represent the tsar himself, and we will not surrender."

"The tsar is dead," Rimsky-Korsakov said. "As I understand it, he has been succeeded by his heir, Princess Anna. Prince Golitsyn is her agent, and the legitimate voice of Saint Petersburg. You, Mademoiselle, have been declared a heretic by the patriarch himself, and your accomplices share your crimes. Furthermore, you harbor the criminal Menshikov and have kidnapped Tsarevna Elizavet."

"That is outrageous!" Hercule snapped from behind her left shoulder. "You little, bearded pig! I—"

"A moment, Hercule," Adrienne said quietly.

She summoned Uriel to her.

Yes, Adrienne?

I must be certain I have your aid against these ships and whatever other forces may be marshaled against us.

The malakus seemed to sigh. *I prefer not to attract attention just yet, but if there is no other way—yes.*

My trail ends here. If I am to pick it up again—and find my son, as you desire—I must win this battle.

As I said, Uriel said.

But this time, do it as I command it. Do you understand?

I understand.

She nodded and returned her attention to the governor.

"Enough of this," she said softly. "Governor, prepare to surrender your city."

"You must be joking."

"Look out your window," she replied.

She picked one of the flying frigates and severed all but one of the spirits that kept it aloft. It dropped—not quite like a stone. It was distant but not so distant that she couldn't hear the wails of the crew. The ship would hit hard, probably hard enough to split its hull, but most on board ought to survive.

The governor had vanished from the view of the mirror, but he soon returned, stroking his beard and chewing even more frantically at his lip.

"I will give no second warning," Adrienne told him. "The next ship will drop straight from the sky, so that I need not fight the crew as infantry when my soldiers secure your fortress. By our reckoning, you have only fifty or so troops at your disposal, anyway. Far, far less than we expected, I must tell you. We were prepared to fight many times that number. What's more, do not count on your angelic weapons—you will find them no more dependable than your ships. Indeed, I give you half an hour to confirm this, and five minutes more to surrender."

She stepped away from the mirror, then quieted it with a pass of her hand.

"*Can* we win, if it comes to it?" she asked.

"Yes," Hercule said with certainty. "If what you said about their weapons is true, yes. I have a hundred and half again fighting men, more than twice what they have, unless they have some hidden away." He cocked his head. "Which is what worries me. Where have their troops all gone? There should be many, many more."

"Well," Adrienne replied, "that is one of the things we are here to learn."

The magic mirror flickered in all the colors of the rainbow, a sign that someone was trying to speak from the other end. She waved it on. It was, as she had expected, the governor.

"I have no choice," he said harshly. "I surrender the city to you. But I warn you—there will be consequences, and though you command every demon in hell, you will not avoid them."

"Nor would I wish to try, Governor," she replied. "The sooner these consequences appear before me, the sooner I can dissolve them. Recall your ships and expect troops under my authority within the hour."

"Adrienne," Crecy said softly, "look."

She followed the direction of the redhead's finger. In the distance, the mist coruscated yellow and orange, a plume of color racing away at high speed.

"Golitsyn. Swedenborg. The metropolitan."

"The wheel, at the very least," Crecy cautioned.

Can you stop them, Uriel?

No. I am weak, now. There was . . . resistance. From this moment on I am under siege; it will remain so until this matter is resolved, or until I die. What I warned you of has come to pass: I have been noticed.

It was necessary. She paused. *Thank you.*

The entity did not answer.

New Moscow was a ghost town; they saw that almost immediately. Its streets were nearly empty, and more than half the houses were abandoned.

"Some plague, perhaps, or attacks by the Indians?" Hercule speculated.

"Questions to put to the governor, not to me."

Everything was built of wood, and in that way only, it did

resemble Moscow, which had few stone structures. The governor's house, the statehouse, and the church were the largest; squat buildings with attempts at onion domes on the towers. The streets were unpaved and ankle-deep in mud. It stank almost as much as Adrienne remembered Paris stinking.

The governor and his staff waited to receive them, swords held flat in their palms, ready for surrender. Adrienne watched silently as her men collected them.

Rimsky-Korsakov was a little taller in person than she had expected, but he flinched more.

"What will you do with us now?" he asked.

"I'm placing you and all of your officers under house arrest and forbidding you any contact with magic mirrors, aetherschreibers, or anything of that sort, though I'm sure any damage along those lines is already done. Will you invite me into your statehouse? We have things to discuss."

Rimsky-Korsakov nodded and led the way.

Seated at a polished cedar table, Adrienne sipped some tea the governor's servant brought them and looked the fellow in the eye.

"First things first. Where is everyone?"

"I don't know what you mean."

"This town could hold five times as many people as I see. Barracks that could house five hundred contain fewer than fifty. Don't play the innocent with me. Where have they gone? And while we're at it, my scouts have discovered another colony, some hundred miles north. What is it?"

"A Mongol settlement, with a Chinese fortress."

"It seems even emptier than *this* town. Why? Are they in the same place your own people are?"

He shrugged. "It is not my business to ask where the Chinese have gone. Go ask them yourself."

"I suggest you cooperate, little pig," Hercule growled.

The governor looked defiant and fearful and said nothing.

"He *is* cooperating, Hercule," Adrienne chided. "His men have gone to the east, into the interior. Isn't that right, Governor? You've been left defenseless against *me*, because something of much greater importance is happening out there. Yes?"

"What traitor told you this?"

"You did, just now. I was merely guessing." She turned away from his face as it crumpled in dismay. "Hercule, begin searching this building, then move on to the governor's house and the church—"

"You *cannot* search the church!" Rimsky-Korsakov shouted.

"It will be done respectfully, but it will be done. I *am* a heretic, remember?"

"You will burn in hell."

"*You* will burn here, if you continue in this way; and afterward I venture the two of us will meet in hell, for I doubt very much that you are a good man. What has become of your tsar, and what part did you play in the matter?"

"I was not involved in the affair of the tsar."

"Tell me of it, and save yourself considerable agony."

"I will not."

"*I* will."

They all turned at the new voice. Adrienne actually found herself gaping, for three reasons. The first was that the man who stood there, firmly escorted by two of Adrienne's Lorraine guard—had spoken in French. Second, he wore the black robes of a Jesuit priest. Third—she knew him.

"Pierre Castillion!"

The priest—a man of some forty years with a narrow, ascetic face—blinked. "I know you, Mademoiselle?"

He did not recognize her. But then, why should he?

"I know you, more properly, but that for another time. You were saying?"

"Don't listen to him," Rimsky-Korsakov snapped in Russian. "Whatever he is saying, it is bound to be some papist lie."

"Hush," Adrienne told the governor, "or I will have you gagged."

"Don't hurt him, please," Castillion said. "He is merely a pawn in this game. He is not responsible."

"We are all responsible, Father Castillion, all of us. Now what do you have to say about our tsar?"

"He is not here. He was here, but he has gone."

As her initial shock began to fade, Adrienne noticed other things. Castillion looked tired—no, more than tired, haggard. And he was bleeding from a cut on his forehead.

"Did my men give you that?" she asked.

"No, Mademoiselle. I was set upon by rogues on my journey here."

"From where?"

"The Chinese outpost to the north."

"That's more than eighty miles away."

"Indeed. I still have friends in Peking, you see, and they told me you were coming. I walked here to meet you."

"My apologies, Father," Adrienne said. "I will not ask you to testify in this state." She turned to Crecy. "Secure the governor and his men. The father and I will return to our ship, where I can be assured he will be cared for in safety."

"Your wish," Crecy replied. "Come, gentlemen, let us see what sort of accommodations we may offer you in your own town. Better than you had planned for us, I'll guess."

A few hours later—fed, his wound cleaned, and in new clothes, Castillion looked considerably better.

"Please take your time," Adrienne told him. "Our cause is urgent, but a few extra hours or so will make little difference."

"I cannot agree with you," the priest replied, "which is why I walked here. But I thank you for your hospitality." He paused. "How *do* I know you, lady?"

She wondered again whether she should tell him, finally decided to. "Don't you remember teaching me arithmetic? I sat in the first row."

"You were at Saint Cyr?" he asked, eyes lighting. Then they suddenly shone even more brightly. "Wait! Adrienne . . . de Mornay de—ah—" He clasped his hands together. "It escapes me."

"Montchevreuil," she finished.

"You must have been only fifteen or so. I was so young myself—By our savior, I *do* remember you. Very quiet. Very pensive. You always knew the answers and never would say them." He shook his head. "I *must* know how you came to your present condition. It is beyond imagining!"

"No more strange than finding an old teacher of mine in the New World," she said. "Your story first, then mine."

He nodded briskly and began telling her his tale. She found herself savoring his voice. She, Crecy, and Hercule spoke French when they were alone, as she did also with some of her Lorraine guard, though many of them were more comfortable with German. But Father Castillion had a rustic accent, not the Parisian one that Crecy and Hercule owned. It was musical, soft and trilling, not unlike her grandfather's accent—or her own, when she let the courtly training slip. It was both familiar and almost forgotten.

"After Saint Cyr I taught at the college of Louis le Grande—but my heart was always on travel. I read Leibniz's work on China, and it was then that I knew where our Lord was calling me." He smiled ruefully. "It was more difficult explaining that to Rome, however, for they always seem to have some other idea of what God has said, and besides, there was trouble with the Jesuits in China. They had a tendency, it was said, to become—strange. But at last, in the year 1719, I got my wish, and I sailed to Peking, and thus began a life I could not—for all of my reading—have ever imagined. I do not think I should say much of that now—I would digress, and digress again, until all important points were obliterated."

He took a sip of the coffee she had provided for him, and closed his eyes. "Coffee! So many years since I have tasted it. What a wonder! I cannot imagine where you find it."

"Africa," Adrienne said simply.

"Ah, yes. With your flying ships. Of course. I am behind the times. I hope you can catch me up, when convenient. I hear—I am given to understand—France is no more."

"Not as such. The people survive, however, if not their kings. Please go on, Father."

"Yes, you see? Digression. Well, the emperor of China suffers the Jesuits for a variety of reasons. He has no fear or care that we might convert all his subjects—it is unimportant to him what faith his people hold. Indeed, there are many faiths in China. Though I have become convinced that the root of Chinese law and ritual has its root in Christ—" He broke off. "You see? There I go. No, the only thing I need to mention here is that we were helpful to the emperor when it came to negotiating with European powers. Some years ago, the tsar of Russia was involved in just such a negotiation, and I was present."

"This would be the resettling of the Mongols to the New World?"

"Many of them, yes. The ruling dynasty in China, you see—the Ch'ing—were, a hundred years ago, themselves barbarians not much different from the Mongol and Juchen tribes. They are thus well aware of the threat that such tribesmen pose to their own empire. Twelve years ago, when the world became stranger and colder, that threat increased tenfold, for the Mongols and their kin were forced toward China by the climate itself. Thus, the Russian offer of aid could not be ignored even by the proud Ch'ing. So, Russians and Mongols settled here, and for years all was well. The Chinese maintained several outposts on these coasts, to *know* that all was well. Due to certain studies of my own—you see, I will not bore you with them just now—I fell out of favor with both the Chinese court and my own order. By coming here, I was able to continue my work and avoid any persecutions. Frankly, the Chinese simply do not care what happens beyond their borders if they do not see an obvious effect to themselves.

"So here I came. And about two years ago, things began to change again."

Adrienne leaned forward, intent on the story.

"More ships than ever came from Russia, and there were rumors of much construction—of airships and other arcane things. Many of the natives were enslaved to this end, and the Mongol settlers were drawn into it for trade. This was a hunters' paradise for them, you see, but there were still things they wanted which they could not kill with an arrow. And—there was the prophet."

"Prophet?"

"I'm ahead of myself. The Chinese outpost, where I lived and worked, grew very quickly in size. While many of those settled here pursued the life of their forefathers, crossing the mountains to the rich, horse-loving plains that lie beyond them, others thought to make for themselves an empire, not unlike the Chinese one. They built their military might. In time, they nearly came to blows with the Russian settlements—but then the prophet came, uniting them."

"Again, this prophet."

"He was a boy—a European boy, perhaps Russian—who was raised in the care of a khan named Orcha. Orcha would never say where he got the boy, or call him anything but 'son.' From a very early age, however, the boy performed miracles of all sorts. People had dreams, summoning them to him. Finally, when the troops assembled and marched down the coast to this place, the boy stepped out between the two armies, between their very guns, and he spoke in a voice that everyone heard. He told them to forget the differences of the Old World, that it was time to make a new one, and to cleanse the New World of every bad thing from Europe and from Asia. I cannot describe exactly what he said, but he was understood in all languages. And the angels—the angels were with him, all about him, everywhere. It was deeply moving, Mademoiselle. Deeply. I wept.

"And so the army kept building, now jointly. Native tribes

were recruited and armed, and more fabulous weapons came from Russia. Mostly from the church, from the Old Believers, who thought of the boy as a saint. I, myself, began to grow troubled. I saw and heard of things—of great machines and weapons of war—that seemed somehow more demonic than angelic. This sudden appearance of angels, their sudden presence in our lives, was suspicious to me. It remains so, and the feeling grows stronger each day.

"Then came a day when the army began to march, and near that time, I hear, the tsar arrived in one of his flying ships.

"Imagine my surprise—they tried to arrest him. I did not see this, you understand, only heard about it. There was a battle; the tsar fled into the interior. I have heard nothing of him since."

"And the prophet?" Her throat felt tight. She had no doubt whatsoever who the "prophet" was.

"He marched with the army, almost two years ago."

"For what purpose? What do they hope to conquer? The whole of the continent?"

The priest's voice dropped very low. "It is my belief, lady, that the prophet does not lead the army to conquer but rather to kill. I think he is the Antichrist, come to lead the army of darkness. I believe—I fear—that the end of time is at hand."

Adrienne tried to look serious but felt a sort of giddy humor. She knew she shouldn't—perhaps, at last, she was going mad. But if one more person she met on this strange journey told her that the end of the world was coming, and that her son was the cause of it, she would surely burst out laughing. Not because she didn't believe it, but because—like all things repeated too often, thought on too long—it had ceased to make sense to her.

7.

The Frames

The Cowetas confiscated everything: their aegises, their weapons both scientific and mundane, their horses, the portable aetherschreiber Franklin had brought along for communicating with Nairne and the rest. He argued about that last, pressing the point that he should be allowed to at least inform his government of what had happened; but it was another argument he lost. In the end, stripped down to their breeches, they were led into the round central building and warriors set outside.

"What now?" Robert asked.

"Only God knows," McPherson replied. "I expect the worst."

"And the worst is?" Robert asked.

"The Coweta are mighty fond of torture."

A shadow fell through the doorway. Franklin looked up into Sterne's smiling face. "Not quite what I wanted, Mr. Franklin," he said with good humor. "I'm under orders to bring you back, preferably alive. It looks to me as if my new allies might . . . spoil that." He drew a small silver snuffbox from his pocket and took a pinch. He was returning it to his coat when an expression of dismay overcame his features.

"Dear me—how rude. Would you care for some?"

"No, thank you. But if you're granting requests, I would very much like to see your neck broken."

"Ah, ever the humorist, eh, Mr. Franklin? I suppose you'll

be witty to the end, what? Excellent. Give the savages a good show. Let them see how an Englishman dies. Good man."

"And what for you, now?" Franklin asked. "You flew here, I suppose."

"Oh, bravo. Now you wear your scientific mask, eh? Yes. Wide about, of course, to avoid your tricky devices, but it was quite a pretty tour. And now? It's off to New Paris, I think—I've alliances to make there as well." Sterne settled down into a crouch. "I should tell you that the war is not going well for your folk. We've punched an army in almost to your Fort Moore, and the resistance wasn't exactly what we thought it would be. It seems we have some quite surprising weapons—surprising to your backwoodsmen, at least. With the Coweta here to keep them from retreating farther west, I think we can conclude that this campaign will last only a little while longer."

"You are allied with demons, Sterne. You ought to know that."

Sterne's smile spread across his face, and with breathtaking suddenness, a red orb, much like an eye, formed above his head. "I know quite well whom I fight for, Mr. Franklin, so save your breath. Indeed, I owe you a debt from an old friend of mine. You may remember him. Trevor Bracewell?"

"I remember him," Franklin snarled. "A traitor to mankind, like yourself. A murderer and a rogue. He got his justice, and you will, too."

"Did he?" Sterne smiled broadly. "Was it justice that he died for a crime he did not commit?"

"He murdered my brother, in most foul manner."

"No, he did not. He set the fire. *I* did the killing, slipped my long blade here into your sweet brother's heart." He patted the smallsword at his side. "I just missed you in Boston—I was to rendezvous with Bracewell the same afternoon you killed him. No matter—things have ways of working out, don't they?" He leaned in and kissed Franklin on the cheek. "You've been a naughty boy, Ben. You've tampered with what ought not to be bothered, and now a lot of men will die. I leave you to contemplate your errors." He stood and dusted his breeches. "This wilderness is a dirty place," he complained. "One hopes the French will have more amenities and less dust. I think I can strike a good bargain with them, don't you? If not, well, there they are, just on the coast and not so strong for all their pretense. I hear they've become quite silly there, as the French tend to do. Anyway, this is all just . . . distraction. Even war will be meaningless soon enough."

"Yes? Then why bother with it? I'll take your surrender here and now," Franklin said.

"Very droll! I said soon—for now, both war and diplomacy have their uses. Good day, Mr. Franklin."

The orb above Sterne's head vanished, but his eyes gleamed red for an instant.

"I've dissected a few of your kind, you know," Franklin told Sterne's retreating back. "I know why your eyes gleam so, why your strength is so great. It's small modifications they make to you, when you are very young. Stronger bones, extra oculatum in the eye so you can see at night. But whatever they have told you, you are still human. When they are done with the rest of us, they will turn on you. You can still defy them."

"Defy them? Like poor Euler? Yes, I know you have him. No thank you, Mr. Franklin. I know a great deal more about my situation than you do, you know. I know what my reward will be, in the end, and it is quite worth waiting for. Now, finally—you do have the ability to keep a conversation engaged!—I go."

And he did.

"Well," Robert said, after a moment, "there's what I like about fellahs like him."

"What's that?" Franklin asked glumly.

"Well, now that y' put it *that* way," Robert mused, "not a damned thing."

* * *

Over the next few hours, there was a great deal of conversation out in the square. McPherson didn't catch enough to translate, but after a few hours a group of warriors came in and laid rough hands on them.

"Tell chief Chekilli I need to speak to him," Franklin shouted. "It's most important—" One of the warriors buffeted him in the head so hard that he felt his teeth rattle and smelled the bright copper of blood in his nose.

"Sons of bitches!" Robert howled. "Fight me, y' cowards! Any one of y'r, any weapons!"

One of his captors answered him by clubbing him with a wooden weapon that resembled a cutlass with a heavy ball on the end. Robert groaned, and they dragged him out.

Once outside, Franklin saw what the Coweta had been about for the past several hours. A number of square frames had been erected, each made of two eight-foot posts sunk in the ground with cross pieces at top and bottom. They were carried to these—kicking or limp, depending—and lashed to them, spread-eagle, with tough rawhide bands.

"This is where things get bad." McPherson grunted. The tough ranger's voice quavered noticeably, which did more to panic Franklin than anything else. "Try to stay brave," the ranger went on. "Try not to weep or beg. If you're brave, they might kill you faster."

"That's not that result I'm hoping to achieve."

"It will be," McPherson said. "It will be. I'm sorry, Mr. Franklin. I should have seen this coming. Sorry, fellows."

"It's not your fault," Franklin replied.

Franklin thought the torture would begin immediately, but once they had them strung up, the Coweta seemed in no great hurry to begin. Of course, being hung as they were was torture in and of itself. Franklin's hands and feet went numb, while his shoulders felt as if they were being slowly torn apart.

Around them, village life went on. The women were busy—pounding corn in big mortars made of logs, weaving baskets of split cane. The men, on the other hand, mostly sat about on the porches and smoked. At one point a few of them got up and played a game involving rolling a stone wheel and spears. As near as Franklin could tell, they would bowl the stone wheel along the flat earth of the square and then toss spears after it. Whoever came closest was the winner.

The stakes were the colonists' possessions.

Franklin came to in the cool of evening, realizing that the heat must have roasted his senses. The sky was beautiful, layers of color like a storehouse full of Venetian silk. He wondered if it was the last sunset he would ever see.

"Damn you!" The shout came from down the line. It sounded like Robert. Franklin wearily turned his head.

A group of children—boys and girls mixed—were wielding long cane switches, laughing and hollering. They were smacking Robert and one of the rangers. As they struggled feebly in their bonds, the children laughed even louder. Then they moved to the next man down the line.

Franklin got his turn soon enough.

"Don't," he murmured.

One boy, perhaps ten, looked at him with quick, intelligent eyes, then picked up a rock. It hit Franklin on the forehead, a pain as sudden as lightning, followed by a slow dripping down the side of his face. The beating with the canes wasn't so bad, after that.

After the children, the women came by, singly and in clumps. They slapped the men on the frames, spit on them, and cut them shallowly on arms and cheeks with cane knives.

Once it was dark, the harassment stopped, and all Franklin could hear was the labored breathing of his companions and the occasional distant cry of an owl. He hung there, hoping it was a nightmare, praying to awaken.

8.

The Prophet

Adrienne reached a trembling hand to touch the painting. She found only a flat surface, roughened a bit by the texture of the paint. Without sight, it would mean nothing to her, could not chill her to her marrow. She would not recognize her son.

But recognize him she did, there and in the half a hundred other images of him that ornamented the room. Here he was surrounded by angels, there by shining creatures executed in what must be a Chinese style. In another, the boy himself bore wings and a halo.

She stood in a temple whose god was Nicolas.

Again, she shivered, her earlier perverse humor completely fled. If the malakim could make such changes in a child like Crecy—born of natural parents—what had they been able to do with her boy? He was conceived shortly before her hand became what it was, a conduit to the aether, a thing of no world. If Uriel changed her body so, what had become of the child within her?

Uriel didn't know, or pretended not to.

"You see?" Father Castillion said softly. "They will follow him anywhere."

"So will I," she answered shortly. "So will I."

Castillion gave her a worried look, but she ignored it.

They left the shrine and walked back into the muddy streets of New Moscow. Those streets were more trafficked today, as those who had been confined on the airships took their liberty. Many had even taken up temporary residence in the abandoned houses, which was odd, as they could not be as comfortable as their quarters aboard ship. Larger, perhaps, but also colder and not as well furnished.

She noticed another thing. Many of her people avoided her when they saw her coming.

"So you intend to go on?" Father Castillion asked mildly.

"Of course. I have not found my son and I have not found the tsar. I *must* go on."

"You truly believe that the prophet is your son?"

"I have no doubts. He has much of his father in him, and something of me. His is the face I saw in my vision."

"A vision given to you by a devil."

"The death, as I call it. Yes."

"Why would such a creature carry your son's face within it?"

She paused. The day was clear. In the distance a mountain seemed to float on the horizon, a world unto itself, like the moon. The day before it hadn't been visible at all, for the mist and clouds. "I do not know," she replied. "But I do know that my son is in danger, surrounded by those who would ill use him. I know that I shall find him."

Crecy found her poring over texts a few hours later.

"I've found Swedenborg's laboratory, I think," the redhead told her. "Someone's, anyway."

"Good! Is there anything left in it?"

"It was abandoned in a hurry, and the place is cluttered. I can't really say if they left anything of importance."

"Let's go."

Six of the Lorraine guards fell in with them as they made their way back through the streets. "Why so many guards, Crecy? The town is occupied mostly by our own people."

"I no longer trust our own people, Adrienne. One of them is a murderer. Others think *you* are. I also do not trust this town. It may not be as abandoned or unwatched as we think. Taking it was altogether too easy."

"I will trust your instincts, then. Is this it?"

They stood before a low building of split cedar planks. It looked fairly snug and, like the shrine, a little bit alien. It certainly was not a Russian house, nor yet European. Was it native in design or something the Siberians brought with them?

Also like the shrine to her son, its door was large and round, though without the elaborate carving.

The alchemical lanthorn painted the interior ochre, but the scent was all cedar, prickly and pleasant but covering more disturbing scents she could not quite identify. Several long tables were littered with standard alchemical apparatus—a furnace, carefully insulated by brick from the wooden structure, crucibles, and glassware. One table held an articulator connected to a vox next to which was an odd pair of spectacles, thick lensed and set in heavy metal frames.

"What's this?" Crecy asked, indicating the vox. It was a brass funnel with a fine tympanum fixed in its base.

"It's a voice box—a device like a talos, made to allow the malakim to speak in earthly voice—like the head that Bacon built, all those years ago."

"I thought Swedenborg heard angels in his head, as you do."

"I suspect he only hears one, as you did in your youth or as King Louis did. Even if he ingested philosopher's mercury, it is difficult for more than one of them to adjust to a human mind without recourse to some—device." She lifted her hand as an exhibit. "The more lofty the spirit in question, the more true that is; and I suspect that Swedenborg is trying to communicate with the loftiest spirits of all, and they with him." She lifted the glasses curiously and fitted them upon her nose. They were Swedenborg's, for they smelled of the perfume he scented himself with, something like plums.

As she put them on, matter vanished, revealing the vortices and tensions of the aether. For an instant, she could only imagine that somehow her hand had been activated, but then she understood that it was, of course, the glasses themselves. Swedenborg had developed his own method of both seeing and communicating with malakim of all sorts.

She took the glasses off. Perhaps she could find some of his notes among these things.

"Hold there!" Crecy's voice snapped. Adrienne glanced up to see a pale young man, staring at them wide-eyed. His mouth worked, but only nonsense came out. Crecy had drawn her *kraftpistole* and had it pointed at him, and the Lorraine guards were likewise ready.

"Are you Swedenborg's assistant?" Adrienne asked mildly. He was bald, whiter than any man she had ever seen. His eyes were blue—all blue, with no whites. A sudden suspicion struck her even as he leapt forward.

Crecy's weapon jetted straight through the young man's chest and out his back, which did not seem to much perturb him, though his form billowed like a particularly dense puff of smoke expanding. He contracted, however, just in time for the next round of missiles—this time from the Lorraine guards—to punch through him, drawing long streamers of substance from his back to trace the path of the bullets.

Crecy yanked Adrienne out of the way, her sword pulling free. Adrienne opened the eyes of her hand.

What she saw was unlike anything she had ever seen before. It was, for certain, a malakus, but even the simplest of their kind was more complex in form than this. The harmonies in this one were as simple and regular as the parts of a machine. She felt she could take it apart and reassemble it, given time.

And then she saw the link, the thin strand that burrowed off into the distance, and she understood.

Meanwhile, the thing had walked straight through Crecy, or, rather, flowed around her. It now did the same to Adrienne, feeling like nothing so much as a gust of air, contained in one place. It kept running, past them, through the door.

Crecy fired again, but it had no more effect than her first attack.

Adrienne snapped the link she saw and watched the thing

collapse. It retained its form, which sent a small, confirming chill up her back.

"What *is* that?" Crecy asked.

"A new kind of malakus, an artificial one. A talos that builds itself."

"What?"

"I need a moment to think. Gather that thing in a bag or sack of some sort and bring it to my laboratory on the ship. Then seek out my students. I want them to see this."

"Where is Elizavet?"

Linné, Breteuil, and Lomonosov indicated that they did not know. Crecy shrugged. "She was last seen with Mr. Linné, here, helping him gather wildflowers.

"Really?" Émilie commented, a bit of ice in her voice.

"That was this morning," Linné said in an uncomfortable tone. "I have not seen her since."

Adrienne sighed. "Well, no doubt it involves some sort of mischief. She will hear I want her soon enough, and there is no time to spare. Prepare yourselves—I'm going to show you something rather odd."

Crecy had wrapped the "man" in sheets. Now Adrienne unwrapped it, an easy thing, for it did not weigh very much.

Linné's mouth dropped in horror. Émilie and Lomonosov retained a more clinical attitude.

"What is it?" Lomonosov asked.

"You tell me."

"Is it safe?" asked Émilie.

"Yes."

They began to poke and prod at the thing, gasping as they found themselves able to push their fingers into it.

"There is a surface tension," Lomonosov observed. "It takes some pressure to puncture it. How much does it weigh?"

"Just under ten pounds."

"Extraordinary."

Linné was still white, trembling a bit. "God did not make that," he muttered.

"No, he did not," Adrienne agreed. "No more than he makes taloi or flying ships."

"No malakus has so much material substance. The most any of them has ever manifested was less than a pound."

"It might just be a new variety," Émilie countered.

"It might," Adrienne said, "but I think Linné is correct. I think this is a new invention of man—or jointly of man and malakim, more likely. A meeting of our two sciences. You remember our speculation that greater malakim make lesser ones from their own substance? I think this thing was made by Swedenborg—from the substance of a malakus, with its permission and cooperation. And whatever device he used to make it, he also used to manufacture this substance."

"He can make malakim that are manifest in matter?" Linné asked.

"Not *very* manifest," Lomonosov remarked, poking at the "body" again.

"No," Émilie said, "this is exponentially greater than anything that exists in nature. This creature has more substance than the strongest wind of a tempest. If it were larger, or if its substance were very hot or very cold . . ."

"Émilie sees the danger," Adrienne replied. "And besides, he might be able to achieve yet higher densities of matter than this. Even if he can't, this is very serious. I think this poor thing is only an experiment, intentionally made innocuous. Its substance is mostly gas and phlegm."

"That in itself is proof that this represents innovation," Linné stated, excitement finally overcoming the revulsion that had been coloring his voice. "No natural malakus contains more than one substance."

"True," Adrienne said. "And further, as Émilie implied, there is no particular reason why its substance could not be lux and gas, or lux and damnatum, or some other volatile combination. It could even be made unstable, like an alchemical lanthorn, reacting to unleash the properties of the matter it contacts. It increases the power of the malakim to meddle with matter more than tenfold, which is not a good thing at all."

"I wonder . . ." Lomonosov mused, tapping his finger on the table.

"Go ahead."

"I have been speculating—Sir Isaac's last publications concerning matter. He had come to the conclusion that matter itself is rather insubstantial, that even the densest matter is most porous, with great space relative to the actual atoms. I have followed some of his speculations—I did not bring it up earlier as it seemed of little consequence. But now . . ." He paused a moment. "I think it can be demonstrated that Newton did not go far enough—that matter is not an arrangement of forces with bits of solid substance scattered in it here and there, but that there is really no such thing as 'matter' at all. All of its properties can be explained by reference to the ferment itself. What we have called 'atoms' may be nothing more than the intersections of forces, or perhaps the emanation points for them, the places where affinities are born."

"That's preposterous," Linné said.

"On the face of it, yes. And yet we know that gravity, which gives things weight, is not a substance, not a solid thing, but an immaterial force. Why then must we suppose that the things that it acts upon are material?"

Linné pinched his arm. "This is real. It is tangible."

"Is gravity unreal, then, since you cannot pinch it?"

"This is interesting speculation," Adrienne said, "and I see how it may be important to the subject at hand. It would suggest that the difference between us and the malakim is less than we suspect."

"It goes to what I said earlier," Lomonosov said, a boyish enthusiasm bubbling out with the words. "The malakim are composed of different sorts of affinities than we—those nearer God, those of the least-limited sort. I propose matter is also affinity—of the *most* limited sort. You see? In which case, creating something such as we see before us is not to do with mediating between the realm of matter and the realm of spirit, but of transforming up and down a scale that grades from those grossest affinities we *perceive* as matter to those we *imagine* as spirit. Think! Through philosophers' mercury we transform the motions of 'matter' into pulsations of 'spirit.' Why should the transformation be so simple if they are truly unlike things?"

Adrienne nodded, her attention fixed on her hand. "It would explain much," she murmured. "It might explain how a hand could be manufactured from dream."

"Mademoiselle?"

She shook herself. It was time to consult Uriel again, to sort through his science of lies for what he might know about the thing on the table.

Before she could dismiss them, however, Hercule appeared in the doorway. He was breathing heavily, and his cravat was spattered scarlet.

"Hercule? What has happened? Are you well?"

"A scrape, nothing more. It's Menshikov. Someone released him. He has rallied a number of supporters, and more go to him each moment."

"How many?"

"His followers have seized one of the ships, the *Ivan*. None of your guard has gone over, of course, but many from the attached regiment have. They may have as many fighting men as we do."

"But not as many ships."

"No. But they have captured the statehouse, and, I believe, liberated the governor and his staff."

"What is this? How can Menshikov have been colluding with the governor?"

"I don't think he was. I think he saw a chance to seize

power from you and he took it. The governor's men round out his numbers nicely."

"The idiot. What does he hope to accomplish?"

"You ask that of Menshikov?"

"Where is he?"

"The statehouse, I believe."

"Then he will have the governor's magic mirror," she said grimly. "It is time, I think, for Prince Menshikov to learn a lesson in what power actually is."

Her fury carried her upward to the bridge as surely as the most powerful affinity. How dare he, after all she had done for him? And how dare her followers turn on her? It was unbelievable. How long had it been since one of her followers disobeyed her, much less flew against her?

Menshikov's smug face was awaiting her when she reached the magic mirror.

"Good afternoon, Empress of the Air," he said.

"Menshikov, you have gone mad. I can crush you like an insect."

"That will mean harming your followers, which I expect will make those who still foolishly cling to the hem of your garment think twice about whom they choose to serve."

"Not so. I can be quite selective when I wish."

"Indeed. But how selective? Selective enough to kill me and not the tsarevna? I wonder." He stepped back, to reveal Elizavet, her clothing in disarray, one wrist bound to Menshikov's and the other tied behind her back. She looked angry and frightened.

"Menshikov, you have certainly sealed your fate. The tsar will forgive you much, but for this you will die by the knout."

"Peter is dead, you stupid bitch. If not, where is he? Not here, in their prisons. Not in China. Not anywhere. Golitsyn and his traitors have killed him. It is for us to pick up the pieces, to take Russia back; and yet here you are, like a character is some silly fairy tale, crossing seven mountains and seven seas in search of the firebird. No more, you hear? I will not go with you, and neither will those who stand with me. Do what you will, you will not win them back. They know you for the treacherous murderess you are."

"The same murderess who saved you from the knout, Menshikov? I wonder—did some follower of yours kill Irena, just so you might contrive this occasion? It seems like you."

"Does it? Then you do not know me well." His voice changed a bit. "Listen, Adrienne. We have the same enemies, you and I. The Golitsyns, the Dolgurukys, the Old Believers. We should be working together, not fighting like this. I have a plan I think will make us both happy."

"Menshikov, you are correct—we do have the same enemies. One of them is *you*. You plot your own death, which makes you a doubly stupid enemy. Any one of my people who wishes to stay here with you may do so. But you will release Elizavet, and you will release her now. I will say no other word to you until you do."

"I will not. She is the only assurance I have that you will not assassinate me."

As promised, Adrienne did not speak to him again. She merely smiled, the coldest, cruelest smile she could twist her mouth to, and waved the mirror off.

"I want her back, and I want a plan for retrieving her within the next quarter of an hour."

"And then what?"

"Then we push on, with whoever is loyal to us. We still have most of the ships. I will not be deterred by this rebellion. If they want to stay in this godforsaken place, they may. We get Elizavet, we go."

Adrienne wrapped light and motion around them and made truce with gravity, so that they came to earth more lightly than feathers.

Menshikov's guards saw nothing until it was far too late. It confirmed what Adrienne thought: Menshikov had no alliance with unseen powers. He was operating, not from a position of strength, but from ignorance and arrogance.

Bullets turned and phlogiston licked about them. The molten-silver spray of a Fahrenheit gun curled like spume meeting the prow of a fast-moving ship. Menshikov's soldiers, more than a dozen of them, died in the ensuing retaliation, and they died without death cries. Her djinni crowded the air, stifling the motions men know as sound.

It was thus that they came upon Menshikov still oblivious—though one of his bodyguards sensed something, looking up in time to see the distortions approaching. He joined his companions in the other life, as Menshikov gaped, thrust Elizavet in front of him like a shield, and drew his *kraftpistole*.

"Show yourselves, or I kill her. I will take a bride with me to the grave."

Adrienne allowed the forces obscuring them to dissipate. Menshikov's face twitched, but he otherwise maintained his composure. He was no coward, Menshikov.

"I break my word," Adrienne said. "I will speak to give you one more warning. Release her and live. I can boil your blood without harming her. I will do it."

"You will do it anyway."

"Then why haven't I?"

"The hell with you," he snapped and pulled the trigger. Elizavet heard the sound and sucked in a breath.

But nothing happened. Adrienne smiled. "You should not have chosen an alchemical weapon, Prince. A simple pistol would have been much more trouble for me."

"I was just . . . joking, you know," he said weakly. "I never meant to hurt her." He slumped, then, and the weapon fell from his hands. "It was all a joke," he muttered "Menshikov, the clown."

"Hercule, go cut Elizavet free of this fool."

Hercule stepped forward with knife and severed the rope.

Elizavet, sobbing at last, threw herself into his arms. He backed away from Menshikov, who straightened his back and thrust his chin up.

"Do what you will. Kill me if it pleases you."

"That would be too easy for you. I have no wish to end your suffering, Menshikov. Let the wives and children of those who died defending you do your suffering for you. Let them wonder why, if I am the evil one you make me out to be, you live when their loved ones died."

Menshikov's hard eyes gleamed with a sudden hope. "You mean to let me live?"

Adrienne could only laugh at that. She was still laughing as she took Elizavet from Hercule, and they retraced their path to the ship, boarding more conventionally by basket.

They were halfway up when Uriel spoke to her.

Something is coming, he said.

What do you mean?

Something I don't understand. Space—distance and dimension—are difficult things for me. I have trouble evaluating them. But something is near you, powerful and weird.

Adrienne opened her otherworld eyes and gazed about at the night sky. The gravity of the stars shone though the clouds, an infinitude of vortices that made a Persian rug of the sky. The sea was mostly sameness, with only subtle ripplings in its form. The air was similar, though it was hatched with the forces that worked through it.

And yet she did see something, near the horizon, where the mountains ought to be. It was something strange and simple, a blankness almost.

"By God!" Hercule choked.

She blinked, let her normal sight reassert itself, and followed Hercule's rare, terrified gaze.

Something came over the mountain, blacker than the night, but with a heart like a furnace, twisting, a great drain in the sky with fire pouring down it.

"By God, what is that?"

She, too, was frozen for the moment, then licked her dry lips and replied. "It is what we spoke of earlier. It is one of Swedenborg's engines. You were right, Hercule, this was all merely a trap, something to slow us until *that* could arrive."

She reached over and grasped his hand. It was the first time they had touched since before Irena died. He did not return her grip, but he did not shake it off, either.

"It's so wonderful to be right, once in a while," he muttered.

Nearby, Father Castillion broke into fervent prayer.

9.

Keres

"Fire!"

Oglethorpe felt like Zeus, calling the lightning. But the hill he commanded was somewhat less than Olympus, and after the redcoats were done falling, they sent their own bolts right back up, drumming the ancient oaks and hickory, ripping into the rich black loam—but not into his men. Trees eight feet in diameter made good shields.

"That got their attention," Parmenter whooped.

Oglethorpe nodded, peeking out from behind the tree. The redcoats had formed ranks again right in the open heart of the old fields, despite the fact that they certainly couldn't see the Continental Army above them. All around him, Indians, rangers, and dragoons slunk from tree to tree, hunting for a better angle for the next volley.

When Oglethorpe felt cowardly, he reminded himself that the army that had once outnumbered them two to one now had four times their number, despite the plenitude of redcoats they had emptied. More troops had arrived from Charles Town, probably ferried there by airship—which meant that Unoka had failed in his mission.

Or abandoned it, a nastier part of him thought.

"Fire!" he shouted again, and a hundred or so muskets bellowed.

Again, the return volley; and again it left him and his men untouched. Below, the redcoats closed ranks where their fellows had fallen.

"They're draggin' up ordnance." Parmenter grunted. "Looks like the wildfire guns."

James saw the long tubes Parmenter had noticed, carried by taloi, two to a gun.

"We'll retreat over the hill," he said. "We already know how these work." They had received a nasty surprise two days before, when the weapons were first used. They jetted a viscous, burning substance for unlikely distances. He had lost thirty men in the last exchange.

Fortunately they were big, and took a few minutes for even the supernaturally strong automatons to get into place. Now that he knew what they were, it was a simple matter to hit fast and hard, then vanish back into the forest.

The signal for retreat went back, but Oglethorpe himself kept watching. They still had a few minutes before the guns could threaten. He called the drummer over, a boy scarcely more than fourteen.

"Beat the 'Grenadiers March,' " he said, "to taunt 'em."

The boy nodded, and without a single worried glance down the hill, began beating the tune. His rangers caught the sound, and as they retreated, they whooped and shouted insults down the hill.

Aside from insulting them, Oglethorpe's fondest hope was that one of the redcoat commanders would lose his temper and lead a charge up the hill. *He* sure as the devil would, if he were in their situation.

Instead, they sent up another useless volley as the taloi situated the guns.

"That's enough, boy—go on over the hill."

"I'll wait for you, sir."

"Do *not* question my command. Go!"

Still beating the march, the boy followed his orders.

Oglethorpe unlimbered his flintlock, took careful sight on the fellow who seemed to be supervising the automatons, and squeezed the trigger.

The redcoat took two steps, head turning this way and that,

as if he thought one of his own men had struck him with a fist. Then he looked down at his coat.

One thing about the redcoats—you didn't usually see them bleed at this distance. But you could see them fall, which the fellow did after another confused second or two, though by that time two soldiers had rushed up to support him.

The first of the wildfire guns shot then, and a trail of blazing oil—or whatever it was—splashed up through the trees toward him. It missed by thirty yards, but just the same, he figured it time to go. He slung the musket over his shoulder and started up the hill at a brisk pace. The guns *whoosh*ed behind him, but he didn't look back.

His men cheered as he joined them on the ridge, and he acknowledged them with a wave as he found his steed and mounted. Tomochichi, already on his horse, gave him a nod.

"We'll devil 'em into chasing us up here yet," he said. "Once we've got 'em in the hills, I daresay we can do some good work."

"They have restraint, but no other sort of sense," Tomochichi said. "Will they even take cover when we attack?"

"Not if we're lucky. It's not how they fight in Europe."

"Your men are European."

"Most were born here, and have been fighting with Indians and Spanish their whole lives. I was trained on the Continent, and at first could not understand the American method of fighting myself."

"You do it well enough now."

"Yes. I don't like it, though. I'm a man for the hard charge, not for this sort of skulk fighting. But winning is more important than my sensibilities."

"*We* count it an honorable way to fight," Tomochichi reminded him.

"I know," Oglethorpe replied. "And—"

He never finished the thought, for at that instant a pillar of flame exploded scarcely four yards from him, and then three more. It deafened him—for all of the gaping mouths and rearing mounts, he heard nothing but the biggest damn church bells in the world, right in his ear.

He fought for control of his mount, furious. How had his scouts missed the redcoats placing guns high enough to reach them here? Seeking cannon would do it, if they had something to seek, but—

Then a shadow passed over, and he saw an airship like the one that had attacked Fort Moore. And another, and another.

Adrienne studied the approaching storm. "This is a very bad thing," she said.

"Ah," Hercule said, "ah. And here I, with no scientifical training, was not worried in the least. How fortunate that I have a philosopher to enlighten me. What say you to *this*, demoiselle de logick? What say we take our ships and leave, *now,* before this 'very bad thing' has opportunity to prove to us just how bad it *is*? What say you to that?"

"It seems in no great hurry," Adrienne observed. "We will not leave until all the ships are ready and everyone back aboard."

"That will take several more minutes. Minutes we may not have."

"What have they done?" Crecy asked in a voice that sent little chills up Adrienne's spine, as even the sight of the thing did not. "What in the name of all unholy have they *done*?"

The storm was sliding down the mountain, as if an egg had been broken on the misty peaks, an egg with a sun for a yolk. It left behind it a trail of white vapor several miles wide. The eye grew brighter and larger as it moved, gone from its original sulking red to the color of lightning.

Adrienne referred to her instruments and revised her first opinion of the storm's speed: it looked slow only because of distance. She now calculated it was moving some thirty or forty miles an hour, which was around the top speed of the airships. For the moment, it was following the contours of the land, but they had already seen it airborne. Hercule might be right—it might be able to move more quickly in the air.

"What is it doing?" Crecy asked.

Adrienne studied it, trying to understand it herself.

"I see two vortices," she said after a moment, "one on top of the other, joined at the eye—that burning point. The bottom one turns clockwise and draws matter in. Not all matter, but a certain compound—I think it is the substance of graphite, or coal. The trees and soil become vapor when it leaves them, or they catch fire from the heat first and the dark ash of the smoke is sucked in. That spirals into the center, where—I'm not sure *what* is happening there. It's not exactly transmutation—it's as if the ferments themselves are being crushed together, mangled into a new substance. Much heat and lux are released—you see that part—and a hurricane of gas and some new substance comes whirling out anticlockwise."

"Poisonous gases?"

"Perhaps. It does not really matter, because they are so hot they would kill any living thing."

"My God."

"I imagine God has little to do with this. This is one of Swedenborg's engines. It is also alive—a malakus."

"A destroying angel." Crecy's voice was flat. "An old dream of theirs, made finally real."

"If you have held anything back concerning this, you should speak now, Veronique."

"I keep nothing from you," Crecy replied softly. "Nothing like this has ever existed before save in the darkest desires of the *malfaiteurs*."

"Thanks to Swedenborg, it exists now. What could he have been thinking? He is not an evil man."

"He doesn't have to be," Crecy replied. "He only need be gullible. I'm with Hercule. We should leave. Now."

"When all are aboard," Adrienne repeated absently.

She was mesmerized by the beauty of it, the sheer audacity

of scale. The substance of graphite was a universal one in living things. She had studied it and written a small treatise on it some years before. It was present in the earth and plants and beasts, even in the very atmosphere. Diamonds were made of it. When this thing finally quenched its thirst, nothing living would remain on Earth—nothing composed of matter, that is. The malakim would be immune to its appetites.

In her paper, she had speculated that graphite was the substance into which God had breathed life—the clay metaphorically referred to in Genesis. If that was so, then life would not only end, it could never exist again. That aspect of God's creation would be undone forever.

She had never bothered herself to conceive of something like this—another unforgivable stupidity, for evidently Swedenborg had.

She heard a soft gasp; Linné and Émilie had joined her at the rail.

"There is a new sort of angel for you, Linné. How will you name it?" she asked softly.

He didn't answer. By now the fringes of the monster had reached the outer settlements of New Moscow, and it seemed to gather speed. The burning eye was far too bright to stare at directly, even obscured by the ash swirling in and the inferno rushing out. It was still miles away, but she could smell it. It was a sharp smell, metallic, not at all like smoke.

"A new genus?" Linné asked finally, his voice thick with fear. "As we discussed, a creation, like the taloi? Is it then the same?"

"You are the namer," she said.

"Angelos keres," he murmured. "*Keres* for the Greek bringers of death." His voice was shaking.

"Well done," Adrienne told him. "Don't forget to write it down."

The ship was beginning to sway with the force of the wind. They were all now sweating, for the approaching air was steaming.

"All are aboard, Adrienne! For pity's sake!" Hercule seemed unable to look at the thing chewing toward them. She had never known a braver man than Hercule, but everyone had a different breaking point when it came to terror. Some men who would sneer into the mouth of a cannon would run cursing from a spider. To her, however dangerous, the keres was beautiful. But to Hercule, or anyone who could not see its full complexity, it must appear more unnatural than any spider.

"Let's go, then," she said.

The airships below were already rising to join them as their own lumbered into forward motion, swaying unsteadily. Above, the ruby globes with their captive ifrits howled a thin counterpoint to their approaching cousin.

"Heading?" Hercule asked.

"Inland. Over the mountains."

"That's where that thing just came from."

"I know."

"God damn it all," Hercule snapped, but he did as she directed.

They rose as quickly as they dared, and the heat followed them up as the keres gorged on New Moscow. Even as it did so, she saw two spots of red fire rise above—the airship Menshikov had stolen and another—one of the governor's.

"It seems the prince has lost his taste for this province," Crecy remarked dryly.

Adrienne returned her attention to the keres. From above, even to the unaided eye, its spiral structure was obvious. So was its trail—a path that looked very much like snow. It even lay on the landscape like snow—nothing that resembled trees, houses, or people remained along its path—only the curves of the earth itself.

"It's rising," Crecy shouted. "It's coming after us."

"So it is." Adrienne felt her first tingle of real fear.

The keres turned and stood on its edge like a wheel—much as they had first seen it. It turned a bit more so that it was aimed at them, like a giant target seeking its arrow, and began to rise, pushed up by its own heat and the force of its exhalations. It sounded like a grinding wheel amplified a million times. Loud, but not so loud that she could not hear the screams of her shipmates as it rose to take them.

10.

Red Paths

Ben Franklin was a god.

Not *the* God, of course, not the Creator—that distant, omnipotent being who hears prayers as rarely as an emperor hears the complaints of the least peasant in his country. No, Franklin was one of the clerkish gods, low on the ladder, busy with the daily task of looking after the planet Earth. Just now he was sifting through stacks of paperwork that seemed to grow larger by the instant. He signed the usual forms that would bring summer into autumn, initialed several memos to the god of the solar system, put through a request for more stardust.

He picked up the next document, squinting his eyes. They had been failing for the past several years. It was time, perhaps, to begin wearing glasses. He had tried reading glasses but disliked them because he had to take them off to see anything at a distance, which was a nuisance. What he needed was glasses that could help with both. Maybe two sorts of lenses in the same frame, the stronger lenses below, where the eyes naturally went when reading. . . .

Then he noticed the sheet he was staring at.

Provision for ye annihilation of the Towne of London by means of a Comet.

A chill clutched his godly heart. He could imagine, with divine imagination, exactly what that meant. A bar of light creeping with deceptive slowness down the sky. A horizon of flame. The terror as a light brighter than the sun washed over the million people in the City of Science, as they looked up for the last time.

Nope. He wasn't going to sign that.

And then he noticed that he already had.

He rushed to his window and threw it open, saw the terrible star descending.

Well, he was a god, wasn't he? He leapt from the window and began bounding across the earth in titanic leaps, arms outstretched. At first it went well, but then his feet touched ever more lightly on the ground, so he couldn't get purchase. He tried harder, but the faster he tried to run, the less contact he could get with the ground.

And all the while, he felt something awful coming behind him. He could not look over his shoulder, either, could not bear what he knew he would see. The gleaming red eyes of the devil, the floating orbs of his diabolic servants. He knew who followed him, risen from the dead, unkillable. It was Bracewell, now wearing the face of Sterne.

Or was he wearing a stern face?

A hysterical little laugh ached its way out of his chest. He should hide, but there was no place, and he felt the horror coming ever closer to his back, heard Bracewell-Sterne's sickening laugh.

He suddenly realized he had forgotten all about the comet. Frantically he looked up again, just in time to see a hemisphere of light rise on the horizon, and then a black column, lifting forever into the sky. Suddenly he could not breathe in the ash-thickened air. He could not breathe, and the warlock was upon him, and still he could not turn to see. He tried to scream, but it caught in his throat, kept there as if by a hand pressed over his mouth.

Then he did feel it—a hand—and awoke, thrashing in the dark, his heart trying to kill itself by battering against his breastbone.

"Hsst! Quiet, señor! I have come to rescue you!"

His body was slow to hear that, for the hand over his mouth

still frightened it; but then his mind caught up slowly, and he relaxed. The hand came away.

He was still hanging in the frame, as he had been for two days. Now and then they had been brought water and a little sour cornbread. Now and then children beat them and women threw urine on them.

The real torture still hadn't begun. Franklin had almost begun to wish it would.

Suddenly one of his arms sagged free, and it hurt more than anything had hurt him in a long time. He heard himself groan.

"Shh!" his benefactor hissed, cutting the rest of his bonds. Franklin fell from the frame like a child's puppet. The smell of dark earth filled his head, and he thought of worms and bare bones.

Enough of that. Marshaling his willpower, he lifted his head and noticed other shadows moving about the frames.

"Who—who are you?" Franklin managed.

"It is I, Don Pedro de Salazar de Ivitachuca," the voice proclaimed very softly. "And it is my honor to rescue you from these wretched heathens. But you must help me, too. Do you understand?"

"I do," Franklin whispered.

"Good. In a moment, we will creep from here. My man Francisco will be your guide, while I go about diverting the foe. You must be very silent, you understand?"

"Yes."

Moonlight spilled from behind a cloud, and Franklin caught glimpses of the rangers, readying themselves. As Don Pedro ghosted away, someone else squatted unsteadily nearby.

"Robin?"

"Aye. Here, take this." He pressed something in Franklin's hand. A little ax, such as Indians and rangers carried. He found he could barely get his hand to close on it.

"This is the best we have?"

"A couple of pistols. I thought they would go better in the

hands of the rangers. Not to worry—if we actually have to fight out of the village, I suspect it won't matter how we're armed."

"I suspect you're right. What about the guards?"

"They have grins on their throats. Our Apalachee friends seem pretty accomplished at this sneak warfare."

A third person joined them.

"Francisco, me," he said. "You hold on my shirt, stay close, yes?"

"Yes."

"Okay," McPherson said from somewhere near. "Let's go at it, boys. Let yar feet be specters."

Franklin had done his share of sneaking—stealing into Prague castle, filching a book from a Jewish wizard, most recently in the harbor at Charles Town. But always he had been aided by his inventions. Tonight he had nothing but darkness to render him invisible, in unknown territory, surrounded by leagues of enemies.

He glumly reflected that even with his aegis, he had usually managed to get a bit tripped up.

They started across the square. A cool breeze wove around them, but Franklin was still wet with sweat, his shirt clinging to his skin as if he had been swimming.

To Ben's ears, their party sounded like a herd of elephants. A dog somewhere agreed and began yapping.

Of course, the dogs here howled 'most all night, but this one had a knowing sort of bark. How long could it be before someone noticed?

He felt better once they got through the palisade, though he knew he had no right to. They still had a long way to go. He gripped the ax, thinking that here he had finally learned something about the use of a sword—only to be placed in the position of having to use yet another unfamiliar weapon.

But, as Robert said, if he had to actually *use* it, things were done anyhow.

They had just entered a narrow lane of darkness when gunfire erupted and shrill shrieks. First just a few, but then many more.

The gunfire escalated.

"Run," Francisco said.

They did, and it was curiously like his dream. No, it was worse, because in a dream Franklin always had some distant sense that he *was* dreaming . . . and a tiny but real comfort that he would awaken.

Here was no such comfort. Though his feet had plenty of purchase, the only thing he could make out at all was Francisco's shirt a few feet in front of him, and that more by tactile sense than sight.

Then they broke into a clearing. The half moon was already behind the trees—when it set, the night would be even darker. Ahead horses whickered, and more shadows bounded to their feet.

"Our men," Francisco informed him.

Franklin couldn't see how many there were, but it seemed a fair number. Things were looking up.

Until the men they were approaching began firing their guns, that is.

The night sang to Red Shoes as he trailed his paddle in the water. The water was so smooth, his vision so clear, that it looked as if his stolen canoe was sailing upon a river of stars, for he could see their pale reflections blurred by the passage of water, broken by the ripples his vessel made.

Grief's eyes held starlight, too. She was watching him, more still than the river, like the carved figurehead of an English ship, though facing in and not away.

"Are your bonds too tight?" he asked softly.

She did not answer, but instead eclipsed the light in her eyes with heavy lids and lay back into the bow of the canoe.

Red Shoes shrugged and returned his attention to the night.

Ten years before, in Venice, he had heard music unlike any he had ever known. The songs of the Choctaw were spare, chants with a single melody accompanied by a pair of sticks for rhythm, sometimes a rattle, most rarely a water drum. The music in Venice had been many songs together at once, played on many instruments of cleverly captured wind and chirping strings. As complicated as science, its rhythms and harmonies were—to him—elusive, alien, and beautiful.

Tonight, the night sang so. It pulsed with the cadences of frogs, soared with the crooning of whippoorwills, the wild cries of shriek owls and their witchy kin. All of this he had noticed before, of course—but now there was more, a structure he had never heard that put it all in place. It was beauty, and he stayed caught in it, not thinking but only being—until he heard the voice.

He was annoyed when the voice interrupted the song, calling him from the channel of the river to the backwater cane swamps, where the glassy columns hissed and rattled like ghostly snakes. But he followed the voice because he knew it was one he ought to answer. It was time.

Red Shoes.

I am coming, scalped man. I am coming to kill you.

The swamp stank of rot, as if its surface was the bloated skin of a corpse, the canoe a sharp blade opening it. He paddled on, into shadow, until one of the shadows stood.

"Here I am," the scalped man said. "I've been waiting for you."

"You've been awaiting your death."

The scalped man chuckled, very low. "Why should you want to kill me? We are brothers, you and I, and you are the elder brother."

"We are no kin."

Again, the laugh. "Feel your strength, brother, like the deep roots of a tree. You made a shadowchild and sent it to your people, to warn them, I guess. I tell you now, it was destroyed like all the rest. Did it weaken you? You made a hundred more to serve you here—I see them there about you, your hungry children. Were you weakened, drained—did you grieve, as once you did, when your messenger died?"

"No."

"You don't find that strange?"

"I do."

"Were you attacked, as you thought you would be—by me, by my spirits, by those who travel with the Sun Boy? You were not, because they know you now. *I* know you."

"You attacked my messenger, as you just said."

"The attack was by mindless things, set to watch, before you became what you are."

"I know you, scalped man. My enemy. You tried to kill me—you wounded me. You and yours chased my friends. You still chase them."

Now the scalped man laughed low and deep. "You really don't know, do you? How have you blinded yourself, brother?"

"What are you yowling about?"

"Think! Why is the woman there in the canoe with you bound? Why did you lash her hands and feet with rawhide?"

"She tried to run away. I was worried she would be killed, lost and alone in this country. I bound her for her own good."

"Ah, yes. But when did she try to escape? Why?"

"She—she wasn't as strong as I thought she was. She got sick, and then she tried to run." He straightened. "I'm tired of your questions. I'm going to kill you now."

"If I am to die, indulge me just a little further, Red Shoes. *When* did she get sick?"

This was annoying, but for some reason his desire to kill the scalped man had waned. Perhaps because there was no longer any need to fear him. The scalped man was a nothing to him, an insect.

Of course, he reminded himself, even an insect, carelessly trod underfoot, could cause sickness with its ghost. It would not do to keep his eye too far from his foe.

"Try to remember," the scalped man urged again. "When did she try to escape? Why?"

Pushing down his anger, Red Shoes turned one eye inward and remembered.

11.

Apollo

As fire splashed all around him and the flying machines whined above, Oglethorpe had a vivid recollection of visiting a glassblower's once, when he was a boy, of the glistening, smooth forms taking shape in the molten crystal. Here it looked as if someone was blowing men and horses of glass, so thickly did the burning stuff cover them. The lack of sound made it all the more unreal.

The men were in total panic, as well they should be. Grimly, he pulled his pistols, took aim at the next ship to pass over, and fired. He thought he saw a tiny spark fleck the metal. He fired again.

Shoving the empty guns into the holsters on his saddle, he drew his Fahrenheit pistol from his belt.

Then it occurred to him that the infantry and cavalry below surely knew of the aerial attack—which meant that they would be on their way.

He galloped around, yanking men by the arm, pointing them down the next hill. They needed to put some distance between themselves and the valley the redcoats occupied, and they needed, by damn, to get from the sight of these airships.

He tried to ignore the burning wretches on the ground, some still crawling, their eyes already evaporated.

It took forever, it seemed, to get them all moving in a common direction. If he got the chance, he might point out later to Tomochichi that this was where the European way was better: the redcoat troops had the discipline to stand and wait for orders even while the sky rained hellfire on them, and when the order came they would march through the curtains of fire to where they were directed.

Like machines, he thought. Like the taloi.

By the time they regrouped at the top of the next ridge, Oglethorpe's hearing was coming back, and some order had returned. He sent Parmenter around for a quick count, then set rear guards, as they began toiling down the next hill. Leagues were what they needed now. He noticed that most of his men spent so much time looking up through the trees, wondering when death would envelop them with fiery embrace, that they couldn't guide their horses. Even after a few hours with no sign of the flying machines, there were more upcast eyes than in a caravan of pilgrims.

Parmenter galloped up. "The head count is fifty-six," he said.

"Fifty-six?" Oglethorpe said, stunned. "I have whittled two hundred men down to fifty-six?"

"Sir, we've accounted for at least three hundred redcoats. And I'm sure some of the men are merely scattered, and will find us soon."

"Fifty-six."

"Yes, sir."

Oglethorpe digested that in silence, wondering what Prince Eugène of Savoy might have done with fifty-six men against—how many?

"Sir, I've a few worries to discuss."

"Hmm? Yes, of course, Lieutenant. Go on."

"The airships, sir. They must know we no longer have our devil gun. If they didn't before, they do now. Which means they will surely bring in their larger craft."

"They might suspect we are tricking them."

"They might. Or they might have captured the Maroons, or the Maroons might have gone to them with it—"

"I've asked you not to voice suspicions like that."

Parmenter looked stubborn, but he took another line. "All I'm saying is that we can expect more worries from the air, sir."

"Thank you for making glass clear, Mr. Parmenter."

"My pleasure, General," Parmenter replied without heat. "Another thing—how well do our scouts know this territory?"

"I don't even know which ones are alive. Chief?"

Tomochichi had been following the conversation silently. "Not well," he said. "This is Coweta territory. I came through here in my youth, but have no good map of it in my head."

"That's my worry," Parmenter said. "The redcoats have the best map—the land itself. They can fly over it and figure where they ought to be. Or where *we* ought to be."

"What do you mean?"

"Before, we were drawing *them* in, making them go where *we* wanted. I think they've changed breeches with us. Now we're goin' where they want *us* t' go."

Oglethorpe sighed wearily. "That's probably right, Mr. Parmenter."

They got their confirmation a few hours later, when they tried to work their way back south and east. They ran straight up against a well-armed cavalry, one that could not possibly have gotten there by separating from the main army. Airships again.

They exchanged a few shots and fell back, now reduced to fifty-four. The cavalry did not pursue with speed, but Oglethorpe felt them back there, driving them.

"Yes, Mr. Parmenter," he allowed, "you are most certainly correct. They lead us by the nose now."

"What shall we do about it?"

"Go, I expect. Acquit ourselves as best we can. Our aether-schreiber was destroyed in that set-to on the hill, so I'll want a few of your rangers to try and slip through, to get the news out. A few might make it."

"Sir, you should go."

"Don't waste any time on that," Oglethorpe told him. "You won't convince."

By mid-morning of the next day, they could see the trap. Their high ground gave way to an open savanna bounded by a river on the west and low but rugged mountains on the north. Across the plain, near the river, they could make out a picket of men and ordnance. Hovering over the plain itself were two of the big airships. They looked almost like sailing ships, suspended beneath orbs of a sulky red color.

"We would more easily punch through those behind us," Parmenter said, as they took it all in from the trees.

"They would merely move a greater force to block us or drop grenades on us again when we engage. Even if they cannot always see us through the trees, they will know where their own troops are." He raised his voice so all of the men could hear.

"No, we have three choices: surrender, try to scatter into the woods, or attack. All you men who know me can guess which one I'm in favor of. But I will count none of you cowards if you choose another way, especially you men with wives and children. I'm an old bachelor, with no one to mourn me, so naturally the choice is, for me, an easy one."

"I'm with you, sir," Parmenter said quietly.

"No one can count the days allotted until after they are spent," Tomochichi added. "If this is the last of mine, it is good."

He saw fear—but not cowardice—on the faces of several of the men, but none asked to be excused.

"Masters Kelly, Callahan, Henderson."

"Sir?" they answered in unison.

"I've chosen you three to slip out, if you can, in case the other scouts don't make it through." Also because he knew they had big families and no close kin to help support them.

"General," Henderson said, "I reckon you think it a kindness—"

"Not at all, Mr. Henderson. I think it an order."

"Then call me a traitor if you must, sir, but my family is better served by me fightin' here."

"I reckon we all feel that way," Callahan added.

Oglethorpe tried to suppress a fierce smile, but he couldn't. "Very well, gentlemen. Should you survive this, I may hang you, but for now—check your weapons."

When they had done so, he drew his Fahrenheit pistol and his broadsword. They trotted out of the forest together.

They were met, first, with eerie silence. They had ridden nearly a hundred yards before guns of the distant red line even moved to aim at them.

Oglethorpe raised his sword high, whirled it thrice, and shouted at the top of his lungs. "For God and America!"

And charged.

"Can you stop it?" Crecy asked, gazing at the monstrous thing rising below them. The air was charged with dizzying heat and a frighteningly unnatural scent. The sky vibrated like a drumhead.

Adrienne crinkled her brow in concentration. "Stop it? No. But, let me think—how does it know to chase us?"

"I don't understand you."

"Whatever else it is, it is a malakus, a thing unused to seeing and judging things made of matter. It knows to chase our ships, somehow, which means it has been taught to recognize them, to tell them apart from trees or houses or other things of wood."

"That makes sense."

"But its understanding cannot be very discerning. What if it had two groups of ships to follow? Or three?"

"It does, and it's chasing us—not Menshikov."

"Exactly," Adrienne replied. "It simply chose the largest group." She whirled toward the wheelhouse. "Hercule! Have the other ships maneuver as close as possible to us. I have an idea."

"I heard you. But if your reasoning's sound, shouldn't we scatter?"

"No. That might confuse it *too* much. I want to give it as clear a choice as possible, and I want it to follow Menshikov, since you'll notice his ships are headed in the opposite direction from ours. Bring the ships together!"

Hercule sprang into motion, sending the signals out by flag and schreiber. The rest of the fleet began drifting toward them, until they were in a tight cluster, each vessel no more than thirty yards from another.

"Closer," Adrienne said. "I want the hulls touching."

"In this wind? Impossible."

"Look there, Hercule," she said, pointing at the keres. It was gaining only slowly, but it did not have to catch them—only come near enough for the outer fringes of it to touch them. Then the ships and their bodies would come apart—if they were not already dead from the heat. "Surviving *that* is what is impossible. Anything is reasonable compared to that."

So much sweat covered Hercule's face that it seemed that his flesh was already bubbling into blisters. When he swiped at it with his cuff, it became a glossy sheen.

"As you say." He gave the orders.

Instants later a sickening tremor ground through the ship. Linné, not holding firmly enough, was slammed into the rail and flung half over before Crecy caught him with her sure, strong hands. Others weren't so lucky. A young sailor fell into the narrow space between two ships and was caught and crushed into a paste as surely as if he had fallen into a giant's mortar.

Another concussion, this one as sharp as a cannon hit, bucked the ship. Spars and cables snapped.

The scent of woodsmoke reached her nostrils as the undersides of the ships began to smolder.

She closed her mortal eyes and went to the world of insubstance, where she worked a deception, masking each ship with the other, creating a sphere that blended and merged their substance, like a prism in reverse, making white light of many colors.

It was illusion only—the ships did not really merge. But the impression they made on the aether did. She held it, as the ships and their crews screamed around her and fire rose below. She worked the operation in her head, like a rosary, like needlework, over and over, until it fell in time with her heart, with the pulse in her neck, until she began to lose herself and wondered why she needed mortal eyes at all, or flesh.

Her work faded behind her, like the world, and she fluttered like a moth in the darkest, largest night of all. No stars, no lamps, no moon rose to attract her, only lighter black or a dark, dark gray. She moved toward that.

In that thinner night, holes appeared, like eyes, and then a line that might be a nose. As she watched a portrait formed, ash smeared on lampblack. She recognized the face.

"Nicolas?" she heard someone ask, and then knew it was herself.

Her own voice answered her, but the words did not come from her. "*Nico-less.* What is that name? It is an old name. I have heard it before."

"Nicolas? My son? Is it you?"

Deep in the black sockets, almost invisible sparks flashed.

"Who calls me son? I know my mother's voice. You are not my mother. You are—" a pause "—an old dream of mine, maybe. Something like that."

"Nicolas!" Adrienne felt a tremor, her heart humming like a violin string. "It *is* your name. I *am* your mother. I am coming for you."

The face frowned, and the sparks grew in number and magnitude. "I was told to expect you. I was told to expect your lies. I'm leaving."

The face began to fade, and Adrienne felt sudden panic. She had found him, somehow, across the aether. She could not lose him now.

"Wait!" she begged. "Wait! I am mistaken. I thought you

were someone else. But I would like—I would like to talk to you."

This time, the voice sounded hesitant. "Talk? About what?"

"About you. About anything you wish. What . . . what can I call you?"

"You may *not* call me the name you used before."

"I will not. It was a mistake."

"You may call me . . . Sun Child."

She saw herself, suddenly, in a grotto in Versailles, staring at a statue with her face. The statue was of Thetis, a mistress of Apollo. In the same grotto stood a statue of Apollo, and his face was that of Louis XIV. Louis, who had raped her—not by force of arms, but because he was the king, was certain that no woman could or would refuse him. Louis, the Sun King.

Louis, the father of her son.

"May I call you . . . Apollo?" she asked.

"What means that?"

"It means 'the sun.' "

"It is good, then. Tell me more of this name."

"It is Greek, the name of an ancient god, who drove a chariot across the sky."

"I ride such a chariot," the voice said, softening somehow. "I see most wondrous things. They are pleasing to me. The country I pass over pleases me, the chosen land. It is pleasing to purify it."

"What do you mean?"

There came a pause. "My nurse returns," he said. "I shall tell her of you."

"Have you—have you ever had a secret friend, Apollo?"

"Not—not in a long time. My mother used to be my secret friend, but now she isn't secret."

"Why don't *we* be secret friends?"

"Why?"

"For the fun of it—for the secret."

The face scrunched, as if pondering. "That pleases me very well," it remarked. "But if that's the case, I must go now. I will call on you later—if I may." He sounded almost shy.

"Later, then," Adrienne replied, as the ash swirled and was swallowed by pitchy darkness. She heard a roaring like distant surf, felt heat prick her skin. She remembered, suddenly, what she had been doing, and realized with horror that she must have failed.

Red Shoes remembered.

The day after sending the shadowchild to his people, he found the tracks of the Mongols. They weren't hard to find; after all, they were the predators, not the prey—or at least they thought they were. The panther does not hide her tracks.

But they were no longer the panther, which they discovered the next day when he caught them and killed them all. It was a simple matter, really, to loosen the lightning in their armor, their weapons, their blood. It had once been beyond him—this sort of magic—but no longer. The shadow of the great snake pulsed in his heart and belly, and little was beyond him now.

After that, he and Grief continued on, now tracking Flint Shouting, Tug, and the tsar. This trail was a little harder to follow, but when there were no tracks he still had their scent, and it led him surely through forests that were growing to be more like forests, grasslands that came more infrequently and in smaller expanses.

After two days they reached a place where the weight of a small river gently bent the earth into a shallow valley, from which the smoke of cooking fires streamed into a still blue sky. On the cleared, high ground above the water clustered some fifteen houses made of grass—Wichita houses, like those he had seen before.

As they rode leisurely down the hill, riders came out to meet them. Amongst them, with his new, clear sight, he saw Flint Shouting.

Flint Shouting saw Red Shoes, too, and let out a jubilant whoop.

"You lucky Choctaw!" he yelled, as they came closer. "You survived after all!"

Something about that irritated Red Shoes, but he kept it to himself. After all, Flint Shouting had only done what he had told him to. "I did," he affirmed.

"I have a war party ready to go after the Mongols," Flint Shouting said proudly.

"That's good work, but no longer necessary," Red Shoes said.

Flint Shouting's face bunched like a frog preparing to hop. "Really?"

"Yes. I dealt with them."

"How? I thought you were all out of strength."

"I found more."

Flint Shouting leaned over to clasp his arm. "Good! Good! You shall tell us the story! Though I wish I could have killed a few more myself. We had to fight, you know—some of them caught up with us. We only made it here yesterday." He gestured grandly. "The village of my birth," he said.

"Your people seem to have forgiven you," Red Shoes observed.

"Hmm? Oh, yes. There are still a few who want to cut off my nose, but things are better now. They missed me, I think, and their anger has cooled."

Another rider was coming up the slope—Tug, looking a little silly on his Mongol pony. He was grinning like a split-open pumpkin.

"Damn good t' see you!" he called as he drew near. "Damn good!" He hopped off and in two bounds had reached Red Shoes, who soon found himself lifted from his horse and riding on the big man's shoulders, a crowd of Wichita children all around them, whooping and screaming. He whooped, too, but it was as if the part of him that was glad to see Tug again was far away, a sort of dream.

His whole life as a man was a dream, one he was waking from.

That night they feasted, and he ate as he had not in months. His appetite surprised him, but his satisfaction came from the feeling in his belly, not from the taste. The food itself was flavorless. After the meal, he watched Tug stumble about, trying to dance, mostly failing but obviously enjoying himself. The former pirate tried to draw Red Shoes into it, but as the night wore on, he felt ever more gravid, hot, listless.

The tsar didn't join in, either.

"Our pursuit is really dead?" Peter asked, picking at what remained of a bowl of buffalo stew.

"Yes."

"Killed by your magic?"

"Yes."

The tsar nodded. "I owe you more each day. I know the gratitude of a king means little to you, but you have it."

"On the contrary, Tsar Peter, it means much to me. I want your people far from my country. Perhaps, in your gratitude, you will remember that."

"I want the same thing."

"Do you? What if they win? What then?"

"As I said before," Peter said, "it isn't taking the land—it's holding it. We could never hold this wild country, not if every Russian bore arms. And why should we? What can we get from it that we could not get more profitably by trade?"

Red Shoes nodded distractedly.

"Our friend Flint Shouting seems quite important here," the tsar noticed.

"It's his people. Of course, these same people were torturing him to death not long ago, so best stay wary."

The tsar threw up his hands. "It's hard to worry, right now. I feel better than I have in weeks. I feel strong. Do these people have strong drink?"

"You mean like wine or brandy?"

"Exactly so."

"No."

The tsar made a face. "Well, they ought to have it."

Red Shoes thought of the destruction the bitter waters had wrought in his own homeland and among the little nations crouched around New Paris. He didn't say anything.

"I wish to dance with them," the tsar said, pointing at the circular dance in progress. "Is it permitted?"

"Of course. You see that Tug does so."

"Indeed." The tsar clasped his arm. "Again—my thanks, both for my rescue and for adventures I could never have dreamed of, even in my youth." He rose and joined the dancing. Nothing he did even remotely fit into what the Wichita were doing, but they seemed amused by his efforts.

Red Shoes knew that on another day he would have been amused, too. But something was wrong with him. He was feeling more torpid than ever. He got up and wandered into the darkness outside the village, trying to understand.

He turned at a slight sound. Tug was following him.

"You mad at me, fellah?" the sailor asked when they were alone. "I knew I should have come back f 'r yuh. Damn—but you said—"

"You did the right thing, Tug," he said softly. "You did exactly the right thing. Don't feel bad about it."

"Then what's the matter? Y' han't said three words all evenin'."

Red Shoes closed his eyes, saw again the expanse of his tail, the black rattles humming at the end of it.

"I—Listen to me, Tug. Something's happened. I've swallowed something, and its burning me inside. Do you understand?"

"No. Not a damn bit."

"Just—" He couldn't feel his feet on the ground anymore. "Tug, I need you to do something. If anything happens to me—"

"Wat d' y' mean? You sick?"

"I think so. If anything happens, you have to take the tsar

away from here. To Carolina or New Paris. You have to let the other white men know what's happening out here. You have to find Benjamin Franklin and Nairne and tell them. You understand me? Make Flint Shouting go with you, as a guide."

"What's wrong with you?"

"Maybe nothing. Just leave me alone for a while."

Tug stood there for a few minutes. "Red Shoes, I owe y' my life more times 'n' I can count. More 'n that, you're a mate, an' though I've said that of quite a few, y'r the best friend I've ever owned. 'Drot you, but tell me what's goin' on."

"I will when I know, Tug. I swear it. Now go find one of these Wichita women. There ought to be one or two curious about white men."

"More like ten," he said. "But if y' need me—"

"I only need to be alone," Red Shoes told him. "Please."

"Well, if that's the right of it. I'll see y' in the mornin'."

"Yes."

When Tug was gone, Red Shoes stood trembling, gazing up at the stars, hating them for no reason that he could name.

He walked back into the village the next morning, without having slept. A few women and children were already stirring, and an old man whose flesh was covered with little tattoos—each shaped like a small cross—watched Red Shoes approach through narrowed eyes. He had shadowchildren—small, weak ones. One of them was sniffing curiously at Red Shoes.

"You are something strange," the old man said in the trade language.

"Really? What am I, grandfather? Tell me. I would like to know, myself."

The old man stared at him for a few moments, then cleared his throat.

"A long time ago, there was a flood that covered the world. Do you remember it?"

"I've heard of it. How could I remember it?" But suddenly he did remember something, a surging rage, a mighty effort to split the skin of the world, to suck it back into the mud, to thwart Hashtali. He remembered boiling and a weight of waters greater than the sea.

He didn't tell that to the old man.

"Before the flood," the old man said, "four children were born. Their father was a chief, and as they grew, they became monsters. At first they were just a little rough on the other children, but since their father was a chief, they were tolerated. In time they killed and ate one of their playmates, and people understood that the children were bad. But by then it was too late. They grew up, taller than trees, and they could reach down and grab people wherever they went. Finally they got so tall they could reach anywhere in the world, but they couldn't reach their own feet. They had grown together, like a giant tree with a different face for each direction. They could not walk around anymore.

"So the only safe place to live, you see, was right at their feet. That's where our ancestors went to live. If they wandered out too far, though, the monsters could still reach them. That's why the flood came, eventually, to kill the four monsters before they grew all the way to the sky and started pulling down the stars."

That was wrong, Red Shoes knew. The flood hadn't come to kill the giants, but *because* of them. Or maybe—

Maybe all these years he had been wrong.

Wrong about what? What were these thoughts, these memories? Sparks flashed behind his eyes, and his skull hurt as if it were breaking apart. He flexed his great wings, and the sound of his thousand rattles filled the heavens.

The old man noticed. "*You* are growing," he said. "*You* are growing tall."

Suddenly everything snapped into focus, and the pain was gone. "But I am not yet so tall that you can hide at my feet," Red Shoes said. He smiled grimly as he lit a fire in the old man's veins, watched his eyeballs burst like ripe plums as the steam inside him boiled out.

The watching children screamed. He killed them, too.

He didn't like the houses, so he set them on fire. Then the warriors woke up and came for him, and he popped them like flint corn on a hot rock, first one by one, then in numbers.

That was what Red Shoes remembered.

12.

Cavalries

Francisco pushed Franklin flat beneath the whining bullets. Behind him, someone shrieked in agony as three more muskets went off. People were shooting at him from both directions.

"Keep low," Francisco shouted and then, ignoring his own advice, leapt up.

Someone hurtled from the darkness to meet him, and suddenly Francisco and someone else were straddling over Franklin, shouting and grappling. As Franklin kicked against the ground, sliding away from them, he heard a peculiar, meaty sound and a gurgle, and one of the two shapes fell.

The other bent quickly toward him, and he saw the silhouette of an ax against the stars.

And then Robert—Franklin knew him by his cursing—was suddenly standing over him, too, and this time there was a sound almost exactly like a pumpkin splitting after having been dropped. Something wet splattered on Ben's face.

"Up, Ben!" Robert shouted.

"But they're shooting—"

"That's Don Pedro's men, knocking down Cowetas. Come on!"

There was a sudden moment of quiet, and then more pandemonium. Don Pedro's men had either reloaded or, more likely—given the heartbeats in which this had all taken place—drawn new weapons. Blazing sparks lit the night again.

"Wait, Robin. Francisco!" He knelt at the two bodies near

him, realizing he didn't know which was which. They were both Indians, both dressed much alike, at least in the darkness.

It did not matter, for they were both dead as stones.

It seemed to take forever to get mounted. The hubbub in the near distance continued, but all the warriors unfortunate enough to choose the right direction in which to search for the fugitives seemed to be either dead or fled.

Ben's horse followed the one in front of it at a trot.

Oglethorpe watched the ships grow nearer, still waving his sword and shouting his defiance. He aimed to pass right under the big airships and then straight on to the kneeling line of redcoats between him and the river. With any luck at all, they might be able to take a few of the bastards with them.

But then he caught a motion from the corner of his eye, saw another body of horse bearing down out of the mountains to his right.

And they did not wear red. He shouted in exultation, thinking at first by their dark faces they might be the Cherokee, at long last fulfilling their promise to help; and for that instant, he thought his men might actually have a chance. But then it registered how few the newcomers were—twelve or so at the most. Not much of an addition, hardly a drop in the ocean.

"Great God!" Parmenter cried.

Oglethorpe jerked his eyes from the horsemen in time to see the airships fall. They made an impressive sound as they bounced and splintered.

"Unoka!" Oglethorpe shouted, for now he could see the little African, brandishing the devil gun in the air, hear the triumphant cries of the Maroons as they flowed into his charge and became one with them.

Almost without thinking, Oglethorpe wheeled his charging men through the wreckage of the airships, which now shielded them from the infantry beyond. When they came from amongst the hulks, they had only fifty yards to go.

Of course, fifty yards could be a damn long way when you were facing a line of muskets. A wall of smoke puffed toward them. Parmenter grunted, but held his saddle—everyone else was behind him, so Oglethorpe couldn't see how many died in that first volley.

The second rank fired while the first rank reloaded.

But they were now close enough so that two volleys was all the enemy got; and Oglethorpe drove straight into the bayonets, firing his pistol, slashing with the broadsword.

The ranks were thin. They had been spread to give maximum firepower, not to absorb a charge which, by all rights, should never have come anywhere near them. Still, Oglethorpe counted it a miracle—a true, honest miracle—when they were suddenly through, and there was the river and beyond it the welcoming haven of the forest.

With no letup, he plunged into the stream, his men behind him. Bullets kicked spume in the water so it looked like every fish in the river was spitting; but with sudden, fierce joy, he knew for sure that God was on his side. They had already done the impossible—having come this far, they would make it all the way.

His newfound faith got more reinforcement an instant later, as guns began barking from the forest beyond the river—and these guns were not aimed at them but at the redcoats.

By the time he was free of the river and in the sheltering trees, he was actually laughing. What else could he do? The redcoats were retreating across the field, double time.

Later he found time to thank God more formally, with a long and earnest prayer. Not only had he given them a miracle, but of his fifty-four remaining men, only five had been killed in the mad dash, though many, Parmenter included, were wounded. Unoka had lost two.

Their allies across the river were Coweta, and that's about

all he knew. Tomochichi was deep in parley with them, and would be for some hours.

Having thanked God, he had someone else to thank.

The Maroons kept to their own campfire, of course, easily found by the noise they made. When he reached it, he saw the black men ringed around Unoka, who was singing in his own language. His men gave answering calls, clapping their hands or beating sticks in strange rhythms; and Oglethorpe felt transported to a continent he had never seen, to the wild jungles that had given many of these men birth.

As he listened to the strange music, his throat caught. It was both triumphant and melancholy. Surely they missed their homeland as much as he missed England. Just as surely, they were determined that their home was now here, in America.

He stood mesmerized, not thinking to intrude, but after a time they noticed him standing there.

"Come an' talk to us, General!" Unoka shouted. "Tell us about you crazy charge!"

"I didn't come here to say anything about me," Oglethorpe said. "I came to tell you that, by damn, you are men such as I have never known. And I have never been prouder to ride with anyone."

Unoka nodded. "Didn't t'ink we were comin', did you?"

"We thought you met with ill chance."

"T'at we did, time an' time again, an' we got behind, always two paces behind. But we caught up, didn't we?"

"Damned if you didn't," Oglethorpe said. "And damn glad I am. And if you gentlemen will permit it, I would like to shake the hand of every last one of you."

Morning brought soberer reflection. Two more of his men had died of their wounds. The Coweta had pitched in out of anger at the redcoats and admiration for the courage of the Colonials, but they made it clear that the war still wasn't theirs. What Tomochichi did get out of them was a few guides who knew the area, who assured them that they could get them to the margravate, flying eyes or no.

"It's what we ought to do," Parmenter said. "We did what we set out to, an' then some."

"I quite agree," Oglethorpe murmured.

"I count this a victory," Parmenter said, wincing as he tried to sit up. A bullet had shattered two ribs but seemed to have missed his vitals.

Oglethorpe thought about all his men who would never count anything again. He clapped the ranger on the shoulder lightly. "Many more victories like this," he said, "and we will have no need of a defeat."

"I know you're right, sir, but whatever comes, it was glorious, wasn't it?"

"That is was, Mr. Parmenter. That it was."

Pain brought Adrienne back, sharp stinging pain on her cheeks, and she opened her physical eyes to Crecy drawing her hand back for another slap. The redhead hesitated. "Adrienne?"

"Why are you hitting me, Veronique?"

"You were—you were gone from us."

Adrienne noticed that she was no longer on the deck of the airship. She was in her cabin, her clothes loosened.

Her head hurt, very much.

"How long?"

"Nine hours."

"And how long have you been slapping me?"

"Nine hours, on and off. I've never seen you like that."

"I've never experienced that either." She rubbed her forehead. "Did it work? Did we escape the keres?"

"It must have. We still live, and the monster went off after Menshikov's ships."

Adrienne nodded, feeling faint. "I hope he gives it a good chase," she said.

"After all he has done?"

"Of course. The longer it chases him, the longer it will be before we must face it again."

"Ah. And yet we follow the source of it, do we not? How can we know this army we chase does not have a hundred of those things?"

"We don't," Adrienne replied. "Certainly they have more than one. They may have far worse things."

"With creatures like that," Crecy said, "I don't see why they need an army at *all*."

Adrienne shrugged. "A question for Uriel, when he comes to me again. I suspect that this has more to do with the factions of the malakim than it has to do with a sensible plan of conquest. For whatever reason, some of them are reluctant to destroy humanity outright—I think they would rather have us kill ourselves. That engine could swallow cities, but it was sent with a singular purpose—to destroy New Moscow and ourselves."

"It left quite a trail, coming here. We're following it backward, toward the east."

"You see? I've been told the dark engines are of recent invention. Perhaps this was the first test of them. If they had been using them since the army set out, two years ago, there would be nothing of this continent left."

"But they have them now," Crecy said.

"Yes. And so we must learn to destroy them."

"What if they cannot be destroyed?"

Adrienne smiled grimly. She had spoken to her son. He was real, he was alive, and she could find him again. Anyone who got in the way of that courted disaster, no matter what sort of engine they had with them.

"If there is one thing that life has taught me, Veronique," she said softly, "it is that *anything* can be destroyed."

Epilogue

Weeping Lightning

Red Shoes came back from memory to find the scalped man before him, chuckling. He waggled a finger at Red Shoes. "Yes, I saw the village you destroyed. It still smokes. Crows and buzzards pick at the corpses of the warriors, the women, the children, the old men. A fine job."

"They were my enemies," Red Shoes said.

"And who are your friends?"

"Tug. Flint Shouting."

"The ones you follow now."

"Yes."

"Think, Red Shoes. You killed the Mongols. You killed the Wichita. What are your friends fleeing, when their pursuers are all dead?"

"I don't know. I wish I did."

"You know. They are fleeing *you*."

And it suddenly made sense. Of course they had run from him. Who wouldn't? Flint Shouting had tried to turn and fight Red Shoes, but Tug had smacked the Wichita over the head. Red Shoes remembered that. Good old Tug, doing what he had asked. He must have figured that this was the "something" Red Shoes feared would happen to him.

In any case, the scalped man was right—he should have known. What *had* blinded him?

But he knew the answer to that, too. Something in him was afraid—or remembered being afraid—of this sort of thing.

Something in him was like Grief, sickened by what he had done at the Wichita village.

Part of him, yes—the fingernail of one hand was a part of him, too, but not a large part. Yet this had been large enough to paint the truth black.

He would have to attend to that. What use this power if mortal weakness made him fear to use it?

He nodded to the scalped man. "It is true, what you said. Do you have anything else true to say, or have you used up all such words?"

"Do you still plan to kill me?"

"Not just now. I can do that anytime I want."

"Indeed, you can. What *will* you do now?"

"Find my friends and prove to them that they need not fear me. Find my people and protect them from what is coming."

"The best way to be safe from it is to join with it," the scalped man said.

"Perhaps. I will decide when the time comes. You have helped me just now, but I have not forgotten how treacherous your kind are. I do not trust all of your advice."

"May I travel along with you?"

"No."

"May I follow you?"

"Do what pleases you, but remember I may change my mind and kill you at any moment."

For the rest of the night, the only sound he made was the lick of his paddle into the river. He tried to sort out what had become of him. He didn't feel very different—he still felt like himself, like Red Shoes. He had known persons hollowed out by the spirits, walking skins with no human minds in them. That wasn't what he was.

It seemed, when he thought back, that he had changed when he made the messenger shadowchild. That was when he understood how very powerful he was, when the strength he had swallowed began to quicken.

There were legends among his people of orphans who one day learned that they were the bastard children of Thunder, who—after a few tests—suddenly came into their legacy and power. He felt a bit like that, as if he had finally earned the use of something that had always been in him, that he had always deserved.

He caught Grief staring at him again and remembered another legend.

"Can I untie you now? Will you try to run?" he asked.

Given her recent behavior, he didn't expect her to answer; but after a brief hesitation, she did. "Where I go?" she asked dully.

He drew a knife and cut the rawhide thongs on her hands and feet. "This way you can swim if we overturn. But keep your promise."

"I will."

And again she lapsed into silence, which wasn't what he was after.

"At the Wichita village—you were—sick," Red Shoes ventured.

"Yes. You killed them all. The little children."

"When did a warrior ever flinch from killing?"

"You weren't warrior. They not die at the hands of warrior. You tornado, grass fire. Plague."

"Would you blame those things for killing?"

"I would blame the sorcerer who sent them."

"Ah. May I tell you a story?"

"How could I stop you?"

"There was an orphan boy who had no luck, no hunting magic, no kin, nothing. One day he went off into the woods, to succeed or to die. In the night, a peregrine falcon came into the circle of his fire, pursued by a horned owl. The falcon asked the boy to protect him, while the owl demanded he give the falcon up to him. The owl, a great sorcerer, promised the boy all the powers of the night if he should leave the falcon to him.

"But the boy protected the falcon, who gave him the power of his eyes, and his sharp breast, with which to strike prey like a war club. The falcon made the orphan into a great hunter, a war prophet.

"We tell that story to our children. We tell them the orphan's choice was the correct one—owls are accursed beings, nightgoers. And the boy benefited from helping the falcon. *But*—" He paused meaningfully. "—Who knows what the boy would have gotten if he had chosen the *owl*?"

"You do," Grief replied.

He grinned. "Yes, I do. People like me, when we are very, very young—a voice calls us away, and we go. I remember it very well. It was the little man, *kwanakasha*, also called *bohpoli*, the thrower. He offered me two choices—a bag of herbs and a war club. It was really no choice at all—either way I would have ended as an accursed being, a plague to all people.

"But my uncle was attentive. He noticed me, speaking to this companion no one else could see. He was wise and powerful. Our people—the wise ones, the sacred fire makers and the prophets—have long known a simple fact. Some children are suited for these spirits, but even so the spirit must stroke the mother just so, make small changes in the child so he can receive them. The thing is—the very changes that allow them to speak to us, to raise us in secret though we are surrounded by family—those same changes make it possible to turn against them. To cut them up, put them back together, use them to manipulate the shadows of our souls and to make magic that owes nothing directly to them. I did this, with my uncle's help. I denied the easy power, and took what was hard. In a sense, I chose the falcon, you might say."

"I not think so. I think you choose owl from very start. But you not know until now."

"I am not an accursed being, Grief. I have been good."

"You not who you were, Red Shoes."

He smiled briefly. "Did you know me so well?"

"I watched you."

"Why?"

She didn't answer.

"Maybe I'm not who I was," he went on. "Nor am I who I will be. This is the test of the *kwanakasha* all over again. Again they try to make me their servant, this time by presenting a greater power. Again I foil them, steal their fire, use it for my own purposes."

"Scalped man call you *brother*."

"The scalped man fears me. The scalped man wants to bend me to his will, by trickery since he cannot by strength. I laugh at him."

"You slaughtered whole village."

"I will slaughter many more than that, if need be, to keep my people safe, to stop this army."

Grief seemed to consider that. "It is said among my people that sorcerer's greatest power is he can travel without his heart," she murmured. "Do you people also say?"

"Yes."

"Do you think you have a heart?"

"Maybe I don't. Maybe that's the difference you notice. If so, I'm better off without it."

Grief trailed her hand in the water. "After my kin die, I wish I had no heart. If I know how to become sorcerer, to cut out my heart and hide far from body, I would do, if get power for revenge. I would still do it. You show me how?"

"Not and leave you alive, I fear."

She nodded a little sorrowfully. "*You* my best chance for revenge, then. Will you kill them who kill my people?"

"Yes."

"You frightened me," she continued. "I try to run away. I not try again." She flung droplets from her fingers out onto the dark mirror of the river. "Where we going?"

He nodded downstream. "This will take us to the Okahina, the Great Water Road."

"I've heard of."

"My people live beyond it. That's where we are going."

"What you do when you get there?"

"With my people, I will throw back this army. They will fall as thick as leaves in the autumn. The Water Road will run red, and they will have to give it a new name. And I will face this Sun Boy, and if he has his heart in him, I will tear it out. After that—I don't know. One part of their idea may be right. It may be that we should destroy all the white and black men. It may be that we should push them into the sea, just as this army aims to do. Or . . ." He considered not telling her, but then did so anyway. "Or it may be that the days allotted to the world are done, that it is time to shatter the bowl of the sky and begin again."

"What you mean?" she asked, her voice peculiar.

He shrugged. "I don't know," he said, remembering the flood again. Someone had tried to do it before. "Something I heard somewhere. It is of no real concern. It will happen or not."

"My people have stories, too," Grief said. "One is about man who fight terrible serpent, horned serpent. To do this, he get power of thunderbirds, who dwell in the mountains. He find them, and they gave him the power. He destroy serpent, but the thunderbird mystery still in him, and his body not—ah—hold it. He weep lightning—first sometimes, then always. Whenever he look someone—family, friends, lovers—he weep lightning, they die. He too strong."

"What became of him?"

"He not die. He wander yet, rag tied on face so not open eyes."

Red Shoes considered it. "An interesting story. Beautiful, in its way. Thank you for it. But do not fear—my lightning stays in me until I will it to come forth. As you see." And he widened his eyes at her.

"At first," she cautioned, "at first."

Later they pulled ashore and built a fire. He watched the planes of her face in the flickering light.

"You didn't answer me. Why did you watch mc so?"

She met his gaze. "Because you watch me."

"Did I?"

"Yes."

"Why do you think I did that?"

For answer, she stood and unhitched her skirt, then pulled her chemise over her head. Now the firelight played along the whole long column of her, and for an instant he was in Venice, puzzling at a marble statue of a woman, naked—in a city full of people obsessed with covering their bodies. Two strange moments, come together.

He watched her approach, but did not rise. She walked closer, until they were nearly touching.

He could feel the heat radiating from her skin. Her musky, smoky scent filled his head. Gradually, by small degrees, he leaned until his cheek touched her thigh, as if some force were pulling them together, was still pulling, would not be satisfied until their bodies had crushed and mingled into one.

"It is not this simple, what I want from you." He sighed.

"I know that," she said, and sank slowly down against him, so that his cheek brushed across her belly, her breasts, finally came to rest in the hollow of her neck. She came farther, engulfing him in her scent, in the brassy fire of her skin.

The sun found Franklin and the rest through a curtain of fog, beside a broad, swift stream. They paused to wait for better light, and for the first time Franklin had a look at his benefactors.

There were twelve of them, and Franklin knew two of them instantly—Voltaire and Euler.

"Voltaire?" he ventured. "I thought I left you with a job to do."

"Good morning, my friend. Never fear—I brought pen, ink, and paper. It seemed to me that there could be nothing so inspirational for writing a declaration of freedom than the experience of nature, where all things are free."

"Ah. Then you organized this expedition for your own benefit?"

"Ah, no. I organized nothing—as always, I'm a mere tagalong."

"Then I don't understand what spurred it, though I am more than grateful."

"Our friend, the Don of Ivitachuca, is responsible, though Nairne endorsed it. Scarcely a day after you left, Mr. Priber had intelligence of airships among his beloved Cherokee. He hurried off to mend any problems there, but not before directing our attention toward the Coweta, which his spies were sure was the next destination of the fliers. The Don was all afire, demanding that he be allowed to ride to your rescue. Nairne agreed, of course."

"Why did I get no word of this on the aetherschreiber?"

"We sent it, but never got confirmation from you."

"I never saw any such message." Franklin rubbed his jaw. "That's bad, for that means they have some method of interrupting—and most likely reading—our communications. I suspected this, but that makes it no happier to know. Oh, well—our important communiqués go in cryptogram, at least. And what is Euler doing here?"

Euler heard and answered for himself. "I think I can still be of help to you but none to your army, as they do not trust me."

"I cannot claim that *I* trust you," Franklin said.

"But you can keep an eye on me, no?"

"*That's* true," Franklin allowed.

The rest of the rescue party seemed to be Apalachee warriors. They affected the same mixture of European and Indian style as their leader, though some tended much to the Indian side. The same could be said, probably, of their ancestry. Some bore strikingly European features, though all were some degree of copper in hue. A few even sported small goatees, the first facial hair Franklin had ever seen on Indians.

Hoofbeats and a shrill war cry sent them all turning, though by the time Franklin managed his horse, a palisade of muskets had already been erected.

It was with great relief that he recognized Don Pedro, who pranced his fine Spanish stallion into their midst, holding aloft four bloody scalps.

"Now the Coweta know the Apalachee have been among them!" the Don shouted. "Let there be no doubt of how we treat our enemies! Let there be no doubt that the cowardly Coweta have learned!"

He was answered by the salute of every Apalachee musket.

"Ah," Voltaire said, wincing and patting his ears. "I misunderstood! I thought our goal was to escape the Coweta, not summon them hither."

McPherson was close enough to catch that. "They can't have much doubt of where we went anyway," he said. "A group this size can hardly travel without sign. They'll come or not, depending on whim."

"They'll want revenge, won't they?"

"Revenge, yes. But to their way of thinking, they needn't take their revenge on us in particular. They can have it by killing *any* Englishman or Apalachee."

"That's an odd way of thinking."

McPherson shrugged. "Not so different from what we know, if you think close. War is nation against nation. In European armies, officers are considered inviolate, yet they are the ones who direct the action. What man in the English infantry ever knew the Frenchman he killed? When did it ever have to do with personal grudges?"

"Yes, and I find that odd, too," Franklin replied. "There is nothing logical about war."

"A fine thing to say just after you start one," Voltaire commented.

"Aye," Franklin agreed glumly.

Don Pedro trotted his mount up to Ben. "I hope you are well, my friend."

"Thanks to you and yours, yes. I cannot find enough thanks to offer."

"You may thank us by giving us the privilege of accompanying you to New Paris," the Don replied.

Franklin looked to McPherson, who nodded imperceptibly.

"We are the ones who would be honored," Franklin said, trying not to gag at the sight of the bloody parcels still clutched in Don Pedro's fist.

"God is with us," the Apalachee assured him. "He will protect us from the heathen, even as he protected Moses."

Franklin agreed aloud, but couldn't help but wish the Don had chosen a different comparison. After all—Moses himself had never made it to the promised land.

But they were alive, and free, and only just barely tortured, and for the moment he could be pretty happy with that.

Read on—for a preview of

The Shadows of God

The explosive conclusion of
The Age of Unreason

by J. Gregory Keyes

New Paris

Benjamin Franklin crouched low on hands and knees, pressing his face toward the ash gray soil. The forest surrounding him chirped, clicked, and hummed lazily in the soggy noontime heat.

A sudden rattling in the branches made him look up, for the forest had proven deceptive, these last few months. Sleepy it might be, but it dreamed of panther, Indian ambush, rattlesnake, and the corpse of Benjamin Franklin.

But it was only a flight of green parakeets, settling into a live oak. For the moment, the forest was not trying to kill Franklin. A Spaniard, this forest: disdaining to do much of anything between noon and three o'clock. So this was a good time to pry at the land's secrets. Franklin knelt a little lower, wishing the Coweta hadn't taken his hand lens when they tried to torture him to death. He needed it now. He continued his work with squinting eyes, sat up briefly, scribbled in his book, then peered back at the dirt.

When he heard the footsteps behind him, it was too late. Or would have been, if it hadn't been a friend.

"Reading our futures there, Sir Wizard?"

Franklin didn't turn. "Hello, Voltaire," he said, the belated tingle of alarm fading. "They fascinate me. Look at them."

The Frenchman crouched beside him, his long arms folded on narrow knees, a merry grin on a face that was mostly pointed chin. "I take it you mean the ants?" he said.

"Of course. See here, how they form a train to supply their city? I followed this one back—it goes to the corpse of an opossum, some twenty yards in that direction. For ants, that would be a distance of leagues, I should think. And here—these that so fiercely guard the citadel when I threaten it. Like guards or warriors."

"By 'citadel' I assume you mean this little mound of earth."

"Yes. But, again, if you give an ant the stature of a man, how impressive does his mound become?"

"Modestly so if size is the only quality you note. Even so, it would be only a very *large*, uneven, unlovely mound of earth. Nothing to be compared to, say, the Louvre or the Sistine Chapel."

"The ants do not build to impress you, my friend. Given our relative proportions, which would have more space for living and working? This mound, with its tight-packed tunnels, or the Sistine Chapel, with its vaulted ceilings—space mostly wasted in vain grandeur? The ant's eye is all toward efficiency."

"Ah. They are perhaps German, then, or English. There are no French ants, I suppose?"

"Butterflies I suppose to be French," Franklin replied good-naturedly. "Fireflies and lacewings."

"Would that you were right." The philosopher sighed. "But it was no horde of butterflies that laid waste Europe, no lacewing that left that hole where once London was."

"No, I suppose not," Franklin said absently. He bent to watch two ants meet. They seemed to exchange information of some sort, then scurried off purposefully.

"No empty greetings or pleasantries, I'll wager," Franklin murmured, "no small comments. It's all business with them. The food is *there*, danger is *here*, the south tunnel needs repair."

"You admire them, then?"

Franklin looked up at last, his brow furrowed slightly. "They interest me. Each time we stop, I try to find one of their cities, and indeed they are everywhere. It is not so much to say, I think, that below our feet, scarcely noticed, is an empire we are all but unaware of. Seen from the right prospect, the world could be said to be ruled by ants."

"Yes? And yet now that you have brought them to my notice, I could destroy their great city there. I could bring this outpost of empire to naught."

Franklin dusted his hands on his breeches and stood. "Four days ago we passed over ground still smoking. Everything green was burned, and all four-footed things had either fled or succumbed. I found ant cities there scorched black by what must have been terrific heat—and yet they were there. Knock down a mound, and it will be refurbished in the space of a day or two. And then there are the million cities elsewhere, scattered over all the world. For all our greater size and knowledge, I can think of no way we could destroy the race of ants, not utterly."

"Now I see your studies have a more than theoretical bent," Voltaire said. "Who do you liken to the ants—mankind or the malakim?"

The very word still sent a tremor through Franklin. He wished his old mentor, Sir Isaac, had named them differently—from the Latin or Greek rather than from the Hebrew. The latter held too much of the fear and fire of the Old Testament.

But then, the malakim *were* fear and fire.

"We are their ants, I think," Franklin replied, "living beneath their heels, usually unnoticed. Occasionally *we* notice *them*—and worship them as gods, angels, or devils. And occasionally they notice us in turn and grind us beneath their heels."

"But never all of us, no more than we could grind out all the ants. Is that what you're saying?"

"They've failed until now. But we haven't learned the trick of setting the ants against each other, to pit one city against another and send warriors to the deepest chambers of their catacombs. But the malakim seem to have perfected the science of turning man against man. There are men happily inventing more ways for those aetheric devils to kill us every day."

Voltaire nodded. "The malakim seem quite determined to exterminate us. More determined than I should be to destroy the kingdom of ants."

"Perhaps if you had been stung enough, you would have a different opinion. I've heard that in the Amazon, there are ants that march as an army and can strip clean a living man in a few heartbeats."

"The ants turning the tables and destroying the man? Would that *we* could be such ants, then, so we might pick clean the bones of our unseen enemy," Voltaire commented. "For—"

"God's sake, are you two at it again?"

Franklin and Voltaire turned to face the new speaker, a handsome fellow with flowing auburn hair, dressed in buckskin breeches and the shabby remains of a burgundy justaucorps.

"Hello, Robin."

Robert Nairne leaned against a tree, folding his arms. "The world is all at war, with the angels themselves against us. We wander starvin' in the wilderness, blood-lusty Indians at our heels, and you fellows are talkin' philosophy t' worms an' such."

Franklin shrugged and grinned. "The mind is an insatiate master—it demands substance even when the belly has none."

"My poor brain has enough to chew on, trying to figure ways to help us come through this alive," Robert commented dryly.

"And right well you do at it," Franklin said cheerfully. "But between you, Captain McPherson and his rangers, and Don Pedro's braves, that's all well covered, I trust. I don't know how to follow a trail or find fresh water, and you've seen me hunt! I'm best used thinking of our higher problems."

"So, have the crawlies told you how to defeat all the armies arrayed against us, with our thirty-odd stout fellows?"

"They certainly give me ideas," Franklin replied, feeling a bit defensive despite his oddly buoyant mood. After all, Robert was right: any sober and sincere thought proved their situation to be a few leagues south of hopeless. And yet . . . yes, Franklin was hopeful. There was no problem that human ingenuity could not resolve. How could dwelling on the negative help them?

Or worrying—say, about his wife, Lenka.

That thought must have changed his expression.

"What?" Robert asked.

"I was just wondering how the war is going. How Lenka is."

"She was well, when I left her," Voltaire said.

"I thought I charged you with keeping an eye on her," Franklin said.

"She's quite a woman, your wife. She can look after herself. *You* were the one who needed rescuing—we were all agreed on that." He paused. "She did feel you neglected her by leaving her behind."

"I nearly got her killed once. I thought it was safer for her to stay back there. I hope I wasn't wrong."

"If I had a woman like that, I would let her make her own decisions."

That stung a little, and Franklin felt a sharp reply in his throat, but he swallowed it down. He wouldn't let his worry and shame speak for him.

"What's done is done. When we reach New Paris, God willing, we will find an aetherschreiber to replace the one the Coweta took from us, and I shall discover how she fares. Until then, I try not to worry. Hope is better tonic than despair."

Robert nodded agreement. Then his gaze went past Franklin, and he suddenly drew the pistol at his belt, perhaps forgetting he had neither powder nor shot.

Franklin turned to follow his friend's determined and worried stare, and saw that the forest was a lighter sleeper than he had hoped.

Franklin, Robert, and Voltaire stood on a small, grassy field, surrounded by mixed cane, brush, and a few lone oaks fringing a forest of enormous pine. Franklin saw the sun glint off steel, and his vision adjusted. In the tall cane crouched men, at least six of them, possibly many more. Indians, the long barrels of their muskets level to the ground, aimed at Franklin and his companions. And these fellows, Franklin was willing to bet, were well supplied with powder.

"What do we do?" he whispered.

"Nothing, if they want us dead," Robert replied. "They have us fair."

"Are they Cowetas? Would they follow us this far?"

"They might. But there is no lack of Indians in this country. They come out of the earth, like this damned cane."

"Or your ants," Voltaire added.

"Perhaps we should call for our companions," Franklin said.

"You wandered some distance from them in your scientific curiosity," Robert said grimly.

"What then?"

"You're the ambassador," Voltaire suggested. "Parley with them."

"Ah. Yes." Franklin licked his dry lips. "Well, I suppose they know we're here already. Robert, put away your weapon. It's useless anyway."

"They don't know that."

"They know you can kill no more than one of them, and probably not that at this range with that popper. Put it away."

Robert did so reluctantly.

Ben stood a little straighter, showing his empty hands.

"Hello there!" he called. "Who do I have the pleasure of addressing? I am Benjamin Franklin, appointed representative of South Carolina, and I am on a mission of peace and diplomacy."

There followed a nerve-racking pause but finally a shout came back from the thicket.

"Parlez-vous français? Je ne parle pas anglais."

"Oui, un petit peu," Franklin replied. *"Je m'appelle Benjamin Franklin, de Carolina Sud—"*

"You are in Louisiana," the fellow replied, still in French. "That is very far from Carolina."

"I've come to treat with the French king," Franklin replied. "I have the papers to prove it."

Another hesitation, and then the voice said, "Come forward, you." Franklin could see the man now, gesturing with his hand. He wore a blue French coat, but his features looked Indian.

"I'm coming," Franklin replied.

"Hold there, Señor Franklin!"

Another man had emerged from behind them—also an Indian—a silver crucifix bobbing at his throat, a rapier hanging jauntily at his side, and barbaric tattoos decorating his exposed flesh.

"Don Pedro!" Franklin exclaimed gladly.

"The same," the Apalachee chieftain replied. He jerked his head toward the Indians in the brush. "What do those skulking scoundrels want?"

"I'm not sure," Franklin admitted. "They speak French."

"Yes?" The Apalachee cleared his throat and called out in that language. "I am Don Pedro Salazar de Ivitachuca, prince and Nikowatka of Apalachee. Stop hiding, you rascals, and face me like a man."

"There are but four of you," the man in the woods replied. "Lay your arms on the ground or suffer the consequences."

"You should take your own advice," Don Pedro replied, and snapped his fingers.

Suddenly, on all sides, the forest began to move as Apalachee warriors seemed to appear magically from behind every tree.

"Much as we despise it," Don Pedro called, "the Apalachee,

too, can skulk. And now, my friend, it is you who are surrounded and outnumbered."

Another long pause, and then the French-speaker stood. "The French king will mislike this behavior on his own lands."

"Take us to him, then," Franklin called back. "That is all we ever desired. Won't you come shake my hand and let us have peace between us? What sense for this warlike behavior, when we are not at war?"

"In these days, everyone is at war," the man replied. "But I am coming."

He emerged from the forest a moment later. Seeing him more closely, Franklin guessed he was half Indian, for his features owed strongly to the European. He wore a silver gorget at his throat and carried an officer's smallsword. Beneath his blue coat, his flesh was bare, save for the flap of a loincloth.

"I am Henri Koy Penigault," he said, when he drew near, "captain of the king's march guard and war captain of the Mobila. Stand your men down, and I will escort you to New Paris."

Franklin clasped his hand. "Captain Penigault, it is a great pleasure. We feared you were Coweta, for they have been trying to murder us since before the last new moon."

"Well, we have that in common at least." Penigault grinned. "An enemy of the Coweta might be a friend of mine. Shall we meet and smoke together?"

Franklin remembered the last time he had smoked the pipe of peace, how near he had come to losing the meal in his belly. But at the moment, his belly was quite empty.

"I would be delighted," he lied.

After the smoke, however, there was brandy and freshly slain venison, and most fingers came off triggers and sword hilts. Franklin and Voltaire sat around a fire, along with Don Pedro and James McPherson, the rugged captain of the Southern Rangers, regarding Penigault and his chief men across the wavering flames. They were a mixed bunch, French and Indian and one Negro.

"My father was French," Penigault said. "My mother was Alibamon. I was schooled in New Paris, but I prefer to live here on the frontier, with my mother's people. We keep the borders, as I told you."

"Thank you for the brandy. I've never tasted the like."

"Good, yes? We make it from persimmons and wild plums. Now, tell me of your adventures with the Cowetas. We are eager for news of them, and of the Carolinas. We hear little these days, what with the war."

"I'll want to know what you know of the war," Franklin said. *Is my wife alive? But they couldn't know that.*

"Not much," Penigault said. "The English king has taken both Carolinas. The margravate of Azilia still stands, but word is for not much longer."

Franklin nodded. "The English king, as you call him, is a pretender to the throne, James Stuart. He took the seaboard colonies by trickery and with the aid of Moscovado troops."

"Moscovado?"

"Russians," Voltaire clarified.

"Ah, yes. Tsar Peter. We have heard of him." There was something in the man's voice, as if he had a secret.

"Yes, well. You may know that years ago the English colonies signed a treaty of mutual protection with Louisiana, with the Cowetas, and with the Spanish in Florida. I've been trying to unite those signatories to fight together against the Pretender and his allies. I went first to the Coweta, and from there was to continue on to New Paris, to treat there with King Philippe."

"The Cowetas are snakes. They attacked you?"

"They had already been approached by emissaries from the Pretender. They outstripped us, you see, for they came on a flying craft—"

"Shaped something like a great leaf and gliding like a buzzard?"

"Yes. You've seen it?"

"We have. We thought it was a lightning hawk—a creature of legend, a sort of demon that eats children."

"You were not far wrong in that. Their craft is engined with a demon of sorts. In any event, they had already struck a bargain with the Coweta king, and he determined that we should die by torture. But my good friend Don Pedro prevented that."

"Praise God, not me," the Apalachee said, sounding nevertheless quite pleased. "It was our Lord gave me the strength and the foresight to rescue you from the heathens." He hunched forward. "I assume, my friend, that you are a baptized man?"

"I am," Penigault acknowledged.

"Then God has delivered us back to Christian lands, as I knew he would."

Penigault acknowledged that with a tilt of his head. "And so you escaped the Coweta," he pressed. "Did you take many scalps?"

"I do not brag," Don Pedro said, "For He-Who-Sits-Above saw it all and knows I tell the truth. I took four scalps myself, and would have taken many more, but it was not for me to risk glorious death that day but to make certain I survived, to deliver Mr. Franklin to his destiny. I see that clearly. We are engaged not merely against the English king or the Russian tsar but against the very forces of hell, and those deceived monarchs merely twitch like puppets for them. Our true enemies are not flesh and blood, but are the damned spirits that ride the wind at night and by day stay hidden in black clouds that crawl in the spaces beneath the world, shunning light."

Penigault, whom Franklin had reckoned a pragmatic sort, suddenly shivered and crossed himself. "The dark things stir," he said. "It is well known. The accursed beings walk amongst us. Old men have died, eaten from within. Strange warnings and signs come from the west, where demons dwell. They say the house of the dead has opened up and the damned come to take all our souls. Is this true, Mr. Franklin?"

Franklin drew his brows together, wondering how to explain. The malakim were indeed both the angels and devils of superstition, but they were more than that. Moreover, science had proved them real, and it rankled him to hear them spoken of in these medieval terms, just as Newton's biblical appellation rankled.

A soft voice spoke from beyond the circle of light.

"It is true."

Franklin peered out and saw faintly red-glinting eyes. Penigault gasped. "A sorcerer."

"Please join us, Mr. Euler," Franklin said.

A young man stepped into the light. His mild eyes, now blue, surveyed them all. "I am Leonhard Euler, gentleman, and I am at your service."

"You are accursed," Penigault said. "I saw your eyes!"

"I was once accursed," Euler said. "I was a warlock of the malakim, a pair of human hands to work their mischief. But I am no longer their tool."

Penigault looked to Franklin for confirmation.

"So he claims," Franklin told the Louisianan. "I once doubted him, but he has been a friend to us. Without Mr. Euler, we would all be dead or captive back in Charles Town." *Which does not mean I trust him,* Ben finished silently. His brother had been killed by a creature like Euler, and that sort of thing was hard to turn his back on.

"Thank you, Mr. Franklin. Those are kind words."

Penigault switched his regard back to Franklin.

"And you—you are a wizard, they say. The wizard of Charles Town."

"I've been called that. I am a man of science, which is the most useful form of wizardry."

"And can you stop these night-goers?"

"Not alone. But with allies, and the spirit of many peoples—yes. I believe I can."

Penigault nodded. "I hope you can convince the king, then. I do hope you can."

"You don't sound optimistic," Voltaire noticed.

"There are reasons I prefer the marches," Penigault said glumly.

"There she is, fellows," McPherson said, "France in America—New Paris." The ranger's voice held a note of good-natured contempt that Franklin hoped Penigault and his fellows didn't catch. After all, Penigault had not only guided them through the silty maze of the lower Mobile River but had obtained the canoes they now traveled in.

Franklin mopped his brow, grimacing at the slimy sweat that seemed to somehow ooze up from the river itself. He peered ahead to see what the ranger found worthy of his disdain. Not that he was expecting much. The last several leagues had taken them past villages—Indian, European, and Negro—more squalid and impoverished than any he had seen in the interior. While some of the *habitants* halfheartedly tilled wilted fields of corn, more came wading into the river, begging for food and brandy—especially brandy.

But even thus introduced, even with expectations lowered, to call the town he saw ahead "New Paris" required a breathtaking amount of wishful thinking.

The muddy shores sloped up from the bay, and houses, scarcely distinguishable from the Indian habitations he had grown accustomed to, spilled down to the water and even walked on stilts to mingle with dilapidated docks. At one long stone quay were moored a sloop, a frigate, two brigantines, and a ragged collection of canoes and pirogues—which, for all he knew, was the sum of the modern French navy. Beyond, south, he could see the squat form of Fort Condé commanding the mouth of the bay. It, at least, looked sturdy, though Franklin knew his eye for such things was questionable.

As for the city itself, the mud huts did give way to larger, more impressive dwellings as the eye tracked farther from the shore. And surmounting all of this was a truly . . . if not grand, at least bizarre structure. It looked like some idiot madman's attempt to construct a chateau. Never in London, Prague, Venice, or anyplace between had Franklin ever seen such a rambling monstrosity, half built of timbers, half of stone, decked in places with a mishmash of columns and towers that even to his untrained eye seemed completely wrong.

But, by God, it was *big*.

"Mon dieu!" Voltaire exclaimed. "It is a parody of Versailles itself!"

"I hope the real one looks a bit better," Ben said.

"The real Versailles was in questionable taste, I'll grant you, though doing such questioning aloud once was a faux pas of the Bastille sort. Next to that—that thing—however, it was sublime." He cocked his head. "Who rules here? Do you know?"

"The last I heard it was Philippe VII. Does that explain anything to you?"

"The former duke of Orléans? No, it doesn't explain much to me. He was a strange little man, flighty, not given much to serious matters, but not known for such dramatic bad taste either. He was a lover of science, though."

"Perhaps that would explain why the upper tier of the palace is crusted with those glowing gargoyles," Ben said. It was almost dusk, and the pale pink glow of alchemical light was clearly visible, both in the castle and outside.

"Here come the gunboats," McPherson said.